D0400564

IT WAS WAR NOW . . .

Twenty Creedmoors thundered in unison from that rocky slope. It seemed to Tom then that hell had indeed broken loose. He had aimed and shot at a running brave. What strange fierceness he felt! His hands shook to spoil his aim and his face streamed with cold sweat. All the men were loading and firing, and he was in the midst of a cracking din. Yet above it all rose a weird piercing sound—the war-cry of the Comanches. Tom thought, as he shuddered under it, that he understood now why hunters had talked of this most hideous and infamous of all Indian yells. . . . It was the war-cry of a wild tribe for life.

Books by Zane Grey

Published by POCKET BOOKS

Most Pocket Books are available at special quantity discounts for bulk purchases for sales promotions, premiums or fund raising. Special books or book excerpts can also be created to fit specific needs.

For details write the office of the Vice President of Special Markets, Pocket Books, 1230 Avenue of the Americas, New York, New York 10020.

THE
THUNDERING
HERD

PUBLISHED BY POCKET BOOKS NEW YORK

POCKET BOOKS, a Simon & Schuster division of
GULF & WESTERN CORPORATION
1230 Avenue of the Americas, New York, N.Y. 10020

Copyright 1925 by Zane Grey, renewed 1953 by Lina Elise Grey

Published by arrangement with Harper & Row, Publishers, Inc.

All rights reserved, including the right to reproduce
this book or portions thereof in any form whatsoever.
For information address Harper & Row, Publishers, Inc.,
10 E. 53rd St., New York, NY 10022

ISBN: 0-671-83593-9

First Pocket Books printing May, 1983

10 9 8 7 6 5 4 3 2 1

Cover art by Mort Kunstler

POCKET and colophon are registered trademarks
of Simon & Schuster.

Printed in the U.S.A.

THE
THUNDERING
HERD

Chapter I

AUTUMN winds had long waved the grass in the vast upland valley and the breath of the north had tinged the meandering lines of trees along the river bottoms. Gold and purple, and a flame of fire, shone brightly in the morning sunlight.

Birds and beasts of that wild open northland felt stir in them the instinct to move toward the south. The honk of wild geese floated down upon the solitudes and swift flocks of these heralds of winter sped by, sharply outlined against the blue sky.

High upon the western rampart of that valley perched an eagle, watching from his lonely crag. His telescopic eye ranged afar. Beneath him on the endless slope and boundless floor of the valley, moved a black mass, creeping with snail-like slowness toward the south. It seemed as long as the valley and as wide. It reached to the dim purple distances and disappeared there. The densest part covered the center of the valley, from which ran wide straggling arms, like rivers narrowing toward their sources in the hills.

Patches of gray grass, dotted with gold, shone here and there against the black background. Always the dark moving streams and blots seemed encroaching upon these patches of grass. They spread over them and covered them. Then other open spaces appeared at different points. How slow the change! Yet there was a definite movement.

This black mass was alive. The eagle was gazing down upon leagues and leagues of buffalo. Acres of buffalo, miles of buffalo, millions of buffalo! The shaggy, irregular, ragged herd had no end. It dominated slopes, and bottomlands, and the hazy reaches beyond.

The vision of the eagle was an organ for self-preservation, not capable of appreciating the beauty and sublimity of the earth and its myriads of wild creatures. Yet with piercing eye the eagle watched from his lonely crag. Boundless void, with its moving coverlet of black, the wide space of sky keen with its cold wind—valley of leagues, with its living heritage of a million years! Wild, primitive, grand was the scene. It was eloquent of the past. The future stretched away like the dim, strange, unknown purple distances, with an intimation of tragedy. But the hour was one of natural fruition, wild life in the open, with the sun like an eye of the Creator, shining over the land. Peace, silence, solitude attended the eagle in his vigil.

Yet a brooding sadness, like an invisible mantle, lay over the valley. Was it the dreamy, drowsy spell of autumn? Was it the pervading spirit of a dying season, reluctant to face the rigor of snow and ice? The fact was that autumn lingered, and nature brooded over some mystery, some problem, some blunder. Life was sweet, strong—scented on the wind, but there was death lurking somewhere, perhaps in the purple shadow of distance to the southward. The morning was bright, golden, glorious, yet it did not wait, and night was coming. So there was more than the melancholy languor of autumn in the still air. A mighty Being seemed breathing there, invisible and infinite, all-encompassing. It kept its secret.

Suddenly the eagle plunged like a thunderbolt from his crag and shot down and down, at last to spread his closed wings, and sail slowly and majestically round and round, over an open grassy patch encircled by buffalo.

In this spot, well toward the center and front of the vast herd, appeared about to be enacted a battle between a monarch and his latest rival for supremacy.

The huge leader, shaggy, brown, ragged, was not a creature of beauty, but he was magnificent. He had twice the bulk of an ox, and stood as high as a horse. His massive head, with the long shaggy hair matted with burrs, was held low, muzzle almost to the ground, showing the big curved short horns widely separated. Eyes of dark fire blazed from beneath the shaggy locks. His great back slowly arched and his short tufted tail rose stiffly erect. A hoarse rumble issued from the cavern of his chest—a roar at the brazen effrontery of this young bull that dared to face him.

Many and many had been the battles of this old monarch. For years he had reigned, so many that he had forgotten the instinct of his youth, when he, like the rival before him, had bearded the king of the buffaloes. He had to fight again, in obedience to that law which respected only the survival of the fittest.

The bull that had challenged the king to battle was also magnificent. He too lowered his huge head, and with short prodigious strokes he pawed tufts of grass and heaps of earth up into the air. His color was a glossy seal brown and he did not have the ragged, worn appearance of the monarch. His shaggy hair hung thick and woolly from head and shoulders and knees. Great rippling muscles swelled on his flanks as he pawed and moved round his enemy. He meant to attack. He shone resplendent. He seemed the epitome of animal vigor and spirit. The bawl with which he answered the roar of the monarch rang clear and hard, like a blast. He possessed something that the old warrior had lost. He had beauty and youth.

The surrounding buffalo did not appear concerned over this impending battle. They were aware of it, for they would raise their shaggy heads from the grass and gaze a moment at the king and his jealous aspirant. Then they would return to their feeding. It was noticeable, however, that the circle did not narrow; if anything, it gradually widened.

The king did not wait for his foe to begin the struggle. He charged. His dash was incredibly fast for so heavy a beast and his momentum tremendous. Square against the lowered head of the young bull he struck. The shock sent forth a sodden crash. The bull staggered under the impact. His whole bulk shook. Then he was lifted, head up, forefeet off the ground, higher, and with grinding clash of horns he was hurled heavily upon his back.

Under the great force of that charge the old monarch went to his knees, and the advantage which might have been his was lost. He heaved in his rage.

Nimbly the young bull rolled over and bounded to his feet, unhurt. Nature had by this time developed him to a perfect resisting force. His front was all bone, covered by matted hair. Swifter than a horse, as quick as a cat, he launched his bulk at his antagonist, and hit him with a shock no less terrific than the one that had opened the battle. But the old warrior received it as if he had been a great oak rooted in the earth.

Then with heads pounding and horns grinding, these beasts, relentless as nature itself, settled down to the wonderful and incredible battle of buffalo bulls. Bent and bowed, always head to head, they performed prodigious feats of ramming and butting, and endeavoring to give each other a fatal thrust with horn.

But under that heavy mat of wool was skin over an inch thick and tougher than hardened leather. These bulls were made to fight. They had extraordinary lung capacity and very large nostrils. Their endurance was as remarkable as their physical structure.

In a cloud of dust they plowed up the prairie, driving the grazing buffalo back and forth, and covering acres of ground in their struggle. The crash of heads and rattle of horns gradually diminished in vigor of sound, indicating that the speed and strength of the rivals were wearing down. Not so their ferocity and courage! It was a battle to death or complete vanquishment. In time the dust cloud blew away on the wind, and then the bulls could be seen in action less strenuous but still savage.

The old monarch was near the end of his last battle. His race was run. Torn and dirt-covered and bloody, he backed before the onslaughts of his foe. His lungs, like great bellows, sent out gasps that were as well utterances of defeat. He could not withstand the relentless young bull. Age must go down. He was pushed to his knees and almost bowled over. Recovering, he wearily fronted that huge battering black head, and then was shoved to his haunches. Again, narrowly, he escaped the following lunge. That was the moment of defeat. He was beaten. The instinct for life took the place of the instinct for supremacy. Backward, step by step, he went, always facing the bellowing young conqueror. There came intervals when he was free of that lowering battering head; and during the last of these he sheered away among the stragglers of the herd, leaving the field to the victor. The old monarch had retired to the ranks and there was a new leader of the herd.

The eagle soared back to his lonely perch, there to clutch the crag with his talons and sweep the valley with crystal eye.

Out to the front of the black mass of buffalo a whirlwind twisted up a column of dust. Funnel-shaped it rose, yellow and spreading, into the air, while it raced across the valley. That, or something as natural, stirred a movement in the foreranks of buffalo. All at once the leaders broke into a run, heading south. The movement, and the growing pound of their hoofs, ran through the herd as swiftly as a current. Then, magically and wondrously, the whole immense mass moved as if one spirit, one mind, dominated it. The throbbing pound of hoofs suddenly increased to a roar. Dust began to rise and blow back, like low clouds of yellow smoke, over the acres, and then the miles of bobbing black backs. The vast herd seemed to become a sea in swift and accelerating action.

Soon a rising pall of dust shrouded the thousands of buffalo, running under what seemed an obscure curtain. The volume of sound had swelled from rhythmic pound and beat to a mighty and appalling roar. Only the battlements of the upper air, assailed in storm by the ripping of lightning, could send back such thunder as now rose from the shaking earth. But this was one long continuous roll. The movement of buffalo in unison resembled a tidal wave and the sound was that of an avalanche. The ground trembled under the thundering herd.

The eagle perched motionless on his crag, indifferent to the rolling chaos beneath him. The valley-wide cloud of dust floated low down. Time passed. Halfway to the zenith rose the sun. Then gradually the tremor of the earth and the roar of hoofs diminished, rolled, and died away. The herd had passed. On his lofty perch the eagle slept, and the valley cleared of dust and movement. Solitude, loneliness, and silence reigned at the solemn noontide.

It was spring of an era many years after the lone eagle had watched the buffalo herd.

An upland prairie country rolled and waved down from snow-capped Rocky Mountains to spread out into the immense eastern void. Over the bleached white grass had come a faint tinge of green. The warm sun had begun its renewal of the covering of the earth. A flock of wild geese, late on their annual pilgrimage, winged swift flight toward the northland. On the ridges elk grazed, and down in the hollows, where murmuring streams rushed, clouded with the blue color of melted snow, deer nibbled at the new tender shoots of grass.

Below the uplands, where the plain began, herds of buffalo dotted the patches and streaked the monotony of the gray vastness. Leagues and leagues it spread, always darker for the increase of buffalo, until all was a dense black that merged into the haze of distance.

A river wended its curving way out across the plains, and in a wooded bend an Indian encampment showed its white tepees, and red blankets, and columns of blue smoke lazily rising.

Hidden in the brush along the river half-naked red men lay in wait for the buffalo to come down to drink. These hunters did not need to sally forth for their game. They had only to wait and choose the meat and the hide that best served them for their simple needs. They did not kill more than they could use.

Along the river bank, far as eye could see, the shaggy monsters trooped down to drink. Bulls and cows and calves came in endless procession. In some places, where the bank was steep, the thirsty buffalo behind pushed the row ahead into the water, whence rose a splashing *mêlée*. The tawny calves, still too young to shed their coats and turn the seal brown of their mothers, bawled lustily as they were shoved into the river.

Near the encampment of the Indians, where trees and brush lined the shore, the buffalo were more wary. They liked the open. But stragglers came along, and the choicest of these fell prey to the deadly arrows of the red men. A shaggy young bull, sleek and brown, superb in his approaching maturity, passed within range of the chieftain of that hunting clan. He rose from his covert, a lean, dark Indian, tall and powerful of build, with intense face and piercing eyes turned toward his quarry. He bent a bow few Indians could have drawn. He bent it till the flint head of the arrow touched his left hand. Then he released the arrow. Like a glint of light it flashed and, striking the bull behind the shoulder, buried half its length there. The animal grunted. He made no violent movements. He walked back as he had come, only more and more slowly. The chief followed him out to the edge of the timber. There other buffalo coming in saw both Indian and wounded bull, but they only swerved aside. The bull halted, and heaving heavily, he plunged to his knees, and then rolled over on his side.

After the hunters came the squaws, with their crude flint and bone implements, to skin the buffalo and cut up the meat and pack it to the encampment.

There the chief repaired to rest on his buffalo hide under a tree, and to think the thoughts and dream the dreams of the warrior. Beyond the white-peaked mountain range lived enemies of his, red men of a hated tribe. Other than remembrance of them he had no concern. His red gods could not tell him of the future. The paleface, who was to drive him and his people into the fastnesses of the arid hills, was unknown and undreamed of. Into his lofty serene mind no thought flashed of a vanishing of the buffalo while yet his descendants lived. The buffalo were as many as the sands of the river bottoms. They had always been; they would always be. The buffalo existed to furnish food, raiment, shelter for the red man.

So the chief rested in his camp, watching beaver at work on the river bank, as tame as were the buffalo. Like these animals, he and his tribe were happy and self-sufficient. Only infrequent battles with other tribes marred the serenity of their lives. Always the endless herds were to be found, to the south or the north. This chief worshiped the sun, loved his people and the wild, lonely land he believed was his; and if there was in his tribe a brave who was liar or coward or thief, or a squaw who broke the law, death was his or her portion.

A straggling band of white men wearily rode and tramped across the great plains centuries before that wonderful level prairie was to be divided into the Western states of America.

These white travelers were the Spanish explorers under the command of the intrepid Coronado. It was a large band. Many of them rode horses—Arabian horses of the purest breed, from which the Western mustang was descended. But most of them walked, wearing queer apparel and armor not suitable to such arduous travel. They carried strange weapons.

Hardy, indomitable, and enduring, this first band of white men to penetrate the great plains and the deserts of the South and West, recorded for history something of their marvelous adventures and terrible experiences and strange sights.

Many hundreds of leagues they traveled, according to their historian, Castaneda, over tremendous plains and reaches of sand, stark and level, and so barren of trees and stones that they erected heaps of the ox dung they found, so that they could be guided back by the way they had come. They lost horses and men.

All the way across these great plains of grass and sand the Spaniards encountered herds of crooked-back oxen, as many as there were sheep in Spain. But they saw no people with the crooked-back cattle. These weary and lost travelers, almost starved, found in the oxen succor they so grievously needed. Meat gave them strength and courage to go on through obstacles none save crusaders could have overcome. Sometimes in this strange country it rained great showers of hailstones as big as oranges; and these storms caused many tears and injuries.

Castaneda wrote:

These oxen are the bigness and color of our bulls. . . . They have a great bunch of hair on their fore shoulders, and more on their fore part than their hinder part, and it is like wool. They have a horse-mane upon their backbone, and much hair, and very long from their knees downward. They have great tufts of hair hanging down their foreheads, and it seemeth they have beards because of the great store of hair hanging down at their chins and throats. The males have very large tails, and a great knob or flock at the end, so that in some respects they resemble the lion, and in some others the camel. They push with their horns; they run; they overtake and kill a horse when they are in their rage and anger. The horses fled from them, either because of their deformed shape, or else because they had never before seen them. Finally it is a foul and fierce beast of countenance and form of body.

Coronado and Castaneda, with their band of unquenchable spirits, were the first white people to see the American buffalo.

Chapter II

ALL during Tom Doan's boyhood, before and through the stirring years of the Rebellion, he had been slowly yielding to the call that had made so many young men adventurers and pioneers in the Southwest.

His home had not been a happy one, but as long as his mother lived and his sisters remained unmarried he had stayed there, getting what education there was available at the little Kansas village school, and working hard on the farm. When Kansas refused to secede to the South at the beginning of the Rebellion, Tom's father, who was a rebel, joined Quantrill's notorious band of guerillas. Tom's sisters were in sympathy with the South. But Tom and his mother held open leaning toward the North. It was a divided family. Eventually the girls married and left home. Tom's mother did not long survive her husband, who was shot on one of Quantrill's raids.

Tom outlived the sadness and bitterness of his youth, but they left their mark upon him. His loyalty to his mother had alone kept him from the wildness of the

time, and their poverty had made hard work imperative. After the war he drifted from place to place,
always farther and farther toward the unsettled country. He had pioneer blood in him, and in his mind he
had settled the future. He meant to be a rancher, a
tiller of the soil, a stockman and a breeder of horses,
for these things he loved. Yet always there was in him
the urge to see the frontier, to be in the thick of wild
life while he was hunting and exploring for that wonderful land which would content him. Thus Tom Doan
had in him a perfect blending of the dual spirit that
burned in the hearts of thousands of men, and which
eventually opened up the West to civilization.

Not, however, until the autumn of 1874 did he
surrender to the call. The summer of that year had
been a momentous one in the Southwest. Even in
years of stress this one stood out as remarkable, and
the tales drifting up from the frontier had thrilled
Tom's heart.

A horde of buffalo-hunters, lured by the wild life and
the development of a commercial market for buffalo
hides, had braved the Indians in their haunts and
started after the last great herds. This had resulted in
an Indian war. The Cheyennes, Kiowas, Arapahoes,
and the Comanches had gone on the warpath. A
thousand warriors of these tribes had made the memorable siege of a small band of buffalo-hunters and
their soldier escort, and after repeated and persistent
charges had been repulsed. The tale of this battle was
singularly thrilling to Tom Doan. Particularly had the
hunting of buffalo appealed to him. Not that he had
ever hunted a buffalo, for in fact he had never seen
one. But stories told him as a boy had fixed themselves
in his mind, never to be effaced.

Early spring found Tom Doan arriving at the outfit-
ting post from which an army of buffalo-hunters were
preparing to leave for the long haul to the south.

The atmosphere of this frontier fort and freighting

station was new to Tom, and affected him deeply. The stir of youthful love of wild tales was here revived. At a step, almost, he had found himself on the threshold of the frontier. Huge freighting wagons, some with six horses attached, and loaded with piles and bales of green buffalo hides, lumbered in from the level prairie land. The wide main street of the town presented a continual procession of men and women, mostly in rough garb of travel, and all intent on the mysterious something that seemed to be in the air. There was a plentiful sprinkling of soldiers, and pale-faced, frock-coated gamblers, and many stylishly dressed women who had a too friendly look, Tom thought. There were places of amusement, saloons and dance halls, that Tom found a peep into sufficient. Dust lay inches deep in the street, and the horses passing along continually raised clouds of it.

The camp on the outskirts of this town soon drew Tom. Here, ranged all around, it appeared, were the outfits of the buffalo-hunters, getting ready to travel south. Tom meant to cast his lot with one of them, but the tales he had heard about the character of some of these outfits made him decide to be careful. According to rumor some of them were as bad as the Comanches.

The first man Tom accosted was a tall, rugged, bronzed Westerner, with a stubby red beard on his lean face. He was encamped under a cottonwood, just bursting into green, and on the moment was busy jacking up the hind wheel of his huge canvas-covered wagon.

"I'll give you a lift," offered Tom, and with one heave he raised the rear end of the wagon.

"Wal!" ejaculated the Westerner, as he rapidly worked up his jack to meet the discrepancy occasioned by Tom's lift. "Reckon you're husky, stranger. Much obliged."

Tom helped him complete the job of greasing the wagon wheels and then asked him if he were a buffalo-hunter.

"I am thet," he replied. "An' what're you?"

"I've come to join one of the outfits. Are there really good wages to be made?"

"Wal, you are new heahaboots," returned the other, grinning. "My early fall hunt netted me five hundred dollars. Late fall then I made four hundred. An' this winter I hunted down on the Brazos, cleanin' up six hundred an' eighty."

Tom was amazed and excited over this specific information, direct from the hunting grounds.

"Why, that's wonderful!" he replied. "A fellow can make enough to buy and stock a ranch. Did you have a helper?"

"Shore—my two boys, an' I paid them wages."

"How much?" inquired Tom.

"Twenty-five a month. Are you lookin' fer a job?" rejoined the Westerner, with an appreciative glance at Tom's broad shoulders.

"Yes, but not for such wages as that. I'd like to go in for myself."

"It's the way to do, if you can buy your own outfit."

Upon inquiry Tom found that outfits were high, and with his small savings he could hardly hope to purchase even an interest in one. It would be necessary for him to hire out to the best advantage, and save his earnings toward buying horses, wagon, and equipment for himself. Nevertheless, opportunity seemed indeed knocking at his door. The rewards of buffalo-hunting, as set forth by the Westerner, were great enough to fire the blood of any young man. Tom experienced a sudden lift of his heart; a new and strong tide surged through him.

At the end of the road Tom came to a small grove of cottonwoods, just beyond the edge of the town; and here he caught the gleam of more canvas-covered vehicles. He found three outfits camped there, apart from one another, and the largest one was composed of several wagons. A camp fire was burning. The smell of wood smoke assailed Tom's nostrils with more than pleasurable sense. It brought pictures of wild places and camp by lonely streams. A sturdy woman was bending over a washtub. Tom caught a glimpse of a girl's rather comely face peering out of the front of a wagon. Two young men were engaged at shoeing a horse. Under a cottonwood two men sat on a roll of bedding.

As Tom entered the grove one of the men rose to a lofty stature and showed himself to be built in proportion. He appeared past middle age, but was well preserved and possessed a bearded, jovial face, with frank blue eyes that fastened curiously upon Tom. The other man had remarkable features—sharp, hard, stern, set like a rock. Down his lean brown cheeks ran deep furrows and his eyes seemed narrowed inside wrinkled folds. They were gray eyes, light and singularly piercing.

Tom had an impression that this was a real plainsman. The giant seemed a man of tremendous force. Quick to form his likes or dislikes, Tom lost no time here in declaring himself.

"My name's Tom Doan," he said. "I want a job with a buffalo-hunter's outfit."

"Glad to meet you. I'm Clark Hudnall, an' this is my friend, Jude Pilchuck," replied the giant.

Whereupon both men shook hands with Tom and showed the interest common to the time and place. Hudnall's glance was a frank consideration of Tom's stalwart form and beardless face. Pilchuck's was a keen scrutiny associated with memory.

"Doan. Was your father Bill Doan, who rode with Quantrill?" he inquired.

"Yes—he was," returned Tom, somewhat disconcerted by this unexpected query.

"I knew your father. You favor him, only you're lighter complexioned. He was a hard rider and a hard shooter. . . . You were a boy when he got——"

"I was fifteen," said Tom, as the other hesitated.

"Were you on your dad's side?" asked Hudnall, curiously.

"No. I was for the North," returned Tom.

"Well, well, them days were tough," sighed Hudnall, as if he remembered trials of his own. Then he quickened with interest. "We need a man an' I like your looks. Have you any hankerin' for red liquor?"

"No."

"Are you alone?"

"Yes."

"Ever hunt buffalo?"

"No."

"Can you shoot well?"

"I was always a good shot. Have hunted deer and small game a good deal."

"What's your idea—throwin' in with a hide-hunter's outfit?"

Tom hesitated a moment over that query, and then frankly told the truth about his rather complicated longings.

Hudnall laughed, and was impressed to the point of placing a kind hand on Tom's shoulder.

"Young man, I'm glad you told me that," he said. "Back of my own reason for riskin' so much in this hide-huntin' is my need to make money quick, an' I've got to have a ranch. So we're two of a kind. You're welcome to cast in your lot with us. Shake on it."

Then Tom felt the mighty grip of a calloused hand that had known the plow and the ax. Pilchuck likewise offered to shake hands with Tom, and expressed himself no less forcibly than Hudnall.

"Reckon it's a good deal on both sides," he said. "The right kind of men are scarce. I know this buffalo-huntin'. It's a hard game. An' if skinnin' hides isn't tougher than diggin' coal, then I was a meathunter on the U. P. an' the Santa Fe for nothin'."

Hudnall called the two younger men from their task of shoeing the horse. Both appeared under thirty, stocky fellows, but there the resemblance ended.

"Burn, shake hands with Tom Doan," said Hudnall, heartily. "An' you, too, Stronghurl. . . . Doan is goin' to throw in with us."

Both men greeted Tom with the cordial good will and curiosity natural to an event of importance to them. It was evident that Burn, from his resemblance to Hudnall, was a son. Stronghurl had as remarkable a physiognomy as his name, and somehow they fitted each other.

"Burn, you'll take Doan with your wagon," said Hudnall. "That fills our outfit, an' we'll be pullin' tomorrow for the Panhandle. . . . Hey, you women folks," he called toward the wagons, "come out an' meet my new man."

The stout woman left off washing at the tub and came forward, wiping her red hands on her apron. She had a serious face that lighted with a smile.

"Wife, this is Tom Doan," went on Hudnall, and next in order he presented Tom to Burn's wife, whom Tom recognized as the young woman he had seen in the wagon. Last to emerge was a girl of eighteen or thereabouts, sister of Burn and manifestly Hudnall's pride. She was of large frame, pleasant faced, and she had roguish eyes that took instant stock of Tom.

Thus almost before he could realize his good fortune, Tom found himself settled with people of his own kind, whom he liked on sight. Moreover, Hudnall had the same pioneer urge which possessed Tom; and the fact that Pilchuck, an old buffalo-hunter, was to accompany them down into Texas, just about made the deal perfect. To be sure, Tom had not mentioned wages or shares, but he felt that he could safely trust Hudnall.

"Where's your pack?" inquired Burn. "An' what have you got in the way of outfit?"

"I left it at the station," replied Tom. "Not much of an outfit. A bag of clothes and a valise."

"Nary horse or gun. Have you any money?" went on Burn, with cheerful interest.

"I've got two hundred dollars."

"Good. Soon as we get this horse shod I'll go uptown with you."

"Well, son," spoke up Hudnall, "I reckon Tom had better let Pilchuck buy gun an' horse an' what else he needs."

"Humph!" ejaculated Mrs. Hudnall. "If I know men you'll all have a say about horses and guns."

"Mr. Doan, wouldn't you like me to help you pick out that horse?" inquired Burn's sister, mischievously.

"Why, yes," replied Tom, joining in the laugh, "I'd like you all to help—so long as I get one I can ride."

The women returned to their tasks while Hudnall went off with Pilchuck toward the town. Left to his own devices, Tom presently joined Burn and Stronghurl, who were not having any easy job shoeing the horse. It was a spirited animal.

"Doan, would you mind fetchin' that bay horse back?" asked Burn, presently pointing toward the other side of the grove, where several canvas-covered wagons gleamed among the trees.

Tom picked up a halter and strode away under the trees, at once pleasantly preoccupied with thought of the most satisfying nature. He came up with the bay horse, which he found eating out of a girl's hand. Tom saw and heard other people close by, but he did not notice them particularly. Intent on the horse, he did not take a second glance at the girl, until she spoke.

"I've caught your horse twice to-day," she said.

"Much obliged. But he's not mine," replied Tom, and as he put the halter over the neck of the animal he looked at the girl.

Her eyes met his. They were large, black as midnight, and they gazed up from a face almost as dark as an Indian's. Her hair was brown and appeared to have a sheen or light upon it.

Tom's glance became what hers was—steady, almost a stare without consciousness, a look of depth and gravity for which neither was responsible.

Then Tom withdrew his glance and attended to knotting the halter. Yet he could see her still. She was of medium height, neither robust nor heavy, yet giving an impression of unusual strength and suppleness for a girl. She was young. Her dress of homespun material looked the worse for wear.

"He's a pretty horse," she said, patting the sleek nose.

"Yes, he is. I hope the horse I've got to buy will be like him," replied Tom.

"Are you a buffalo-killer, too?" she inquired, in quicker tone.

"I expect to be."

"Milly," called a gruff voice, "you're not a hoss thief and you're not makin' up with strangers."

Tom turned hastily to see a big man looming across the camp fire. He wore a leather apron and carried a hammer in his brawny hand. It was impossible that this blond giant could be the girl's father. Even in that moment of surprise and annoyance Tom felt glad of his conviction. The man's face bore a thin yellow beard that could not hide its coarseness and brutality. He had bright, hard blue eyes.

"Excuse me," said Tom, stiffly. "I had to come after Mr. Hudnall's horse." Then turning to the girl, he thanked her. This time her eyes were cast down. Tom abruptly started off, leading the animal.

It did not occur to him that there was anything significant about the incident, except a little irritation at the coarse speech and appearance of the blond man. Nevertheless, that part of it slipped from his mind, and the vague, somehow pleasurable impression of the girl persisted until the serious and thrilling business of choosing horse and gun precluded all else.

The fact that Hudnall and his men left off work, and Pilchuck insisted on being the arbiter of these selections, attested to the prime importance with which they regarded the matter. Hudnall argued with Pilchuck that he knew the merits of horses as well as the latter knew guns.

So they journeyed into town, up the dusty motley-crowded street, rubbing elbows with Indians, soldiers, hunters, scouts, teamsters, men who bore the stamp of evil life upon their lean faces, and women with the eyes of hawks. Pilchuck knew almost everybody, it seemed. He pointed out many border celebrities to Tom's keen interest. One was Colonel Jones, a noted plainsman, who in the near future was to earn the sobriquet "Buffalo Jones," not like his contemporary, Buffalo Bill, for destroying buffalo, but for preserving calves to form the nucleus of a herd. Another, and the most striking figure of a man Tom had ever seen, was Wild Bill, perhaps the most noted of all frontiersmen. He was a superb giant of a man, picturesquely clad, straight as an Indian, with a handsome face, still, intense, wonderful in its expression of the wild spirit that had made him great. Tom thought he had never before seen such penetrating, alert eyes. Pilchuck mentioned casually that not long since, Wild Bill had fought and killed twelve men in a dugout cabin on the plains. Bill got shot and cut to pieces, but recovered. Tom was far from being a tenderfoot, yet he gaped at these strange, heroic men, and thrilled to his depths. Seeing them face to face stimulated and liberated something deep in him.

The supply store where Pilchuck conducted Tom and the others was full of purchasers, and except for absence of liquors in bottles it resembled a border barroom. It smelled of tobacco in bulk; and Tom saw shelves and stacks of plug tobacco in such enormous quantity that he marveled to Hudnall.

"Golly! man, we gotta have chaw tobacco," replied that worthy.

A counter littered with a formidable array of guns and knives appeared to be Pilchuck's objective point.

"We want a big fifty," he said to the clerk.

"There's only one left an' it ain't new," replied this individual, as he picked up a heavy gun. It was a fifty-caliber Sharps rifle. Pilchuck examined it and then handed it over to Tom. "I've seen better big fifties, but it'll do for a while. . . . Next you want a belt an' all the cartridges you can lug, an' both rippin' an' skinnin' knives."

When these purchases were made Tom had indeed about all he could carry. Hudnall then ordered the supplies needed for his outfit, and when that was accomplished Pilchuck led them down the street to the outskirts of town, where there was a corral full of dusty, vicious, kicking horses. It took an hour for Pilchuck and Hudnall to agree on a horse that Tom could ride. Having been a farm hand all his days, Tom was a good horseman, but he was not a bronco-buster. Finally the selection was made of horse, saddle, bridle, blanket, and spurs. When this purchase was paid for Tom laughed at the little money he had left.

"Things come high, an' they ain't worth it," complained Pilchuck. "But we haven't any choice. That's a good horse—young enough, strong, easy gait, but he never saw a buffalo."

"What of that?" asked Tom, with a little check to his elation.

"Nothin'. Only the first buffalo he sees will decide a lot."

Tom regarded this rather ambiguous remark with considerable misgiving and made a mental note of it, so he would not forget.

What with their purchases, and Tom's baggage, which they got at the station, the party had about all they could take back to camp. The afternoon then was a busy one for all concerned. Tom donned rough garb and heavy boots, suitable to life in the open. The change was not made without perception of an indefinable shifting in his spirit. He was about to face the perils of the frontier, and serious and thoughtful as he endeavored to make himself, he could not repress an eager, wild response. He tried out his horse, which he named Dusty, because at that time nothing but a bath could have removed the dust from him. Dusty gave a creditable performance and won the approval of all save Pilchuck. Hudnall, and his daughter, Sally, particularly liked the horse. Tom saw that he could sell or trade at his discretion, and so for the time was well pleased.

The rest of the afternoon he spent helping Burn Hudnall arrange and pack the big wagon that was to transport their precious outfit, and later, out on the plains, haul the hides they expected to get.

"I was tellin' father I'd like to pick up a boy somewhere," said Burn.

"What for?" inquired Tom. "We can take care of this outfit."

"Sure, for the present. But when we get out among the buffalo we'll need some one to drive the wagon an' keep camp while we chase an' kill an' skin buffalo."

"I see. Then the idea will be a main camp kept by your father, and the rest of us in pairs with wagons and outfits will range all over?"

"I reckon that's Pilchuck's idea. From what I can gather there'll be a lot of hustlin' an' movin' when we strike the herds of buffalo."

"I should think it'd be a chase with no time for camp," said Tom.

"Reckon so. Anyways we're bound to know soon," replied Burn, grimly.

At sunset Tom heard the cheery call of the women folk to supper; and he was not far behind Burn in getting to the table, which was a canvas spread on the ground. They all appeared hungry. Hudnall loaded his tin plate, filled his cup, and then repaired to the wagon, and set his supper upon the seat. He was too big to squat on the ground, cross-legged and Indian fashion, but his stature enabled him to stand and eat from the wagon seat. Pilchuck, too, had his peculiar habit. He set his plate down, and knelt on one knee to eat.

They were all excited, except Pilchuck, and though this in no wise distracted from a satisfying of hunger, it lent a sparkle and jollity to the occasion. Tom was not alone in having cut away from the humdrum of settled communities and in cherishing dreams of untrammeled country and future home and prosperity.

After supper he again walked into the town, purposely going alone. He did not pry into his reason. This third visit to the main street did not satisfy his vague longing, whatever it was, and he retraced his steps campward.

When he reached the end of the street passersby became scarce, and for that reason more noticeable. But Tom did not pay attention to any one until he heard a girl's voice. It came from behind him and had a note of annoyance, even anger. A man's reply, too low and husky for coherence, made Tom turn quickly.

A young woman carrying a heavy parcel was approaching, a step or two in advance of a man. It required only a glance to see that she was trying to get away from him.

Tom strode to meet her, and recognized the girl with whom he had exchanged words at the camp adjoining Hudnall's.

"Is that fellow bothering you?" demanded Tom.

"He insulted me," she replied.

Tom broke into swift strides toward the offender.

"Say, you!" he called, forcibly. But the man hurried away, at a pace that would have necessitated running to catch him.

"Never mind. Let him go," said the girl, with a little laugh of relief.

"This town is full of ruffians. You should not have come in alone," was Tom's reply.

"I know. It's happened before. I wasn't afraid—but I'm glad you came along."

"That package looks heavy. Let me carry it," offered Tom.

"Thank you, I can manage very well," she returned.

But he took it away from her, and in so doing touched her hand. The effect on Tom was sudden and profound. For the moment it destroyed his naturalness.

"Well—I—it is heavy—for a girl," he said, awkwardly.

"Oh, I'm very strong," she rejoined.

Then their eyes met again, as they had when Tom had reached for the horse and looked at her. Only this time it seemed vastly different. She looked away, across the open toward the grove where fires gleamed in the gathering twilight. Then she moved. Tom fell into step beside her. He wanted to talk, but seemed unable to think of anything to say. This meeting was not an ordinary incident. He could not understand himself. He wanted to ask her about who she was, where she was going, what relation she bore to the rude man who had called her Milly. Yet not a word could he utter. He could have spoken surely, if he had not been concentrating on the vagueness and uncertainty of himself.

Before they had quite reached the edge of the grove she stopped and confronted him.

"Thank you," she said, softly. "I'll carry it now."

"No. We're still a long distance from your camp."

"Yes—that's why," she returned, haltingly. "You must not go with me. . . . He—my stepfather, you heard him. I—I can't tell you more."

Tom did not yield up the parcel with very good grace. "I may never see you again!" he burst out.

She did not answer, but as she relieved him of the package she looked up, straight and clear into his face. Her eyes held him. In them he read the same thought he had just exclaimed aloud. Then she bade him good night, and turning away, vanished in the gloom of the grove.

Not until she was gone did Tom awake to a realization that this chance meeting, apparently so natural on her part and kindly on his, just an incident of travel, two strangers exchanging a few civilities, was the most significant and appealing and thought-provoking experience of his life. Why had he not detained her, just a moment, to ask for the privilege of seeing her again? Still, he could see her to-morrow. That last look of her big black eyes—what did it mean? His mind revolved many useless questions. He found a seat at the edge of the grove and there he pondered. Night came, dark and cool. The stars shone. Behind him sounded the crackle of camp fires and the voices of men and the munch of horses at their grain.

A strange thing had happened to him, but what was it? A girl's eyes, a few words, a touch of hands! Had they been the cause of this sudden melancholy one moment and inexplicable exaltation the next, and his curiosity about her, and this delving into himself? But he did not call it silly or foolish. Tom was twenty-four years old, yet this condition of mind was new. Perhaps the thrill, the excitement of the prospects ahead, had communicated themselves to an otherwise ordinary incident. The thought, however, he ridiculed. Every moment of his musing tended toward consciousness of a strange, dreamy sweetness inspired by this girl.

Chapter III

WHEN Tom roused next morning to Burn Hudnall's cheery call he found that he had slept later than usual for him.

He rolled out of his bed of blankets under the wagon, and pulling on his boots and washing his face and hands, was ready for breakfast and the eventful day.

The sun had just risen above the eastern horizon. West and southwest the rolling prairie-land shone green and gold under the bright morning light. Near at hand horses and cattle grazed. Far down the clearly defined road canvas-covered wagons gleamed white. Some of the buffalo-hunters were already on their way. Tom stood a moment, watching and thinking, as he drew a deep full breath of the fresh crisp air, feeling that whatever lay in store for him beyond the purple horizon—adventure, hardship, fortune—he was keen to face it.

While at breakfast Tom suddenly remembered his meeting with the girl, Milly. In the broad light of day he did not feel quite the same as in the gloaming of last night. Yet a sweetness stole pervadingly upon him. Glancing through the grove toward the camp where the first meeting with her had taken place, he missed the white wagons. That end of the grove was empty. The wagons were gone—and with them the girl. Tom experienced a blankness of thought, then a sense of loss and a twinge of regret. After this moment he thoughtfully went on eating his breakfast. Nothing was to come of the meeting. Still, her people were buffalo-hunters, too, and somewhere down in that wild country he might see her again. What a forlorn hope! Yet by cherishing it he reconciled himself to the fact that she was gone.

After breakfast his curiosity led him to walk over to where her camp had been; and he trailed the wagon tracks out into the road, seeing that they headed toward the southwest. His grain of comfort gathered strength.

"Our neighbors pulled out early," he remarked, halting where Pilchuck and Hudnall were packing.

"Long before sunup," replied Hudnall. "Did you hear them, Jude?"

"Huh! They'd waked the dead," growled Pilchuck. "Reckon Randall Jett had his reason for pullin' out."

"Jett? Let's see. He was the man with the yellow beard. Come to think of it, he wasn't very civil."

"I heard some talk about Jett uptown," went on Pilchuck. " 'Pears I've met him somewheres, but it's slipped my mind. He's one of the hide-hunters that's got a doubt hangin' on him. Just doubt, it's only fair to say. Nobody knows anythin'. Jett has come out of the Panhandle twice with thousands of hides. He's made money."

"Well, that's interestin'," replied Hudnall. "He's just been married. My wife had some talk yesterday with a woman who must have been Mrs. Jett. She was from Missouri an' had a grown daughter. Married a few weeks, she said. My wife got a hunch this woman an' daughter weren't keen about the hide-huntin' business."

"Well, when you get down on the Staked Plains, you'll appreciate Mrs. Jett's feelings," remarked Pilchuck, dryly.

Tom listened to this talk, much interested, recording it in memory. Then he asked if all the buffalo-hunters followed the same line of travel.

"Reckon they do," replied Pilchuck. "There's only one good road for a couple of hundred miles. Then the hunters make their own roads."

"Do they scatter all over the plains?" went on Tom.

"Well, naturally they hang round the buffalo. But that herd is most as big as the Staked Plain."

Tom had no knowledge of this particular part of Texas, but he did not fail to get a conception of magnitude.

"When do we pull out?" he concluded.

"Soon as we hitch up."

In less than an hour the Hudnall outfit, with three good wagons drawn by strong teams, were on the move. The women rode with the drivers. Tom had the job of keeping the saddle horses in line. They did not want to head out into the wilderness, and on the start were contrary. After a few miles, however, they settled down to a trot and kept to the road.

Soon the gleam of the town, and groves of trees, and columns of smoke, disappeared behind a rolling ridge, and all around appeared endless gray-green plain, bisected by a white road. No other wagons were in sight. Tom found the gait of his horse qualified to make long rides endurable. The lonely land was much to his liking. Jackrabbits and birds were remarkable for their scarcity. The plain appeared endlessly undulating, a lonesome expanse, mostly gray, stretching away on all sides. The soil was good. Some day these wide lands would respond to cultivation.

The Hudnall outfit traveled steadily until about four o'clock in the afternoon, making about twenty-five miles. A halt was called in a grove of elm trees that had long appealed to Tom's eye. It amused him to see the amiable contention between Pilchuck and Hudnall. The former, like all guides and scouts long used to outdoor life, wanted to camp at the first available spot where others had camped. But Hudnall sought a fresh and untrammeled place, driving some distance off the road to a clean glade under spreading elms just beginning to green. A shallow creek ran under the high bank. Birds and rabbits were plentiful here, and cat and coyote tracks showed on the muddy shore.

There was work for everybody and something of confusion. Further experience in making camp was essential before things could be done smoothly and expeditiously.

"I laid out jobs for everybody. Now rustle," was Hudnall's order.

The teams were unhitched and turned loose to drink and graze. Harness and collars were hung upon the front wheels. Tom scouted for firewood, which appeared plentiful, and the ring of his ax resounded through the glade. Hudnall and his son lifted the cook stove and mess box from a wagon, then the cooking utensils and tableware. A level spot was cleaned off, a fire started on the ground and also in the stove, then the meal preparations were turned over to the women. Hudnall erected a tent for himself and his wife. Sally's bed was made in the wagon. Pilchuck helped Stronghurl pitch a tent beside their wagon, but he spread his own bed, consisting of blankets on a tarpaulin, outside under the trees. Burn Hudnall put up a tent for himself and his wife, and Tom unrolled his bed under Burn's wagon.

At sunset they ate supper. The gold and pink of western sky appeared to send a reflection upon the winding stream of water. Everybody was hungry, and even Pilchuck seemed to feel something good in the hour and the place. If there had been any misgivings on the part of the women, they had now vanished. The talk was jolly and hopeful. Sally Hudnall made eyes at Tom, and then, seeing her advances were apparently unobserved, she tried the same upon Stronghurl.

After supper Tom chopped and carried wood for the camp fire that night and for next morning. This done, he strolled along the creek toward the grazing horses. Fresh green grass grew abundantly on the banks and ensured reasonably against the horses' straying that night. Tom decided not to hobble Dusty.

A few hundred yards from camp the creek circled through a grove of larger elms and eddied in a deep pool. Here on a log Tom lingered and indulged in rest and musings. His thoughts seemed to flow and eddy like the stream, without any apparent reason. But when thought of the girl, Milly, recurred, it abided with him. Here in the solitude of this grove he seemed to remember more vividly, and after reviewing gravely all the details concerning her it seemed to him not improbable that she was unhappy and unfortunately situated. "I—I can't tell you more," she had said, hurriedly, in a tone he now realized held shame and fear. Tom meditated over that, and at the end of an hour, when dusk was creeping under the trees, he threw off the spell and retraced his steps toward camp. There was little chance of his ever seeing her again. With resignation to that, and the vague sadness attending it, he put her out of his mind.

Soon a camp fire blazed through the dusk, and seen from afar, with the black shadows of men crossing its brightness, it made a telling picture. Tom joined the circle sitting and standing round it. The air had grown cold, making the warmth most agreeable.

"That 'tarnal smoke follows me everywhere I turn," said Sally Hudnall, as she moved to a seat beside Stronghurl.

"Elm wood ain't so good to burn," observed Pilchuck. "Neither is cottonwood. Smoke smells an' makes your eyes smart."

"Mary has a likin' for hickory," said Hudnall. "Golly! I'll bet I'll never again have apple pie baked over a hickory fire."

"Unless you go back to Illinois," added his wife, dryly.

"Which'll never be, Mary," he replied, with finality.

His words, tinged with a suggestion of failure back there in Illinois, checked conversation for a moment. They all had places dear to look back upon. Pioneers had to sacrifice much. Tom gazed at the circle of quiet faces with more realization and kindness. Buffalo-hunting was but to be an incident. It had dominated his thought. In the background of his mind, in the future, had been the idea of a ranch. With these people home and farm were paramount. Tom wondered if they were not starting out upon an ill-advised enterprise. Not to think of its peril!

Day by day the Hudnall outfit traveled over the prairie, sometimes west, and then south, yet in the main always southwest. They made from fifteen to twenty-five miles a day, according to condition of the road and favorable places to camp. Now and then they passed a freighting outfit of several wagons, heavily loaded with buffalo hides. The days passed into weeks, until Tom lost track of them.

Down here on the great plains spring had surely come. All was green and beautiful. The monotony of the country had been broken up by streams winding away between wooded banks, yet the rolling level seemed to hold generally, viewed from afar. On clear mornings a gray heave of higher ground appeared to the south. What farther north had been an openness and sameness of country now assumed proportions vast and striking.

One sunset, when halt was made for camp in an

arroyo, Pilchuck waived his usual work and rode off up a slope. Reaching the summit, he dismounted and, elevating a short telescope, he looked long to the southward. Later, when he returned to the camp, all eyes fixed upon him.

"See anythin'?" queried Hudnall, impatiently.

Tom felt a thrill merely from the look of the scout.

"Buffalo!" announced Pilchuck.

There was a moment's silence. The women responded more quickly to this good news. Hudnall seemed slow and thick. Burn Hudnall threw down a billet of wood he had held in his hand.

"Buffalo!" he echoed, and the quick look of gladness he flashed upon his father proved how much he had been responsible for this trip.

"How many?" demanded Hudnall, with a long stride toward the scout.

"Reckon I couldn't say, offhand," replied Pilchuck. "Herd is another day's ride south."

Sally Hudnall interrupted her father as he was about to speak again: "Oh, I'm crazy to see a herd of buffalo. Are there lots of them?"

"Tolerable many," replied Pilchuck, with a look of professional pride. "Reckon this herd is about fifteen miles long an' three or four deep!"

Then Hudnall let out a stentorian roar, and that was a signal for equally sincere if not so exuberant a rejoicing from the others.

Next day's travel was the longest Tom had ever endured. The ground was dusty, the sun hot, the miles interminable, and there appeared ahead only the gray-green stretch of plain, leading the eyes with false hopes. But at last, toward sunset, a fringe of winding foliage marked the course of a stream. It seemed a goal. Beyond that water the great herd of buffalo must be grazing. An hour more of weary travel over uneven prairie—for Pilchuck had turned off the road early that morning—brought the outfit down into a coulee, the wildest and most attractive camp site that had yet fallen to them.

Tom made short work of his camp duties that evening, and soon was climbing the highest ridge. He climbed fast in his eagerness. Abruptly, then, he reached the top and looking westward, suddenly became transfixed.

The sun was setting in a golden flare that enveloped the wide plain below. Half a mile from where he stood was an immense herd of huge woolly beasts, wild and strange to his sight, yet unmistakably buffalo. Tom experienced the most tingling thrill of his life. What a wonderful spectacle! It was not at all what he had pictured from tales he had heard. This scene was beautiful; and the huge straggling bulls seemed the grandest of big game beasts. Thousands of buffalo! Tom reveled in his opportunity and made the most of it. He saw that the herd circled away out of sight beyond the other end of the ridge upon which he stood. Long he gazed, and felt that he would never forget his first sight of a buffalo herd.

Upon his return to camp he found that he was not the only one late for supper. Hudnall had been out with Pilchuck. Burn was on the moment coming in with his wife and sister, who were talking excitedly about what they had seen.

"How many did you see?" asked Hudnall, of Tom.

"Oh, I've no idea—all of five thousand—and I couldn't see the end of the herd," replied Tom.

"We saw ten thousand, an' that on the other side of the ridge from you," added Hudnall, tensely. His big eyes were alight and he seemed to look afar. Tom sensed that Hudnall had not responded to the wildness and beauty of the spectacle. He saw thousands of hides to sell.

"Reckon I heard shootin' down the river a couple of miles," said Pilchuck. "There's another outfit on the trail. We'll be lucky if we don't run into a dozen."

"Is this the main herd you spoke of?" inquired Tom.

"No. This is only a little bunch," returned Pilchuck.

Mrs. Hudnall broke up the colloquy. "Are you all daffy about buffalo? Supper's gettin' cold."

"Mary, you'll be fryin' buffalo steak for me to-morrow night," rejoined her husband, gayly.

After supper Hudnall called the men aside for the purpose of consultation.

"Pilchuck an' me are pardners on this deal," he said. "We'll pay thirty cents a hide. That means skin-nin', haulin the hide to camp, an' peggin' it out. No difference who kills the buffalo."

"That's more than you'll get paid by most outfits," added Pilchuck.

Stronghurl and Burn agreed on that figure; and as for Tom he frankly admitted he thought thirty cents a hide was big pay.

"Huh! Wait till you skin your first buffalo," said the scout, grinning. "You'll swear thirty dollars too little."

"Well, my part of this deal is settled. I furnish supplies an' pay for hides," said Hudnall. "Jude here will boss the hunt."

"Not much bossin'," said that individual "We're a little farther south than I've hunted. I rode through here with some soldiers last fall, an' know the country. This bunch of buffalo is hangin' along the river. Reckon there's buffalo for miles. They'll hang around here, unless too many outfits get chasin' them. A good way to hunt is to catch them comin' to drink. Aim to hit behind the shoulder, an' shoot till he drops. Some-times it takes two or three bullets, an' sometimes five on the old bulls. When you hunt out in the open you've got to ride like hell, chase them, an' keep shootin' till your cartridges are all gone."

"That's easy, an' ought to be heaps of fun," said Burn.

"Reckon so. An' don't forget it's dangerous. Keep out of their reach. The real hard work comes in skinnin' an' peggin' out. Before you get good enough at that to make three dollars a day, you'll be sick of the job."

"Three dollars!" echoed Burn, in scorn. "I expect to make five times that much."

Tom had much the same aspiration, but he did not voice it. Pilchuck looked amused and mysterious enough to restrain undue enthusiasm.

"Finally—an' this is a hunch you want to take serious," went on Pilchuck, lowering his voice so the women could not hear. "We might run on to Indians."

That sobered all the listeners.

"Last summer was bad an' fall was worse," he continued. "I don't know now how conditions are or what the Indians are doin.' Reckon somebody, hunters or soldiers, will happen along an' tell us. My belief is there'll be some tough fights this year. But, of course, the redskins can't be everywhere, an' these buffalo are thick an' range far. We may be lucky an' never see a Comanche. But we'll have to keep our eyes peeled all the time an' mustn't get far apart. If we see or hear of Indians, we'll move camp an' stand guard at night."

"Jude, that's stranger talk than you've used yet," responded Hudnall, in surprise and concern.

"Reckon so. I'm not worryin.' I'm just tellin' you. There'll be a heap of hunters in here this summer. An' like as not the soldiers will see what women there are safe to the fort or some well-protected freightin' post."

Tom thought of the dark-eyed girl, Milly. Almost he had forgotten. How long ago that meeting seemed! Where was she now? He convinced himself that Pilchuck's assurance of the protection of soldiers applied to all the women who might be with the hunting bands.

No more was said about Indians. Interest reverted strongly to the proposed hunt to begin on the morrow. Tom fell in with the spirit of the hour and stayed up late round the camp fire, listening to the talk and joining in. Once their animated discussion was silenced by a mournful howl from the ridge-top where Tom had climbed to see the buffalo. It was a strange sound, deep and prolonged, like the bay of a hound on a deer scent, only infinitely wilder.

"What's that?" asked somebody.

"Wolf," replied Pilchuck. "Not a coyote, mind you, but a real old king of the plains. There's a lot of wolves hang with the buffalo."

The cry was not repeated then, but later, as Tom composed himself in his warm blankets, it pealed out again, wonderfully breaking the stillness. How hungry and full of loneliness! It made Tom shiver. It seemed a herald of wilderness.

Tom was the first to arise next morning, and this time it was the ring of his ax and the crash of wood thrown into the camp-fire circle that roused the others. When Stronghurl sallied forth to find the horses, daylight had broken clear; and by the time breakfast was ready the sun was up.

Pilchuck, returning from the ridge-top, reported that buffalo were in sight, all along the river, as far as he could see. They were a goodly distance out on the plain and were not yet working in for a drink.

"I'll take my turn hangin' round camp," said Hudnall, plainly with an effort. "There's a lot to do, an' some one must see after the women folks."

"It'd be a good idea for you to climb the ridge every two hours or so an' take a look," replied Pilchuck, casually. But his glance at Hudnall was not casual. "I'll leave my telescope for you. Don't miss anythin'."

The men saddled their horses and donned the heavy cartridge belts. They also carried extra cartridges in their pockets. Tom felt weighted down as if by a thousand pounds. He had neglected to buy a saddle sheath for his gun, and therefore would have to carry it in his hand—an awkward task while riding.

They rode behind Pilchuck down the river, and forded it at a shallow sand-barred place, over which the horses had to go at brisk gait to avoid miring.

"How're we ever goin' to get the wagons across?" queried Burn Hudnall.

"Reckon we've no choice," replied Pilchuck. "The hides have to be hauled to camp. You see the actual chasin' an' killin' of buffalo doesn't take much time. Then the real work begins. We'll have all the rest of the day—an' night, to skin, haul to camp, an' peg out."

This side of the river bank was more wooded and less precipitous than the other. Buffalo tracks were as thick as cattle tracks round a water-hole. The riders halted at the top of the slope where the level plain began. Out on the grassy expanse, perhaps a mile or more, extended a shaggy dark line like a wall.

"Reckon there's your buffalo," said the scout. "Now we'll scatter an' wait under cover for an hour or so. Hide in the brush or behind a bank, anywhere till some come close. Then burn powder! An' don't quit the buffalo you shoot at till he's down. When they run off, chase them, an' shoot from your horses. The chase won't last long, for the buffalo will run away from you."

Pilchuck stationed Tom at this point, and rode on down the edge of the plain with the other men. They passed out of sight. In that direction Tom could not see far, owing to rising ground. To the southwest, however, the herd extended until it was impossible to distinguish between vague black streaks of buffalo and dim distance.

"Pilchuck said this was only a little bunch!" soliloquized Tom, as he scanned the plain-wide band of beasts.

Dismounting, he held his horse and stood at the edge of the timber, watching and listening. It was a wonderfully satisfying moment. He tried to be calm, but that was impossible. He recognized what had always been deep in him—the love of adventure and freedom—the passion to seek these in unknown places. Here, then,

he stood at his post above the bank of a timber-
bordered river in the Panhandle of Texas with a herd of
buffalo in sight. He saw coyotes, too, and a larger
beast, gray in color, that he was sure was a wolf.
Hawks and buzzards sailed against the blue sky. Down
through the trees, near the river, he espied a flock of
wild turkeys. Then, in connection with all he saw, and
the keenness of the morning which he felt, he remembered the scout's caution about Indians. Tom thought
that he ought to be worried, even frightened, but he
was neither. This moment was the most mysteriously
full and satisfying of his life.

Opposite his point the buffalo did not approach
more closely; he observed, however, that to the eastward they appeared to be encroaching upon the river
brakes.

Suddenly then he was thrilled by gun-shots. Boom!
Boom! . . . Boom-boom! His comrades had opened
the hunt.

"What'll I do now?" he mused, gazing down the
river, then out toward the herd. It presented no change
that he could distinguish. "I was told to stay here. But
with shooting begun, I don't think any buffalo will
come now."

Soon after that a gun roared out much closer, indeed, just over the rise of plain below Tom.

"That's a big fifty!" he ejaculated, aloud.

Far beyond, perhaps two miles distant, sounded a
report of a Sharps, low but clear on the still morning
air. Another and another! Tom began to tingle with
anticipation. Most likely his comrades would chase the
buffalo his way. Next he heard a shot apparently
between the one that had sounded close and the one
far away. So all three of his fellow hunters had gotten
into action. Tom grew restive. Peering out at the herd,
he discovered it was moving. A low trample of many
hoofs assailed his ears. Dust partially obscured the
buffalo. They appeared to be running back into the

gray expanse. Suddenly Tom became aware of heavy and continuous booming of guns—close, medium, and far-away reports mingling. As he listened it dawned on him that all the reports were diminishing in sound. His comrades were chasing the buffalo and getting farther away. After a while he heard no more. Also the dust-shrouded buffalo opposite his position had disappeared. His disappointment was keen.

Presently a horseman appeared on the crest of the ridge that had hidden the chase from him. The white horse was Pilchuck's. Tom saw the rider wave his hat, and taking the action as a signal he mounted and rode at a gallop to the ridge, striking its summit some few hundred yards to the right. Here he had unobstructed view. Wide gray-green barren rolling plain, hazy with dust! The herd of buffalo was not in sight. Tom rode on to meet Pilchuck.

"Tough luck for you," said the scout. "They were workin' in to the river below here."

"Did you kill any?" queried Tom, eagerly.

"I downed twenty-one," replied Pilchuck. "An' as I was ridin' back I met Stronghurl. He was cussin' because he'd only got five. An' Burn burned a lot of powder. But so far as I could see he got only one."

"No!" ejaculated Tom. "Why, he was sure of dozens."

"Reckon he knows more now," returned Pilchuck. "You ride down there an' see how many you can skin. I'll go back to camp, hitch up a wagon, an' try to come back across the river."

The scout rode away, and Tom, turning his horse eastward, took to a trot down the immense gradual slope. After searching the plain he espied a horse grazing, and then a dark shaggy mound which manifestly was a slain buffalo. Tom spurred his horse, rapidly covering the distance between. Soon he saw Burn at work skinning the buffalo.

"Good for you!" shouted Tom, as he galloped up.

"Helluva job—this skinnin'!" yelled Burn, flashing a red and sweaty face toward Tom. "Hey! Look out!"

But his warning came too late. Tom's horse snorted furiously, as if expelling a new and hateful scent, and, rearing high, he came down and plunged so violently that Tom flew one way and his gun another.

Tom landed hard and rooted his face in the grass. The shock stunned him for a second. Then he sat up and found himself unhurt. The surprise, the complete victory of the horse, and the humiliation of being made to root the ground like a pig stirred Tom to some heat.

"Hope you ain't hurt?" called Burn, anxiously, rising from his work.

"No, but I'm mad," replied Tom.

Whereupon Burn fell back and rolled over in the grass, roaring with mirth. Tom paid no attention to his comrade. Dusty had run off a hundred or more paces, and was now walking, head to one side, dragging his bridle. Tom yelled to stop him. Dusty kept on. Whereupon Tom broke into a run and caught him.

"You're a fine horse," panted Tom, as he mounted. "Now you'll—go back—and rub your nose—on that buffalo."

Dusty appeared placable enough, and trotted back readily until once again close to the buffalo. Tom spurred him on and called forcibly to him. Dusty grew excited as he came nearer. Still he did not show any ugliness.

"Don't hurry him," remonstrated Burn. "He's just scared."

But Tom, not yet cooled in temper, meant that Dusty should go right up to the buffalo. This he forced the horse to do. Then suddenly Dusty flashed down his head and seemed to propel himself with incredible violence high into the air. He came down on stiff legs. The shock was so severe that Tom shot out of the saddle. He came down back of the cantle. Desperately he clung to the pommel, and as Dusty pitched high again, his hold broke and he spun round like a top on the rump of the horse and slid off. Dusty ceased his pitching and backed away from the dead buffalo.

Only Tom's feelings were hurt. Burn Hudnall's "Haw! haw! haw!" rolled out in great volume. Tom sat where he had been dumped, and gazing at the horse, he gradually induced a state of mind bordering upon appreciation of how Dusty must have felt. Presently Burn got up, and catching Dusty, led him slowly and gently, talking soothingly the while, nearer to the buffalo, and held him there.

"He's all right now," said Burn.

Tom rose and went back to the horse and patted him.

"You bucked me off, didn't you?"

"Tom, if I were you I'd get off an' lead him up to the dead buffalo till he gets over his scare," suggested Burn.

"I will," replied Tom, and then he gazed down at the shaggy carcass on the ground. "Phew! the size of him!"

"Looks big as a woolly elephant, doesn't he? Big bull," Pilchuck said. "He's the only one I got, an' sure he took a lot of shootin'. You see the buffalo was runnin' an' I couldn't seem to hit one of them. Finally I plunked this bull. An' he kept on runnin' till I filled him full of lead."

"Where are those Pilchuck got?" queried Tom, anxious to go to work.

"First one's lyin' about a quarter—there, to the left a little. You go tackle skinnin' him. It's an old bull like this. An' if you get his skin off to-day I'll eat it."

"I've skinned lots of cattle—steers and bulls," replied Tom. "It wasn't hard work. Why should this be?"

"Man, they're buffalo, an' their skin's an inch thick, tougher than sole leather—an' stick! Why it's riveted on an' clinched."

"Must be some knack about the job, then," rejoined Tom, mounting Dusty. "Say, I nearly forgot my gun.

Hand it up, will you? . . . Burn, I'll bet you I skin ten buffalo before dark and peg them out, as Pilchuck called it, before I go to bed."

"I'll take you up," said Burn, with a grim laugh. "I just wish I had time to watch you. It'd be a circus. But I'll be ridin' by you presently."

"All right. I'm off to win that bet," replied Tom, in cheery determination, and touching Dusty with the spurs he rode rapidly toward the next fallen buffalo.

Chapter IV

DUSTY evinced less fear of the second prostrate buffalo, which was even a larger bull than the huge tough old animal Burn was engaged in skinning.

This time Tom did not take any needless risks with Dusty. Riding to within fifty feet of the dead beast, he dismounted, led the nervous horse closer, and round and round, and finally up to it. Dusty behaved very well, considering his first performance; left to himself, however, he edged away to a considerable distance and began to graze.

Tom lost no time in getting to work. He laid his gun near at hand, and divesting himself of his coat he took ripping and skinning knives from his belt. Determination was strong in him. He anticipated an arduous and perplexing job, yet felt fully capable of accomplishing it and winning his bet with Burn. This buffalo was a monster; he was old and the burrs and matted hair appeared a foot deep at his forequarters; he was almost black.

First Tom attempted to turn the beast over into a more favorable position for skinning. He found, however, that he could scarcely budge the enormous bulk. That was a surprise. There appeared nothing to do but go to work as best he could, and wait for help to move the animal. Forthwith he grasped his ripping knife and proceeded to try following instructions given him. It took three attempts to get the knife under the skin and when he essayed to rip he found that a good deal of strength was required. He had calculated that he must expend considerable energy to make any speed, until practice had rendered him proficient. The considerable energy grew into the utmost he could put forth. After the ripping came the skinning, and in very short time he appreciated all Burn had said. "Helluva job is right!" Tom commented, remembering his comrade's words. But he did not spare himself, and by tremendous exertions he had the buffalo skinned before Burn finished his. Tom could not vouch for the merit of the job, but the skin was off. He could vouch, however, for his breathlessness and the hot sweat that bathed his body. Plowing corn or pitching wheat, jobs he had imagined were hard work, paled into insignificance.

"Say—wonder what pegging out the hide—will be like," he panted, as he sheathed his knives and picked up his gun. Mounting Dusty he rode eastward, scanning the plain for the next dead buffalo.

Presently he espied it, and galloping thither he found it to be another bull, smaller and younger than the others, and he set to work with renewed zeal. He would have to work like a beaver to win that bet. It took violence to make a quick job of this one. That done, Tom rode on to the third.

While he was laboring here Burn rode by and paid him a hearty compliment, which acted upon Tom like a spur. He could not put forth any greater zeal; indeed, he would do wonders if he kept to the pace he had set himself. But as he progressed he learned. This advantage, however, was offset by the gradual dulling of his knives. He had forgotten to bring his steel.

He toiled from one dead buffalo to another. The

breeze died away, the sun climbed high and blazed down upon the plain. His greatest need was water to drink. Hour by hour his thirst augmented. His shirt was so wet with perspiration that he could have wrung it out. The heat did not bother him so much. Gradually his clothes became covered with a lather of sweat, blood, grease, and dust. This, and the growing pangs in his body, especially hands and forcarms, occasioned him extreme annoyance. He did not note the passing of time. Only now and then did he scan the plain for sign of his comrades. Indians he had completely forgotten. Burn and Stronghurl were to be seen at intervals, and Pilchuck, driving the wagon, was with them. Once from a high knoll Tom thought he espied another wagon miles down the river, but he could not be sure. He did, however, make out a dim black blur to the southward, and this he decided was the buffalo herd, ranging back toward the river.

During this strenuous time there were incidents of much interest, if he could only have given them due attention. Buzzards swooped down over him, closer and closer, till he felt the wind of their wings. A lean gray wolf came within range of his gun, but Tom had no time for shooting. He toiled on and the hours flew.

When, late in the afternoon, he tore off the hide that assured him of winning the wager, he was exultant. He was now two miles from the wagon, which he made out was approaching. Only one more buffalo did he find, and this he skinned by the time Pilchuck drove up.

"Wal, if you ain't a Kansas cyclone!" ejaculated the scout, with undisguised admiration. "Seventeen skinned your first day! Doan, I never seen the beat of it."

"I had a bet with Burn," replied Tom, wiping his hot face.

"If you can keep that lick up, young man, you'll make a stake out of this hide-huntin'," returned Pilchuck, seriously.

"Wait till I learn how!" exclaimed Tom, fired by the praise and the hopes thus engendered.

"Reckon I'll cut the hump off this young bull," remarked the scout, as he climbed out of the seat. "Buffalo steak for supper, hey?"

"I could eat hoofs. And I'm spitting cotton," said Tom.

"You forgot a canteen. Son, you mustn't forget *anythin'* in this game," admonished Pilchuck. "Rustle back to camp."

Tom was interested, however, to learn how Pilchuck would cut the desirable hump from the carcass. Long had Tom heard of the savory steaks from the buffalo. The scout thrust his big knife in near the joining of the loin, ripped forward along the lower side as far as the ribs ran; then performed a like operation on the upper side. That done, he cut the ends loose and carved out a strip over three feet long and so thick it was heavy.

"Reckon we can rustle back to camp now," he said, throwing the meat on the pile of hides in the wagon.

"Is that the herd coming back?" queried Tom, pointing from his horse.

"Yes. They'll be in to-night yet to drink. We'll find them here to-morrow mornin'. Did you hear the big fifties of the other hunters?"

"You mean others besides our outfit? No, I didn't."

"There's a couple of outfits down the river. But that's lucky for us. Probably will be hunters all along here soon. Reckon there's safety in numbers an' sure the buffalo are plenty enough."

Tom rode back to camp facing a sunset that emblazoned the western ramparts in gold and purple. The horizon line was far distant and lifted high, a long level upland, at that moment singularly wild and beautiful. Tom wondered if it could be the eastern extension of the great Staked Plains he had heard mentioned so often. Weary as he was from his extraordinary exertions, he yet had spirit left to look and feel and think. The future seemed like that gold-rimmed horizon line.

He reached camp before dusk, there to receive the plaudits of his comrades and also the women folks. Burn was generous in his eulogy, but he created consternation in Tom's breast by concluding, "Wait till you try peggin' out a hide!"

"Aw! I forgot there was more. I've not won that bet yet," he rejoined, dejectedly.

After attending to his horse Tom had just about enough energy left to drink copiously and stretch out with a groan under a tree. Never before in his life had he throbbed and ached and burned so exceedingly. An hour's rest considerably relieved him. Then supper, which he attacked somewhat as if he were a hungry wolf, was an event to be remembered. If all his comrades had not been equally as ravenous he would have been ashamed. Pilchuck got much satisfaction out of the rapid disappearance of many buffalo steaks.

"Meat's no good when so fresh," he averred. "After bein' hung up a few days an' set, we call it, an' fried in tallow, it beats beef all hollow."

Before darkness set in Tom saw Pilchuck peg out a hide. First the scout laid the hide flat and proceeded to cut little holes in it all around the edge. Next with ax and knife he sharpened sticks nearly a foot long. Three of these he drove through the neck of the hide and deep enough into the ground to hold well. Then he proceeded to the tail end and stretched the skin. Tom could well see that skill was required here. Pilchuck held the skin stretched, and at the same time drove one peg, then another, at this end. Following that, he began to stretch and peg the side, eventually working all around. The whole operation did not take long and did not appear difficult.

Tom essayed it with a vim that made up for misgivings. Like the skinning, it was vastly more difficult than it looked. Cutting the holes and making the pegs was easy; however, when it came to stretching the hide and holding it and pegging it all by himself, he found it a most deceiving and irksome task.

Sally Hudnall offered to help Tom, but he declined
with thanks, explaining that he had a wager to win.
The girl hovered round Tom and curiously watched
him, much to his annoyance. He saw that she was
laughing at him.

"What's so funny?" he queried, nettled.

"You look like a boy tryin' to play mumblypeg an'
leap-frog at once," she replied with a giggle.

Tom had to laugh a good-natured acknowledgment
to that; and then he deftly turned the tables on her by
making a dry, casual remark about Stronghurl. The girl
blushed and let him alone to ponder over the intricacies of this hide pegging. No contortionist ever performed more marvels of stretching his body than Tom
achieved. Likewise, no man ever so valiantly stifled
back speech that would have been unseemly, to say
the least, in the hearing of women. His efforts, however, were crowned with the reward of persistence. By
midnight he had the job done, and utterly spent he
crawled into his bed, where at once his eyes seemed to
glue shut.

Next morning he readily answered Pilchuck's call,
but his body was incapable of a like alacrity. He
crawled out of his blankets as if he were crippled. A
gradual working of his muscles, however, loosened the
stiffness and warmed the cold soreness to the extent
that he believed he could begin the day with some
semblance of service.

It was again, in Pilchuck's terse terms, every man
for himself. Tom welcomed this for two reasons, first
that he could go easy, and secondly that he wanted to
revel in and prolong his first real encounter with the
buffalo.

Hudnall changed Tom's plans somewhat by relegat-
ing him to watch camp that day, while he went out
with the other men. He modified this order, however,
by saying that if any buffalo came near camp Tom
might go after them.

Breakfast was over at sunrise. Pilchuck brought out

his heavy ammunition box, with which each hunter was provided, and told Tom he could help a little and learn while he helped. His belt contained more than thirty empty shells that were to be reloaded.

"Reckon I ought to have done this last night," he explained to Hudnall, who was impatient to be off. "You fellows go on down the river. I'll catch up with you."

The three hunters rode off eagerly, and Pilchuck got out his tools for reloading. Tom quickly learned the use of bullet-mold, swedge, lubricator, primer, extractor, tamper, and patchpaper.

"Reckon I'm all set now," affirmed the scout. "You put these tools away for me. An' keep a good lookout. I'm not worryin', but I'd like to know if there's Indians huntin' this herd. Take a look from the ridge with my glass, an' there'll be buffalo on the other side of the river to-day, you can keep in sight of camp an' get a shot."

With that Pilchuck mounted his horse and trotted away through the timber. Tom leisurely set about the few tasks at hand. It pleased him when he was able to avoid Sally's watching eyes. She seemed to regard him with something of disapproval. When the camp chores were finished Tom took the telescope and climbed to the ridge-top. Apparently more buffalo were in sight than on the previous day and about in the same latitude. Tom swept the circle of surrounding country, grey-green rolling plain, the low ridges, the winding river depression, with its fringe of trees. Some miles down the river rose a column of smoke, marking, no doubt, another camp. Far away to the south and west loomed the strange upheaval of land. Clearly defined by the telescope, it appeared to be an escarpment of horizonwide dimensions, gray and barren, seamed by canyons, standing in wild and rugged prominence above the plains.

Not until late in the morning did Tom's watchful gaze espy buffalo approaching camp. Then he was thrilled to see a number of what appeared to be bulls grazing riverward opposite the camp. Hurrying down from the eminence whence he had made this observation, he got his gun and cartridges, and crossing the river he proceeded up the thickly wooded slope some distance to the west of his first stand of yesterday. It looked to him as if the bulls might work down into a coulee which opened into the river depression. He was quite a little time reaching the point desired—the edge of woodland and brink of the ravine—and when he peered from under the last trees he was moved with such an overwhelming excitement that he dropped to his knees.

Out on the open plain, not a hundred yards distant, grazed nine buffalo bulls, the leader of which appeared larger than the largest he had skinned the day before. They had not scented Tom and were grazing toward him, somewhat to the right, manifestly headed for the coulee.

Trembling and panting, Tom watched with strained sight. He forgot he held a "big fifty" in his hands, and in the riotous sensation of that moment he did not remember until from far down the river came a dull boom-boom of guns. It amazed him to see that the buffalo bulls paid no attention to the shooting. He made up his mind then to take his time and await a favorable opportunity to down the leader. They were approaching so slowly that he had ample time to control the trembling of his muscles, though it was impossible to compose himself.

Several of the bulls piled over the little bank into the coulee, and while they were passing within fifty yards of Tom the others leisurely began the descent, the huge bull nodding along in the rear. The near ones passed into the timber, getting farther away from Tom. He had difficulty in restraining his eagerness. Then one bull began to crash in the brush. He made as much noise as an elephant. Tom watched with an intense interest only second to the hot-pressed lust to kill. This bull was crashing against thick brush, and it soon became plain to Tom that the beast was scratching his shaggy hide, tearing out the matts of burrs and the shedding hair. It came away in great tufts, hanging on the sharp broken ends of the brush. This old bull knew what he was about when he charged that thicket of hackberry.

Suddenly Tom was electrified by a puff which assuredly came from the nostrils of a buffalo close to him. He turned cautiously. Behind and below him, closer than fifty yards, the other bulls were passing into the timber. He plainly heard the grinding of their teeth. They were monsters. Instinctively Tom searched for a tree to climb or a place to run to after he fired. What if they should charge his way? He would scarcely have time to reload, and even if he had, of what avail would that be?

Then the monarch wagged his enormous head in line with Tom's magnifying vision. What a wide short face! His eyes stood out so that he could see in front or behind. His shaggy beard was dragging. Tom could see only the tips of the horns in all that woolly mass. Puff! came the sound of expelled breath.

Tom felt he hated to kill that glorious and terrifying beast, yet he was powerless to resist the tight palpitating feverish dominance of his blood. Resting the heavy rifle on a branch, he aimed behind the great shaggy shoulder, and with strained muscles and bated breath he fired.

Like a cannon the old Sharps roared. Crashings of brush, thudding of heavy hoofs, sounded to the right of the cloud of smoke. The other bulls were running. Tom caught glimpses of broad brown backs cleaving the brush down the river slope. With shaking hands he reloaded. Peering under the drifting smoke, he searched fearfully for the bull he had fired at, at first seeing only the thick-grassed swelling slope of the coulee. Then farther down he espied a huge brown object lying inert.

The wildness of the boy in Tom conquered all else.

Leaping up, he broke out of the woods, yelling like an Indian, and charged down the gentle slope, exultant and proud, yet not quite frenzied enough to forget possible peril. From that quarter, however, he was safe. The monarch was heaving his last breath.

Pilchuck rode in at noon that day, in time to see Tom stretch the hide of his first buffalo.

"You got one, hey?" he called, eying the great shaggy hide with appreciation. "Your first buffalo! Wal, it's a darned fine one. They don't come any bigger than that fellow."

Tom had to tell the story of his exploit, and was somewhat discomfited by the scout's remark that he should have killed several of the bulls.

"Aren't you back early?" queried Tom, as Pilchuck dismounted.

"Run out of cartridges," he said, laconically.

"So quick!" exclaimed Tom, staring. "You must have seen a lot of buffalo."

"Reckon they *was* thick this mornin'," returned the scout, dryly. "I got plumb surrounded once an' had to shoot my way out."

"Well? . . . How many did you down?"

"Twenty-one. I think when we count up tonight we'll have a good day. Burn is doin' better than yesterday. . . . Wal, I want a bite to eat an' a drink. It's warm ridin' in the dust. Then I'll hitch up the wagon an' drive down for the hides. Come to think of it, though, I've a job to do before. You can help me."

Later Pilchuck hailed Tom to fetch an ax and come on. Tom followed the scout down into the thickets.

"Cut four strong poles about ten feet long an' pack them to camp," said Pilchuck.

Tom did as he was bidden, to find that the scout had returned ahead of him, carrying four short poles with forks at one end. He proceeded to pound these into the ground with the forks uppermost, and then he laid across them the poles Tom had brought, making a square framework. "We'll stretch a hide inside the poles, loose so it'll sag down, an' there we'll salt our buffalo humps."

Pilchuck then brought in a team of horses and hitched it to the big wagon. "Wal, son," he said to Tom, "I ain't hankerin' after skinnin' hides. But I may as well start. We're goin' to kill more buffalo than we'll have time to skin."

He drove out of camp down the slope into the shallow water. The horses plunged in at a trot, splashing high. Pilchuck lashed out with the long whip and yelled lustily. Any slowing up there meant wheels stuck in the sand. Horses, driver, and wagon were drenched. From the other side Pilchuck looked back. "Fine on a day like this," he shouted.

Not long after he had gone Tom heard one of the horses up the river neigh several times. This induced him to reconnoiter, with the result that he espied a wagon coming along the edge of the timber. It appeared to be an open wagon, with one man in the driver's seat. Another, following on horseback, was leading two extra horses.

"More hide-hunters," Tom decided as he headed toward them. "Now I wonder what's expected of me in a case like this."

When the driver espied Tom come into the open, rifle in hand, he halted the horses abruptly.

"Dunn outfit—hide-hunters," he announced, with something of alarmed alacrity, as if his identity and business had been questioned. He appeared to be a short, broad man, and what little of his face was visible was bright red. He had bushy whiskers.

"I'm Tom Doan, of Hudnall's outfit," replied Tom. "We're camped just below."

"Clark Hudnall! By all that's lucky!" exclaimed the man. "I know Hudnall. We talked some last fall of going in together. That was at Independence. But he wasn't ready and I come ahead."

Tom offered his hand, and at this juncture the horseman that had been behind the wagon rode forward abreast of the driver. He was a fat young man with a most jocund expression on his round face. His apparel was striking in its inappropriateness to the rough life of the plains. His old slouch hat was too small for his large head, and there was a tuft of tow-colored hair sticking out of a hole in the crown.

"Ory, shake hands with Tom Doan, of Hudnall's outfit," said Dunn. "My nephew, Ory Tacks."

"Much obliged to meet you, Mister Doan," replied Tacks, with great aplomb.

"Howdy! Same to you," greeted Tom, in slow, good humor, as he studied the face of this newcomer.

Dunn interrupted his scrutiny.

"Is Hudnall in camp?"

"No. He's out hunting buffalo. I'm sure you're welcome to stop at our camp till he comes in. That'll be around sundown."

"Good. I'm needing sight and sound of some one I know," replied Dunn, significantly. "Lead the way, Doan. These horses of mine are thirsty."

When the travelers arrived at Hudnall's camp, Tom helped them unhitch in a favorable camping spot, and unpack the necessary camp duffle. Once during this work Ory Tacks halted so suddenly that he dropped a pack on his foot.

"Ouch!" he cried, lifting his foot to rub it with his hand while he kept his gaze toward Tom's camp. It was an enraptured and amazed gaze. "Do I see a beautiful young lady?"

Thus questioned, Tom wheeled to see Sally Hudnall's face framed in the white-walled door of Hudnall's prairie wagon. It was rather too far to judge accurately, but he inclined to the impression that Sally was already making eyes at Ory Tacks.

"Oh! There!" ejaculated Tom, hard put to it to keep his face serious. "It's a young lady, all right—Miss Sally Hudnall. But I can't see that she——"

"Uncle Jack, there's a girl in this camp," interrupted Ory, in tones of awe.

"We've got three women," said Tom.

"Well, that's a surprise to us," returned Dunn. "I had no idea Hudnall would fetch his women folks down here into the buffalo country. I wonder if he . . . Tom, is there a buffalo-hunter with you, a man who knows the frontier?"

"Yes. Jude Pilchuck."

"Did he stand for the women coming?"

"I guess he had no choice," rejoined Tom.

"Humph! How long have you been on the river?"

"Two days."

"Seen any other outfits?"

"No. But Pilchuck said there were a couple down the river."

"Awhuh," said Dunn, running a stubby, powerful hand through his beard. He seemed concerned. "You see, Doan, we've been in the buffalo country since last fall. And we've sure had it rough. Poor luck on our fall hunt. That was over on the Brazos. Kiowa Indians on the rampage. Our winter hunt we made on the line of Indian Territory. We didn't know it was against the law to kill buffalo in the Territory. The officers took our hides. Then we'd got our spring hunt started fine— west of here forty miles or so. Had five hundred hides. And they were stolen."

"You don't say!" exclaimed Tom, astonished. "Who'd be so low down as to steal hides?"

"Who?" snorted Dunn, with fire in his small eyes. "We don't know. The soldiers don't know. They *say* the thieves are Indians. But I'm one who believes they are white."

Tom immediately grasped the serious nature of this information. The difficulties and dangers of hide-hunting began to assume large proportions.

"Well, you must tell Hudnall and Pilchuck all about this," he said.

Just then Sally called out sweetly, "Tom—oh, Tom—wouldn't your visitors like a bite to eat?"

"Reckon they would, miss, thanks to you," shouted Dunn, answering for himself. As for Ory Tacks, he appeared overcome, either by the immediate prospect of food, or by going into the presence of the beautiful young lady. Tom noted that he at once dropped his task of helping Dunn and bent eager energies to the improvement of his personal appearance. Dunn and Tom had seated themselves before Ory joined them, but when he did come he was manifestly bent on making a great impression.

"Miss Hudnall—my nephew, Ory Tacks," announced Dunn, with quaint formality.

"What's the name?" queried Sally, incredulously, as if she had not heard aright.

"Orville Tacks—at your service, Miss Hudnall," replied the young man, elaborately. "I am much obliged to meet you."

Sally took him in with keen doubtful gaze, and evidently, when she could convince herself that he was not making fun at her expense, gravitated to a perception of easy conquest. Tom saw that this was a paramount issue with Sally. Probably later she might awake to a humorous appreciation of this young gentleman.

Tom soon left the newcomers to their camp tasks, and went about his own, which for the most part consisted of an alert watchfulness. Early in the afternoon the distant boom-boom of the big buffalo guns ceased to break the drowsy silence. The hours wore away. When, at time of sunset, Tom returned from his last survey of the plains, it was to find Hudnall and his hunter comrades in camp. Pilchuck was on the way back with a load of fifty-six hides. Just as twilight fell he called from the opposite bank that he would need help at the steep place. All hands pulled and hauled the wagon over the obstacle; and hard upon that incident came Mrs. Hudnall's cheery call to supper.

Tom watched and listened with more than his usual

attentiveness. Hudnall was radiant. This day's work had been good. For a man of his tremendous strength and endurance the extreme of toil was no hindrance. He was like one that had found a gold mine. Burn Hudnall reflected his father's spirit. Pilchuck ate in silence, not affected by their undisguised elation. Stronghurl would have been dense indeed, in the face of Sally's overtures, not to sense a rival in Ory Tacks. This individual almost ate out of Sally's hand. Dunn presented a rather gloomy front. Manifestly he had not yet told Hudnall of his misfortunes.

After supper it took the men two hours of labor to peg out the hides. All the available space in the grove was blanketed with buffalo skins, with narrow lanes between. Before this work was accomplished the women had gone to bed. At the camp fire which Tom replenished, Dunn recounted to Hudnall and Pilchuck the same news he had told Tom, except that he omitted comment on the presence of the women.

To Tom's surprise, Hudnall took Dunn's story lightly. He did not appear to grasp any serious menace, and he dismissed Dunn's loss with brief words: "Hard luck! But you can make it up soon. Throw in with me. The more the merrier, an' the stronger we'll be."

"How about your supplies?" queried Dunn.

"Plenty for two months. An' we'll be freightin' out hides before that."

"All right, Clark, I'll throw in with your outfit, huntin' for myself, of course, an' payin' my share," replied Dunn, slowly, as if the matter was weighty. "But I hope you don't mind my talkin' out straight about your women."

"No, you can talk straight about anyone or anythin' to me."

"You want to send your women back or take them to Fort Elliott," returned Dunn, brusquely.

"Dunn, I won't do anythin' of the kind," retorted Hudnall, bluntly.

"Well, the soldiers will do it for you, if they happen to come along," said Dunn, just as bluntly. "It's your own business. I'm not trying to interfere in your affairs. But women don't belong on such a huntin' trip as this summer will see. My idea, talking straight, is that Mr. Pilchuck here should have warned you and made you leave the women back in the settlement."

"Wal, I gave Hudnall a hunch all right, but he wouldn't listen," declared the scout.

"You didn't give me any such damn thing," shouted Hudnall angrily.

Then followed a hot argument that in Tom's opinion ended in the conviction that Pilchuck had not told all he knew.

"Well, if that's what, I reckon it doesn't make any difference to me," said Hudnall, finally. "I wanted wife an' Sally with me. An' if I was comin' at all they were comin' too. We're huntin' buffalo, yes, for a while—as long as there's money in it. But what we're huntin' most is a farm."

"Now, Hudnall, listen," responded Dunn, curtly. "I'm not tryin' to boss your outfit. After this I'll have no more to say. . . . I've been six months at this hide-huntin' an' I know what I'm talkin' about. The great massed herd of buffalo is south of here, on the Red River, along under the rim of the Staked Plain. You think this herd here is big. Say, this is a straggler bunch. There's a thousand times as many buffalo down on the Red. . . . There's where the most of the hide-hunters are and there the Comanches and Kiowas are on the warpath. I've met hunters who claim this main herd will reach here this spring, along in May. But I say that great herd will never again get this far north. If you want hide-huntin' for big money, then you've got to pull stakes for the Red River."

"By thunder! we'll pull then," boomed Hudnall.

"Reckon we've got some good huntin' here, as long as this bunch hangs around the water," interposed Pilchuck. "We've got it 'most all to ourselves."

"That's sense," said Dunn, conclusively. "I'll be glad to stay. But when we do pull for the Staked Plain country you want to look for some wild times. There'll be hell along the Red River this summer.

In the swiftly flying days that succeeded Dunn's joining Hudnall's outfit Tom developed rapidly into a hunter and skinner of buffalo. He was never an expert shot with the heavy Sharps, but he made up in horsemanship and daring what he lacked as a marksman. If a man had nerve he did not need to be skillful with the rifle. It was as a skinner, however, that Tom excelled all of Hudnall's men. Tom had been a wonderful husker of corn; he had been something of a blacksmith. His hands were large and powerful, and these qualifications, combined with deftness, bade fair to make him a record skinner.

The Hudnall outfit followed the other outfits, which they never caught up with, south along the stream in the rear of this herd of buffalo. Neither Dunn nor Pilchuck knew for certain that the stream flowed into the Red River, but as the days grew into weeks they inclined more and more to that opinion. If it was so, luck was merely with them. Slowly the herd gave way, running, when hunted, some miles to the south, and next day always grazing east to the river. The morning came, however, when the herd did not appear. Pilchuck rode thirty miles south without success. He was of the opinion, and Dunn agreed with him, that the buffalo had at last made for the Red River. So that night plan was made to abandon hunting for the present and to travel south in search of the main herd.

Tom took stock of his achievements, and was exceedingly amazed and exultant. How quickly it seemed that small figures augmented to larger ones!

He had hunted, in all, twenty-four days. Three hundred and sixty buffalo had fallen to his credit. But that was not all. It was the skinning which he was paid for, and he had skinned four hundred and eighty-two buffalo—an average of twenty a day. Hudnall owed him then one hundred forty-four dollars and sixty cents. Tom had cheerfully and gratefully worked on a farm for twenty dollars a month. This piling up of money was incredible. He was dazzled. Suppose he hunted and skinned buffalo for a whole year! The prospect quite overwhelmed him. Moreover, the camp life, the open wilderness, the hard riding and the thrill of the chase—these had worked on him insensibly, until before he realized it he was changed.

Chapter V

THERE was just daylight enough to discern objects when Milly Fayre peeped out of the wagon, hoping against hope that she would be able to wave a farewell to the young man, Tom Doan. She knew his name and the names of all the Hudnall party. For some reason her stepfather was immensely curious about other outfits, yet avoided all possible contact with them.

But no one in Hudnall's camp appeared to be stirring. The obscurity of the gray dawn soon swallowed the grove of trees and the prairie schooners. Milly lay back in her bed in the bottom of the wagon and closed her eyes. Sleep would not come again. The rattle of wagon trappings, the roll of the crunching wheels, and the trotting clip-clop of hoofs not only prevented slumber, but also assured her that the dreaded journey down into the prairie had begun in reality.

This journey had only one pleasing prospect—and that was a hope, forlorn at best, of somewhere again seeing the tall, handsome stranger who had spoken so kindly to her and gazed at her with such thoughtful eyes.

Not that she hoped for anything beyond just seeing him! She would be grateful for that. Her stepfather would not permit any friendships, let alone acquaintances, with buffalo-hunters. Five weeks with this stepfather had taught her much, and she feared him. Last night his insulting speech before Tom Doan had created in Milly the nucleus of a revolt. She dared to imagine a time might come, in another year when she became of age, that would give her freedom.

The meeting with Tom Doan last night had occasioned, all in twelve hours, a change in Milly Fayre. His look had haunted her, and even in the kindly darkness it had power to bring the blood to her face. Then his words so full of fear and reproach—"I may never see you again!"—they had awakened Milly's heart. No matter what had inspired them! Yet she could harbor no doubt of this fine-spoken, clear-eyed young man. He was earnest. He meant that not to see her again would cause him regret. What would it mean to her—never to see him again? She could not tell. But seeing him once had lightened her burden.

So in Milly Fayre there was born a dream. Hard work on a farm had been her portion—hard work in addition to the long journey to and from school. She did not remember her father, who had been one of the missing in the war. It had been a tragedy, when she was sixteen, for her mother to marry Randall Jett, and then live only a few months. Milly had no relatives. Boys and men had tormented her with their advances, and their importunities, like the life she had been forced to lead, had not brought any brightness. Relief indeed had been hers during those months when her stepfather had been absent hunting buffalo. But in March he had returned with another wife, a woman hard featured and coarse and unreasonably jealous of Milly. He had sold the little Missouri farm and brought his wife and Milly south, inflamed by his prospects of gaining riches in the buffalo fields.

From the start Milly had dreaded that journey. But

she could not resist. She was in Randall Jett's charge. Besides, she had nowhere to go; she knew nothing except the work that fell to the lot of a daughter of the farm. She had been apathetic, given to broodings and a growing tendency toward morbidness. All the days of that traveling southward had been alike, until there came the one on which her kindness to a horse had brought her face to face with Tom Doan. What was it that had made him different? Had the meeting been only last night?

The wagon rolled on down the uneven road, and the sudden lighting of the canvas indicated that the sun had risen. Milly heard the rattling of the harness on the horses. One of the wagons, that one driven by Jett, was close behind.

Movement and sound of travel became more bearable as Milly pondered over the difference one day had wrought. It was better that she was going on the road of the hide-hunters, for Tom Doan was one of them. Every thought augmented something vague and deep that baffled her. One moment she would dream of yesterday—that incident of casual meeting, suddenly to become one of strangely locked eyes—how all day she had watched Hudnall's camp for sight of the tall young man—how she had listened to Jett's gossip with his men about the other outfits—how thrilled she had been when she had met Tom Doan again. It had not been altogether fear of her stepfather that had made her run off from this outspoken, keen-eyed young man. She had been suddenly beset by unfamiliar emotions. The touch of his hands—his look—his speech! Milly felt again the uplift of her heart, the swell of breast, the tingling race of blood, the swift, vague, fearful thoughts.

The next moment Milly would try to drive away the sweet insidious musing, the ponder over her presence there in this rattling wagon, and what might be in store for her. There had been a break in the complexity of her situation. Something, a new spirit, seemed stirring in her. If she was glad of anything it was for the hours in which she could think. This canvas-topped wagon was her house of one room, and when she was inside, with the openings laced, she felt the solitude her soul needed. For one thing, Jett never objected to her seeking the privacy of her abode; and she now, with her new-born intuition, sensed that it was because he did not like to see the men watching her. Yet he watched her himself with his big hard blue eyes. Tom Doan's eyes had not been like that. She could think of them and imagine them, so kindly piercing and appealing.

This drifting from conjectures and broodings into a vague sort of enchanting reverie was a novel experience for Milly. She resisted a while, then yielded to it. Happiness abided therein. She must cultivate such easy means of forgetting the actual.

Milly's wagon lumbered on over the uneven road, and just when she imagined she could no longer stand the jolting and confinement, it halted.

She heard Jeff's gruff voice, the scrape of the brakes on the wagon behind, and then the unsnapping of harness buckles and the clinking thud of heavy cooking-ware thrown to the ground. Milly opened the canvas slit at the back of her wagon, and taking up the bag that contained her mirror, brush and comb, soap, towel, and other necessities, she spread the flaps of the door and stepped down to the ground.

Halt had been made at the edge of a clump of trees in a dry arroyo. It was hot, and Milly decided she would put on her sunbonnet as soon as she had washed her face and combed her hair.

"Mawnin', girl," drawled a lazy voice. It came from the man, Catlee, who had driven her wagon. He was a swarthy fellow of perhaps forty years, rugged of build, garbed as a teamster, with a lined face that seemed a record of violent life. Yet Milly had not instinctively shrunk from him as from the others.

"Good morning, Mr. Catlee," she responded. "Can I get some water?"

"Shore, miss. I'll hev it for you in a jiffy," he volunteered, and stepping up on the hub of a front wheel he rummaged under the seat, to fetch forth a basin. This he held under a keg that was wired to the side of the wagon.

"Dry camp, Catlee," spoke up a gruff voice from behind. "Go easy on the water."

"All right, boss, easy it is," he replied, as he twisted a peg out of the keg. He winked at Milly and deliberately let the water pour out until the basin was full. This he set on a box in the shade of the wagon. "Thar you are, miss."

Milly thanked him and proceeded leisurely about her ablutions. She knew there was a sharp eye upon her every move and was ready for the gruff voice when it called out: "Rustle, you Milly. Help here, an' never mind your good looks!"

Milly minded them so little that she scarcely looked at herself in the mirror; and when Jett reminded her of them, which he was always doing, she wished that she was ugly. Presently, donning the sunbonnet, which served the double duty of shading her eyes from the hot glare and hiding her face, she turned to help at the camp-fire tasks.

Mrs. Jett, Milly's stepmother, was on her knees before a panful of flour and water, which she was mixing into biscuit dough. The sun did not bother her, apparently, for she was bare-headed. She was a handsome woman, still young, dark, full faced, with regular features and an expression of sullenness.

Jett strode around the place, from wagon to fire, his hands quick and strong to perform two things at once. His eyes, too, with their hard blue light, roved everywhere. They were eyes of suspicion. This man was looking for untoward reactions in the people around him.

Everybody worked speedily, not with the good will

of a camp party that was wholesome and happy, bent on an enterprise hopeful, even if dangerous, but as if dominated by a driving spirit. Very soon the meal was ready, and the men extended pan and cup for their portion, which was served by Mrs. Jett.

"Eat, girl," called Jett, peremptorily.

Milly was hungry enough, albeit she had been slow and, receiving her food and drink, she sat down upon a sack of grain. While she ate she watched from under the wide rim of her sunbonnet.

Did she imagine a subtle change had come over these men, now that the journey toward the wild buffalo country had begun? Follonsbee had been with Jett before and evidently had the leader's confidence, as was evinced by the many whispered consultations Milly had observed. He was a tall, spare man, with evil face, red from liquor and exposure, and eyes that Milly had never looked into twice. Pruitt had lately joined the little caravan. Small of stature, though hardy, and with a sallow face remarkable in that its pointed chin was out of line with the bulging forehead, he presented an even more repulsive appearance than Follonsbee. He was a rebel and lost no opportunity to let that fact be known.

These men were buffalo-hunters, obsessed with the idea of large sums of money to be made from the sale of hides. From what little Milly had been able to learn, all the men except Catlee were to share equally in the proceeds of the hunt. Milly had several times heard argument to that effect—argument always discontinued when she came within hearing.

Milly had become curious about her stepfather and his men. This interest of hers dated back no farther than yesterday, when her meeting with Tom Doan, and a few words exchanged with the pleasant Mrs. Hudnall, and her eager watching of the Hudnall camp, had showed her plainly that Jett's was a different kind of outfit. No good humor, no kindliness, no gay words or pleasant laughs, no evidence of wholesome anticipation! Jett had never been a man she could care for, yet up to the last few weeks he had been endurable. The force of him had changed with the advent of these other men and the journey into unsettled country. In him Milly now began to sense something sinister.

They did not speak often. The business of eating and the hurry maintained by Jett were not altogether cause for this taciturnity. Catlee was the only one who occasionally made a casual remark, and then no one appeared to hear him.

"Rustle along, you-all," ordered Jett, gruffly, as he rose from his meal.

"Do you aim to camp at Wade's Crossin' tonight?" queried Follonsbee.

"No. We'll water an' get wood there, an' go on," returned Jett, briefly.

The other men made no comment, and presently they rose, to set about their tasks. The horses were hitched up while munching their grain out of the nose bags. Milly wiped the plates and utensils that Mrs. Jett hurriedly and silently washed.

"Mother, I—I wish we were not going on this hunt," ventured Milly, at last, for no other reason than that she could not stand the silence.

"I'm not your mother," replied the woman, tersely. "Call me Jane, if the name Mrs. Jett makes you jealous."

"Jealous? Why should I be jealous of that name?" asked Milly, in slow surprise.

"You're no more related to Jett than I am," said Mrs. Jett, pondering darkly. She seemed a thick-minded person. "For my part, I don't like the hunt, either. I told Jett so, an' he said, 'Like it or lump it, you're goin'.' I reckon you'd better keep your mouth shut."

Milly did not need such admonition, so far as her stepfather was concerned. But from that moment she decided to keep both eyes and ears open. Jett's domineering way might be responsible for the discontent of his wife and the taciturnity of his men.

When all was in readiness to resume the journey Milly asked Jett if she could ride on the seat with the driver.

"Reckon not," answered Jett, as he clambered to his own seat.

"But my back gets tired. I can't lie down all the time," remonstrated Milly.

"Jane, you ride with Catlee an' let Milly come with me," said Jett.

"Like hob!" sneered his wife, with a sudden malignant flash of eyes that was a revelation to Milly. "Wouldn't you like that fine now, Rand Jett?"

"Shut up!" returned Jett, in mingled anger and discomfiture.

"You're mighty afraid some man will look at that girl," she went on, regardless of his gathering frown. "How's she ever goin' to get a husband?"

Jett glared at her and ground his teeth.

"Oh, I see," continued Mrs. Jett, without lowering her strident voice. "She *ain't* goin' to get a husband if *you* can help it. I've had that hunch before."

"Will you shut up?" shouted Jett, furiously.

Whereupon the woman lifted herself to the seat beside him. Jett started his team out toward the road. As Pruitt and Follonsbee had driven ahead in their wagon, Milly was left alone with Catlee, who seemed to be both amused and sympathetic.

"Climb up heah, miss," said he.

Milly hesitated, and then suddenly the new turn of her mind obstructed her old habit of obedience and she nimbly stepped to a seat beside the driver.

"Reckon it'll be warmer out heah in the sun, but there's a breeze an' you can see around," he said.

"It's much nicer."

Catlee plied his long lash, cracking it over the horses

without touching them, and they moved off in easy trot. The road lay downhill, and ahead the gray prairie rolled in undulating vast stretches to the horizon.

"Are we going to Indian Territory?" Milly asked the driver.

"Miss, we're in the Territory now," he replied. "I don't know when, but in a few days we'll cross the line into the Panhandle of Texas."

"Is that where the buffalo are?"

"I ain't shore aboot that. I heard Jett say the big herd would be comin' north an' likely run into the hunters somewheres near Red River."

"Will all the hunters go to the same place?"

"Shore they will, an' that'll be where the buffalo are."

Milly did not analyze the vague hope that mounted in her breast. She felt surprised to find she wanted to talk, to learn things.

"Is this strange country to you?" she asked.

"Shore is, miss. I never was west of the Missouri till this trip. Reckon it's goin' to be hard. I met some hunters last night. They was celebratin' their arrival in town, an' I couldn't take too great stock in their talk. But shore they said it was bad down heah where we're goin'. I'm afraid it ain't no place for a girl like you."

"I'm afraid so, too," said Milly.

"Jett ain't your real father?" queried Catlee.

"He's my stepfather," replied Milly, and then in a few words she told Catlee about herself, from the time her mother had married Jett.

"Well, well, that accounts," rejoined Catlee, in tones unmistakably kind. But he did not vouchsafe to explain what he meant. Indeed, her simple story seemed to have silenced him. Yet more than before she felt his sympathy. It struck her singularly that he had stopped talking because he might have committed himself to some word against her stepfather.

Thereafter Milly kept the conversation from personalities, and during the afternoon ride she talked at intervals and then watched the dim horizon receding always with its beckoning mystery.

Sunset time found Jett's caravan descending a long gradual slope ending in a timbered strip that marked the course of a stream. Catlee pointed out two camps to Milly. White wagons stood out against the woodland; fires were twinkling; smoke was rising. The place appeared pleasant and sheltered. Jett drove across the stream, unhitched the horses, and he and Follonsbee watered them and filled the kegs while Pruitt and Catlee gathered firewood, which was tied on behind the wagons.

One of the campers below the crossing came out in the open to halloo at Jett, more in friendly salutation than otherwise. Jett did not reply. He lost no time hooking up traces and harness and getting under way. He led on until nearly dark and halted at a low place where grass appeared abundant.

"Why didn't my stepfather camp back there with the other outfits?" queried Milly, as Catlee halted his team.

"Shore he's not sociable, an' he's bent on travelin' as far every day as possible," replied the driver.

While Milly was busily engaged helping Mrs. Jett round the camp fire, darkness settled. Coyotes were yelping. A night wind rose and, sweeping down into the shallow coulee, it sent the white sparks flying. The morose mood of the travelers persisted. After supper was over and the tasks were finished Milly climbed to the seat of her wagon and sat there. It was out of earshot of the camp fire. Jett's wagon had been drawn up close beside the one she occupied. Heretofore camp had always been pitched in a sheltered place, in a grove or under the lea of a wooded hill. This site was out on the open prairie. The wind swept around and under the wagon, and it needed only a little more force to make it moan. But few stars lightened the cloudy sky. Lonesome, dismal, and forbidding, this prairie land increased Milly's apprehensions. She tried not to think of the future. Always before she had been dully resigned to a gray prospect. But now a consciousness grew that she could not go on forever like this, even if her situation did not grow worse. Of that, she had no doubt. Someone had told her that when she was eighteen years old she would be free to look out for herself. Yet even so, what could she do? She worked as hard for the Jetts as she would have to work for anyone else. Perhaps eventually she might get a place with a nice family like the Hudnalls. Suddenly the thought of Tom Doan flashed into her mind, and then of marriage. Her face burned. She hid it, fearful that even under cover of night someone might see her and read her thoughts. No use to try to repudiate them! She yearned for the companionship of women who would be kind to her, for a home, and for love.

These thoughts became torture for Milly, but only so long as she strove against them. She had awakened. She could not be deprived of her feelings and hopes. Thus her habitual morbid brooding came to have a rival for the possession of her mind. When she went to bed that night she felt not only the insidious inception of a revolt, but also a realization that strength was coming from somewhere, as if with the magic of these new thoughts.

Days passed—days that dragged on with the interminable riding over the widening prairie—with the monotony of camp tasks, and the relief of oblivion in sleep.

Milly always saw the sun rise and set, and these were the only incidents of the day in which she found pleasure. She had exhausted Catlee's fund of stories and his limited knowledge of the frontier. He was the only one in the outfit that she could or would talk to. Follonsbee was manifestly a woman-hater. Pruitt had twice approached her, agreeably enough, yet offensive through his appearance; and she had cut his overtures short. Mrs. Jett's hawk eyes never failed to take note of any movement on her husband's part in Milly's direction, which notice finally had the effect of making Jett surlily aloof. Yet there was that in his look which made Milly shrink. As days and miles passed behind, Jett manifestly grew away from the character that had seemed to be his when Milly's mother married him. Here in this environment harshness and violence, and a subtle menace, appeared natural in him.

Not a day went by now that Jett did not overtake and pass an outfit of two or more wagons bound for the hunting fields. These he passed on the road or avoided at camping grounds. When, however, he met a freighter going out with buffalo hides, he always had spare time to halt and talk.

Jett pushed on. His teams were young and powerful, and he carried grain to feed them, thus keeping up their strength while pushing them to the limit. The gray rolling expanse of Indian Territory changed to the greener, more undulating and ridged vastness of the Panhandle of Texas. Where ten days before it had been unusual to cross one stream in a day's travel, now they crossed several. All of these, however, were but shallow creeks or washes. The trees along these stream bottoms were green and beautiful, lending contrast to the waving level of the plains.

Milly conceived the idea that under happy circumstances she would have found a new joy and freedom in riding down into this wilderness.

One afternoon, earlier than usual, Jett turned for good off the road, and following a tree-bordered stream for a couple of miles, pitched camp in a thick grove, where his wagons and tents could not readily be seen. Evidently this was not to be the usual one-night stand. If it were possible for Jett to be leisurely, he was so on this occasion. After helping unpack the wagons he gave orders to his men, and then saddling one of the horses he rode away under the trees.

It was dusk when he returned. Supper had been timed for his arrival. About him at this moment there was an expansion, an excitement, combined with bluff egotism. Milly anticipated what he announced in his big voice.

"Bunch of buffalo waterin' along here. We've run into the stragglers. It'll do to hang at this camp an' hunt while we wait to see if the big herd runs north."

The announcement did not create any particular interest in his comrades. No one shared Jett's strong suppressed feeling. After supper he superintended the loading of shells and sharpening of knives, and the overlooking of the heavy rifles.

"The old needle gun for me!" he exclaimed. "Most hunters favor the big fifty."

"Wal, the fifty's got it all over any other guns fer shootin' buffs at close range," responded Follonsbee.

"We might have to shoot some other critters at long range—redskins, for instance," commented the leader, sardonically.

Jett's superabundant vitality and force could not be repressed on this occasion. Apparently the end of the long journey had been cause for elation and anticipation, and also for an indulgence in drink. Milly had known before that Jett was addicted to the bottle. Under its influence, however, he appeared less harsh and hard. It tempered the iron quality in him. Likewise it roused his latent sentimental proclivities. Milly had more than once experienced some difficulty in avoiding them. She felt, however, that she need not worry any more on this score, while Mrs. Jett's jealous eyes commanded the scene. Still, Mrs. Jett could not be everlastingly at hand.

It turned out that Milly's fear was justified, for not long after this very idea presented itself, Jett took advantage of his wife being in the wagon, or somewhere not visible, to approach Milly as she sat in the door of the wagon.

"Milly, I'm goin' to be rich," he said in a low hoarse tone.

"Yes? That'll be—good," she replied, bending back a little from his heated face.

"Say, let's get rid of the old woman," he whispered. His eyes gleamed in the flickering firelight, with what seemed devilish humor.

"Who—what?" stammered Milly.

"You know. The wife."

"Mrs. Jett! Get rid of her. . . . I—I don't understand."

"Wal, you're thicker 'n usual," he continued, with a laugh. "Think it over."

"Good night," faltered Milly, and hurriedly slipped into her wagon and tried with trembling fingers to lace up the flaps of the door. Her head whirled. Was Jett merely drunk? Pondering over this incident, she was trying to convince herself that Jett meant no more than ill humor toward his wife, when she heard him speak a name that made her heart leap.

"Hudnall, yes, I told you," he said, distinctly. "His outfit is somewhere in this neck of the woods. I saw his wheel tracks an' horse tracks."

"Wal, how do you know they're Hudnall's outfit?" queried Follonsbee.

"Huh! It's my business to know tracks," replied Jett, significantly. "There's two outfits camped below us. I saw horses an' smoke."

"Rand, if I was runnin' this outfit I wouldn't hunt buffalo anywhere's near Hudnall."

"An' why not?" demanded Jett.

"Say, you needn't jump down my throat. I jest have an idee. Hudnall's pardner, Pilchuck, is a plainsman, an'—"

"Huh! I don't care what the hell Pilchuck is," retorted Jett, gruffly ending the discussion.

Chapter VI

Jett had chosen this secluded camp site, as he had all the others on the way down into the buffalo country, to render his whereabouts less liable to discovery. Anyone hunting for camps along the river would have found him, but the outfits traveling casually by would not have been aware of his proximity.

Next morning he had everybody up at dawn, and never had his dominating force been so manifest.

"Catlee, your job is horses," he said, curtly. "Keep them on this side of the river. The road's on the other side. You'll find the best grass along this strip of timber. Some time to-day I'll ride in an' help you hitch up to haul hides."

To his wife he gave a more significant order.

"Jane, I don't want any fire burnin' except when I'm in camp with the men. You an' Milly keep your eyes open, an' if you see Indians or anybody, slip off in the brush an' hide."

With that he rode off, accompanied by Follonsbee and Pruitt. Manifestly the hunt was on.

Milly, despite apprehension at the possibility of Indians, was glad to see the buffalo-hunters ride away. From what she had heard, this hide-hunting was an exceedingly strenuous business, consuming all of the daylight hours and half of the night. She had accepted her stepmother's sulky aloofness, finding relief also in that. The work given her to do she performed speedily and thoroughly. Then with a book and her sewing she slipped away from camp into the dense growth of underbrush.

By taking time she threaded a way without undue difficulties, and finally came out upon a beautiful grass-covered and flower-dotted bank above the stream. The place delighted her. The camp was within call, yet might have been miles away; the brush leaned over the fragrant shady nook, and above spread the giant elms; the stream widened here at a turn and formed a pool, the only one she had seen on the ride. A wide strip of sand ran along the opposite slope. On that side the wood appeared open, and led gently up to the plain. Milly could see the bright sky line barred by black trunks of trees. The road ran along the edge of the timber, and if any travelers passed she could see them. What would she do if she recognized the Hudnall outfit? The very thought made her tremble. Perhaps such hope dominated her watching there. For the rest, she could have hours alone, to think and dream, or to sew and read, and all the time she could see everything opposite her without being seen herself.

It did not take long for her to discover that this place had much to distract her from meditation or work. Suddenly it awoke in her a feeling that she did not know she possessed. Solitude she had always yearned for, but beauty and nature, the sweetness of sylvan scene and melody of birds, as now revealed to her, had not heretofore been part of her experience. They seemed strangely harmonious with the vague and growing emotion in her heart.

Milly did not read or sew. Wild canaries and song-sparrows and swamp blackbirds were singing all around her. A low melodious hum of many bees came from the flowering brush above. Somewhere under the bank water was softly rippling. A kingfisher flew swiftly downstream, glinting in the sunlight. At the bend of the stream, on a jutting sandbar, stood a heron, motionless and absorbed, gazing down into the water. The warm fragrant air seemed to float drowsily toward her.

The peace and music of this scene were abruptly dispelled by crashing, thudding sounds from the slope opposite. Milly gazed across. Shaggy dark forms were passing from the open plain down into the woods.

"Oh!—buffalo!" cried Milly, at once delighted and frightened. Her heart beat high. Gathering up her book and sewing, she was about to answer to the instinct to run when it occurred to her that she was on a steep bank high above the stream, out of danger. She decided to stand her ground. Sinking low behind a fringe of grass and flowers, she peeped over it, with bated breath and wide eyes.

Everywhere along the sky line of the wooded slope she saw the dark forms, not in a thick troop, but straggling in twos and threes. Lower down the foremost buffalo appeared, scattering dead leaves and raising the dust. A hundred yards below Milly the first buffalo came out of the woods upon the sand and crossed it to drink. Then gradually the line of bobbing brown humps emerged from the trees and grew closer and closer to Milly until she began to fear they would come right opposite to her. What wild, shaggy, ox-like beasts! If she had been fearful at first, she now grew frightened. Yet the wonder and majesty of these buffalo were not lost upon her. On they crashed out of the woods! She heard the splashing of the water. Like cattle at a long trough they lined up to the stream and bent huge woolly black heads.

"If any come close—I'm going to run!" whispered Milly to herself.

It did not appear, however, that she would have to resort to flight. The line of buffalo halted some fifty yards below her position. Thus she managed to avert utter panic, and as the moments passed her fears began to subside. Suddenly they were altogether dispelled. A number of buffalo broke ranks and turned again to the woods, leaving open spaces where tawny little buffalo calves could be seen. Milly experienced a feeling of utmost pleasure. All her life on the farm she had loved the little calves. These were larger, very wild looking, fuzzy and woolly, light in color, and did not appear, like the calves she had seen, weak and wobbly in their legs. These young animals were strong and nimble. Some left their mothers' sides and frisked along the sand a little way, in an unmistakable playfulness, yet unlike any play Milly had ever seen. They lifted themselves off their front feet and gave their heads a turning, butting movement, quite agile, and nothing if not aggressive. Then they fled back to their mothers. Only a few of these calves drank from the stream, and they did not appear thirsty, as did the matured buffalo. Gradually the ranks thinned, and then the last of the grown buffalo turned to the slope. The calves, though loath to leave that enchanting spot, did not tarry long behind. The herd leisurely trooped up the slope and disappeared.

To Milly it did not seem possible that she had actually seen buffalo close at hand. The reality was strikingly different from the impression she had gathered. Huge beasts, yet not ugly or mean! They seemed as tame as cattle. Certainly if unmolested they would never harm anyone. Suddenly the bang of heavy guns rang from far over the slope.

"Oh, Jett and his hunters!" she exclaimed, in quick comprehension. "They are killing the buffalo!"

Not until that moment had the actual killing of buffalo—the meaning of it—crossed Milly's mind. Bang—bang—bang came the shots. They made her shrink. Those splendid beasts were being killed for their hides. Somehow it seemed base. What would become of the little calves? There dawned in Milly's mind an aversion for this hide-hunting. If the meat was to be used, even given to the hungry people of the world, then the slaughter might be condoned. But just to sell the hides!

"Tom Doan is a hide-hunter, too," she soliloquized. "Oh, I'm sorry! . . . he looked so nice and kind. I guess I—I don't care much about him."

What a man's vocation happened to be was really a serious matter to a woman. Milly recalled that one of the troubles between her mother and Jett had been his hatred of farm labor. Manifestly this hunting buffalo was to his liking, and perhaps he did not call it work.

Thus the incident of the buffalo coming down to drink had upset Milly's short period of revel in the sylvan place. Even when the muddy water cleared out of the stream, and the dust clouds disappeared from the woods, and the melody of birds and bees was renewed Milly did not recover the happy trend of feeling. Realization of the fact that Tom Doan was a hide-hunter had spoiled everything. Milly tried to read, and failing that she took up her sewing, which occupation had the virtue of being both necessity and pastime. For an hour or more the bang-bang of guns upon the plain above disturbed her. These reports appeared to get farther and farther away, until she could not hear them any more.

Some time after this, when she was returning to the dreamy mood, she heard a crashing of brush opposite and below her. Listening and peering in this direction, where the wood was thicker, she waited expectantly for buffalo to appear. The sound came at regular intervals. It made Milly nervous to become aware that these crashings were approaching a point directly opposite her. A growth of willows bordered the bank here, preventing her from seeing what might be there.

Then she heard heavy puffs—the breaths of a large beast. They sounded almost like the mingled panting and coughing of an animal strangling, or unable to breathe right.

Another crash very close sent cold chills over Milly. But she had more courage than on the first occasion. She saw the willows shake, and then spread wide to emit an enormous black head and hump of a buffalo. Milly seemed to freeze there where she crouched. This buffalo looked wild and terrible. He was heaving. A bloody froth was dripping from his extended tongue. His great head rolled from side to side. As he moved again, with a forward lurch, Milly saw that he was crippled. The left front leg hung broken, and flopped as he plunged to the water. On his left shoulder there was a bloody splotch.

Milly could not remove her eyes from the poor brute. She saw him and all about him with a distinctness she could never forget. She heard the husky gurgle of water as he drank thirstily. Below him the slow current of the stream was tinged red. For what appeared a long time he drank. Then he raised his great head. The surroundings held no menace for him. He seemed dazed and lost. Milly saw the rolling eyes as he lurched and turned. He was dying. In horror Milly watched him stagger into the willows and slowly crash out of sight. After that she listened until she could no longer hear the crackling of brush and twigs.

Then Milly relaxed and sank back into her former seat. Her horror passed with a strong shuddering sensation, leaving in her a sickening aversion to this murderous buffalo hunting.

The sun mounted high and the heat of the May day quieted the birds. The bees, however, kept up their drowsy hum. No more buffalo disturbed Milly's spasmodic periods of sewing and reading and the long spells of dreaming. Hours passed. Milly heard no horses or men, and not until the afternoon waned towards its close did she start back to camp. To retrace her steps was not an easy matter, but at last she wound her way through the brush to the open space. Camp was deserted, so far as any one stirring about was concerned. Milly missed one of the wagons.

Some time later, while she was busy making her own cramped quarters more livable, she heard the voices of men, the thud of hoofs, and the creak of wheels. With these sounds the familiar oppression returned to her breast. Jett would soon be there, surly and hungry. Milly swiftly concluded her task and hurried down out of her wagon.

Presently the men came trooping into camp on foot, begrimed with dust and sweat and manifestly weary. Catlee was carrying a heavy burden of four guns.

Jett looked into his tent.

"Come out, you lazy jade," he called, roughly, evidently to his wife. "A buffalo wolf has nothin' on me for hunger." Then he espied Milly, who was in the act of lighting a fire. "Good! You'd make a wife, Milly."

"Haw! Haw!" laughed Follonsbee, sardonically, as he threw down hat, gloves, vest, and spread his grimy hands. "No water! Gimme a bucket. If I had a wife there'd be water in camp."

"Huh! You hawk-faced Yankee—there ain't no woman on earth who'd fetch water for you," taunted Pruitt.

"Wal, if Hank thinks he can teach Jane to fetch an' carry he's welcome to her," responded Jett.

This bluff and hearty badinage, full of contention as it was, marked a change in the demeanor of Jett and his men. Catlee, however, took no part in it. He was connected with Jett's outfit, but did not belong there.

Mrs. Jett then appeared among them, and her advent, probably because of Jett's remark, occasioned ill-suppressed mirth.

"I heard what you said, Rand Jett," she retorted, glaring at him. "You can't make me welcome to any man, much less a hide thief like Hank Follonsbee."

"Shut your face," returned Jett, in an entirely different tone. "You know your job. Rustle to it."

That ended the approach to humor. When Follonsbee fetched the water they all washed and splashed with great gusto. This pleasant task finished, they showed plainly what little leisure was now possible to them, for they got their kits and began reloading shells and sharpening knives.

"Catlee, you clean the guns," ordered Jett.

While thus busily engaged they talked of the day's hunt—of the half hour of shooting that was fun and the eight hours of skinning that was labor—of the hide-stretching still to do before sleep could be thought of. Milly listened with keen ears in the hope they might drop some word of the Hudnall outfit, but she spent her attention in vain.

Presently Mrs. Jett called, "Come to supper."

"Or you'll throw it out, huh?" queried Jett, rising with alacrity.

They ate hurriedly and prodigiously, in silence, and each man reached for what he wanted without asking. Jett was the first to finish.

"Fill up, you hawgs," he said to his comrades; "we've work to do.—Jane, you an' Milly clean up—then go to bed. We'll be just outside the grove, stretchin' hides."

Milly lay awake a long while that night, yet did not hear the men return. Next day they had breakfast before sunrise and were off with a rush. Milly spent quiet hours on the shady bank, where the sweetness and music were undisturbed. Another day passed in which she saw nothing of the men except at the morning and evening meal hours. Jett and his helpers were settling into the strenuous routine of hide-hunting.

On the fourth day they broke camp and traveled twenty miles down the same side of the river, to halt in the only clump of trees Milly had noted for hours.

Next morning Jett's men were again hunting buffalo. That night they did not return until long after dark. Milly had gone to bed, but she heard their gruff, weary voices.

The following day was again one of breaking camp and traveling south. Milly observed that the country changed, while yet it seemed the same; and she concluded that it was the vastness and wildness which grew. Next morning she heard shooting up until noon. She was so grateful to be left alone that the hours seemed to fly. There was always a place where she could hide near camp, and Jett seldom forgot to mention this. As they journeyed farther south his vigilance as well as his excitement increased day by day. From the camp-fire talk Milly gathered that both the number of buffalo and of hunters were augmenting. Yet Jett appeared to have established the rule of traveling one day and hunting the next. As he progressed the work grew more arduous. There was no road over this endless plain, and the level stretches were cut up, sometimes necessitating the unloading and reloading of the wagons. May warmed to June. The plain was now one wide rolling expanse of green, waving gently to every breeze; the stream courses were marked by a line of deeper green, trees now in full foliage. Herds of buffalo began to show to the east of this stream Jett was following. His hunting, however, he did on the west side, where Milly understood the buffalo ranged in larger numbers.

At length Jett traveled two days southward and then crossed the stream to its west bank. Following it down on that side, he was halted by a large river.

"Ha, boys, here's the Red, an' it's our stampin' ground this summer," he rolled out, sonorously.

For a camp he chose a spot hard to reach, as well as hard to espy from above. A forest of timber and brush bordered both sides of this Red River, and once down in it neither river nor plain could be seen. Jett spent the remainder of that day making permanent camp. Follonsbee, whom he had sent on a reconnoitering ride up the river, returned about sunset.

"Believe I saw fifty square miles of buffalo," he announced, impressively, sitting in his saddle and gazing down at the leader.

"Huh! I took that for granted," replied Jett. "How far did you go?"

"Reckon about five miles up an' climbed a big bluff above the river. Could see for miles. An' shore that sight stumped me. Why, Rand, I couldn't see the end of buffalo, an' I was usin' the telescope, too!"

"That's more to the point—how many outfits could you spot?" demanded Jett, impatiently.

"Wal, I spotted enough, an' some to spare," drawled the other. "West of the bluff I seen camp smokes all along the river, as far as I could see."

"Any camps close?"

"Only two between ours an' the bluff," replied Follonsbee. "Then there's one on the point across the creek. Reckon outfits are strung down the river, too. Buffalo everywhere."

"Ahuh! It's the main herd. Now, I wonder will they run north."

"Reckon so. But if they do they'll turn back."

"You figger on their bein' blocked by the gang of hide-hunters behind us?"

"Prezactly. We couldn't be in a better stand. This big herd is massed in a triangle. River on the south; Staked Plain on the west, an' on the third side thousands of hunters."

"Yes. It seems that way. Mighty big bit of country, but it *is* a trap."

"Where do the Indians come in your calculatin'?" queried Follonsbee.

"Nowhere. If they get mean the buffalo-hunters will band together an' do what the soldiers couldn't do—chase the damned redskins up in their Staked Plain an' kill them."

"Wal, it looks like a hell of a summer, huh?"

"I reckon so, all around. It means the end of the buffalo, an' that means peace with the Indians, whether they fight or not."

"Rand, this is the huntin' ground of Comanches, Cheyennes, Kiowas, an' Arapahoes. The land an' the buffalo are theirs."

"Theirs—hell!" exploded Jett, in contempt.

"Shore I know your sentiments," returned Follonsbee, rather shortly. "Like most of these hide-hunters, you say wipe the redskins off the earth. To me it looks like a dirty trick. I'd rather steal from a white man than an Indian. . . . But I'm givin' you my idee for what it's worth. We'll have to fight."

Jett appeared for the moment in a brown study, while he paced up and down, swinging a short rope he had in his hand.

"If the Indians are on the war-path, as we hear, won't they wait till this bunch of hunters has a big store of hides on hand—before startin' that fight?" he queried, shrewdly.

"I reckon they would," admitted Follonsbee.

"An' when they do come raidin', we're goin' to get the hunch in plenty of time, aren't we?" went on Jett.

"We shore have a fine stand. With hunters east an' west of us, an' millions of buffalo out there, we can't hardly be surprised."

"Wal, then, what's eatin' you?" growled Jett.

"Nothin.' I was just gettin' things clear. We're agreed on the main points. Now one more. The sooner we make a big stake, the better?"

Jett nodded a significant acquiescence to that query, and then went about his tasks. Follonsbee, dismounting, took the saddle off his horse. Soon after that Mrs. Jett called them to supper.

At this camp Milly lost her wagon as an abode, a circumstance, on the moment, much to her displeasure. The wagon, being high off the ground, and with its box sides, had afforded more of protection, if not comfort. Jett had removed hoops and canvas bodily and had established them as a tent, a little distance from the main camp. Milly pondered apprehensively over this removal by some rods from the rest of the tents. Perhaps Mrs. Jett had inspired this innovation, and if so, Milly felt that she would welcome it. But she had doubts of every move made by the leader of the outfit.

Upon entering the improvised tent Milly found that she could not stand erect, but in all other particulars it was an improvement. She could lace both doors tightly, something impossible when the tent was on the wagon. She unrolled her bed and made it up. Then she unpacked and unfolded her clothes and hung them conveniently at the back. Her bag, with its jumbled assortment of things she had thought so poor, now, in the light of this wild travel, assumed proportions little short of precious. She could have been worse off— something which before had never crossed her mind. Without soap, linen and muslin, a sewing kit, mirror, a few books, and many other like articles, she would have found this camp life in the wilderness something formidable to face.

When she went outside again daylight was still strong and the afterglow of sunset was spreading in beautiful effulgence over the western sky. Milly gazed about her. It appeared that a jungle lay between camp and the river. Jett and his men were in earnest and whispered council, with guns and tools and ammunition for the moment forgotten. Mrs. Jett sat a forlorn and sullen figure in front of her tent. Milly needed and wanted exercise. She began to walk around the camp. No one paid any heed to her. Indeed, since reaching the buffalo fields, she had become a negligible attraction, for which she was devoutly thankful.

Summer had indeed come to this northern part of Texas. The air was drowsy and warm. She found a few belated flowers blossoming in a shaded place. A spring bubbled from under a bank, and as she passed it frogs plumped into the water. She heard the mournful cooing of turtledoves.

Milly found a trail that evidently made short cut of the distance up to the plain, and she followed it, not without misgivings. Jett, however, did not call her, and emboldened by this she ventured on. The slope was gradual and covered by heavy timber. Her heart began to beat and her breath to come and go quickly. She felt her stagnant blood enliven to the call made upon it. She saw a flare of gold and rose sky beyond the black tree trunks. It was not so very far from camp—this first level of the plain. She wanted to see the great herd of buffalo. Thus engrossed, she went on to the edge of the timber, and halted there to gaze outward. A wonderful green plain stretched away to the west, rising gradually. It was barren of animals. The rich colors of the afterglow were fading. Was that a level purple-gray bank of cloud along the horizon or a range of upland hills?

A clip-clop of trotting horse made her start sharply. Wheeling, she espied a rider close upon her. He had come from round a corner of the wooded slope.

Milly took backward steps, meaning to slip out of sight. But the rider had seen her. Coming on so quickly, while she was slow in moving, he rode right upon her, and uttering an exclamation of surprise, he leaped from the horse.

Sight of him down on the ground where Milly could see him better gave her a galvanizing shock. Was this tall young man the image of her dreams? She stared. He took a step forward, his ruddy face lighting. He seemed strange somehow, yet she knew him. His eyes pierced her, and she suddenly shook with a sure recognition of them.

"Milly!" he cried, incredulously. His tone held the same wonderful thing that was in his look.

"Oh—it is you!" burst out Milly, all at once beside herself. She ran straight to meet him.

"Milly! Say—what luck!—I'd given up ever seeing you again," he said, trying to hold her hands.

"Tom—Doan!" she ejaculated in realization. She felt the hot blood flame in her face. Shamed and frightened, yet tingling with a joy nothing could check, she backed falteringly away. His glad eyes held her gaze, though she strove to avert it. Had he changed? His face was thinner, darker, a red bronze where it had been clear tan.

"Sure it's Tom Doan," he replied in delight. "So you remembered me?"

"Remembered—you?" faltered Milly. "I—I——"

A loud halloo from the wooded slope below interrupted her. It was Jett's voice, calling her back to camp.

"That's Jett," she whispered, hurriedly. "He must not see you."

"Go back. You've time. He's far off," replied Doan.

"Oh yes—I must go."

"Listen—just a second," he whispered, following her, taking her hand. He seemed intense. "Hudnall's camp is only a few miles up the river. I'm with him, you know. Meet me here to-night when the moon comes up. That'll be early."

"Here—at night?" murmured Milly, tremulously. The idea was startling.

"Yes. At moonrise. Promise!" he entreated.

"I'll come."

"Don't be afraid. I'll be waiting for you—right here. . . . Go back to camp now. Don't give yourself away."

Then he shot her a bright, intent look and strode noiselessly away, leading his horse into the grass.

Milly wheeled to run down into the woods, almost coming to disaster in her excitement. It was farther to camp than she thought and some parts of the trail necessitated care in the gathering twilight. Jett did not appear to be coming after her. In a few moments she recovered from her breathless headlong precipitation.

The flicker of a camp fire shone through the woods, and that would have guided her had she lost the plain trail. Thoughts and emotions relative to the meeting with Tom Doan were held in abeyance. She must hurry back to camp and allay Jett's suspicions or fears concerning her. Dusk had fallen when she reached camp, which she approached leisurely. She saw Jett and all his outfit grouped round the camp fire.

"Where've you been?" he asked, gruffly.

"Walking under the trees," she replied, easily.

"Why didn't you answer me?"

"Do I have to yell because you do?" she returned.

"Haw! Haw! Haw!" roared Follonsbee, and he gave Pruitt a dig in the ribs.

"Wal," continued Jett, evidently satisfied, "when it gets dark that's your bedtime. Jane can set up all night if she likes."

"Because I've no need of sleep, eh?" demanded the woman, sarcastically.

"Why, you're a handsome jade," responded Jett.

Milly found in the situation a development of her own resourcefulness. She did not want this hour after supper to appear different from any other; so she stood a moment back of the circle of light, watching the camp fire, and then going to where the water pail stood she took a drink. Leisurely then she moved away to her tent. How fortunate now that it stood apart from the others!

Milly crawled inside to flop down on her bed. For a moment the self-restraint under which she had been taut lingered by reason of its very intensity. Then suddenly it broke. In the darkness of her tent she was safe. Thought of Jett and his outfit flashed into oblivion.

"Oh—what has happened? What have I done? What am I going to do?" she whispered to herself.

It all rushed back, strong and sweet and bewildering. She had to fight feeling in order to think. Some incredibly good instinct had prompted her to stray away from camp. Tom Doan! She had met him. In all that wide vast wilderness the one and only person she had met was the one she yearned for. She had spoken to him; she had promised to meet him later when the moon rose.

Tremendous as was the import of these facts, it did not seem all. What had happened? With mounting pulse she forced herself to recall everything, from the moment she had heard the horse. How she strung out the sensations of that meeting! Had she felt them all then? No—some of them, the deeper ones, were an augmenting of those which had been thoughtless. Could she ever gather into one comprehensive actuality the wildness of amaze, joy, and hope that had constituted her recognition of Tom Doan? What had gone on in her mind all these endless days? Futile to try to understand why! She had almost run straight into his arms.

"Oh, I—I had no time to think!" she whispered, with her burning face buried in the blankets.

Night and darkness and silence and loneliness could not help Milly now. She was in the throes of bursting love. Unawares it had stolen insidiously into all her waking and perhaps sleeping hours—and then, in an unguarded moment, when chance threw Tom Doan again into her presence, it had brazenly surprised her into betrayal. She knew now. And she lay there suffering, thrilling, miserable, and rapturous by turns. It was a trying hour. But it passed and there followed another mood, one wanting only proof, assurance of her wild dream, to border on exquisite happiness. She forgot herself and thought of Tom.

She saw him as clearly as if she had been gazing at him in the light of the sun. Older, thinner, graver, harder his face came back to her. There were lines he had not had, and a short fuzzy beard, as fair as his hair. There had been about him the same breath of the open plain and the buffalo and gunpowder and sweating brow that characterized Jett and his men. This could account for the hardness, perhaps for every change in him.

Only his eyes and the tone of his voice had seemed the same. And in recalling them there flooded over her a consciousness of the joy he had expressed at meeting her again. He had been as happy as she. It was impossible to doubt that. Without thought of himself or of what he was doing he had answered as naturally to the meeting as she had. Friendlessness, loneliness always had engendered a terrible need for love; and this raw life in the buffalo-fields, in the company of hard men and a woman who hated her, had but added a yearning for protection. Milly could understand; she could excuse herself. Yet that did not help much. It was all so sudden.

Absorbed in her new-born emotions, Milly had no cognizance of the passing of the hours. But when the gloom inside of her tent lightened and the canvas showed shadows of leaves moving and waving, she realized that the moon had risen. Trembling all over, she listened. The camp was silent. When had the men gone to bed? Only the murmur of insects and soft rustle of wind kept the silence from being dead. She peeped out. Low down through the trees a silvery radiance told of a rising moon. As Milly watched, with a growing palpitation in her breast, a white disk appeared and almost imperceptibly moved upward, until half the great beautiful moon sailed into her sight, crossed by black branches of trees.

"It's time to go," she whispered, and felt a cold thrill. She realized her danger, yet had no fear. If discovered in the act of meeting a lover she would surely be severely beaten, perhaps killed. But nothing could have kept Milly from keeping that tryst.

Cautiously she crawled out on hands and knees, and then away from the tent, keeping in the shadow. A log on the camp fire flickered brightly. She saw the pale gleam of the tents and her keen ear caught heavy breathing of one of the tired sleepers. At length she rose to her feet and, moving away silently, she lost sight of all round the camp except the fire. Then she circled in the direction of the trail that led up the slope.

Her nervous dread of being caught passed away, leaving only excitement. She did not know where to look for the trail, except that it started somewhere at the base of the slope behind the camp. She would find it. How big and black the elms! Shadows lay thick. Only here and there showed the blanched patches of moonlight. A stealthy step, a rustling, halted her and gave a different tingle to her pulse. Some soft-footed animal stole away into the obscurity. Relieved, she moved slowly to and fro, peering in the grass at her feet, searching for the trail. She remembered that it had led down to the spring and not to Jett's camp. As the spring lay east she worked that way. At last she stepped into the trail and then her heart throbbed faster. He would be waiting. What should she say?

As she climbed with swift steps the shadows under the trees grew less dense. Then she faced a long aisle where her own shadow preceded her. Beyond that she passed into thicker timber where it was dark, and she had to go slowly to hold to the trail. An incautious step resulted in the sharp cracking of a twig. It startled her. How lonely and wild the woods!

Milly reached level ground, and there not far was the end of the trees, now standing out clear and black against a wide moonlit plain. She glided faster, drawn in spite of herself, hurrying to meet him. Vague were her conjectures: sweet were her fears. She ran the last few yards.

As she entered the zone of moonlight and stood expectantly, peering everywhere, she felt the terrible importance of that moment. He was her only friend. Where was he? Had she come too early? If he had not . . . Then a tall dark form glided out into the moonlight.

"Milly!" came the low, eager voice. He hurried to her, drew her back into the shadow.

Milly's strained eagerness and the intensity of purpose that had brought her there suddenly succumbed to weakness. His presence, his voice, his touch changed her incomprehensibly. In desperation she tried to cling to her resolve not to be like she had been at that first meeting there.

"I thought you'd never come," he said.

"Am I—late?" she whispered.

"It's no matter, now you're here," he replied, and took her into his arms.

"Oh—you mustn't," she entreated pushing back from him.

"Why, what's wrong?" he queried, in sudden concern.

In a silence fraught with exquisite torture for Milly she stood there, quivering against him. He put a hand under her chin and forced her head up, so that he could see her face.

"Girl, look at me," he ordered, and it was certain that he shook her a little. "Don't you know what I mean?"

Milly felt that she must drop then. Almost the last of her strength and courage had vanished. Yet she was impelled to look up at him, and even in the shadow of the trees she saw the fire in his eyes.

"How could I know—when you've never told—me?" she whispered, haltingly.

"I love you—that's what," he flung at her. "Do you have to be told in words?"

How imperative that was he could never have understood. It quite robbed her of will. She swayed to him with her head on his breast.

"Milly, did I take you in the wrong way?" he asked, bending over her.

"How—did you take—me?"

"That you must care for me." Fear and anxiety vied with a happy masterfulness in his voice.

"Do *you* have to be told in words?"

"No," he answered, low, and bent to her lips. "But tell me both ways."

Milly might have yielded to his importunity had his ardor left her any force. But she could only lean against him and cling to him with weak hands, in happiness that was pain. For a while then he held her in silence.

"What's your name?" he asked, suddenly.

"Mildred Fayre," she found voice to reply.

"How old are you?"

"Seventeen—nearly eighteen."

"Did you ever love any other man before me?"

"Oh no!"

"Ah, then you do?" he queried, bending to kiss her cheek.

"Don't you know that I do?"

"Will you be my wife?" he flashed.

"Yes," she whispered.

"When?"

"The very day I am of age—if you want me so soon."

"Want you!—I've wanted you so badly I've been sick, miserable. It was not so terrible at first. It grew on me. But I loved you from the moment I said I might never see you again. Do you remember?"

"Yes, Tom Doan, I remember as well as you."

"Oh, you do? Well, when did you love me. I'm curious. It's too good to be true. Tell me when."

"Since the instant I looked over that horse to see you standing there."

"Milly!" He was incredulous, and as if to make sure of his good fortune he fell to caressing her.

Later then, sitting against one of the trees, with his arm round her waist, Milly told him the story of her life. She did not dwell long on the poverty and hard work of her childhood, nor the vanishing hopes and ideals of her school days, nor the last sordid months that had been so hard to endure.

"You poor girl! Well, we must have been made for

each other," he replied, and briefly told his own story. Life had been hard work for him, too, full of loss, and lightened by little happiness. Evidently it hurt him to confess that his father had been a guerilla under Quantrill.

"I always was a farmer," he concluded. "I dreamed of a fine ranch, all my own. And I'm going to have it. Milly, I'm making big money in this buffalo-hide business. I'll be rich. I'll have you, too!"

Milly shared his rapture and did not have the heart to speak of her disapproval of his killing buffalo, nor of her fear of Jett. She embraced joy for the first time.

The night hours wore on and the moon soared high in the heavens, full, silvery white, flooding the plain with light. Out there coyotes were yelping their sharp wild notes. From the river bottom came the deep bay of a wolf. An owl hooted dismally. All of this wildness and beauty seemed part of Milly's changed and uplifted life.

"Come, you must go back to your camp," said Doan at length.

"Oh—must I? I may never see you again!" she whispered.

"Plague me with my own words, will you?" he retorted, and his kisses silenced her. "Will you meet me here to-morrow night, soon as your folks are asleep?"

"Yes."

"Come then. It grows late. Lead the way down, for I'm going as far as I dare with you."

Within sight of the pale gleam of the tents he bade her good-by and silently stole back into the shadow of the slope. Milly as stealthily reached her tent and slipped into it, full of heart and wide awake, to lie in her bed, realizing that in gratefulness for the changed world and the happiness she would now never relinquish, she must go back to the prayers of her childhood.

Chapter VII

At dawn the singing of wild canaries awakened Milly Fayre. There must have been a flock of them that had alighted on the elm tree which sheltered her tent. She listened, finding in the sweet treble notes an augury for her future. How good to awaken to such music and thought.

A loud hoarse yawn from the direction of camp proclaimed the rising of one of the men. Soon after that a sharp ring of Jett's ax drove away the canaries. Rays of rosy light penetrated the slit of Milly's tent, final proof that another day had come. Milly felt a boundless swell of life within her. Never before had any day dawned like this one! She lingered in her bed long after the crackling of the camp fire and the metallic clinking of Dutch oven and skillet attested to the task of breakfast.

"Hey, Milly, you're gettin' worse than the old lady!" called out Jett, in voice for once without gruffness. "Are you dead?"

"I'm very much alive," replied Milly, almost in glee at the double meaning of her words.

"Pile out, then," added Jett.

Milly did not hurry so much as usual; a subtle courage had stirred in her; she felt inspired to outwit Jett. Yet she meant to pretend submission to his rule. Her hope was strong that the arduous toil of hunting and skinning buffalo would continue to leave Jett little time in camp, and none to molest her with evil intentions. He was too obsessed to make money to spare time for drinking.

"Wal, the bombardin' has begun," Follonsbee was heard to say.

"Some early birds that's new to buffalo huntin'," replied Jett. "My experience is you get only so much shootin' in a day. I reckon, though, with the stragglin' bunches of this big herd rompin' to an' fro, we'll hear shootin' all day long."

The men were gone when Milly presented herself at the camp fire. She ate so little that Mrs. Jett noted the absence of her usual appetite.

"Are you sick?" she asked, with something of solicitude.

"No. I just don't feel hungry," replied Milly.

"You've got a high color. Looks like a fever," said the woman, her bright bold eyes studying Milly's face. "Better let me mix you a dose of paregoric."

"Thanks, no. I'm all right," returned Milly. But despite her calm assurance she was intensely annoyed to feel an added heat in her flushed cheeks. It might not be so easy to fool this woman. Milly divined, however, that it was not beyond the bounds of possibility for Mrs. Jett to be sympathetic regarding Tom Doan. Still, Milly dare not trust such impulsive premonition. She performed her accustomed tasks more expeditiously and even better than usual, then repaired to her tent.

After that the interminable hours faced her. How many till moonrise! They seemed everlasting and insupportable. She could neither read nor sew; all she could do was to sit with idle hands, thinking. At

length, however, she discovered that this very thinking, such as it had come to be, was happiness itself.
She had only the short morning and evening tasks
now, and all the hours to wait here in this permanent
camp for the stolen meetings with Tom Doan. Hours
that would become days and weeks, even months, all
to wait for him! She embraced the fact. Loneliness was
no longer fearful. She had a wonderful secret.

The morning was still and warm, not so hot as on
other days, by reason of a cloudily hazed sky. The
birds had gone away, and there was not a sound close
at hand. But from the plain above and from across the
stream that flowed into the Red River, and from all
around it seemed, when she concentrated her attention, there came the detonations of guns. None were
close by, and most appeared very distant. They had no
regularity, yet there were but few intervals of perfect
silence. On the other hand, sometimes a traveling
volley of reports would begin away in the distance and
apparently come closer and then gradually withdraw
to die away. A few shots together appeared a rare
occurrence.

"At every shot perhaps some poor buffalo falls—
dead—or dying like that great crippled bull I saw.
Augh!" exclaimed Milly, in revulsion at the thought.
"I'd hate to have Tom Doan grow rich from murdering
buffalo. . . . But he said he did not kill many—that he
was a skinner."

Then her ears seemed to fill with a low murmur or
faint roar, like the rumble of distant thunder. At first
she thought a storm was brewing out toward the
Staked Plain, but the thunder was too steady and
continuous. In surprise, she strained her hearing.
Long low roar! What could it be? She had heard about
the rumble of an earthquake and for a moment felt fear
of the mysterious and unknown force under the earth.
But this was a moving sound that came on the still
summer air. It could be made only by buffalo.

"The thundering herd!" exclaimed Milly in awe. "That's what Jett called it."

She listened until the roar very slowly receded and diminished and rolled away into silence. Still the shooting continued, and this puzzled Milly because it was reasonable to suppose that if the hunters were pursuing the herd the sound of their guns would likewise die away.

Milly wandered round the camp, exploring places in the woods, and several times resisted a desire to go up the trail to the edge of the plain. Finally she yielded to it, halting under cover of the last trees, gazing out over the green expanse. It was barren as ever. The banging of guns appeared just as far away, just as difficult to locate. Milly wished she could climb high somewhere so that she might see over the surrounding country.

Nearby stood a tree of a kind she did not know. It had branches low down and rose under one of the tall elms. Milly decided she would be much less likely to be seen up in a tree; besides, she could have her desire gratified. To this end she climbed the smaller tree, and from it into the elm, working to a high fork not easily attained. Then she gazed about her, and was so amazed and bewildered by the panorama that she had to exert her will to attend to any particular point of the compass.

Westward the green prairie rose in a grand fan-shaped slope of many leagues, ending in the horizon-wide upheaval of bold gray naked earth which the hunters called the Staked Plain. It was as level-topped as a table, wild, remote, austere, somehow menacing, like an unscalable wall.

In the middle of that vast stretch of green plain there were miles and miles of black patches, extending north and south as far as eye could see. Though they seemed motionless at that distance Milly recognized them as buffalo. Surely they could not be parts of the herd whence came the low, thundering roar.

Far to the left, along the shining green-bordered river, there appeared a belt of moving buffalo, moving to the southwest, and disappearing in what seemed a pall of dust. By turning her ear to that direction and holding her breath Milly again caught the low roar, now very faint. Much banging of guns came from that quarter. Out on the plain from this belt were small herds of buffalo, hundreds of them, dotting the green, and some were in motion.

Then Milly espied thin threads of black moving across the river. Buffalo swimming to the southern bank! These were several miles away, yet she saw them distinctly, and line after line they extended, like slender bridges, across the river until they, too, vanished in the curtain of dust. South of the river the boundless plain showed irregular ragged areas of black, and meandering threads, leading into the haze of distance. Eastward Milly gazed over a green river-bottom jungle, thick and impenetrable, to the level prairie blackened with buffalo. Here were straggling lines moving down toward the river. Altogether, then, the surrounding scene was one of immense openness, infinite waving green prairie crossed by widely separated streams, and made majestic by the domination of buffalo—everywhere buffalo, countless almost as the grasses of the prairie.

"What a pity they must die!" murmured Milly. For in the banging of the guns she heard the death knell of this multiplicity of beasts. She had seen the same in the hard, greedy, strong faces of Jett, and buffalo-hunters like him. Nature with its perfect balance and adjustment of the wild beasts was nothing to Jett. He would kill every buffalo on the plains for the most he could get, if it were only a bottle of rum.

Milly pondered over vague ideas in her developing mind. God might have made the buffalo to furnish the Indians and white men with meat and fur, but surely not through the sordidness of a few to perish from the earth.

Above Milly, in the blue sky, and westward till her sight failed, were huge black birds, buzzards, sailing high and low, soaring round and round, till the upper air seemed filled with them. Buzzards! Birds of prey they were—carrion-eaters, vultures that were enticed from their natural habits, from the need for which nature created them, to fall foul on this carnage left by the hunters.

Some of these uncanny birds of prey swooped down over Milly, and several alighted in a tree not far distant. Solemn, repulsive, they inspired in Milly a fear of the thing called nature. Were they necessary?

She did not long remain up there in her perch, and she discovered that descent was not so easy as climbing. Nevertheless she got by the worst of it without mishap, and then she breathed easier.

The thud of hoofs below caused her to stop abruptly. Horsemen were somewhere close at hand. Owing to the thick foliage she could not see what or where they were. Circling the trunk of the tree with her arm she leaned against it, making sure of her balance. She was still thirty feet from the ground, adequately hidden by bushy leaves, unless some one looked upward from directly beneath her. It was natural to suppose these riders were buffalo-hunters. Presently she espied them, indistinctly through the network of branches. They were riding from the north, evidently having come along the stream. To Milly's consternation they halted their horses almost directly under her. Then she made out that they were soldiers. She need have no fear of them, yet she did not like the idea of being discovered.

"Captain," spoke up one, "there's a good spring down this trail. I'd like a drink of fresh cold water.— Here, one of you men take some canteens down and fill them. The trail leads to the spring."

One of the half dozen soldiers dismounted, and collecting several canteens from his companions he lounged off out of sight.

"Ellsworth, you know this Red River country?" spoke up another soldier.

"Reckon I do, though not very well down this far," came the reply. "This is God's country compared to the Staked Plain. I know that well enough."

"Well, I figure we're on a wild-goose chase," said another, evidently an officer. He had dismounted to fling himself under one of the trees. He removed his sombrero to reveal a fine, strong, weather-beaten face, with mustache slightly gray. "We can never persuade these hide-hunters to go to the fort on account of Indian raids."

"Reckon not. But we can persuade them to send their women to a place of safety. Some of the fools have their women folk. For my part, I'd like to see these hunters band together against the Indians."

"Why?"

"Well, they're a hard lot and Lord only knows how many there are of them. They'll do what we soldiers never could do—whip that combination of redskin tribes."

"Better not say that in the colonel's hearing," said the officer, with a laugh.

"I wouldn't mind. Reckon I've hinted as much. I'm serving on scout duty, you know. But one thing's sure, these hide-hunters have started a bloody mess. And it's a good thing. This section of Texas is rich land. It's the stamping-ground of the Indians. They'll never give it up till the buffalo are gone. Then they'll make peace. As it is now they are red-headed as hell. They'll ambush and raid—then run back up into that devil's place, the Staked Plain."

"I'll bet you we get a taste of it before this summer ends."

"Like as not. If so, you'll remember the campaign," said the other, grimly.

Presently the soldier returned with the canteens, which manifestly were most welcome.

"There's a camp below, sir," said the soldier.

"Buffalo outfit, of course?"

"Yes. Three wagons."

"Did you ask whose outfit it is?"

"No one about camp, sir."

The officer got to his feet, and wiping his heated face, he stepped to his horse.

"Ellsworth, we've passed a good many camps of hide-hunters, all out in the open or along the edge of the timber. What do you make of an outfit camped way down out of sight. That's a hard pull for loaded wagons."

"Hunters have notions, same as other men," replied the scout. "Maybe this fellow wants as much protection as possible from storm and dust. Maybe he'd rather get out of the beaten track."

"Colonel's orders were to find trace of hide thieves," said the officer, thoughtfully. "That stumps me. They're hundreds of these outfits, all traveling, killing, skinning together. How on earth are we going to pick out thieves among them?"

"You can't, Captain," returned the scout, decidedly. "That'll be for the hunters themselves to find. As I said, they're a hard lot and jumbled one. Outlaws, ex-soldiers, adventurers, desperadoes, tenderfeet, plainsmen, and pioneers looking for new ground, and farmers out on a hunt to make money. I reckon most of them are honest men. This hide-hunting is something like the gold rush of '49 and '51, of course on a small scale. Last summer and fall there were hide thieves operating all through the Panhandle. A few of them got caught, too, and swung for it. This summer they'll have richer picking and easier. For with the Indian raids to use as cover for their tracks how can they be apprehended, unless caught in the act?"

"But, man, you mean these robbers waylay an outfit, kill them, steal the hides, burn the camp, and drive off to let the dirty work be blamed on Indians?"

"Reckon that's exactly what I do mean," replied Ellsworth. "It's my belief a good many black deeds laid to the Indians are done by white men."

"Did you tell the colonel that?"

"Yes, and he scouted the idea. He hates Indians. Got a bullet in him somewhere. I reckon he'd rather have bad white men on the plains than good Indians."

"Humph!" ejaculated the officer, and mounting his horse he led the soldiers west along the edge of the timber.

Milly waited a good while before she ventured to descend from her perch; and when she reached the ground she ran down into the woods, slowing to a walk when within sight of camp. She repaired to her tent, there to lie down and rest and think. She had something to ponder over. That conversation of the scout and officer had flashed grave conjectures into her mind. Could her stepfather be one of the hide thieves? She grew cold and frightened with the thought; ashamed of herself, too; but the suspicion would not readily down. Jett had some queer things against him, that might, to be sure, relate only to his unsociable disposition, and the fact, which he had mentioned, that he did not want men to see her. Milly recalled his excuse on this occasion, and in the light of the soldiers' conversation it did not ring quite true. Unless Jett had a personal jealous reason for not wanting men to see her! Once she had feared that. Of late it had seemed an exaggeration.

Fearful as was the thought, she preferred it to be that which made him avoid other camps and outfits, than that he be a hide thief and worse. But her woman's instinct had always prompted her to move away from Jett. She was beginning to understand it. She owed him obedience, because he was her stepfather and was providing her with a living. Nothing she owed, however, or tried to instill into her vacillating mind, quite did away with that insidious suspicion. There was something wrong about Jett. She settled

that question for good. In the future she would listen
and watch, and spy if chance offered, and use her wits
to find out whether or not she was doing her stepfather
an injustice.

The moon took an unconscionably long time to rise
that night, Milly thought. But at last she saw the
brightening over the river, and soon after, the round
gold rim slide up into the tree foliage.

Her task of safely leaving camp this evening was
rendered more hazardous by the fact that Jett and his
men were near the camp, engaged in laborious work of
stretching and pegging hides. They had built a large
fire in a wide cleared space to the left of the camp.
Milly could both see and hear them—the dark moving
forms crossing to and fro before the blaze, and the
deep voices. As she stole away under the trees she
heard the high beat of her heart and felt the cold
prickle of her skin; yet in the very peril of the moment—for Jett surely would do her harm if he caught
her—there was an elation at her daring and her revolt
against his rule.

Halfway up the trail she met her lover, who was
slowly coming down. To his eager whispered "Milly"
she responded with an eager "Tom," as she returned
his kiss.

Tom led her to a grassy spot at the foot of a tree
which was in shadow. They sat there for a while, hand
in hand, as lovers who were happy and unafraid of the
future, yet who were not so obsessed by their dream
that they forgot everything else.

"I can't stay long," said Tom, presently. "I've two
hours pegging out to do to-night. Let's plan to meet
here at this spot every third night, say a half hour after
dark."

"All right," whispered Milly. "I always go to my
tent at dark. Sometimes, though, it might be risky to
slip out at a certain time. If I'm not here you wait at
least an hour."

So they planned their meetings and tried to foresee and forestall all possible risks, and from that drifted to talk about the future. Despite Tom's practical thought for her and tenderness of the moment, Milly sensed a worry on his mind.

"Tom, what's troubling you?" she asked.

"Tell me, do you care anything for this stepfather of yours?" he queried, in quick reply.

"Jett? I hate him. . . . Perhaps I ought to be ashamed. He feeds me, clothes me, though I feel I earn that. Why do you ask?"

"Well, if you cared for him I'd keep my mouth shut," said Tom. "But as you hate him what I say can't hurt you. . . . Milly, Jett has a bad name among the buffalo outfits."

"I'm not surprised. Tell me."

"I've often heard hints made regarding the kind of outfits that keep to themselves. On the way south some freighter who had passed Jett ahead of us gave Pilchuck a hunch to steer clear of him. He gave no reason, and when I asked Pilchuck why we should steer clear of such an outfit he just laughed at me. Well, to-day Pilchuck found Jett skinning a buffalo that had been killed by a big-fifty bullet. Pilchuck knew it because he killed the buffalo and he remembered. Jett claimed he had shot the buffalo. Pilchuck told him that he was using a needle gun, and no needle bullet ever made a hole in a buffalo such as the big fifty. Jett didn't care what Pilchuck said and went on skinning. At that Pilchuck left, rather than fight for one hide. But he was mad clear through. He told Hudnall that hunters who had been in the Panhandle last summer gave Jett a bad name."

"For that sort of thing?" inquired Milly, as Tom paused.

"I suppose so. Pilchuck made no definite charges. But it was easy to see he thinks Jett is no good. These plainsmen are slow to accuse any one of things they can't prove. Pilchuck ended up by saying to Hudnall:

'Some hunter will mistake Jett for a buffalo one of these days!' "

"Some one will shoot him!" exclaimed Milly.

"That's what Pilchuck meant," rejoined Tom, seriously. "It worries me, Milly dear. I don't care a hang what happens to Jett. But you're in his charge. If he *is* a bad man he might do you harm."

"There's danger of that, Tom, I've got to confess," whispered Milly. "I'm afraid of Jett, but I was more so than I am now. He's so set on this hide-hunting that he never thinks of me."

"Some one will find out about you and me, or he'll catch us. Then what?" muttered Tom, gloomily.

"That would be terrible. We've got to keep any one from knowing."

"Couldn't you come to Hudnall's camp to live? I know he'd take you in. And his wife and daughter would be good to you."

Milly pondered this idea with grave concern. It appealed powerfully to her, yet seemed unwise at this time.

"Tom, I could come. I'd love to. But it surely would mean trouble. He could take me back, as I'm not of age. Then he'd beat me."

"Then I'd kill him!" returned Tom, with passion.

"He might kill you," whispered Milly. "Then where would *I* be? I'd die of a broken heart. No, let's wait a while. As long as he's so set on this hunting I have little to fear. Besides, the women out here with these buffalo-hunters are going to be sent to the fort."

"Where'd you hear that?" demanded Tom, in amaze.

Milly told him of the impulse that had resulted in her climbing the tree, and how the soldiers had halted beneath her, and the conversation that had taken place. She told it briefly, remembering especially the gist and substance of what the officer and scout had said.

"Well! That's news. I wonder how Hudnall will take

it. I mustn't give way where I heard it, eh, little girl. It'd be a fine thing, Milly. I hope the soldiers take all you women to the fort quick. I wouldn't get to see you, but I could endure that, knowing you were safe."

"I'd like it, too, and, Tom, if I am taken I'll stay there until I'm eighteen."

"Your birthday is to be our wedding day," he said.

"Is it?" she whispered, shyly.

"Didn't you say so? Are you going back on it?"

His anxiety and reproach were sweet to her, yet she could not wholly surrender her new-found power or always give in to her tenderness.

"Did I say so? Tom, would you quit murdering these poor buffalo for me, if I begged you?"

"What!" he ejaculated, amazed.

"Would you give up this hide-hunting business for me?"

"Give it up? Why, of course I would!" he responded. "But you don't mean that you will ask it."

"Tom dear—I might."

"But, you child," he expostulated, "the buffalo are doomed. I may as well get rich as other men. I'm making big money. Milly, by winter time—next year surely, I can buy a ranch, build a house, stock a farm—for you!"

"It sounds silly of me, Tom. But you don't understand me. Let's not talk of it any more now."

"All right. Only tell me you'll never go back on me?"

"If you only knew how I need you—and love you—you'd not ask that."

Milly, upon her stealthy approach to camp, observed that the men had finished their tasks and were congregated about the fire, eating and drinking. The hour must have been late. Milly sank noiselessly down in her tracks and crouched there, frightened, and for the moment unable to fight off a sense of disaster. She could do nothing but remain there until they went to bed. What if Jett should walk out there! He and his comrades, however, did not manifest any activity.

"No—not yet. We'll wait till that Huggins outfit has more hides," declared Jett, in a low voice of finality.

"All right, boss," rejoined Follonsbee, "but my hunch is the sooner the better."

"Aw, to hell with buffalo hides," yawned Pruitt. "I'm aboot daid. Heah it's midnight an' you'll have us out at sunup. Jett, shore I'm sore, both body an' feelin'. If I knowed you was goin' to work us like this heah I'd never throwed in with you."

"But, man, the harder we work the more hides, an' the less danger——"

"Don't talk so loud," interrupted Follonsbee.

"It shore ain't me shoutin'," replied Pruitt, sullenly. "If I wanted to shout I'd do it. What's eatin' me is that I want to quit this outfit."

Jett shook a brawny fish in Pruitt's face, that showed red in the camp-fire light.

"You swore you'd stick, an' you took money in advance, now didn't you?" demanded Jett in a fierce whisper.

"I reckon I did. I'm square, an' don't you overlook that," retorted Pruitt. "It's you who's not square. You misrepresented things."

"Ahuh! Maybe I was a little overkeen in talkin'," admitted Jett. "But not about what money there is in this deal. I know. You'll get yours. Don't let me hear you talk quit any more or I'll know you're yellow."

For answer Pruitt violently threw a chip or stick into the fire, to send the sparks flying, and then rising, with one resentful red flash of face at Jett, he turned and swaggered away towards his tent, without a word.

"Bad business," said Follonsbee, shaking his head pessimistically. "You've no way with men, Rand. You'd get more out of them if you'd be easy an' patient, an' argue them into your opinions."

"Reckon so, but I can't stand much more from that damned rebel," growled Jett.

"He's harder to handle than Catlee," went on Jett. "He's beginnin' to see a hell of a risk in your way of hide-huntin'. Catlee ain't wise yet. He's as much a tenderfoot as Huggins or a lot more of these jay-hawkers who're crazy to get rich off the buffalo. I was afraid of these two fellars, an' I said so."

"We had to have men. We'd lost a week waitin'," complained Jett.

"Yes, but it'd have been better to wait longer, till you got the right men."

"Too late now. I'll make the best of it an' try to hold my temper."

"Good. Let's turn in," replied Follonsbee, and rose to go toward the tents. Jett spread the fire and followed him. Soon the camp appeared dark and deserted.

Milly crouched there under the big elm until she was sure Jett had crawled into his bed, and then swiftly and noiselessly she covered the ground to her own tent. In the interest of this colloquy among the men she had forgotten her fright. That, in her opinion, had been strange talk for honest hunters. Yet she could only surmise. While she was revolving in her mind the eventful disclosures of the day sleep overtook her.

Days passed. They flew by, it seemed to Milly. The idle hours that fell to her lot were yet not many nor long enough for these ravenous hide-hunters. She watched in the daytime and listened at night, yet the certainty of what she feared did not come.

Her meetings with Tom Doan continued regularly as the third nights rolled round, without hitch or mishap; and in them Milly seemed to grow into the fullness of a woman's feeling. They talked of their love, of their marriage, and their plans for a home. There was little else to talk about except the buffalo, and the status of Jett and his men. Milly always suffered a pang when Tom, forgetting her love of all animals, raved about how many buffalo he had killed and skinned. Once she got blood on her hand from one of his boots, which she had inadvertently touched, and she was so sick and disgusted over it that she spoke sharply. Almost they quarreled. As for the truth concerning Jett, all Milly's observation and Tom's inquiry could not satisfy them as to what was the actual truth.

More days went fleeting by, ushering in hot July, more hide-hunters along the river brakes, and, what seemed incredible, more buffalo.

"They're massin' up an' makin' ready for a hell of a stampede one of these days," declared Jett, in his booming voice.

One night Milly was awakened by an unusual sound. Horses were snorting and stamping in camp. She peeped out. A wagon with two teams hitched to it stood just beyond the waning camp fire. Jett's burley form held the driver's seat; Follonsbce, rifle in hand, was in the act of climbing beside him; Pruitt stood on the ground, evidently intent on Jett's low, earnest voice. Milly could not distinguish what was being said. Jett drove away into the gloom of the woods. Where could he be going at this hour of the night? Milly could only conclude that he was driving out for another load of hides. Perhaps Jett had made trips before, unknown to her.

Next day disclosed the odd fact that Jett had not returned. Pruitt and Catlee evidently pursued the hunting as heretofore, and did not commit themselves to any words in Milly's presence. Sunset and supper time found Jett still absent. On the following morning, however, Milly learned that he had returned in the night and was asleep in his tent. She repaired to her own quarters and remained there till noon, when she saw him ride away. That afternoon Milly wandered around, as usual, with apparently no object in view, and eventually approached the glade where Jett kept his hides. She hated to go near it because of the unpleasant odor, the innumerable flies, and the sickening evidence of slaughtered buffalo.

The glade had been cleared farther on the side

toward the stream, and everywhere were buffalo hides, hundreds and hundreds of them, some pegged out to dry, others in piles shaded by cut branches. Milly, because of her former reluctance to visit this place, had no record in her mind of quantity of hides, so she could not tell whether or not there had been a sudden and suspicious addition.

The day after that Jett loaded two wagons with hides, and with Catlee driving one of them they set off for a freighting station. They were gone five days, during which Milly had the most peaceful time since she had left the settlements. Twice she was with Tom, and they made the best of their opportunity. Mrs. Jett during this period was almost amiable. Follonsbee and Pruitt worked about as before.

When Jett returned, his presence, or something connected with it, seemed to spur his men to renewed efforts. Early and late they were toiling at this game. Tom Doan had told her that the great drive of buffalo was on. Milly, however, had not needed this information. She could see and hear.

No daylight hour was without its trampling thunder! Somewhere on one side of the river or other a part of the great herd was always in motion. Dust blew thick over the sky, sometimes obscuring the sun. And an unfavorable breeze, which fortunately occurred but seldom, brought a stench that Milly could not endure. By day the guns banged east, north, south, west, as if a battle were raging. Crippled buffalo limped by the camp, with red tongues hanging out, making for the brakes of the river, to hide and die. By night the howl of coyotes was sleep-preventing and the long-drawn deep, wild bay of wolves filled Milly with a haunting fear.

Chapter VIII

ONE day in July a band of soldiers rode into Hudnall's camp. The officer in charge got off his horse and appeared to be a lithe, erect man of forty, with a stern bronzed face.

"Who's the owner of this outfit?" he inquired.

Hudnall strode forward. "I am. Clark Hudnall's my name."

"Glad to meet you," replied the officer. "I'm Captain Singleton of the Fourth Calvary, stationed at Fort Elliott. This is my scout, Ellsworth. We've been detailed to escort buffalo-hunters to the fort or one of the freighting posts. The Indians are raiding."

"But I don't want to go to the fort," protested Hudnall, obstinately.

"You'll stay here at your own risk," warned Singleton.

"We never expected anything else," returned Hudnall, bluntly. "If you want to know, you're the first soldiers we've seen."

"Have you women with you?" inquired the officer.

113

"Yes. My wife an' daughter an' my son's wife."

"Didn't you know any better than to fetch women out here in this Indian country?" went on Singleton, severely.

"We heard bad rumors, sir, but didn't believe them, an' I may say we've had no trouble so far."

"You've been lucky. Did you know Huggins?"

"Can't say I do—by name," rejoined Hudnall, reflectively.

"Huggins had the outfit several miles below here. One helper at least with him, maybe more. Their camp was raided, burned—hides stolen. No trace of Huggins or his helper."

"Indians?" queried Hudnall, sharply.

"Very likely. We've found no trace of Huggins or his man. They might have escaped to some other outfit or to a freighting post. But that's doubtful. West of here twenty miles or more a band of Comanches attacked some hunters, and were driven off. Unless you buffalo men camp together some of you are going to be killed."

"We'll fight," declared Hudnall, determinedly.

"But you must take your women to a place of safety," insisted the officer.

Hudnall called his wife and daughter. They came forward from their quarters, accompanied by Burn Hudnall's wife. Evidently they had heard something of the conversation; fear was manifest in their faces.

"Ladies, pray do not be frightened," said the officer, courteously. "There's no need for that right now. We're here to escort you to a place where you will be safe while your men folks are hunting. It is *not* safe for you here. Any day Indians might ride down on you when you are alone in camp."

Despite Singleton's courtesy and assurance, the women were alarmed, and gathering round Hudnall they began to talk excitedly.

"Captain, you an' your men make yourselves at home while we talk this over," said Hudnall.

Pilchuck and Tom Doan, just in from skinning buffalo, stood near during this conversation. Tom welcomed sight of soldiers, and he intended to inform Captain Singleton of the two women in Jett's camp.

"Say, Ellsworth," said Pilchuck to the soldier scout, "if this Huggins outfit was killed by Indians they'd not have disappeared. Comanches don't bother to bury or hide white men they've killed."

Ellsworth leaned close to Pilchuck. "Reckon it doesn't look like redskin work to me, either."

Pilchuck swore under his breath, and was evidently about to enter into earnest consultation with the soldier scout when Hudnall called him and Tom. They held a brief council. It was decided that Stronghurl and Pilchuck, with the addition of the outfit, Dunn and Tacks, would remain in camp, while Hudnall, Burn Hudnall, and Tom, accompanied by the women, would go with the soldiers. Hudnall did not consider it needful to send them all the way to Fort Elliott; the nearest freighting post, Sprague's, some three days' journey, would be safe and far enough. Hudnall intended to take advantage of this opportunity to freight out his buffalo hides, of which he had a large number.

"Reckon it may work out best, after all," he averred, brightening. "I'll run no risk losing the hides, an' then we'll soon be in need of supplies, 'specially cartridges."

How dense he seemed to the imperative side of the issue—safety for the women! But he was not a frontiersman. He was brave, though foolhardy.

"We'll pack an' leave early to-morrow," he informed Singleton.

"We'll catch up with you, perhaps before you get to the military road," said the officer.

"I don't know that road, an' with Pilchuck stayin' here I might lose my way," returned Hudnall, in perplexity.

"The military road runs from Fort Elliott to Fort

Dodge. You'll strike it about eighteen miles northwest."

"Reckon you can't miss it," added Pilchuck. "An' there's water aplenty."

Hudnall invited Captain Singleton and his soldiers to have supper, which invitation was accepted, much to Tom Doan's satisfaction. He wanted to think over what was best to say to Captain Singleton about the Jett outfit.

There was indeed bustle and rush around the Hudnall camp that afternoon, part of which work was the preparation of a hearty supper. It was cooked and eaten long before sunset. Afterward Tom found occasion to approach the officer.

"Captain, may I have a—a word with you—about something very important?" he inquired frankly, despite a certain embarrassment he could not help.

"Certainly, young man. What can I do for you?" he replied, with keen gray eyes on Tom.

As they withdrew a little, Tom lost his hesitation and briefly told who he was, what he was doing in Hudnall's outfit, and thus quickly reached the point.

"Captain, please let what I tell you be confidential," he went on, earnestly. "It's about a girl with the Jett outfit. She's Jett's stepdaughter. They're camped below the bluff at the mouth of White Creek, several miles down."

"Jett outfit," mused the officer. "I've heard that name. I know where his camp is—down in the woods. Hidden."

"Yes. Well, I—I'm in love with this girl, Milly Fayre—engaged to her. We expect to be married when she's eighteen. And I'm afraid for her—afraid of Jett more than the Indians. So is Milly. He'll not like this idea of sending his women to the fort or anywhere away from him. You see, he's got a wife, too, no relation to Milly—and he has them do the camp work. He's a hog for this hide-hunting. Then there are two hard nuts with him, Follonsbee and Pruitt. It's not an outfit like ours, Captain, or most any along the river. I can't honestly bring anything bad against Jett, unless it's that he's a brute and is after Milly. I know that. She won't admit it, but I can feel how she feels. She ought to be taken to the fort or wherever our women go— and please, Captain, don't fail to bring her. If you ask her you'll find out quick that she knows what's best for her."

"Suppose you ride down there with us," suggested Singleton.

"I'd like to, but I'd better not," replied Tom. "Jett knows nothing of me yet. Milly thinks it best he doesn't know until she's free. He might harm her. And if he ever lays a hand on her I'll kill him."

"What'd you say your name is?" inquired the officer.

"Tom Doan."

"All right, Tom, I'm for you and Milly. Here's my hand on it."

"Then you'll fetch her along?" queried Tom, trying to content himself, as he gripped the hand of this fine and soldierly man.

"If she's still there."

"I saw her last night—we've been meeting secretly. She's there."

"Then you will see her to-morrow again, for we'll catch you on the road," replied the officer, with a smile.

"We can never thank you enough," returned Tom, with emotion.

It was indeed with a thankful heart that he saw Singleton and his soldiers, leading their packhorses, ride off down the river. After that Tom worked as never before, and not only got all his work done, but considerable of the others'. The Hudnall outfit went to bed late and got up early. By the time the July sun was blazing over the prairie the three heavily laden wagons were moving toward the northwest. Tom had the biggest load of hides in his wagon. The women rode on the drivers' seats with Hudnall and his son.

The route lay along the swell of the slope as it gently dipped to the river, then up on the level prairie and northwest toward the far escarpment of the Staked Plain, a sharp gray landmark on the horizon. Tom followed fairly good wagon tracks until they all appeared to converge in one well-trodden road. Here for hours good time was made. Tom did not mind the heat or the flies or the dust. Over and over again he had counted the earnings Hudnall owed him, and the sum staggered him. Hundreds of dollars! But splendid as that was, it shrank into insignificance at the good fortune of having Milly safely away from Jett and the Indians.

Hudnall made a noon stop at a shady crossing of a little stream. Here the horses were watered and fed and the travelers partook of a light meal. When the journey was resumed Tom could no longer resist the desire to look back along the road in the hope that he might see the soldiers coming. Really he did not expect them before camp that night, yet he was unable to keep from looking back.

All through this morning's travel they had skirted the ragged edge of the buffalo herd. Long, however, had they passed out of hearing of the guns of the hunters. Then early in the afternoon they ran into a large herd coming from the north. It was not a grazing herd, nor could it be called a stampeding herd; but the movement was steady and rapid. Hudnall drove way off the road to try to get round the leaders; this move, however, resulted in the three wagons being caught and hemmed in, with a stream of buffalo passing on both sides.

Tom believed it was a rather ticklish situation. The herd did not appear to be more than a mile wide, but the end toward the north was not in sight. The wagons were halted to wait until the herd had passed. The buffalo split round the wagons, probably fifty yards on each side, and they loped along lumberingly, not in any sense frightened. They raised dust enough to make the halt very uncomfortable, and noise enough to make it necessary to shout in order to be heard.

Tom's dissatisfaction had to do solely with the fact that Hudnall had gotten far enough off the road to miss the soldiers, if they came up presently. Hudnall, however, did not mind the halt, the discomfort, the loss of time, or the probable risk, should the buffalo become frightened.

To Tom's utter amaze, Hudnall presently took up his gun, and picking out bulls running somewhat away from the massed herd, he dropped four in as many shots. On that side the herd swerved away, the inside ranks pressing closer toward the middle, but they did not stampede. Then Burn Hudnall, not to be outdone by his father, dropped three buffalo on his side. The shooting served only to widen the oval that encompassed the wagons. Then the intrepid and indefatigable hunters proceeded to skin the slain beasts, regardless of the trampling mass passing so closely by.

Tom, contrary to his usual disposition, did not offer to help; and when Hudnall yelled something unintelligible he waved his hand at the herd.

It required two hours for the herd to pass the wagons, and another hour for the Hudnalls to complete skinning the seven they had shot. The women complained of the hot sun and the flies and the enforced wait. Tom spent a good deal of that last hour standing on top of the huge pile of hides in his wagon, scanning the horizon in the direction of the Red River camps.

"Hey, Tom, you might have helped along," said Hudnall, as he threw the wet hides up on his wagon.

"You might have been run down, yourself," retorted Tom.

"Father, I think Tom's scared of the Indians the soldier talked about," remarked Sally Hudnall, a little maliciously. She had never quite forgiven Tom for being impervious to her charms.

"Tom afraid? Nope, I can't savvy that," replied her father, in his hearty way.

"Well, he's looking back all the time," said Sally, with conviction.

Her tone, more than the content of her words, brought to Tom's mind a thought that when the soldiers did come along with Milly, there might result an embarrassing situation. What was he to say in explanation of his acquaintance with Milly? A moment's reflection convinced him that no explanation was necessary, nor need the Hudnalls know just yet of his engagement to her. Still, Milly had not been consulted; she would be overjoyed to see him and to meet the Hudnalls; and she was young, impulsive. How would she act? Tom told himself that he did not care the least what she said or did, but all the same an unusual situation for him seemed impending.

As Hudnall led off toward the road, Tom allowed Burn to fall into second place, leaving him to take up the rear, and from this position he could look back to his satisfaction.

Soon they were in the road again, and late in the afternoon turned into the military road Captain Singleton had indicated. Here the horses could travel, mostly at a trot. Tom had craned his neck sidewise so many times looking backward that he had put a crick in it, all to no avail. The soldiers did not put in an appearance. Tom began to worry. Suppose Jett had gotten wind of their coming and had moved camp! Might not the Comanches have raided Jett the same as Huggins! Tom had rather a bad hour along the military road.

At sunset the Hudnall wagons began to draw near a richly green depression of the prairie, where a stream wound its way. And when Hudnall, now far in the lead, turned off the road, Tom was suddenly compelled to pay some attention to the foreground.

Horses were grazing in the grass; tents shone white against the background of green trees; a camp fire sparkled, and round it stood men. Soldiers! Tom's heart gave a leap. Captain Singleton had forged ahead, probably during the delay caused by the buffalo herd.

Tom urged his team to a trot and soon caught up with Burn Hudnall, who turned off the main road towards the camp. Tom followed closely, to be annoyed by the fact that Burn's wagon obstructed his view. Once or twice Tom caught a glimpse of the tents and the fire; yet, peer keenly as he could, he did not discern any women. His heart sank. If Milly was there she would be out watching the wagons drive up. Tom passed from joy to sadness. Yet hope would not wholly die. He kept looking, and all the time, up to the very halt, Burn's wagon prevented him from seeing everything. Therein lay his one hope.

"Hey, Burn, don't you an' Tom drive smelly hides right in camp," yelled Hudnall.

Thus admonished Tom wheeled his team away from the camp. Burn turned also, thus still obstructing Tom's vision. But there had to be an end to it some time. The next time Tom looked up, after he had halted the team, he was probably fifty yards from the camp fire.

He saw soldiers in dusty blue, Hudnall's stalwart form, all three of the Hudnall women, and then a girl in gray waving an excited hand at him. Tom stared. But the gray dress could not disguise the form it covered. Milly! He recognized her before he saw her face.

With surging emotions Tom leaped off the wagon and strode forward. In the acute moment, not knowing what to expect, trying to stifle his extraordinary agitation, Tom dropped his head until he came to the half circle of people before him. Their faces seemed a blur, yet intent, curious on him. Milly stepped into clear sight toward him. She was pale. Her eyes shone large and dark as night. A wonderful smile transfigured her.

Tom felt the need of an effort almost beyond him—to greet Milly without betraying their secret.

But Milly was not going to keep any secrets. He felt that, saw it, and consternation routed his already weakened control.

"Oh, Tom!" she cried, radiantly, and ran straight into his arms.

Only this was terrible, because she forgot everybody except him, and he could not forget them. She almost kissed him before he had wit enough to kiss her first. With that kiss his locked boyish emotions merged into one great gladness. Realizing Milly, he stepped beside her and, placing his arm round her, moved to face that broadly smiling, amazed circle.

"Mrs. Hudnall, this is my—my girl, Milly Fayre," he said.

"Tom Doan! For the land's sake!" ejaculated the kindly woman. "Your girl! . . . Well, Milly Fayre, I'm right happy to make your acquaintance."

She warmly kissed Milly and then introduced her to Sally and Mrs. Burn Hudnall. That appeared to be sufficient introduction for all present.

Hudnall was the most astonished of men, and certainly delighted.

"Wal, Milly, I reckon Tom Doan's boss is sure glad to meet you," he said, and shook her hand with a quaint formality. "Would you mind tellin' me where this scallywag ever found such a pretty girl?"

"He found me—out here," replied Milly, shyly.

"Ah!" cried Sally Hudnall. "Now I know why Tom used to slip away from camp almost every night."

"An' leave off peggin' buffalo hides till the gray mornin'," swiftly added Hudnall. "I always wondered about that."

Amid the laughter and banter of these good people Tom stood his ground as long as possible; then, seeing that in their kindly way they had taken Milly to their hearts, he left her with them and hurried to unhitch the team he had driven.

Burn Hudnall followed him. "You buffalo-skinnin' son of a gun!" he exclaimed, in awe and admiration. "She's a hummer! By gosh! you're lucky! Did you see Sally's face? Say, Tom, she was half sweet on you. An' now we know why you've been so shy of women."

Upon returning to camp, Tom met Captain Singleton, who had a smile and a cordial handshake for him.

"Well, lad, I fetched her, but it was no easy job," he said. "She's a sweet and pretty girl. You're to be congratulated."

"Was Jett hard to manage?" queried Tom, intensely interested.

"Yes, at first, I had trouble with him. Rough sort of man! Finally he agreed to let her come to the freighting post until the Indian scare quieted down. He wouldn't let his wife come and she didn't want to. She struck me as being almost as able to take care of herself as any man."

"Well!" exclaimed Tom, blankly.

"Lad, don't worry," replied the officer, understanding Tom's sudden check of enthusiasm and warmth. "This Indian scare will last. It'll grow from scare to panic. Not until the buffalo are gone will the Indians quit the warpath. Maybe not till they're dead."

On the second day following, about noon, the Hudnall outfit, with their escort, arrived at Sprague's Post, which was situated on a beautiful creek some miles below Fort Elliott. Here the soldiers left the party and went on their way.

Sprague was one of the mushroom frontier posts that had sprung up overnight. It consisted mainly of a huge one-story structure built of logs, that served as sutler's store, as well as protection against possible Indian attacks. The short street was lined with cabins, tents, and shacks; and adjacent to the store were acres and acres of buffalo hides piled high. There were a dance hall, several saloons, a hotel and restaurant, all in the full blast. Buffalo outfits, coming and going, freighters doing the same, in considerable number, accounted for the activity of this post. The sutler's store, which was owned by Sprague, was a general supply center for the whole northern section of Texas.

Hudnall engaged quarters for the women folk, including Milly, that seemed luxurious after their camping experience. Sally Hudnall was to share her room, which had board floor and frame, roofed by canvas, with Milly; and the other Hudnall women had two rooms adjoining, one of which would serve as a kitchen. Hudnall had only to buy stove, utensils, supplies and fuel, to establish his wife and companions to their satisfaction.

Tom could hardly have hoped for any more, and felt that he would be always indebted to the Hudnalls. Fortune had indeed favored him by throwing his lot in with theirs.

Hudnall sold his hides to Sprague, getting three dollars each for the best robe cowhides, two dollars and a half for the bulls, and one dollar and seventy-five cents for the rest. His profits were large, as he frankly admitted, and he told Tom he thought it only fair to pay more for skinning. As for Tom, the roll of bills given to him for his earnings was such that it made him speechless. At the store he bought himself much-needed clothing and footgear, and a new rifle, with abundance of cartridges. Nor did he forget to leave some money with Mrs. Hudnall, for Milly's use, after he had gone. But he did not tell Milly of this.

"Tom," said Hudnall, seriously, when they had turned the horses loose in the fine grama grass outside of town, "I never saw the beat of this place right here for a ranch. Did you? Look at that soil!"

Tom certainly had not. It was rich prairie land, rolling away to the horizon, and crossed by several winding green-lined streams.

"Gee! I'd like to shove a plow into that," added Hudnall, picking up the turf. "Some day, Tom, all this will be in wheat or corn, or pasture for stock. Take my hunch, boy, we haven't seen its beat.. We'll run up a cabin, at the end of this hunt, an' winter here. Then by another spring we can tell.''

Tom found Sprague's Post the most interesting place that he had ever visited, and considerably much too wild, even in daytime. Dance hall and gambling hell, however, had only momentary attraction for him. Sprague's store was the magnet that drew him. Here he learned a great deal.

The buffalo south of the Brazos and Pease Rivers had at last turned north and would soon fall in with the great herd along the Red River. This meant that practically all the buffalo in the Southwest would concentrate between the Red River and the Staked Plain—an innumerable, tremendous mass. The Comanches were reported to be south of this herd, traveling toward the Red; and the Kiowas were up on the Staked Plain, chasing buffalo east; Cheyennes and Arapahoes, whose hunting ground had always been north of this latitude, were traveling south, owing to the fact that the annual migration of buffalo had failed this year. Failed because of the white hunters! An Indian war was inevitable.

Tom heard that Indian Territory was now being guarded by United States marshals; Kansas had passed laws forbidding the killing of buffalo; Colorado had done likewise. This summer would see all the buffalo hunters congregated in Texas. That meant the failure of the great herds to return north into Indian Territory, Kansas, and Colorado. The famous hunting grounds along the Platte and Republican Rivers would be barren. It seemed a melancholy thing, even to Tom, who had been so eager to earn his share of the profits. It was a serious matter for the state legislatures to pass laws such as this. No doubt Texas would do the same.

Tom reasoned out this conclusion before he learned that at this very time the Texas Legislature was meeting to consider a bill to protect buffalo in their state. So far it had been held up by remarks credited to Gen. Phil Sheridan, who was then stationed at San Antonio,

in command of the military department of the
Southwest. Sprague gave Tom a newspaper to read,
and spoke forcibly.

"Sheridan went to Austin an' shore set up thet
meetin'. Told the Senators an' Representatives they
were a lot of sentimental old women. They'd make a
blunder to protect the buffalo! He said the hunters
ought to have money sent them, instead of discourage-
ment. They ought to have medals with a dead buffalo
on one side an' a dead Injun on the other."

Tom was strongly stirred by the remarks credited to
General Sheridan, and he took the newspaper to the
Hudnalls and read the passage:

"These buffalo-hunters have done more in the
last year to settle the Indian trouble than the
entire regular army has done in thirty years. They
are destroying the Indians' commissary. Send
them powder and lead! . . . Let them kill, skin,
and sell until the buffalo are exterminated. Then
the prairie can be covered with speckled cattle!"

"Great!" boomed Hudnall, slapping his big hand
down. "But darn it—tough on the Indians!"

Tom was confronted then with a strange thought; he,
like Hudnall, felt pity for the Indians, yet none for the
buffalo. There was something wrong in that. Later,
when he told Milly about what he had heard, and
especially Hudnall's expression of sympathy, she said:

"Tom, it's because of the money. You men can't see
right. Would you steal money from the Indians?"

"Why, certainly not!" declared Tom, with uplift of
head.

"You are stealing their food," she went on, seriously. "Their meat—out of their mouths. Not because
you're hungry, but to get rich. Oh, Tom, it's wrong!"

Tom felt troubled for the first time. He could not
laugh this off and he did not have any argument
prepared to defend his case.

"Tom Doan," she added, very sweetly and gravely, "I'll have something to say to you—about killing buffalo—when you come to me on my eighteenth birthday!"

Tom could only kiss her for that speech, subtle, yet wonderful with its portent as to her surrender to him; but he knew then, and carried away with him next morning, the conviction that Milly would not marry him unless he promised to give up buffalo-hunting.

Chapter IX

As Tom drove his team after the Hudnalls, southward along the well-beaten military road, he carried also with him a thought of his parting from Milly—and something about her words or looks was like the one bitter drop in his sweet cup.

Early as had been the hour, Milly with the Hudnall women had arisen to prepare breakfast and see their men folk off. Hudnall and Burn were having their troubles breaking away from wives, daughter, and sister, so they had no time to note the poignancy of Milly's farewell to Tom.

At the last she had come close to Tom, fastening her trembling hands to his hunting coat. She looked up into his eyes, suddenly wonderful, strange.

"Tom, you are all I have in the world," she said.

"Well, dear, I'm all yours," he had replied, tenderly.

"You must not stay away long."

"I'll come back the very first chance," Tom had promised.

"You should not leave me—at all," she had whispered then, very low.

"Why Milly, you're safe here now," he expostulated.

"I'll never be safe until—until Jett has no right over me."

"But he will not come for you. Captain Singleton and Sprague say the Indian scare has just begun."

"Tom—I'll never be safe—until *you* take me."

"Dearest . . ." he had entreated, and then Hudnall boomed out, "Come on, break away, you young folks." And there had been only time for a last embrace.

Milly's last look haunted Tom. How big, black, tragic her eyes! How beautiful, too—and their expression was owing to love of him. His heart swelled until it pained. Was it right to leave her? He could have found work at Sprague's. A remorse began to stir in him. If he had only not been so poor—if he had not been compelled to hunt buffalo! He realized that he was returning to the buffalo fields no longer free, bearing the weight of a great responsibility,—a lonely girl's happiness, perhaps her life.

The summer morning was warm, colorful, fragrant with soft breeze off the prairie, full of melody of birds, and bright with the rising sun. But Tom did not respond as usual. The morning passed, and the hot afternoon was far spent before he could persuade and argue himself into something of his old mood. Common sense helped him. The chances of his returning to find Milly safe and well were very much greater than otherwise; yet he could not forget the last few moments they had been together, when under stress of fear and sorrow she had betrayed Jett's real status and her own fatalism. All that day Milly was in his thoughts, and afterward, when he lay in his bed, with the dark-blue, star-studded sky open to his sleepless gaze.

It took Hudnall only two days and a half, hauling light wagons, to return to the Red River camp. Condi-

tions were identically the same as before the trip.
Pilchuck and his three helpers had killed and skinned
three hundred and twenty-five buffalo during Hudnall's absence. The chief of the outfit was delighted;
and late in the afternoon as it was, he wanted to go
right at the slaughter.

"Take it easy," growled Pilchuck. "We want some
fresh grub an' some news."

Manifestly, Pilchuck and his associates had not
fared well since the departure of the women folk.
"Dam the pesky redskins, anyhow," he complained to
Hudnall. "Who's goin' to cook?"

"We'll take our turn," replied Hudnall, cheerfully.

"Lot of fine cooks we got in this outfit," he growled.
"Wal, there's one consolation, anyway—reckon we
won't have to eat much longer."

"An' why not?" demanded Hudnall, in surprise. "I
fetched back a wagon load of grub."

"Wal, we're goin' to be scalped by Comanches
directly."

"Bosh!" boomed Hudnall, half in anger. "You
plainsmen make me sick. You're worse than the soldiers. All this rant about Indian raids! We've been out
over two months an' haven't seen a single Indian,
tame or wild."

The scout gazed steadfastly at Hudnall, and the
narrow slits of his eyes emitted a gray-blue flash, cold
as light on steel.

"It's men like you who can't savvy the West, an'
won't listen, that get scalped by Indians," he said,
with a ring in his voice.

Hudnall fumed a moment, but his good nature pre-
vailed and he soon laughed away the effect of Pilchuck's hard speech. Dread he seemed to lack.

Next morning Tom followed the others of the Hudnall outfit out to the chase, which they returned to with
redoubled energy and a fiercer determination. Con-
crete rewards in shape of gold and greenbacks paid to
them by Hudnall were the spurs to renewed effort.

Tom started that day badly. Just as he came within range of the first buffalo and aimed at it he thought of Milly's reproachful dark eyes and he wavered so that he crippled the beast. It escaped into the herd. Tom was furious with himself for wounding a buffalo that could only limp away to die a lingering death. After that he put squeamishness out of his mind and settled down into the deadly and dangerous business of hide-hunting.

The day was one of ceaseless and strenuous labors, extending long after dark. Bed was a priceless boon; memory had little opportunity; sleep was something swift and irresistible.

Thus was ushered in the second phase of Tom Doan's buffalo-hunting.

The vast herd of buffalo, reported by Pilchuck to be several miles wide and more miles in length than any conservative scout would risk estimating, never got farther north than the vicinity of the Red River.

Gradually it was driven west along the river to the North Fork, which it crossed, and then, harassed by the hunters behind and flanked on the west by the barren rise of the Staked Plain, it turned south, grazing and traveling steadily, to make the wide and beautiful Pease River divide in ten days.

Here began a fearful carnage. Hudnall's outfit fell in with the thick of the buffalo-hunters, many of whom had been a year at the game. They were established in name and manifestly proud of that fact. "Raffert's, Bill Stark's, Nebraska Pete's, Black and Starwell, Bicker-dyke's, Uncle Joe Horde, Old Man Spaun, Jack and Jim Blaise," and many other names became household words in the Hudnall camp.

Tom kept eyes and ears open for news of the Jett outfit, but so far had not been successful in learning its whereabouts. There were hundreds of gangs strung along the river for many miles, and by far not all of the buffalo were in the great massed herd.

On a tributary of the Pease it was decided by Pilchuck and Hudnall to make permanent camp until fall.

"I want four thousand hides by November," boomed Hudnall, rubbing his huge hands.

"Easy. I'll show you how to kill a hundred tomorrow in three hours," replied Pilchuck.

"When we'll freight back to Sprague's?" queried Tom, anxiously.

Thus each man voiced the thing most in his thoughts.

Next day Pilchuck outdid his boast in the estimated time, killing one hundred and eighteen buffalo—a remarkable feat. But he had a fast, perfectly trained horse; he was daring and skillful; he rode his quarry down and made one shot do the work.

Day by day Tom Doan killed fewer buffalo. He did not notice the fact until it was called to his attention. Then, going over his little book of record, which he kept faithfully, he was amazed and chagrined to discover that such was the case. He endeavored to right the falling off, only to grow worse. He wavered, he flinched, he shot poorly, thus crippling many buffalo. It made him sick. The cause was Milly. She dominated his thoughts. The truth was that Milly had awakened him to the cruelty and greed of this business and his conscience prevented him from being a good hunter.

Hudnall solved the knotty problem for Tom, very much to his relief.

"Tom, you've lost your nerve, as Pilchuck says," said the chief. "But you're the best skinner he ever saw. You're wastin' time chasin' an' shootin' buffalo. We're killin' about as many as we can skin, an' we could kill more. Pilchuck can, anyhow. Now you follow us an' skin buffalo only. We'll pay you thirty five cents a hide."

"You bet I take you up," declared Tom, gladly. "I didn't know I'd lost my nerve, but I hate the killing."

"Wal, it's begun to wear on me, to be honest," sighed Hudnall. "I'd rather push a plow."

Next moment he was asking Tom to make accurate estimate of the stock of ammunition on hand. Tom did his best at his calculation and reported: three hundred forty-six pounds of St. Louis shot-toner lead in twenty-five pound bars; about five thousand primers; five cans of Dupont powder, twenty-five pounds to a can; and three cans of six pounds each.

"Jude, how long will that last us?" inquired Hudnall of Pilchuck, who had heard Tom's report.

"Wal, let's see. I reckon August, September, October—unless we have to fight Indians," replied the scout.

"Ho! Ho! There you go again," derided Hudnall. "This Injun talk is a joke."

With this skinning job Tom soon found himself in better spirits, and worked so effectively that he won golden praise from his employers.

"Shucks! What a scalper of redskins that boy would make!" declared Pilchuck. "He can keep a knife sharp as a razor an' cut with it like a nigger."

If Tom had been able to get some leisure he would have found much enjoyment in the permanent camp. It was situated on a beautifully wooded bench above the wild brakes of a tributary to the larger river near by, and game abounded there. Down in the brakes were bear, panther, wildcats in numbers too plentiful for wandering around without a gun. The wide belts of timber appeared to be full of wild turkey and deer. Antelope, tame as cattle, grazed on the prairie; and in the wake of the buffalo slunk hordes of howling coyotes. Bands of big gray wolves, bold and savage, took their toll of the buffalo calves.

The diet of buffalo steak was varied by venison and antelope meat, and once with wild turkey. This last trial of a changed menu resulted disastrously for Tom. It happened to be his turn as cook and he had killed several wild turkeys that day. Their flesh was exceedingly bitter, owing to a berry they lived on, which was abundant in the brakes. Pilchuck, who suffered with indigestion, made sarcastic remarks about Tom's cooking, and the other men were vociferous in their disapproval. Unfortunately Tom had not cooked any other meat.

"Tom, you're a valuable member, but your cookin' is worse than your shootin'," remarked Hudnall, finally. "We'll relieve you of your turn an' you can put that much time to somethin' else. . . . No offense, my lad. You just can't cook. An' we can't starve to death out here. Reckon when you come to ranchin' you'll be lucky to have that pretty black-eyed Milly."

"Lucky!" exploded Burn Hudnall, who it was hinted suffered a little from being henpecked. "Say, he *is* an' he doesn't savvy it."

"Wal, we're all pretty lucky, if you let me get in a word," said the scout, dryly. "Here we've been days in hostile country, yet haven't been molested."

"There you go again!" protested Hudnall, who had become wearied of Indian talk.

"Wal, am I scout for this outfit or just plain plugger of buffs?" queried Pilchuck.

"You're scout, an' pardner, an' everythin', of course," replied Hudnall. "Your scoutin' for buffalo couldn't be beat, but your scoutin' of redskins, if you do any, hasn't worried me."

"Wal, Hudnall, I don't tell you everythin'," rejoined Pilchuck. "Yesterday, ten miles below on the river, I met a bunch of Kiowas, braves, squaws, kids, with ponies packed an' travois draggin'. They didn't look sociable. To-day I saw a band of Comanches tearin' across the prairie or I'm a born liar! I know how Comanches ride."

"Jude, are you tryin' to scare me into huntin' closer to camp?" asked Hudnall.

"I'm not tryin' or arguin'," responded the scout. "I'm just tellin' you. My advice to all of you is to confine your huntin' to a radius of five or six miles. Then there'd always be hunters in sight of each other."

"Jude, you an' Burn an' I killed one hundred ninety-eight buffalo yesterday on ground no bigger than a fifty-acre farm. But it was far off from camp."

"I know. Most hunters like to kill near camp, naturally, for it saves work, but not when they can kill twice as many in the same time farther out."

"I'll kill mine an' skin them an' haul them in," replied the leader.

"Wal, wal," said Pilchuok, resignedly, "reckon advice is wasted on you."

Tom, in his new job, worked out an innovation much to Hudnall's liking. He followed the hunters with team and wagon, and through this hit by accident upon a method of skinning that greatly facilitated the work. Taking a forked stick, Tom fastened it to the middle of the hind axletree, allowing the other sharpened end to drag. Tying a rope to the same axle and the other end to the front leg of a dead buffalo, Tom would skin the upper side down. Next he would lead the horses forward a little, moving the beast. The stick served the purpose of holding the wagon from slipping back. Then he would skin down the center of the sides, and stop to have the team pull the carcass over. Thus by utilizing horse power he learned to remove a hide in half the time it had taken him formerly.

Often the hunters would kill a number far exceeding Tom's ability to haul to camp. But with their help all the hides were removed generally the same day the buffalo were slain. If Tom could not haul all back to camp, he spread them fur side up, to collect the next day. Tom particularly disliked to skin a buffalo that had been killed the day before; because the bloating that inevitably occurred always made the hide come off with exceeding difficulty. Like all expert skinners, Tom took pride in skinning without cutting holes in a hide.

Tom often likened the open ground back of camp on the prairie side to a colossal checkerboard, owing to the many hides always pegged out in regular squares.

Five days from the pegging process these hides would be turned fur side up for a day, and turned again every day until dry. They had to be poisoned to keep the hide bugs from ruining them. As the hides dried they were laid one over the other, making as huge piles as could be handled. To tie these bundles strips of wet buffalo hide were run through the peg-holes of the bottom and top hides, and pulled very tight. All bull hides were made into one bundle, so marked; and the others sorted according to sex, age, and quality. Taken as a whole, this hunting of buffalo for their hides, according to the opinion of all hunters, was the hardest work in the world.

One morning a couple of drivers, belonging to Black and Starwell's outfit, halted their teams at Hudnall's camp, and spread a rumor that greatly interested the leader. They were freighting out thirteen hundred hides to Sprague's. The rumor had come a few days before, from hunters traveling south, to the effect that Rath and Wright of Dodge City was going to send freighters out to buy hides right at the camps. This would afford the hunters immense advantage and profit. The firm was going to pay regular prices and do the hauling.

These loquacious drivers had more news calculated to interest Hudnall. It was a report that the Kansas City firm, Loganstein & Co., one of the largest buyers of hides in the market, was sending their hides to Europe, mostly to England, where it had been discovered that army accouterments made of leather were much better and cheaper when made of buffalo hide. This would result in a rise in prices, soon expected, on the buffalo hides.

All this excited Hudnall. He paced the camp-fire space in thought. Ordinarily he arrived at decisions without vacillation, but this one evidently had him bothered. Presently it came out.

"I'll stay in camp an' work," he said, as if answering a query. "Tom, you an' Stronghurl shall haul all the hides we have to Sprague's. You can see our women folks an' bring back the straight of this news. Let's rustle, so you can go with Starwell's freighters."

The journey to Sprague's Post was an endless drive of eight long, hot glaring days; yet because each day, each hour, each minute, each dragging step of weary horses bore Tom closer to Milly, he endured them joyfully.

Making twenty-five miles the last day, Tom and his companions from the Pease River reached Sprague's late at night, and camped in the outskirts of the settlements, where showed tents and wagons of new outfits. Early next morning Tom and Stronghurl were besieged by prospective buffalo-hunters, intensely eager to hear news from the buffalo fields. Invariably the first query was, were the buffalo really herded by the millions along the Red, Pease, and Brazos Rivers? Secondly, were the Indians on the warpath? Tom answered these questions put to him in the affirmative; and did his best with the volley of other interrogations, many of them by tenderfoot hunters. He remembered when he had been just as ignorant and raw as they were now.

Thus, what with bringing in the horses, breakfast, and satisfying these ambitious newcomers, Tom was held back from rushing to see Milly. Stronghurl said he would see the Hudnalls later. At last, however, Tom got away, and he had only to hurry down the almost deserted street of the post to realize that the hour was still early. He was not conscious of anything save a wonderfully warm and blissful sense of Milly's nearness—that in a moment or so he would see her.

Tom's hand trembled as he knocked on the canvas door of the Hudnall quarters. He heard voices. The door opened, to disclose Mrs. Hudnall, wary-faced and expectant.

"For the land's sake!" she cried, her expression changing like magic. "Girls, it's Tom back from the huntin' fields."

"You bet, and sure glad," replied Tom, and could hardly refrain from kissing Mrs. Hudnall.

"Come right in," she said, overjoyed, dragging him into the kitchen. "Never mind Sally's looks. She just got up. . . . Tom, I know from your face all's well with my husband."

"Sure. He's fine—working hard and making money hand over fist. Sent you this letter. Stronghurl came, too. He'll see you later."

Sally Hudnall and Mrs. Burn Hudnall welcomed Tom in no less joyful manner; and the letters he delivered were received with acclamations of delight.

Tom looked with eager gaze at the door through which Sally had come, expecting to see Milly. But she did not appear.

"Where's Milly?" he asked, not anxiously, but just in happy eagerness.

His query shocked the Hudnall women into what seemed sudden recollection of something untoward. It stopped Tom's heart.

"Milly! Why, Tom—she's gone!" said Mrs. Hudnall.

"Gone!" he echoed, dazedly.

"Yesterday. Surely you met her on the road south?"

"Road south?" . . . No, no," cried Tom, in distress. "Jett! Did he take her away?"

"Yes. He came night before last, but we didn't know until mornin'," continued Miss Hudnall, hurriedly. "Had his wife an' two men with him. Jett sold thirty-four hundred buffalo hides an' had been drinkin'. . . . He—well, he frightened *me*, an' poor Milly. I was never so sorry for any one in my life."

"Oh, I was afraid he'd come!" burst out Tom, in torture. "Milly said I shouldn't leave her. . . . Oh, why, why didn't I listen to her?"

"Strange you didn't meet Jett," replied Mrs. Hud-

nall. "He left with three wagons yesterday afternoon.
They went straight down the military road. We
watched them. Milly waved her scarf for a long time.
. . . She looked so cute an' sweet in her boy's
clothes."

"Boy's clothes?" ejaculated Tom, miserably.
"What do you mean?"

"Jett came here in the mornin'," went on Mrs.
Hudnall. "He was soberin' up an' sure looked mean.
He asked for Milly an' told her that she was to get
ready to leave with him in the afternoon. His wife
wasn't with him, but we met her later in Sprague's
store. She struck us as a fit pardner for Jett. Well,
Milly was heart-broken at first, an' scared. We could
see that. She didn't want to go, but said she'd have to.
He could take her by force. She didn't say much. First
she wrote you a letter, which I have for you, an' then
she packed her clothes. When Jett came about three
o'clock he fetched boy's pants, shirt, coat, an' hat for
Milly. Said on account of Indians scarin' the soldiers
the military department were orderin' women out of
the buffalo fields. Jett was disguisin' his women in
men's clothes. Milly had to have her beautiful hair cut.
Sally cut it. Well, Milly dressed in that boy's suit an'
went with Jett. She was brave. We all knew she might
come to harm, outside of Indians. An' we felt worse
when Sprague told us last night that this Mrs. Jett had
been the wife of an outlaw named Hardin, killed last
summer at Fort Dodge. That's all."

"Good heavens! it's enough!" declared Tom,
harshly, divided by fear for Milly and fury at himself.
"What can I do? . . . I might catch up with Jett. But
then what?"

"That's what I'd do—hurry after her," advised Mrs.
Hudnall. "Somehow you might get her away from
Jett. Tell my husband. He'll do somethin' . . . Tom,
here's Milly's letter. I hope it tells you how she loves
you. For you're all the world to that child. She was
cryin' when she gave it to me."

"Thank you," said Tom, huskily, taking the letter and starting to go.

"Come back before you leave," added Mrs. Hudnall. "We'll want to send letters an' things with you."

"An' say, Tom," called Sally from the doorway, "you tell Dave Stronghurl if he doesn't run here to me pronto it'll be all day with him."

"I'll send him," returned Tom, and hurried back to camp, where he delivered Sally's message to Dave.

"Aw, I've all the time there is," drawled Dave, with an assured smile.

"No! We'll be leaving just as quick as I can sell these hides for Hudnall."

"Wal, I'll be goshed! What's the rush, Tom? . . . Say, you look sick."

"I am sick. I'm afraid I'm ruined," replied Tom, hurriedly, and told Dave his trouble.

His comrade swore roundly, and paced a moment, thoughtfully. "Tom, mebbe it ain't so bad as it looks. But it's bad enough. I'd hate to see that girl fall into the hands of the Indians."

"Indians? Dave, it's Jett I'm afraid of. He's bad and he means bad. . . . I—I think I'll have to kill him."

"Wal, quite right an' proper, if he's what you say. An' I'll back you. Let's see. We'd better rustle. You tend to sellin' the hides an' what else Hudnall wanted. An' I'll tend to Sally."

With that Stronghurl paid some elaborate though brief attention to his personal appearance, then strode off toward the post. Left alone, Tom hurriedly tore open Milly's letter. It was written in ink on good paper, and the handwriting was neat and clear. Tom thrilled at his first sight of Milly's writing.

SPRAGUE'S POST
July 19.

DEAR TOM:

It is my prayer you get this letter soon—surely some day. Jett has come for me. I must go. There isn't anything else I can do. But if you or Mr. Hudnall were here I'd refuse to go and let Jett do his worst.

He'll surely take me back to the buffalo camps, and where they are you will be somewhere. I know you will find me.

I'm scared now and my heart's broken. But I'll get over that and do my best to fool Jett—to get away from him—to save myself. I've bought a little gun which I can hide, and if I have to use it to keep him from harming me—*I will do it*. I love you. You're all I have in this world. God surely will protect me.

So don't feel too badly and don't lose hope. Don't ever give up looking for me. Whenever you pass a camp you haven't seen before, look for a red scarf tied somewhere in sight. It'll be mine.

MILLY.

Tom sat there with clenched hands and surging heart. The letter at once uplifted him and plunged him into the depths. He writhed with remorse that he had ever left her alone. The succeeding moments were the most bitter of his life. Then another perusal of Milly's letter roused his courage. He must be true to the brave spirit that called to him; and he must hope for the best and never give up seeking her, though he realized how forlorn it was.

Tom sold Hudnall's hides at a higher figure than Hudnall had received for his first batch. Sprague not only corroborated the rumors that had been the cause of Hudnall sending Tom out, but also added something from his own judgment. The peak of prices for hides had not been reached. He offered so much himself that Tom wondered whether or not Hudnall would sell at all to the buyers from Dodge City. Tom gathered that there was now great rivalry among the several firms buying hides, a circumstance of profit to the hunters.

"I'll give you another hunch," said Sprague. "After

the hides, the bones of the carcasses will fetch big money. I just heard thet a twenty-mile pile of buffalo bones along the Santa Fe railroad sold for ten dollars a ton. For fertilizer!''

"You don't say!" exclaimed Tom, in surprise. "What'll Hudnall think of that? But, Sprague, it isn't possible to haul bones from the Red River country in quantity enough to pay."

"Reckon that seems far fetched, I'll admit. But you can never tell."

"Now about the Indian scare," went on Tom, anxiously. "What's your honest opinion? Is it serious?"

"Doan, listen," replied Sprague, impressively. "Believe what the scouts an' plainsmen say. They know. The whole half of Texas is bein' run over by a lot of farmers—hide-hunters for the time bein'. They don't know the West. An' some of them will be killed. That's the least we can expect."

"Then—these hide thieves. What do you know about them?" inquired Tom.

"Not much. Thet's not my business. I'm buyin' hides from anybody an' everybody. I can't afford to be suspicious of hunters."

"Did you know the little girl, Milly Fayre, who was staying with Mrs. Hudnall?"

"Shore did, an' I took to her pronto. Mrs. Hudnall told me aboot Jett bein' her stepfather, an' was packin' her off with him, togged out as a boy. I sold Jett the boy's clothes, but didn't know then what he wanted them for."

"She's engaged to marry me. She hates Jett and is afraid of him."

"So thet's the story!" ejaculated the sharp-featured Westerner, with quick gesture of comprehension. "Doan, I ain't sayin' much, but this deal looks bad."

"It looks terrible to me. Is Jett just a—a rough customer?"

"Doan, what he may be doesn't matter, I reckon," returned Sprague, in a low voice. "But take this hunch from me. Follow Jett an' get your girl out of his clutches—if you have to kill him. Savvy?"

Tom had seen the same dancing light gleam, sharp as fiery sparks, in the eyes of Pilchuck, that now shot from Sprague's.

"Yes—I savvy," replied Tom, swallowing hard.

An hour later he was driving his team at a brisk trot south on the military road, and Stronghurl was hard put to it to keep up with him.

Chapter X

RISING early and driving late, Tom Doan, with Stronghurl keeping in sight, traveled southward over the prairie toward the buffalo fields. He made it a point always to reach at night the camp of outfits that had been ahead of him. Thus every day was a dragging one of anxious hope to catch up with Jett, and every sunset was a time fraught with keen, throbbing excitement. Always, however, his search among the outfits ended in bitter disappointment.

A remarkable thing about this journey was that every outfit he passed on the way put on more speed and tried to keep him and Stronghurl in sight. Tom considered it just as well that they did so, for they were fast penetrating into the Indian country.

Early on the ninth morning of that long journey Tom and Stronghurl forded the Pease River, at a dangerous crossing, and entered the zone of slaughter. No live buffalo were in sight, but the carcasses left by the advancing hunters polluted the summer air and made of the prairie a hideous shambles. They passed thou-

sands and thousands of bone piles and rotten carcasses; and as they advanced the bone piles became
fewer and the solid carcasses more. Coyotes in
droves, like wild dogs, fought along the road, regardless of the wagons. Indeed, many of them were so
gorged that they could not run. And as for buzzards,
they were as thick as crows in a Kansas cornfield in
October, likewise gorged to repletion.

The wake of the hide-hunters was something to
sicken the heart of the stoutest man and bring him face
to face with an awful sacrifice.

Tom verified another thing that had long troubled
him and of which he had heard hunters speak. For
every single buffalo that was killed and skinned there
was one which had been crippled and had escaped to
die, so that if ever found its hide would be useless. In
every ravine or coulee or wash off the main line of
travel Tom knew, by investigation of those near where
he and Stronghurl camped or halted at noon, there lay
dead and unskinned buffalo. If he saw a hundred, how
many thousands must there be? It was a staggering
arraignment to confront the hide-hunters.

Toward noon of that day herds of live buffalo came
in sight, and thereafter grew and widened and showed
movement. Tom eventually overhauled a single wagon
drawn by four horses, and drew up beside it asking the
usual query.

"Whoa, thar!" called the stout old driver to his
team. "Jett? No, I ain't heard that name. Hev you,
Sam?"

His companion likewise could not remember such a
name as Jett.

"We've met up with lots of outfits an' never heerd
nary name a-tall," added the former.

Then Tom asked if they had seen an outfit of three
large wagons, three men, a woman, and a boy.

"Big outfit—wal, I reckon. Was the boss a yaller-
bearded man?"

"Yes, that's Jett," replied Tom, eagerly.

"Passed us this mawnin' back a ways. I recollect sure, 'cause the boy looked at us an' waved a red kerchief. He had big black eyes."

"Milly!" breathed Tom, to himself. "Thank you, men. That's the outfit I'm after."

He drove on, urging the tired horses, and he was deaf to the queries his informants called after him upon their own account. Hope and resolve augmented in Tom as he traveled onward. Jett was hurrying back to the main camps, and he would not be hard to locate, if Tom did not catch up with him on the road. Milly's letter lay in the breast pocket of Tom's flannel shirt, and every now and then he would press his hand there, as if to answer Milly's appeal. He drove so persistently and rapidly that he drew far ahead of Stronghurl and the string of outfits which followed.

Miles farther, with straggling herds on each side, and then the boom-boom-boom of heavy guns! From the last ridge above the river he saw a pall of dust away to the west. Here there was action. But it must have been miles away. The river meandered across the prairie, a wide strip of dark green cottonwood and elm. In an hour Tom reached it. Not yet had he come in sight of a three-wagon outfit. With keen eyes he searched the dusty road to make sure that no wheel tracks swerved off without his notice.

Not long after this time he drew near the zones of camps, and presently passed the first one, new since he had come by that way about two weeks before. It was now August.

Tom's misery had diminished to a great extent, and he could contain himself with the assurance that Milly would be somewhere along this tributary of the Pease River.

Boom-boom-boom boomed the big fifties, not louder than at first, yet more numerous and on both sides of the river. Tom rolled by camp after camp, some familiar to him, most of them new. But no red scarf adorned any tent or wagon to gladden his eye. Miles he drove along the river, passing many more camps, with like result. The hunters were returning from the chase; a gradual cessation in gun-fire marked Tom's approach to Hudnall's outfit. It was now impossible to see all the camps; some were too far from the road; others down in the widening brakes of the river. There were wagon tracks that turned off the main road to cross the river. Tom found no sign of Jett's outfit; yet, though much disappointed, it did not discourage him. Jett would be among the hunters after this main herd.

Before sunset he drove into Hudnall's camp.

"If it ain't Tom!" yelled Burn, who was the first to see him.

But Hudnall was the first to get to Tom, and almost embraced him, so glad and amazed was he.

"Back so soon? Gosh! you must have come hummin'!" he rolled out, heartily. "Say, we've had great huntin'. Hard, but just like diggin' gold. What'd you get for my hides?"

"Fifty cents more on every hide," replied Tom, producing an enormous wad of bills. "Maybe I'm not glad to get rid of that! And here're letters. There are newspapers, magazines, and other stuff in a basket under the seat."

"How's my women folks?" asked Hudnall, fingering the greenbacks.

"Just fine. You couldn't hope for better. But my—but Milly was gone," answered Tom.

"Milly? Who's she? Aw yes, your girl. I'd forgotten. . . . Say, Doan, you're thin, you look used up. Trip wear you out?"

Hudnall was all kindliness and solicitude now.

"No. Worry. I'll tell you presently. . . . Dave is somewhere along behind, heading a whole caravan of new hide-hunters."

"The more the merrier. There's room an' we don't see any slackin' up of buffalo," said Hudnall. "Pilchuck got two hundred an' eighty-six day before yesterday. That's his top notch. But he says he'll beat it.

Tom, I forgot to tell you we'll pay you for drivin' out the hides. Five dollars a day, if that's all right?"

"Much obliged," replied Tom, wearily, as he sank down to rest. "Guess I'm fagged, too. You see, I tried to catch up with Jett. He left Sprague's a day ahead of me with Milly."

"The hell you say!" ejaculated Hudnall, suddenly losing all his animation. "We've heard bad rumors about that Jett outfit. You must take Milly away from them."

"Couldn't get track of Jett until to-day," went on Tom. "He was just ahead of me, though I couldn't see his wagons. He hit the river along about mid-afternoon and he's somewhere."

"Wal, we'll find him, an' don't you worry. These camps are no place for women folks. I've come to seein' that, Tom."

"What's happened since I left?" queried Tom.

"Son, if I believed all I heard I'd be pullin' stakes for Sprague's," declared Hudnall. "Reckon some of it's true, though. All I seen for myself was some Kiowas that got killed at the forks of the river above. They raided a camp, an' was crossin' the river when some hunters on the other side piled them up, horses an' all."

"Believe I expected to hear worse," replied Tom, soberly.

"Wash up an' take a rest," advised Hudnall. "I'll look after the horses. Reckon we'd better hold off supper a little. Pilchuck's always late these days. He likes the evenin' hunt an' I don't see any sign of Stronghurl."

"Dave was in sight when I struck the river," said Tom. "Then I slowed up. So he can't be far behind, unless he broke down."

Later, after a bath and shave and the donning of clean clothes, Tom felt somewhat relieved in body. His mind, however, was busy, pondering, clouded; and so it must continue until he had found Milly.

Pilchuck rode in after sunset, a dust-covered, powder-begrimed figure, ragged, worn, proven, everything about him attesting to the excessive endeavor that made him a great hunter. His jaded horse was scarcely recognizable; froth and sweat and dust had accumulated in a caked lather, yellow and hard as sun-baked mud, over front and hind quarters.

"Howdy, Doan!" was his greeting to Tom, with the offer of a horny, grimy hand. "As a freighter you're A number one. Reckon you look sorta washed out—an' washed up, too. Shore you're spick an' span. I'll go fall in the crick, myself."

"Did you have a good day?" asked Tom, after returning his greeting.

"Huh! Not much. I dropped fourteen bulls early, then got jammed in a herd an' had to quit shootin'. Wasn't no stampede or mebbe my story would never have been told. But the pesky bunch took me more'n twenty miles along Soapberry, an' when I did get clear of them I run plumb into some mean-lookin' Kiowas. They was between me an' camp. I had to head off west a little. They rode along for a couple of miles, keepin' on the wrong side of me, an' then seein' I was sure alone, they took after me."

The scout abruptly ended his narrative there, and went about his tasks. Tom, strange to realize, took the incident with a degree of calmness that seemed to him to be an acceptance of times grown heroic and perilous.

A little later Dave Stronghurl drove into camp with weary team, and tired himself, yet unusually loquacious and robustly merry for him. Tom could tell that Dave had something on his mind and awaited results with interest. Hudnall greeted Dave in the same cordial way as he had Tom, asked the same questions, made the same statements about the hide-hunting and news of camp. And he also took charge of Dave's team.

"Get any line on Milly?" asked Dave, as he peeled

off his shirt. "By gum! you shore rustled across the prairie to-day."

Tom was glad to acquaint his comrade with the trace he had obtained of Jett's outfit. Dave vented his satisfaction in forceful, though profane, speech.

While he was performing his ablutions Dunn and Ory Tacks drove in with the day's total of hides, eighty-six, not a good showing. Dunn threw the folded hides out on the open ground some rods from camp, while Tacks unhitched the team.

Hudnall, swift and capable round the camp fire as elsewhere, had a steaming supper soon ready, to which the six men sat down hungry as wolves and as talkative as full mouths would permit.

Ory Tacks had now been some weeks in the buffalo fields. Not in the least had it changed him, except that he did not appear to be quite so fat. Toil and danger had no power to transform his expression of infantile glee with life and himself. He wore the old slouch hat jauntily and, as always, a tuft of tow-colored hair stuck out through a hole in its crown.

Ory plied Tom with queries about Sprague, obviously leading up to something, but Tom, being both hungry and thoughtful, did not give him much satisfaction.

Forthwith Ory, between bites, turned his interest to Stronghurl, with the difference that now he was more than eager.

"Mr. Strongthrow," he began, as usual getting Dave's name wrong, "did you see my—our—the young lady at Sprague?"

"No, she was gone with Jett, I'm shore sorry to say," replied Dave.

"Miss Sally gone!" ejaculated Ory.

"Naw, I meant Tom's girl, Milly Fayre," replied Dave, rather shortly.

"But you saw Miss Sally?"

"Shore did."

"Haven't you a letter for me from her?" inquired Ory, with astonishing naïveté.

"What?" gaped Dave, almost dropping a large bite of biscuit from his mouth.

"You have a letter for me from Sally," said Ory, now affirmatively.

"Boy, do you reckon me a pony-express rider, carryin' the mail?"

"Did you see much of her?" inquired Ory, with scrupulous politeness.

"Nope. Not a great deal."

"How long were you with her? I'm asking, because if you saw her for even a little she'd have given you a message for me."

"Only saw her about thirty minutes, an' then, 'cause Tom was shore rarin' to leave, Sally an' me was busy gettin' married," replied Dave, with vast assumed imperturbability.

It had the effect to crush poor Ory into bewildered silence; he sank down quite staggered. Tom wanted to laugh, yet had not quite the meanness to let it out. Hudnall looked up, frowning.

"Dave, that's no way to tease Ory," he reproved, severely. "Ory's got as much right to shine up to Sally as you. Now if she sent him a letter you fork it over."

Dave got red in the face.

"She didn't send none," he declared.

"Are you sure?" added Hudnall, suspiciously. "I ain't placin' too much confidence in you, Dave."

"So it 'pears. But I'm not lyin'."

"All right. An' after this don't make any fool remarks about marryin' Sally, just to tease Ory. It ain't good taste."

"Boss, I wasn't teasin' him or talkin' like Ory's hair sticks through his hat," returned Dave, deliberately.

"What?" shouted Hudnall.

"Me an' Sally was married."

"You was married!" roared Hudnall, in amaze and rage.

"Yes, sir. There was a travelin' parson at Sprague, an' Sally an' me thought it a good chance to marry. So we did."

"Without askin' leave of me—of her dad?"

"You wasn't around. Sally was willin'—an' we thought we could tell you afterward."

"Did you ask her mother? She was around."

"Nope. I wanted to, but Sally said her mother didn't think I was much of a match."

"So you just run off with my kid an' married her?" roared Hudnall, beside himself with rage.

"Kid! Sally's a grown woman. See here, Hudnall, I didn't reckon you'd be tickled, but I shore thought you'd have some sense. Sally an' me would have married, when this huntin's over. I wanted some one to take care of my money, an' keep it, case I get killed out here. So what's wrong about it?"

"You big Swede!" thundered Hudnall. "You didn't ask *me*. That's what. An' I'm a mind to pound the stuffin's out of you."

Stronghurl was not profoundly moved by this threat.

"If you feel that way, come on," he replied, coolly. He was a thick, imperturbable sort of fellow, and possibly, Tom thought, he might be a Swede.

Pilchuck was shaking with silent mirth; Ory Tacks was reveling in revenge; Burn Hudnall sat divided between consternation and glee; old man Dunn looked on, very much amazed; and as for Tom, he felt that it looked mightily like a fight, yet he could not convince himself it would go that far.

"Come on, huh?" echoed Hudnall, boomingly, as he rose to his lofty height. He was twice the size of Stronghurl. He could have broken the smaller, though sturdy, bridegroom in short order. Slowly Stronghurl rose, at last seriously concerned, but resigned and forceful.

"Reckon you can lick me, Hudnall," he said "an' if it's goin' to make you feel better let's get it over."

For answer Hudnall seemed to change, to expand, and throwing back his shaggy head he let out a stentorian roar of laughter. That eased the situation. Pilchuck also broke out, and the others, except Dave, joined him to the extent of their mirth. Hudnall was the last to recover, following which he shoved a brawny hand at Stronghurl.

"Dave, I was mad, natural-like, but you takin' me serious about fightin' over Sally was funny. Why, bless your heart, I'm glad for Sally an' you, even if you didn't ask me, an' I wish you prosperity an' long life!"

Stronghurl's armor of density was not proof against this big-hearted and totally unexpected acceptance and approval, and he showed in his sudden embarrassment and halting response that he was deeply moved. Nor did he take the congratulations of the rest of the outfit as calmly as might have been supposed he would, from his announcement of the marriage. Ory Tacks showed to advantage in his sincere and manly overture of friendliness.

What with this incident, and the news of Sprague to be told to Hudnall and Pilchuck, and their recital of the hunting conditions to Tom and Dave, the outfit did not soon get the day's hides pegged down, or to their much-needed beds.

Next morning Hudnall made the suggestion that each and all of the outfit would ride out of their way to look over new camps and to inquire of hunters as to the whereabouts of Randall Jett.

"Tom, we can't stop work altogether, but we can all spare some time," he said. "An' I'll drive the wagon out an' back, so you'll have time to ride along the river. It's my idea we'll find Milly pronto."

"Then what?" queried Tom, thrilling deeply with this good man's assurance.

"Wal, you can leave that to me," interposed Pilchuck, dryly. Tom was quick to sense something in the scout's mind which had not been spoken.

But that day and the next and the following passed fleetly by without any trace of Jett's outfit. Ten miles up and down the river, on the west bank, had been covered by some one of Hudnall's outfit. No three-wagon camp had been located.

"Shore Jett must be across the river," averred Pilchuck. "There's outfits strung along, an' enough buffalo for *him*."

"What'll I do?" queried Tom, appealingly.

"Wal, son, you can't work an' do the job right," replied the scout. "I'd take a couple of days off. Ride down the river twenty miles or so, then cross an' come back on the other side. If that don't fetch results ride up the river, cross an' come back. Ask about Indians, too, an' keep your eyes peeled."

Tom's saddle horse, Dusty, had been ridden by Burn Hudnall and Pilchuck also during Tom's absence, and had developed into a fleet, tireless steed only second to Pilchuck's best buffalo chaser. Next morning Tom set off, mounted on Dusty. Well armed, with a small store of food, a canteen of water, and a field-glass, he turned resolute face to the task before him.

In less than two hours he had passed the ten-mile limit of his search so far, and had entered unfamiliar country where camps were many, and buffalo apparently as thick as bees round a hive. But very few of the camps had an occupant; at that hour all the men of each outfit were engaged up on the prairie, as the incessant boom of guns proved. How Tom's eyes strained and ached to catch a glimpse of the red scarf Milly said she would put up wherever she was! What bitter disappointment when he espied a blanket or anything holding a touch of red!

From each camp Tom would ride up the prairie slope to a level and out toward the black-fringed, dust-mantled moving medium that was buffalo. Thus he came upon hunters, skinners, teamsters, all of whom gave him less cordial greeting than he had received from hide-hunters before he went north. It took some moments for Tom to make his sincerity felt. These men were rushed for time, and a feeling of aloofness from strangers had manifestly passed south from camp to camp. Not one of them could or would give him any clue to Jett's outfit.

"Air you lookin' fer hide thieves?" queried one old grizzled hunter.

"No. I'm looking for a girl who has been brought down here by a man named Jett."

"Sorry. Never heard of him. But if you was lookin' fer hide thieves I'd be damn interested," replied the hunter.

"Why?" asked Tom, curiously.

"Because I had eleven hundred hides stole from my camp," he replied, "an' ain't never heerd of them since, let alone seein' hide or hair."

"Too bad. Is there much of this dirty work going on?"

"How 'n 'll can we tell thet?" retorted the man. "Thar's forty square miles of buffler, millin' an' movin', too. Nobody can keep track of any one. It's all mad rush. But some dirty sneaks air gittin' rich on other men's work."

Very few men Tom encountered, however, had any words to spare; and before that day was over he decided not to interrogate any more. It went against his grain to be regarded with hard, cold, suspicious eyes. There was no recourse for him but to search till he met Jett or found his camp. That struck him as far from a hopeless task, yet his longing and dread were poignant. He went on until he had passed the zone of camps and had drawn out of hearing of the boom-boom-boom of the big fifties. Not by many miles, though, had he come to the end of the buffalo herd.

It was the middle of the afternoon, too late for Tom to reach camp that day. He crossed the stream, now a clear shallow sandy-bottomed little watercourse, running swiftly. He was probably not many leagues from its source up in the bluffs of the Staked Plain, stark bald-faced heave of country, frowning down on the prairie.

Tom took the precaution to sweep the open stretches in front with his field-glass. All that he saw there were buffalo, near and far, everywhere, dots and strings and bands, just straggling remnants of the immense herd back over the stream.

A good trail, with horse tracks in it, followed the course of the water east, and led along the edge of the timber and sometimes through open groves. But Tom did not come to a road or see a camp or man or horse. The prairie was a beautiful grassy level, growing brown from the hot sun. Bands of antelope grazed within range of his gun, as tame as cattle; deer trotted ahead of him through the timber; wild turkeys by the hundreds looked up at his approach and made no effort to run. He saw bear and panther tracks in the dust of the trail.

Sunset overtook Tom and still he rode on. Before dark, however, he espied a thick clump of timber in which he decided to spend the night. Finding a suitable place well down from the trail, he unsaddled Dusty and led him to the stream to drink, then picketed him with a long lasso on a grass plot.

Twilight stole down into the grove while Tom ate some of the meat and bread he had taken the precaution to bring. No fire was necessary, as the air was close and sultry; besides, it might have attracted attention. He spread his saddle blankets for a bed, placed his saddle for a pillow, and with weapons at his side he lay down to sleep.

This was the first night he had been alone on the Texas prairies. It was novel, strange, somehow exhilarating, and yet disturbing. His anxiety to find Milly had led him far from the hunters' camps, into wild country, where he must run considerable risk. His state of mind, therefore, rendered him doubly susceptible to all around him.

Dusk mantled the river brakes. The night insects had begun their incessant song, low, monotonous, plaintive. And frogs joined in with their sweet, mellow, melodious trill. In spite of these sounds silence seemed to reign. Solitude was omnipresent there. Tom found it hard to realize that the extermination of America's most numerous and magnificent game beast was in frenzied operation along this river; that bands of Indians were on the warpath, and hide-robbers foraging secretly. Here the night and place were lonely, sad, provocative of such thoughts as had never before disturbed Tom.

By and by his attention was attracted at intervals by soft padded steps somewhere near, and the cracking of twigs down in the brakes, and the squealing of raccoons. Once a wild cry startled him, so nearly like a woman's scream was it, and he recognized it as the rare cry of a panther. He had heard hunters at the camps tell of it. Gradually his nervousness wore away. These creatures of the wilderness would not harm him; he had only to fear those beings made in his own image.

The night, the stars, the insects, the stealthy denizens of the brush, the soft, drowsy, sultry summer darkness with its dim flare of sheet lightning along the horizon, the loneliness and freedom of the open country—these worked on Tom's mind and from them he gathered a subtle confidence that there was something stronger than evil in men. Milly would not be lost to him.

At last Tom slept. He was awakened by the scratching and clucking of wild turkeys, so close that he could have tossed his hat among them. The sun was red in the east. He had slept late. To eat his meager breakfast, water and saddle his horse, fill his canteen, were

but the work of a few moments, and then he was on his
way again, alert, cautious, not to be misled by his
ardor.

Tom traveled ten miles farther east before his ears
again throbbed to the boom of the big buffalo guns.
Scattered herds grazed out on the prairie, but appeared unmolested by hunters. The shooting came
from across the river. Five miles farther on, however,
Tom reached the zone of camps on that side, and heard
the boom of guns.

Between that point and the river bluffs, which he
recognized as landmarks near Hudnall's present location, he found and rode through seven camps of
buffalo-hunters. Wagons, tents, reloading kits, mess
boxes, bales of hides, squares and squares of hides
pegged out—these were in no wise different from the
particulars of the camps opposite.

But Tom did not find what he sought. He crossed the
river and rode towards Hudnall's with a heavy heart.

The afternoon was far spent, still it was too early for
Tom not to be surprised to see his comrades in camp.
There appeared to be other hunters—a group, talking
earnestly.

Tom urged his tired horse to a trot, then a lope.
Something was wrong at Hudnall's. He felt it. There
came a cold tightening round his heart. Reaching
camp, Tom flung himself out of the saddle.

Ory Tacks, the nearest to Tom, as he advanced
toward the men, was crying. Dunn sat near him,
apparently dazed. Burn Hudnall's head was buried in
his arms. Stronghurl and Pilchuck were in conversation with a group of seven or eight men, among whom
Tom recognized hunters from adjoining camps. It was
significant to behold these men all carrying their rifles.
More significant was Pilchuck's face, hard, cold, forbidding, with his thin lips set in tight line and his eyes
almost narrowed shut.

"What's—happened?" burst out Tom, breathlessly.

Burn Hudnall raised a face Tom could never forget. "Father was murdered by Indians."

"Oh, my God—no!" cried Tom, in distress.

"Yes. . . . I saw him killed—an' I just got away—by the skin of my teeth," replied Burn, in a dreadful voice.

"How? When? Where?" panted Tom, shocked to his depths.

"It was father's carelessness. Oh, if he had only listened to Pilchuck. . . . Mebbe two hours ago. I was west of here four or five miles when I saw a band of Indians. They were ridin' towards us. I was skinnin' a bull an' was concealed behind the carcass. Father was off a quarter of a mile, ridin' round a small bunch of buffalo, shootin' fast, an' blind to anythin' else but buffalo. I yelled my lungs out. No use! He couldn't hear. I got to my horse an' was thinkin' of runnin' over to save father, when I saw I was too late. . . . The Indians rode like the wind. They ran down on father. I saw puffs of smoke an' heard shots. Father fell off his horse. Then the Indians circled round him, shootin', yellin', ridin' like naked painted devils. . . . Presently they quit racin', an' rode into a bunch, round where he lay. Some of them dismounted. Others rode toward the wagon an' team. These Indians saw me an' started for me. I tell you I had to ride, an' they chased me almost into camp. . . . Tom, I know what it is to hear the whistle of bullets!"

"He's out there—on the prairie—dead?" gasped Tom.

"Certain as death," replied Burn, solemnly. "Who's to tell mother an' Sally?"

"But—but we must go out there—to see—to find out——"

"Pilchuck's taken charge, Tom," replied the other. "He says the Indians were Comanches an' in pretty strong force. We're to wait till morning, get a bunch of men together, an' then go out to bury father."

Tom was stunned. The catastrophe as persistently portended by Pilchuck and corroborated by Sprague had at last fallen. Splendid, fine, kindly Hudnall was dead at the hands of revengeful savages. It was terrible. To be warned of such a thing was nothing, but the fact itself stood out in appalling vividness.

"Let's rustle supper while it's daylight," said Pilchuck, coming over. "We don't want a camp fire tonight. Reckon there's hardly any danger of attack, but we want to stand guard an' not take any chances."

Camp tasks had to go on just the same, and Tom helped Dunn and Ory Tacks. The other hunters turned to leave with an understanding that they were to stand guard at their camps, and return in the morning.

"Starwell, we'll plan to-morrow after we bury Hudnall," said the scout.

"One only plan," replied the other, a lean, dark, forceful looking Westerner whom Tom felt he would not care to cross. "We buff-hunters must band together an' trail them Comanches."

"Reckon you're right, Star," returned Pilchuck, grimly. "But there's no rush. Them redskins have done more'n kill Hudnall, I'll bet you. They've been raidin'. An' they'll strike for the Staked Plain. That means we've got to organize. If there's a hell of a place in the world it's shore the Staked Plain."

Supper without the cheerful presence of Hudnall would have been a loss, but the fact that he lay dead, murdered, surely mutilated, out there on the prairie, was monstrous to Tom. He could not eat. He wandered about camp, slowly realizing something beyond the horror of the calamity, a gradual growth from shock to stern purpose. No need to ask Pilchuck what was in his mind! The plainsman loomed now in Tom's sight big and strong, implacable and infallible.

Tom stood guard with Stronghurl during the earlier watches of the night; and the long-drawn mournful howl of the prairie wolf had in it a new significance. This wild West was beginning to show its teeth.

Chapter XI

Morning came, and Pilchuck had the men stirring early. When Tom walked out to the camp fire dawn was brightening, and there was a low roll of thunder from the eastward.

"We're in for a thunderstorm," he said to the scout, who was cooking breakfast.

"Storm, mebbe, but not thunder-an'-lightnin' storm," replied Pilchuck. "That sound you hear is new to you. It's a stampede of buffalo."

"Is that so? . . . Say, how like thunder!"

"Yep, we plainsmen call it the thunderin' herd. But this isn't the main herd on the rampage. Somethin', most likely Indians, has scared the buffalo across the river. They've been runnin' south for an hour. More buffalo over there than I had an idee of."

"Yes, I saw miles of scattered herds as I rode up the river," said Tom.

"I smell smoke, too, an' fact is, Doan, I don't like things a damn bit. If the main herd stampedes—holy Moses! I want to be on top of the Staked Plain. Reckon, though, that's just where we'll be."

"You're going after the Comanches?" inquired Tom, seriously.

"Wal, I reckon. It's got to be done if we're to hunt buffalo in peace."

Burn Hudnall presented himself at the camp fire, his face haggard with grief; but he was now composed. He sat at breakfast as usual, and later did his share of the tasks. Not long afterward Starwell and his men rode into camp, heavily armed and formidable in appearance.

"Jude, what you make of that stampede across the river?" he asked, after greetings were exchanged.

"Wal, I ain't makin' much, but I don't like it."

"We heerd shootin' yesterday at daylight down along the river from our camp," returned Starwell. "Small-bore guns, an' I don't calkilate hunters was shootin' rabbits for breakfast."

"Ahuh! Wal, after we come back from buryin' Hudnall we'll take stock of what's goin' on," said Pilchuck. "By that time camp will be full of hunters, I reckon."

"Hardy rode twenty miles an' more down the river, gettin' back late last night. He said there'd be every outfit represented here this mornin'."

"Good. We kept the horses picketed last night, an' we'll be saddled in a jiffy."

Burn Hudnall led that band of mounted men up on the prairie and southwest toward the scene of yesterday's tragedy. The morning was hot; whirlwinds of dust were rising, like columns of yellow smoke; the prairie looked lonesome and vast; far out toward the Staked Plain showed a dim ragged line of buffalo. Across the river the prairie was obscured in low covering of dust, like rising clouds. The thunder of hoofs had died away.

Tom Doan, riding with these silent, somber men, felt a strong beat of his pulse that was at variance with the oppression of his mind. He was to be in the thick of wild events.

In perhaps half an hour the trotting horses drew within sight of black dots on the prairie, and toward these Burn Hudnall headed. They were dead and unskinned buffalo. Presently Burn halted alongside the first carcass, that of a bull, half skinned.

"Here's where I was, when the Indians came in sight over that ridge," said Burn, huskily. "Father must be lyin' over there."

He pointed toward where a number of black woolly dead buffalo lay scattered over the green plain, and rode toward them. Presently Pilchuck took the lead. His keen eye no doubt had espied the corpse of Hudnall, for as he passed Burn he said, "Reckon it'd be more sense for you not to look at him."

Burn did not reply, but rode on as before. Pilchuck drew ahead and Starwell joined him. The riders scattered somewhat, some trotting forward, and others walking their horses. Then the leaders dismounted.

"Somebody hold Burn back," shouted Pilchuck, his bronze face flashing in the sunlight.

But though several of the riders, and lastly Tom, endeavored to restrain Burn, he was not to be stopped. Not the last was he to view his father's remains.

"Reckon it's Comanche work," declared Pilchuck, in a voice that cut.

Hudnall's giant body lay, half nude, in grotesque and terrible suggestiveness. He had been shot many times, as was attested to by bullet holes in his torn and limp limbs. His scalp had been literally torn off, his face gashed, and his abdomen ripped open. From the last wound projected buffalo grass which had been rammed into it.

All the hunters gazed in silence down upon the ghastly spectacle. Then from Burn Hudnall burst an awful cry.

"Take him away, somebody," ordered Pilchuck. Then after several of the hunters had led the stricken son aside the scout added: "Tough on a tenderfoot!

But he would look. Reckon it'd be good for all new-comers to see such a sight. . . . Now, men, I'll keep watch for Comanches while you bury poor Hudnall. Rustle, for it wouldn't surprise me to see a bunch of the devils come ridin' over that ridge."

With pick and shovel a deep grave was soon dug, and Hudnall's body, wrapped in a blanket, was lowered into it. Then the earth was filled in and stamped down hard. Thus the body of the careless, cheerful, kindly Hudnall was consigned to an unmarked grave on the windy prairie.

Pilchuck found the tracks of the wagon, and the trail of the Comanches heading straight for the Staked Plain.

"Wal, Star, that's as we reckoned," declared the scout.

"Shore is," replied Starwell. "They stole wagon, hosses, gun, hides—everythin' Hudnall had out here."

"Reckon we'll hear more about this bunch before the day's over. Must have been fifty Indians an' they have a habit of ridin' fast and raidin' more'n one place at a time."

"Jude, my idee is they'd not have taken the wagon if they meant to make another raid," said Starwell.

"Reckon you're right. Wal, we'll rustle back to camp."

More than thirty hunters, representatives of the outfits within reaching distance of Hudnall's, were assembled at camp when the riders returned from their sad mission. All appeared eager to learn the news, and many of them had tidings to impart.

An old white-haired hunter declared vigorously: "By Gord! we air goin' to give the buffalo a rest an' the Injuns a chase!"

That indeed seemed the prevailing sentiment.

"Men, before we talk of organizin' let's get a line on what's been goin' on," said Pilchuck.

Whereupon the hunters grouped themselves in the shade of the cottonwoods, like Indians in Council. The scout told briefly the circumstances surrounding the murder of Hudnall, and said he would leave his deductions for later. Then he questioned the visiting hunters in turn.

Rathbone's camp, thirty miles west, on a creek running down out of the Staked Plain, had been burned by Comanches, wagons and horses stolen, and the men driven off, just escaping with their lives. That had happened day before yesterday.

The camp of two hunters, names not known, had been set upon by Indians, presumably the same band, on the main branch of the Pease. The hunters were out after buffalo. They found wagons, hides, tents, camp destroyed; only ammunition and harness being stolen. These hunters had made their way to the main camps.

An informant from down the river told that some riders, presumably Indians, had fired the prairie grass in different widely separated places, stampeding several herds of buffalo.

Most of the representatives from the camps up the river had nothing particularly important to impart, except noticeable discontent in the main herd of buffalo, and Starwell's repetition of the facts relating to the shots he and his camp-mates had heard yesterday morning.

Whereupon a lanky man, unknown to Pilchuck's group, spoke up:

"I can tell aboot thet. My name's Roberts. I belong to Sol White's outfit across the river. We're from Waco, an' one of the few outfits from the South. This mawnin' there was a stampede on our side, an' I was sent across to scout around. I crossed the river aboot two miles above heah. Shore didn't know the river an' picked out a bad place. An' I run plumb on to a camp that was so hid I didn't see it. But I smelled smoke an' soon found where tents, wagons, an' hides had been burnin'. There was two daid men, scalped, lyin' stripped, with sticks poked into their stomachs—so I hurried up this way to find somebody."

"Men, I want a look at that camp," declared Pilchuck, rising. "Some of you stay here an' some come along. Star, I'd like you with me. Roberts, you lead an' we'll follow."

Tom elected to remain in camp with those who stayed behind; he felt that he had seen enough diabolical work of the Comanches. Burn Hudnall likewise shunned going. Ory Tacks, however, took advantage of the opportunity, and rode off with Pilchuck. Tom tried to find tasks to keep his mind off the tragic end of Hudnall and the impending pursuit of the Indians.

Pilchuck and his attendants were gone so long that the visiting hunters left for their own camps, saying they would ride over next day. Worry and uncertainty were fastening upon those men who were not seasoned Westerners. They had their own camps and buffalo hides to consider. But so far as Tom could ascertain there was not a dissenting voice against the necessity for banding together to protect themselves from Indians.

About mid-afternoon the scout and the newcomer from across the river returned alone. Pilchuck was wet and muddy from contact with the river bank; and his mood, if it had undergone any change, was colder and grimmer.

"Doan, reckon I'm a blunt man, so get your nerve," he said, with his slits of piercing eyes on Tom.

"What—do you mean?" queried Tom, feeling a sudden sinking sensation of dread. Bewildered, uncertain, he could not fix his mind on any effort.

"This camp Roberts took me to was Jett's. But I think Jett got away with your girl," announced Pilchuck.

The ground seemed to fail of solidity under Tom; his legs lost their strength, and he sat down on a log.

"Don't look like that," ordered Pilchuck, sharply. "I told you the girl got away. Starwell thought the

Indians made off with her. But I reckon he's wrong there."

"Jett! Milly?" was all Tom could gasp out.

"Pull yourself together. It's a man's game we're up against. You're no tenderfoot any more," added Pilchuck, with a tone of sympathy. "Look here. You said somethin' about your girl tyin' her red scarf up to give you a hunch where she was. Do you recognize this?"

He produced a red scarf, soiled and blackened.

With hands Tom could not hold steady to save his life he took it.

"Milly's," he said, very low.

"Reckoned so myself. Wal, we didn't need this proof to savvy Jett's camp. I'd seen his outfit. These dead men Roberts happened on belonged to Jett's outfit. I recognized the little sandy-haired teamster. An' the other was Follonsbee. Got his name from Sprague."

Then Tom found voice poignantly to beg Pilchuck to tell him everything.

"Shore it's a mess," replied the scout, as he sat down and wiped his sweaty face. "Look at them boots. I damn near drowned myself. Wal, Jett had his camp in a place no Indians or buffalo-hunters would ever have happened on, unless they did same as Roberts. Crossed the river there. Accident! . . . Doan, this fellow Jett is a hide thief an' he had bad men in his outfit. His camp was destroyed by Comanches all right, the same bunch that killed Hudnall. But I figure Jett escaped in a light wagon, before the Indians arrived. Follonsbee an' the other man were killed *before* the Indians got there. They were shot with a needle gun. An' I'm willin' to bet no Comanches have needle guns. All the same they was scalped an' mutilated, with sticks in their bellies. Starwell agreed with me that these men were killed the day or night before the Indians raided the camp."

"Had Jett—gotten away—then?" breathlessly asked Tom.

"Shore he had. I seen the light wheel tracks an' Milly's little footprints in the sand, just where she'd stepped up on the wagon. I followed the wheel tracks far enough to see they went northeast, away from the river, an' also aimin' to pass east of these buffalo camps. Jett had a heavy load, as the wheel tracks cut deep. He also had saddle horses tied behind the wagon."

"Where'd you find Milly's scarf?" asked Tom, suddenly.

"It was tied to the back hoop of a wagon cover. Some of the canvas had been burned. There was other things, too, a towel an' apron, just as if they'd been hung up after usin'."

"Oh, it is Milly's!" exclaimed Tom, and he seemed to freeze with the dreadful significance it portended.

"So much for that. Shore the rest ain't easy to figure," went on Pilchuck. "I hate to tell you this part, Doan, because—wal, it *is* worryin' . . . I found trail where a bleedin' body, mebbe more'n one, had been dragged down the bank an' slid off into the river. That's how I come to get in such a mess. The water was deep there an' had a current, too. If we had hooks an' a boat we could drag the river, but as we haven't we can only wait. After some days corpses float up. I incline to the idee that whoever killed Follonsbee an' the other man is accountable for the bloody trail leadin' to the river. But I can't be shore. Starwell thinks different from me on some points. Reckon his opinion is worth considerin'. In my own mind I'm shore of two things—there was a fight, mebbe murder, an' *somebody* rode away with the girl. Then the Comanches came along, destroyed the camp, an' scalped the men."

"An' say, scout," spoke up Roberts, "you're shore forgettin' one important fact. The Indians left there trailin' the wagon tracks."

"Ahuh, I forgot that," replied the scout, averting his

gaze from Tom's. "Jett had a good start. Now if he kept travelin' all night——"

"But it looks as if he had no knowledge of the Indians comin'," interrupted Tom, intensely.

"Shore. All the same, Jett was gettin' away from somethin'. He'd rustle far before campin'," continued the scout, doggedly bent on hoping for the best.

This was not lost on Tom nor the gloomy cast of Pilchuck's lean face. Tom could not feel anything save black despair. Either Jett had the girl or the Indians had her—and the horror seemed that one was as terrible as the other.

Tom sought his tent, there to plunge down and surrender to panic and misery.

Next morning the hunters round their early camp-fires were interested to hear a low thunder of running buffalo. It floated across the river from the south and steadily grew louder.

"That darned herd comin' back," said Pilchuck, uneasily. "I don't like it. Shore they're liable to cross the river an' stampede the main herd."

An hour later a hunter from below rode in to say that buffalo by the thousands were fording the river five miles below.

Pilchuck threw up his hands.

"I reckoned so. Wal, we've got to make the best of it. What with raidin' Comanches an' stampedin' buffalo we're done for this summer—as far as any big haul of hides is concerned."

Men new to the hunting fields did not see the signs of the times as Pilchuck and the other scouts read them; and they were about equally divided for and against an active campaign against the Indians.

A good many hunters along the Pease continued their hide-hunting, indifferent to the appeal and warning of those who knew what had to be done.

The difficulty lay in getting word to the outfits

scattered all over northern Texas. For when the buffalo-hunters organized to make war upon the marauders, that meant a general uprising and banding together of Comanches, Kiowas, Arapahoes, and Cheyennes. Also there were Apaches on the Staked Plain, and they, too, according to reports, were in uneasy mood. Therefore buffalo-hunters not affiliated with the war movement, or camping in isolated places unknown to the organizers, stood in great peril of their lives.

Investigation brought out the fact that a great number of hunters from eastern Texas were on the range, not in any way connected with the experienced and time-hardened band camped on the trail of the main herd. Effort was made to get word to these eastern hunters that a general conference was to be held at Double Fork on a given date.

Over three hundred hunters attended this conference, including all the scouts, plainsmen, and well-known frontier characters known to be in the buffalo country. Buffalo Jones, already famous as a plainsman, and later known as the preserver of the buffalo, was there, as strong in his opinion that the Indian should be whipped as he was in his conviction that the slaughter of buffalo was a national blunder.

It was Jones's contention that the value and number of American buffalo were unknown to the world—that the millions that had ranged the Great Plains from Manitoba to the Rio Grande were so common as to be no more appreciated than prairie-dogs. Their utilitarian value was not understood, and now it was too late.

The Indians knew the value of the buffalo, and if they did not drive the white hunter from the range, the beasts were doomed.

"Only the buffalo-hunters can open up the Southwest to the farmer and cattleman," averred Jones. "The U. S. army can't do it. . . . But what a pity the buffalo must go! Nature never constructed a more perfect animal."

The buffalo, according to Jones, was an evolution of the Great Plains, and singularly fitted to survive and flourish on its vast and varied environment. He estimated the number as ten million. The blizzard of Montana or the torrid sirocco of the Staked Plain was no hindrance to the travel of the buffalo. His great, shaggy, matted head had been constructed to face the icy blasts of winter, the sandstorms and hot gales of the summer. A buffalo always faced danger, whatever it might be.

Different men addressed the council, and none were more impressive than Pilchuck.

"Men, I've lived my life on the plains. I've fought Indians all down the line from Montana. I've seen for a long time that we buffalo-hunters have got to fight these Southern tribes or quit huntin'. If we don't kill off the buffalo there'll never be any settlin' of northern Texas. We've got to *kill* the Comanches, an' lick the Kiowas, Cheyennes, an' Arapahoes. I reckon we'll have to deal with Apaches, too. . . . Now the Indians are scattered all over, same as the buffalo-hunters. We can't organize one expedition. There ought to be several big outfits of men, well equipped, strikin' at these Indians already on the warpath. . . . We hunters along the Pease River divide will answer for that section. There's a bunch of Comanches been raidin', an' are now hidin' up in the Staked Plain. Outfits ought to take care of the Brazos River district an' also the Red River. . . . Now there's one more point I want to drive home. Camps an' outfits should be moved close together in these several districts that expect to send out fightin' men. An' an equal or even strong force should be left behind to protect these camp posts. Last, I shore hope the tenderfoot hunters will have sense enough to collect at these posts, even if they won't fight the Indians. For there's goin' to be hell. This will be a fight for the buffalo—the Indians fightin' to *save* the buffalo an' the white men fightin' to *kill* the buffalo. It'll be a buffalo war, an' I reckon right hereabouts, halfway between the Brazos an' Fort Elliott, will see the hottest of it. I just want every man of you who may be on the fence about fightin', an' mebbe doubtin' my words, to go out an' look at the *acres an' acres* of buffalo hides, an' then ask himself if the Indians are goin' to stand that."

The old scout turned the tide in favor of general arming against the tribes on all points of the range. Then Pilchuck, with his contingent from the Pease River, left for their own camps, four days' travel, determined to take the field at once against the Comanches.

They visited every camp on the way south and solicited volunteers, arriving at Pease River with twenty-seven men ready to follow Pilchuck to the end. One of these was a friendly Osage Indian scout called Bear Claws by the men; another a Mexican who had been a scout in the United States army service and was reported to know every trail and water hole in the wild Staked Plain.

But Pilchuck, elated by his success in stirring up the hunters to the north, was fated to meet with a check down on the Pease River. Seventy-five of the hundred hunters who had agreed to take part in the campaign backed out, to Pilchuck's disgust. Many of these had gone back to hunting buffalo, blind to their danger or their utter selfishness. Naturally this not only held up Pilchuck's plan to start soon on the campaign, but also engendered bad blood.

The site of Hudnall's camp was now the rendezvous of from twenty to thirty outfits, most of which had failed the scout. At a last conference of hunters there Pilchuck, failing to persuade half of these men to fall in line, finally delivered a stinging rebuke.

"Wal, all I got to say is you're hangin' behind to make money while some of us have got to go out an' fight to protect you."

One of these reluctants was a young man named Cosgrove, a hard-drinking loud-mouthed fellow with whom Tom Doan had clashed before, on the same issue.

Tom had been a faithful and tireless follower of Pilchuck, as much from loyalty to the cause as from desire for revenge on the Comanches, whom he was now convinced had either killed or carried off Milly Fayre. No authentic clew of Jett's escape or death had been found, but vague rumors of this and that, and more destroyed camps toward the north, especially a one-night-stand camp with a single wagon and but few horses, had at last stricken Tom's last remnant of hope.

Accordingly, Tom's state of mind was not conducive to tolerance, especially of such greed and selfishness as was manifested by some of the hunters.

Cosgrove was louder than usual in voicing his opinions.

"Aw, to hell with the Indians," he said. "I'm a-goin' to keep on huntin' buffalo. It's nothin' to me who goes off on wild-goose chases."

"Cosgrove, you won't be missed, that's sure," retorted Tom.

"What d'ye mean?" demanded the other, his red, bloated face taking on an ugly look. He swaggered over to Tom. There was a crowd present, some thoughtful, many indifferent.

"I mean we don't want such fellows as you," replied Tom.

"An' why not? Didn't Pilchuck just ask me?"

"Sure. He's asked a couple of hundred men, and lots of them are like you—*afraid to go!*"

"What!" shouted Cosgrove, hotly.

"We'll be better off without cowards like you," returned Tom, deliberately standing up, strung for any move.

"You're a liar!" flashed Cosgrove, advancing threateningly.

Tom knocked him down. Then, as Cosgrove, cursing with rage, scrambled to his knees and drew his gun, the crowd scattered away on each side. All save Pilchuck, who knocked the half-leveled gun out of Cosgrove's hand and kicked it far aside.

"Hyar!" yelled the scout, sternly. "You might get hurt, throwin' a gun that way. I'm advisin' you to cool down."

"He needn't, far as I'm concerned," spoke up Tom, ringingly. "Let him have his gun."

Pilchuck wheeled to see Tom standing stiff, gun in hand.

"You young rooster!" ejaculated Pilchuck, in surprise and disapproval. "Put that gun up an' rustle back to camp."

Thus had Tom Doan at last answered to the wildness of the buffalo range.

Worse, however, grew out of that incident, though it did not affect Tom Doan in any way.

One of Pilchuck's lieutenants was a Texan known on the range as Spades Harkaway, a man to be feared in a quarrel. He had been present when Tom had knocked down young Cosgrove, and later he had taken exception to the talk of a man named Hurd, who was in the same outfit with Cosgrove.

Rumor of a fight reached Hudnall's camp that night, but not until next day were the facts known. Hurd had denounced Pilchuck's campaign, which had brought sharp reply from Harkaway. Bystanders came between the men at the moment, but later the two met again in Starwell's camp. Hurd had been imbibing red liquor and Harkaway had no intention of avoiding trouble. Again the question of Pilchuck's Indian campaign was raised by Hurd and coarsely derided. To this Harkaway had answered, first with a flaming arraignment of those hunters who meant to let Pilchuck's company stand the brunt of the fighting, and secondly with short, cutting contempt for Hurd. Then the latter, as the story came, had shot at Harkaway from behind other men. There followed a bad mess, in which the Texan killed Hurd and crippled one of his friends.

These fights traveling along the shortened lines of camp, brought the question to a heated pitch and split the hunters in that district. The majority, however, turned out to be on the side of the Hurd and Cosgrove type. Pilchuck had over fifty men to take on his campaign, and about the same number to remain behind to protect camps and hides. These men were to continue to hunt buffalo, but only on limited parts of the range near the camps, and always under the eyes of scouts patrolling the prairie, with keen eyes on the lookout to prevent surprise. Over twenty outfits, numbering nearly seventy-five men, who had not the nerve to fight Indians or to remain on the range, left that district for Fort Elliott and Sprague's Post, to remain until the Indian trouble was ended.

Chapter XII

PILCHUCK'S band contained fifty-two men, most of whom owned, or had borrowed Creedmoor Sharps 45-caliber rifles for this expedition. These guns were more reliable and of longer range than the big fifties. Each man took at least two hundred loaded cartridges. Besides that, reloading tools and extra ammunition were included in the supplies. Four wagon loads of food and camp equipment, grain for horses, and medical necessities, were taken in charge of the best drivers.

This force was divided into three companies—one of twenty men under Pilchuck, and two, of sixteen men each, under old buffalo-hunters. This was to facilitate camping operations and to be in readiness to split into three fighting groups.

Tom Doan was in Pilchuck's company, along with Stronghurl, Burn Hudnall, Ory Tacks, Starwell, Spades Harkaway, the Indian called Bear Claws, Roberts, and others whom Tom knew. There were at least eight or ten hunters, long used to the range, and grim, laconic men who would have made any fighting force formidable.

Pilchuck, Bear Claws, Starwell, and Tom formed an advance guard, riding two miles ahead of the cavalcade. Both the scout and Starwell had powerful field-glasses. The rear guard consisted of three picked men under Harkaway. The route lay straight for the Staked Plain and was covered at the rate of fifteen miles a day. At night a strong guard was maintained.

On the fourth day the expedition reached the eastern wall of the Staked Plain, a stark, ragged, looming escarpment, notched at long distances by canyons, and extending north and south out of sight. This bold upheaval of rock and earth now gave at close hand an inkling of the wild and inhospitable nature of the Staked Plain.

The tracks of Hudnall's wagon led into a deep-mouthed canyon down whose rugged bottom poured a clear stream of water. Grass was abundant. Groves of cottonwood trees filled the level benches. Game of all kinds abounded in these fastnesses and fled before the approach of the hunters. Before noon of that day a small herd of buffalo, surprised in an open grassy park, stampeded up the canyon, completely obliterating the wagon tracks Pilchuck was following, and all other signs of the Comanches.

This flight of the buffalo, on the other hand, helped to make a way where it was possible to get the four wagons of supplies up on the Staked Plain. Many horses and strong hands made short work of this labor.

Tom Doan gazed in fascination at the wild, strange expanse before him, the Staked Plain, which though notorious of reputation, was so little known. He had expected to find it a gray level plain of sand. Sand there was, assuredly, but many other things at the same time, as appeared manifest in the sand dunes and bluffs and the ragged irregular brakes, and patches of grass, and wide areas of brush. In Tom's opinion, hunting Indians up there was indeed the wild-goose chase which the expedition had been stigmatized by many of the hunters who had remained behind.

Nevertheless, the Mexican scout led straight to the spot where there had recently been a large encampment of Comanches. They had been gone for days, no doubt having gotten wind of the campaign against them. The tracks of Hudnall's wagon were found again.

As it was now late in the day, camp was pitched here, with the three forces of hunters close together. By dark, supper was finished, the horses were picketed and herded, guards were on duty, and Pilchuck was in council with his two scouts and the more experienced of his men. It was decided to hold that camp for the next day, and send out detachments with the scouts to try and locate the Comanches.

Round the camp fire that night Tom made the further acquaintance of Spades Harkaway, and found him a unique character, reticent as to himself, but not unwilling to talk about Texas, the buffalo, and the Indians. He had twice crossed the Staked Plain from its western boundary, the Pecos River, to the headwaters of the Brazos on the east.

"Thet name Llano Estacado means Staked Plain," said the Texan. "It comes from the early days when the Spanish Trail from Santa Fe to San Antone was marked by '*palos,*' or stakes. There was only two trails across in them days an' I reckon no more now. Only the Indians know this plain well an' they only run in heah to hide awhile. Water an' grass are plentiful in some parts, an' then there's stretches of seventy miles dry an' bare as a bone. Reckon aboot some of the wildest an' roughest holes in Texas are up heah, as shore you-all will find oot."

Harkaway claimed the Llano Estacado was shaped like a ham, with a north-to-south trend, about four hundred miles long, and more than half as much wide. It was a tableland, resembling more the Russian steppes than the other upland districts known in the

West. Its height above the prairie was perhaps a thousand feet. Some of its most pronounced characteristics, that had helped to make its ill fame, were enumerated and described by the Texan as tremendous obstacles to overcome on an expedition like Pilchuck's.

"Thar's bare patches too big to see across," he specified, "an' others growed over with mesquite so thick thet ridin' it is impossible. Thar's narrow deep canyons thet can only be crossed in places miles apart. Then I've seen, myself, canyons thet opened out wide an' full of jumbles of broken cliff, where no man could go."

Higher up on the Staked Plain there were levels of a hundred miles in length, like a gravel floor, treeless, grassless, waterless, where the wind swept all before it. There were zones where ponds of water lay at times, a few of them permanent, sulphurous, or salty, and at dry seasons unfit to drink for man or beast. Near the southern end of this strange steppe was a belt of glistening white sand dunes, many miles wide, impassable for a horse, and extremely perilous for a man. Not, however, from lack of water! For here the singular nature of the Staked Plain was more than unusually marked. Permanent ponds lined by reeds and rushes existed in the very region of sand dunes. Along the whole eastern escarpment of the Staked Plain, for three hundred miles, the bold rock rim was cut and furrowed by the streams that had their sources in this mysterious upland.

Late next day the Mexican scout returned with the information that he had found the main encampment of the Comanches. He had been on a reconnoiter alone. Bear Claws and Pilchuck, who had essayed to follow the tracks of Hudnall's wagon, had actually lost all sign of them. For miles they had trailed the marks of the iron-shod wheels over an area of hard-packed gravel, only to lose them further on in tough, short, springy grass that after the recent rain left no trace.

"The Indian says he can find the wagon tracks by making a wide circle to get off the grass," Pilchuck informed Starwell, "but that might take days. Besides, the Indians sent the wagon off their main trail. Reckon they expected pursuit. Anyway, we'll not risk it."

When Pilchuck made this decision he did not yet know that the Mexican had located the Comanches. Upon consulting with him the information came out that a large band of Indians had been encamped in a canyon, and undoubtedly their lookouts had seen him.

This was verified next day, after a hard ride. An Indian band, large enough to have hundreds of horses, had hastily abandoned the encampment in the canyon and had climbed up on the plain, there to scatter in all directions. Plain trails were left in several cases, but these Bear Claws would not pay any attention to. The Mexican sided with him. They concentrated on dimmer trails over harder ground to follow.

It was after dark when Pilchuck and his men got back to camp, hungry and weary from a long day in the saddle. Next morning camp was moved ten miles to the west, to a secluded spot within easy striking distance of the place where Bear Claws had left off trailing the night before.

That day the Osage Indian lost track of the Comanches for the reason that the trail, always dim, finally vanished altogether. Three days more of searching the fastnesses within riding distance of this camp availed nothing. Camp had to be moved again, this time, at the Indian's suggestion, across the baffling stretch of plain to a wild and forbidding chaos of ruined cliffs, from which center many shallow canyons wandered for some leagues.

"Reckon we've got to rely on our field-glasses to see them before they see us," said Pilchuck.

When the sun rose high enough next morning to burn out the shadows Pilchuck stood with his scouts and some of his men on the crest of the rocky wilderness.

"Shore that's a hole!" he ejaculated.

Far and wide heaved the broken billows of gray rock, like an immense ragged sea, barren, monotonous, from which the heat veils rose in curtains. Here and there a tufted cedar raised its dwarfed head, but for the most part there was no green to break the stark nudity. Naked eyes of white men could only see the appalling beauty of the place and enable the mind to grasp the deceiving nature of its distance, size and color. Pilchuck took a long survey with his field-glass.

"Reckon all them meanderin' gorges head in one big canyon way down there," he said, handing the glass to Starwell.

"I agree with you, an' I'm gamblin' the Comanches are there," replied Starwell, in turn handing the glass to the man nearest him.

Tom had a good look at that magnified jumble of rocks and clefts, and the wonder of its wildness awed and thrilled him.

Standing next to Tom was Bear Claws, the Osage Indian, and so motionless, so striking was he as he gazed with dark, piercing eyes across the void, that Tom marveled at him and felt the imminence of some startling fact. Pilchuck observed this, also, for as he stood behind the Indian he watched him steadily.

Bear Claws was over six feet tall, lithe, lean, erect, with something of the look of an eagle about him. His bronze, impassive face bore traces of vermillion paint. Around his neck was the bear-claw necklace from which the hunters had nicknamed him. In the back of his scalp-lock, a twisted knot of hair, he had stuck the tail feathers of a prairie bird. Bright bracelets of steel shone on his wrists. He was naked to his beaded and quilled breech-clout.

"Me," he grunted, reaching for Pilchuck's field-glass, without taking his fixed gaze from what held him. With both hands then he put the glass to his eyes.

"Ugh!" he exclaimed, instantly.

It was a moment of excitement and suspense for the watching men. Pilchuck restrained Starwell's impatience. Tom felt a cold ripple run over his body, and then as the Indian said, "Comanches!" that ripple seemed suddenly to be strung with fire. He thought of Milly Fayre.

Bear Claws held the glass immovable, with stiff hand, while he stepped from behind it, and drew Pilchuck to the exact spot where he had stood. His long-reaching arm seemed grotesque while his body moved guardedly. He was endeavoring to keep the glass leveled at the exact spot that had held him.

Pilchuck fastened hard down on the glass, that wavered slightly and then gradually became still. To the watching men he evidently was an eternity. But at last he spoke: "By thunder! he's right. I can just make out . . . Indians on trail—goin' down—head of that canyon all these rock draws run into. . . . Starwell, take a look. . . . Hold there, over that first splinter of cliff, in a line with the high red bluff—an' search at its base."

Other glasses were now in use and more than one of the hunters caught a glimpse of the Comanches before they disappeared.

A council was held right there. The distance was approximately ten miles, yet incredibly the Osage Indian had seen something to make him take the field-glass and verify his wonderful keenness of vision. The Mexican scout knew the topography of the rough rock waste and guaranteed to place Pilchuck's force within striking distance of the Comanches by dawn next day.

Thereupon the hunters retraced their steps from that high point and returned to camp. Pilchuck took the scouts to search for a well-hidden pocket or head of a box canyon where wagons and horses not needed could be concealed to advantage and protected by a small number of men. This was found, very fortunately, in the direction of the Indian encampment, and several miles closer. The move was made expeditiously before dark.

"Reckon this is pretty good," said Pilchuck, with satisfaction. "We're far enough away to be missed by any scout they send out to circle their camp. That's an old Indian trick—to ride a circle round a hidin' place, thus crossin' any trail of men sneakin' close. It hardly seems possible we can surprise a bunch of Staked Plain Comanches, but the chance shore looks good."

In the darkest hour before dawn forty grim men rode out of camp behind the Mexican and Pilchuck.

Tom Doan rode next to Bear Claws, the fifth of that cavalcade, and following him came Spades Harkaway. No one spoke. The hoofs of the horses gave forth only dull, sodden sounds, inaudible at little distance. There was an opaque misshapen moon, orange in color, hanging low over the uneven plain. The morning star, white, luminous, like a marvelous beacon, stood high above the blanching velvet of the eastern sky.

They traveled at walk or trot, according to the nature of the ground, until the moon went down and all the stars had paled, except the great one in the east. This, too, soon grew wan. The gray of dawn was at hand. Dismounting in the lee of a low ledge, where brush grew thick and the horses could be tied, Pilchuck left two men on guard and led the others on foot behind the noiseless Mexican.

In less than a quarter of a mile the Mexican whispered something and slipped to his hands and knees. Pilchuck and his followers, two and three abreast, kept close to his heels. The fact that the Mexican crept on very slowly and made absolutely no sound had the effect of constraining those behind him to proceed as stealthily. This wrought upon the nerves of the men.

Tom Doan had never experienced such suspense. Just ahead of him lay the unknown ground never seen by him or any of his white comrades, and it held, no one knew how close, a peril soon to be encountered.

The dawn was growing lighter and rows of rocks

ahead could be distinguished. The ground began to slope. Beyond what seemed a gray space, probably a canyon, rose a dim vague bulk, uneven and woolly. Soon it showed to be canyon slope with brush on the rim.

Tom, finding that he often rustled the weeds or scraped on the hard ground, devoted himself to using his eyes as well as muscles to help him crawl silently. Thus it was that he did not look up until Pilchuck's low "Hist!" halted everybody.

Then Tom saw with starting eyes a deep bend in a wonderful gully where on a green level of some acres in extent were a large number of Indian tepees. A stream wound through the middle of this oval and its low rush and gurgle were the only sounds to accentuate the quiet of the morning. Hundreds of Indian ponies were grazing, standing, or lying down all over this meadow-like level. Not an Indian appeared in sight. But as the light was still gray and dim there could not be any certainty as to that.

Pilchuck raised himself to peer over a rock, and he studied the lay of the encampment, the narrow gateways of canyon above and below, and the approaches from the slope on his side. Then he slipped back to face the line of crouching men.

"By holdin' high we're in range right here," he whispered, tensely. "Starwell, take ten men an' crawl back a little, then round an' down to a point even with where this canyon narrows below. Harkaway, you take ten men an' go above, an' slip down same way. Go slow. Don't make noise. Don't stand up. We can then see each other's positions an' command all but the far side of this canyon. That's a big camp—there's two hundred Indians, more if they have their families. An' I reckon they have. Now Indians always fight harder under such conditions. We're in for a hell of a fight. But don't intentionally shoot squaws an' kids. That's all."

With only the slightest rustle and scrape, and deep

intake of breath, the two detachments under Starwell and Harkaway crept back among the stones out of sight. Then absolute silence once more reigned.

Pilchuck's men lay flat, some of them, more favorably located than others, peering from behind stones. No one spoke. They all waited. Meanwhile the gray dawn broadened to daylight.

"Ugh!" grunted Bear Claws, deep in his throat. His sinewy hand gripped Tom's shoulder.

Tom raised his head a couple of inches and he espied a tall Indian standing before a tepee, facing the east, where faint streaks of pink and rose heralded the sunrise. Tom felt a violent start jerk over his whole body. It was a hot burst of blood. This very Comanche might have been one of the murderers of Hudnall or, just as much a possibility, one of the despoilers of Jett's camp, from which Milly Fayre had disappeared. That terrible loss seemed to Tom far back in the past, lengthened, changed by suffering. It was nothing less than hate with which Tom watched that statuesque Indian.

Presently another Indian brave appeared, and another, then several squaws, and in a comparatively short time the camp became active. Columns of blue smoke arose lazily on the still air. The ponies began to move about.

What an endless period it seemed to Tom before Harkaway and Starwell got into their positions! Tom wondered if Pilchuck would wait much longer. His blood beat thick at his temples; his throat was dry; and a dimness of eye bothered him every few seconds.

"Ugh!" exclaimed Bear Claws, and this time he touched Pilchuck, directing him toward a certain point in the encampment.

At that juncture there pealed out a singularly penetrating yell, most startling in its suddenness and nerve-racking with its terrible long-drawn and sustained wildness.

"Comanche war-cry!" hissed Pilchuck. "Some

buck has glimpsed our men below. Wait! We want the shootin' to begin below an' above. Then mebbe the Indians will run this way."

Scarcely had the scout ceased his rapid whisper when a Sharps rifle awoke the sleeping echoes. It came from Starwell's detachment below.

In an instant the Indian camp became a scene of wild rush and shrill cry, above which pealed sharp quick shouts—the voice of authority. A heavy volley from Starwell's men was signal for Harkaway's to open up. The puffs of white smoke over the stone betrayed the whereabouts of both detachments. A rattle of Winchesters from the camp told how speedily many of the Indians had gotten into action.

Despite Pilchuck's orders, some of his men began to fire.

"All right, if you can't wait. But shoot high," he shouted.

Twenty Creedmoors thundered in unison from that rocky slope. It seemed to Tom then that hell had indeed broken loose. He had aimed and shot at a running brave. What strange fierceness he felt! His hands shook to spoil his aim and his face streamed with cold sweat. All the men were loading and firing, and he was in the midst of a cracking din. Yet above it all rose a weird piercing sound—the war-cry of the Comanches. Tom thought, as he shuddered under it, that he understood now why hunters had talked of this most hideous and infamous of all Indian yells.

In a few moments the first blending roar of guns and yells broke, and there intervened a less consistent din. Pandemonium reigned down in that encampment, yet there must have been many crafty Indians. Already the front line of tepees was in flames, sending up streaks of smoke, behind which the women and children were dimly seen running for the opposite slope. A number of frightened mustangs were racing with flying manes and tails, up and down the canyon, but the majority appeared to be under control of the Indians and coralled at the widest point. Soon many braves, women and children, dragging packs and horses, were seen through or round the smoke on the opposite slope.

The Comanche braves below then lived up to their reputation as the most daring and wonderful horsemen of the plains. To draw the fire of the hunters numbers of them, half naked demons, yelling, with rifles in hands, rode their mustangs bareback, with magnificent affront and tremendous speed, straight at the gateway of the canyon. They ran a gauntlet of leaden hail.

Tom saw braves pitch headlong to the earth. He saw mustangs plunge and throw their riders far. And he also saw Indians ride fleet as the storm-winds under the volleys from the slope, to escape down the canyon.

No sooner had one bunch of rider braves attempted this than another drove their mustangs pell-mell at the openings. They favored the lower gate, beneath Starwell's detachment, being quick to catch some little advantage there. The foremost of four Indians, a lean wild brave, magnificently mounted, made such a wonderful target with his defiance and horsemanship that he drew practically all the fire. He rode to his death, but his three companions flashed through the gateway in safety.

"Hold men! Hold!" yelled Pilchuck, suddenly at this juncture. "Load up an' wait. We're in for a charge or a trick."

Tom Doan drew a deep breath, as if he were stifling. His sweaty powder-begrimed hands fumbled at the hot breech of his Creedmoor. How many times had he fired? He did not know, nor could he tell whether or not he had shot an Indian.

Following with sharp gaze where the scout pointed, Tom saw through smoke and heat the little puffs of white, all along behind the burning front line of tepees. There were many braves lying flat, behind stones, trees, camp duffle, everything that would hide a man.

Bullets whistled over Tom's head and spanged from the rocks on each side of him.

"Watch that bunch of horses!" called Pilchuck, warningly. "There's fifty if there's one. Reckon we've bit off more'n we can chew."

Dimly through the now thinning smoke Tom could see the bunch of riders designated by Pilchuck. They were planning some audacious break like that of the braves who had sacrificed themselves to help their families to escape. This would be different, manifestly, for all the women and children, and the young braves with them, had disappeared over the far slope. It was war now.

"Jude, they're too smart to charge us," said a grizzled old hunter. "I'll swear thet bunch is aimin' to make a break to git by an' above us."

"Wal, if they do we'll be in a hell of a pickle," replied the scout. "I'll ask Bear Claws what he makes of it."

The Osage readily replied, "No weyno," which Tom interpreted as being anything but good for the hunters.

The Mexican urged Pilchuck to work back to higher ground, but the scout grimly shook his head.

Suddenly with remarkable swiftness the compact bunch of Indian horsemen disintegrated, and seemed to spill both to right and left.

"What the hell!" muttered Pilchuck.

One line of Comanche riders swerved below the camp, the other above, and they rode strung out in single file, going in opposite directions. Starwell and Harkaway reserved their fire, expecting some trick. When halfway to each gate the leader of each string wheeled at right angles to head straight for the slope.

"By God! they're goin' between us!" ejaculated Pilchuck. "Men, we've shore got to stick now an' fight for our lives."

At two hundred yards these incomparable riders were as hard to hit with bullets as birds on the wing. Starwell's detachment began to shoot and Harkaway's followed suit. Their guns were drowned in the dreadful war-cry of the Comanches. It seemed wilder, more piercing now, closer, a united sound, filling the cars, horrid yet not discordant, full of death, but for all that a magnificent blending of human voices. It was the cry of a wild tribe for life.

It lifted Tom's hair stiff on his head. He watched with staring eyes. How those mustangs leaped! They crossed the open level below, the danger zone of leaden hail, without a break in their speeding line. When they reached the base of the slope they were perked to their haunches, and in a flash each one was riderless. The Comanches had taken to the rocks.

"Ahuh! I reckoned so," growled Pilchuck.

"Pretty slick, if I do say it. Men, we've got crawlin' snakes to deal with now. You shore have to look sharp."

This sudden maneuver had the same effect upon the Starwell and Harkaway detachments as it had on Pilchuck's. It almost turned the tables on the white men. How grave it was perhaps only the experienced plainsmen realized. They all reserved their fire, manifestly directing attention to his new and hidden peril. The Comanches left in camp, a considerable number, redoubled their shots.

"Men, reckon it ain't time yet to say every one for himself," declared Pilchuck. "But we've shore got to crawl up to the level. Spread out, an' crawl flat on your bellies, an' keep rocks behind you."

Thus began a retreat, fraught with great risk. Bullets from the Winchesters spanged off the rocks, puffing white powder dust into the air. And these bullets came from the rear. The Comanches on each side had vanished like lizards into the maze of boulders. But every hunter realized these Indians were creeping, crawling, worming their way to places of advantage, keeping out of sight with the cunning natural to them.

Tom essayed to keep up with Bear Claws, but this was impossible by crawling. The Osage wriggled like a snake. Pilchuck, too, covered ground remarkably for a large man. Others crawled fast or slowly, according to their abilities. Thus the detachment, which had heretofore kept together, gradually disintegrated.

It had been a short two hundred yards from the top of this slope to the position the hunters had abandoned. Crawling back seemed interminable and insurmountable to Tom. Yet he saw how imperative it was to get there.

Some one was close behind Tom, crawling laboriously, panting heavily. It was Ory Tacks. As he was fat and round, the exertion was almost beyond his endurance and the risks were great. Tom had himself to think of, yet he wondered if he should not help Ory. Roberts crawled a little to Tom's left. He too was slow. An old white-haired buffalo-hunter named Calkins had taken Pilchuck's place on Tom's right. The others were above, fast wriggling out of sight.

A bullet zipped off a stone close to Tom and sang into the air. It had come from another direction. Another bullet, striking in front of him, scattered dust and gravel in his face. Then bullets hissed low down, just over the rocks. The Comanches were not yet above the hunters. Calkins called low for those back of him to hurry, that the word had been passed back from Pilchuck.

Tom was crawling as flat as a flounder, dragging a heavy gun. He could not make faster time. He was burning with sweat, yet cold as ice, and the crack of Winchesters had the discordance of a nightmare.

"Doan," called Roberts, sharply. "The fellow behind you's been hit."

Tom peered around. Ory Tacks lay with face down. His fat body was quivering.

"Ory! Ory! Are you hit?" flashed Tom.

"I should smile," he groaned, lifting a pale face. His old slouch hat was still in place and a tuft of tow-colored hair stuck out through a hole. "Never mind—me."

"Roberts, come help me," called Tom, and began to back down toward Ory. Roberts did likewise, and they both reached the young man about the same time.

"Much obliged to see you," said Ory, gratefully, as they took hold of his arms, one on each side.

Up to that moment Tom had been mostly stultified by emotion utterly new to him. It had been close to panic, for he had found himself hard put to it to keep from leaping up to run. But something in connection with Ory's misfortune strung Tom suddenly and acutely to another mood. Grim realization and anger drove away his fear.

"Drag him; he can't help himself," panted Roberts.

Then began what Tom felt to be the most heartbreaking labor imaginable. They had to crawl and drag the wounded Ory up hill. Tom locked his left arm under Ory's, and dragging his rifle in his right hand he jerked and hunched himself along. Bullets now began to whistle and patter from the other side, signifying that the Comanches to the right had located the crawling hunters. Suddenly, above Tom, boomed a heavy Creedmoor—then two booms followed in succession.

"Good!—It was—aboot time," panted Roberts.

Tom felt the coldness leave his marrow for good. It was fight now. Pilchuck, Bear Claws, the Mexican, and some of the old plainsmen had reached the top of the slope and had opened on the Comanches. This spurred him, if not to greater effort, which was impossible, at least to dogged and unquenchable endurance. Roberts whistled through his nose; his lean face was bathed with sweat. Ory Tacks struggled bravely to help himself along, though it was plain his agony was tremendous.

The slope grew less steep and more thickly strewn with large rocks. Tom heard no more bullets whiz up from the direction of the encampment. They came from both sides, and the reports of Winchesters, sharp and rattling above the Creedmoors, covered a wide half circle. Farther away the guns of the Starwell and

Harkaway forces rang out steadily, if not often. It had become a hot battle and the men were no longer shooting at puffs of white smoke.

Not a moment too soon did Tom and Roberts drag Tacks over the top of the slope into a zone of large boulders from behind which Pilchuck and his men were fighting. For almost at the last instant Tom heard a dull spat of lead striking flesh. Roberts' left arm, on which he was hunching himself along, crumpled under him, and he dropped flat.

"They—busted—me," he declared, huskily, then let go of Tacks, and floundered behind a rock.

Tom by superhuman exertion dragged Ory farther on, behind a long low ledge, from which a hunter was shooting. Then Tom collapsed. But as he sank flat he heard the boy's grateful, "Much obliged, Tom." For a few moments then Tom was deaf and blind to the battle. There was a bursting riot within his breast, an overtaxed heart fluttering to recover. It seemed long that he lay prostrate, utterly unable to lift face or hand. But gradually that passed. Pilchuck crawled close, smelling of sweat, dust, and powder.

"Tom, are you hurt?" he queried, shaking him.

"No—only—all in," whispered Tom, huskily, between pants. "We had to—drag Ory—up here. He's hit; so's Roberts."

"I'll take a look at them," said the scout. "We're shore in better position here. Reckon we can hold the red devils off. Lucky Starwell an' Harkaway are behind them, on both sides. We're in for a siege. . . . Bullets flyin' from east an' west. Peep out mighty careful an' look for an Indian. Don't shoot at smoke."

Tom crawled a little to the left and cautiously took up a position where he could peer from behind the long flat rock. He could see nothing move. An uneven field of boulders, large and small, stretched away, with narrow aisles of gray grass and ground between. The firing had diminished greatly. Both sides were conserving ammunition. Not for several moments did Tom espy a puff of white smoke, and that came from a heavy Creedmoor, four hundred yards or more away, from a point above where Starwell's men had guarded the gateway of the canyon.

Meanwhile as he watched for something to shoot at he could hear Pilchuck working over the wounded men, and ascertained that Roberts had been shot through the arm, not, however, to break the bones, and Ory Tacks had a broken hip. Tom realized the gravity of such a wound, out there in the wilderness.

"I'd be much obliged for a drink of water," was all Tom heard Ory say.

Pilchuck crawled away and did not return. Ory Tacks and Roberts lay at the base of the low ledge, out of range of bullets for the present. But they lay in the sun and already the sun was hot. The scout had chosen a small oval space irregularly surrounded by boulders and outcroppings of rough ledges. By twisting his head Tom could espy eight or ten of Pilchuck's force, some facing east behind their fortifications, others west. Tom heard both profanity and loquacious humor. The Mexican and the Osage were not in sight.

Then Tom peeped out from behind his own covert. This time his quick eye caught a glimpse of something moving, like a rabbit slipping into brush. Above that place then slid out a red streak and a thin blue-white cloud of smoke. Sputt! A bullet hit the corner of his rock and whined away. Tom dodged back, suddenly aghast, and hot with anger. A sharp-eyed Indian had seen him. Tom wormed his way around back of the long rock to the other end. Behind the next rock lay the old white-haired hunter, bare-headed, with sweat and tobacco stains upon his grizzled face.

"Take it easy an' slow," he advised Tom, complacently. "Comanches can't stand a long fight. They're riders, an' all we need is patience. On the ground we can lick hell out of them."

The old plainsman's nonchalance was incredible, yet vastly helpful to Tom. He put a hard curb on his

impetuosity, and forced himself to wait and think
carefully of every action before he undertook it.
Therefore he found a position where he could command a certain limited field of rocks without risk to
himself. It was like peeping through a knot hole too
small for any enemy to see at a distance. From this
vantage point Tom caught fleeting glimpses and flashes
of color, gray and bronze, once a speck of red. But
these vanished before he could bring his rifle into play.

"If you see suthin' move shoot quick as lightnin',"
said the old plainsman. "It might be a gopher or a
cottontail, but take no chances. It's likely to be a two-
legged varmint."

Intense concentration, and a spirit evolving from the
hour, enabled Tom to make considerable progress
toward the plainsman's idea of fighting Comanches.
Tom fired again and again, at the flit of a bird across a
narrow space, at the flash of gun, a gleam of a feather.
But he could never see whether or not he hit an Indian.
Strange to note, however, was the fact that these
fleeting movements of something were never repeated
in the same place. Concentration brought to Tom the
certainty that he was seeing a faint glimpse now and
then of these elusive Comanches. This, with the crack
of Winchesters and hum of bullets, in time bred in him
some semblance of the spirit of the old plainsman. It
was indeed a fight. He had his part to perform. Life
was here, and an inch away sped death. Grim, terrible,
but exalting, and strangely memorable of a vague past!
Tom Doan realized the inheritance he had in common
with men, white or red.

The hours passed swiftly for the fighters. Another
wounded man joined Roberts and Ory Tacks, and the
ordeal must have been frightful for them. Tom forgot
them; so did all the defenders of that position. The
glaring sun poured down its heat. Stones and guns
were so hot they burned. No breeze stirred. And the
fight went on, favorable for the buffalo-hunters because of their fortifications, unfavorable in regard to

time. They were all parching for thirst. By chance or blunder the canteens had been left on the saddles and water had come to be almost as precious as powder. The old plainsman cursed the Staked Plain. Tom's mouth appeared full of cotton paste. He had kept pebbles in his mouth till he was sick of them.

Noon went by. Afternoon came. The sun, hotter than ever, began to slope to the west. And the fight went on, narrowing down as to distance, intensifying as to spirit, magnifying peril to both sides. The Creedmoors from the Starwell and Harkaway forces kept up the bulk of the shooting. They were directing most of their fire down into the encampment, no doubt to keep the Comanches there from joining their comrades on the slope. Mustangs showed on the farther points, and evidently had strayed.

Presently Pilchuck came crawling on hands and knees, without his rifle or coat. A bloody patch showed on his shoulder.

"Tom, reckon I got punctured a little," he said. "It ain't bad, but it's bleedin' like hell. Tear my shirt sleeve off an' tie it around my arm over my shoulder tight."

An ugly bullet hole showed angrily in the upper part of the scout's shoulder, apparently just through the flesh.

"Notice that bullet came from behind," said Pilchuck. "There shore was a mean redskin on your side. He hit two of us before I plugged him. There—good. . . . Now how's the rest of your hospital?"

"I don't know. Afraid I forgot," replied Tom, aghast.

"Wal, I'll see."

He crawled over to the wounded men and spoke. Tom heard Roberts answer, but Ory Tacks was silent. That disturbed Tom. Then the scout came back to him.

"Roberts's sufferin' some, but he's O.K. The young fellar, though, is dyin', I'm afraid. Shot in the groin. Mebbe——"

"Pilchuck! . . . Ory didn't seem bad hurt——"

"Wal, he is, an' if we don't get some water he'll go," declared the scout, emphatically. "Fact is, we're all bad off for water. It's shore hot. What a dumbhead I was to forget the canteens!"

"I'll go after them," returned Tom, like a flash.

"It's not a bad idee," said Pilchuck, after a moment's reflection. "Reckon it'd be no riskier than stayin' here."

"Direct me. Where'd you leave the horses?"

The scout faced south, at right angles with the crossfire from the Comanches, and presently extended his long arm.

"See that low bluff—not far—the last one reachin' down into this basin. It's behind there. You can't miss it. Lucky the rocks from here on are thick as cabbages."

"I can make it," declared Tom, doggedly. "But to get back! That stumps me."

"Easy. You've got to go slow, pickin' the best cover. Reckon the Comanches are all on these two sides of us, but there *might* be some tryin' to surround us."

"Anything more?" queried Tom, briefly.

The scout apparently had no thought of the tremendousness of this enterprise to Tom. It was as if he had naturally expected of Tom what he would do himself if he had not been partially incapacitated. Tom realized he had never in his life received such a compliment. It swelled his heart. He felt light, hard, tense, vibrating to a strange excitation.

"Wal, I can't think of anythin'," replied the scout. "Comin' back be slower'n molasses, an' get the drift of the fight. We're holdin' these redskins off. But I reckon Starwell an' Harkaway have been doin' more. If I don't miss my guess they've spilled blood down in the canyon. Comanches are great on horseback, but they can't stick out a fight like this. If they rush us we're goners. If they don't they'll quit before sunset."

Chapter XIII

MILLY FAYRE rode out of Sprague's Post on the front of a freighter's wagon, sitting between Jett and his wife. The rest of Jett's outfit followed close behind, Follonsbee and Pruitt in the second wagon, and Catlee driving the last.

For as long as Milly could see the Hudnalls she waved her red scarf in farewell. Then when her friends passed out of sight Milly turned slowly to face the boundless prairie, barren of life, suddenly fearful in its meaning, and she sank down, stricken in heart. What she had dreaded was now an actuality. The courage that had inspired her when she wrote the letter to Tom Doan, leaving it with Mrs. Hudnall, was a courage inspired by love, not by hope. So it seemed now.

"Milly, you ain't actin' much like a boy, spite them boy's clothes," said Jett, with attempt at levity. "Pile over in the back of the wagon an' lay down."

Kindness from Jett was astounding, and was gratefully received by Milly. Doing as she was bidden, she found a comfortable place on the unrolled packs of bedding, with her head in a shade of the wagon seat. It developed then that Jett's apparent kindness had been only a ruse to get her away so he could converse with his wife in low, earnest tones. Milly might have heard all or part of that conversation, but she was not interested and did not listen.

Dejectedly she lay there while the steady trot of the horses carried her back toward the distant buffalo range. To be torn from her kind and loving friends at the post and drawn back into the raw hard life led by her stepfather was a bitter and sickening blow. Her sufferings were acute; and as she had become used to hope and happiness she was now ill fitted to cope with misery and dread. She did not think of the future or plan to meet it; she lived in the present and felt the encroaching of an old morbid and fatalistic mood, long a stranger to her.

The hours passed, and Jett's deep, low voice appeared never to rest or cease. He did not make a noon stop, as was customary among the buffalo-hunters. And he drove until sunset.

"Forty miles, bedamn!" he said, with satisfaction, as he threw the reins.

Whether Milly would have it so or not, she dropped at once back into the old camp life, with its tasks. How well she remembered! The smoke of the camp fire made her eyes smart and brought tingling as well as hateful memories.

The other wagons drove up rather late, and once more Milly found herself under the hawk eyes of Follonsbee and the half-veiled hidden look of the crooked-faced Pruitt. Her masculine garb, emphasizing her shapely slenderness, manifestly drew the gaze of these men. They seemed fascinated by it, as if they both had discovered something. Neither of them spoke to her. Catlee, however, gave her a kindly nod. He seemed more plodding in mind than she remembered him.

One by one the old associations returned to her, and

presently her fleeting happiness with the Hudnalls had the remoteness and unreality of a dream and she was again Jett's stepdaughter, quick to start at his harsh voice. Was that harshness the same? She seemed to have a vague impression of a difference in his voice, in him, in all of his outfit, in the atmosphere around them.

A stopping place had been chosen at one of the stream crossings where hundreds of buffalo-hunters had camped that year, a fact Jett growled about, complaining of the lack of grass and wood. Water was plentiful, and it was cold, a welcome circumstance to the travelers. Jett had an inordinate thirst, probably owing to his addiction to rum at Sprague's.

"Fetch some more drinkin' water," he ordered Milly.

She took the pail and went down the bank under the big, rustling, green cottonwoods. Catlee was at the stream, watering the horses.

"I seen you comin', an' I says who's that boy?" he said, with a grin. "I forgot."

"I forgot, too," she replied, dubiously. "I don't like these—these pants. But I've made a discovery, Catlee. I'm more comfortable round camp."

"Don't wonder. You used to drag your skirts round. . . . Gimme your bucket. I'll fill it where the water's clear."

He waded in beyond where the horses were drinking and dipped the pail. "Nothin' like good cold water after a day's hot ride."

"Jett drank nearly all I got before and sent me for more."

"He's burnin' up inside with red liquor," returned Catlee, bluntly.

Milly did not have any reply to make to that, but she thanked Catlee, and taking the pail she poured out a little water, so she would not spill it as she walked.

"Milly, I'm sorry you had to come back with Jett," said Catlee.

She paused, turning to look at him, surprised at his

tone. His bronze face lacked the heat, the dissolute shades common to Jett and the other men. Milly remembered then that Catlee in her opinion had not seemed like the rest of Jett's outfit.

"Sorry? Why?" she asked.

"I know Sprague. He's from Missouri. He told me about you, an' your friend Tom Doan."

"Sprague told you—about—about Tom!" faltered Milly, suddenly blushing. "Why, who told him?"

"Mrs. Hudnall, he said. Sprague took interest in you, it 'pears. An' his wife is thick with the Hudnall women. Anyway, he was sorry Jett took you away—an' so'm I."

Milly's confusion and pain at the mention of Tom did not quite render her blind to this man's sympathy. She forced away the wave of emotion. Her mind quickened to the actuality of her being once more in Jett's power and that she had only her wits and courage to rely upon. This hard-faced, apparently dull and somber man might befriend her. Milly suddenly conceived the inspiration to win him to her cause.

"So am I sorry, Catlee," she said sadly, and her quick tears were genuine. Indeed, they had started to flow at mention of Tom's name. "I—I'm engaged to Tom Doan. . . . I was—so—so happy. And I'd never had—any happy times before. . . . Now I've been dragged away. Jett's my stepfather. I'm not of age. I had to come. . . . And I'm terribly afraid of him.

"I reckon," rejoined Catlee, darkly, "you've reason to be. He an' the woman quarreled at Sprague's. He wanted to leave her behind. For that matter, the four of them drank a good deal, an' fought over the hide money."

"For pity's sake, be my friend!" appealed Milly.

The man stared at her, as if uncomprehending, yet somehow stirred.

"Catlee," she said, seeing her advantage and stepping back to lay a hand softly on his arm, "did you ever have a sister or a sweetheart?"

"I reckon not or I'd been another kind of man," he returned, with something of pathos.

"But you're not bad," she went on, swiftly.

"Me not bad! Child, you're crazy! I never was anythin' else. An' now I'm a hide thief."

"Oh, it's true, then? Jett is a hide thief. I knew something was terribly wrong."

"Girl, don't you tell Jett I said that," replied Catlee, almost harshly.

"No, I won't. I promise. You can trust me," she returned, hurriedly. "And I could trust you. I don't think you're really bad. Jett has led you into this. He's bad. I hate him."

"Yes, Jett's bad all right, an' he means bad by you. I reckon I thought you knowed an' didn't care."

"Care! If he harms me I'll kill him and myself," she whispered, passionately.

The man seemed to be confronted with something new in his experience, and it was dissipating a dull apathy to all that concerned others.

"So that's how a good girl feels!" he muttered.

"Yes. And I ask you—beg you to be a man—a friend——"

"There comes Pruitt," interrupted Catlee, turning to his horses. "Don't let him or any of them see you talkin' to me."

Milly bent over the heavy bucket and, avoiding the dust raised by Pruitt with his horses, she hurried back to camp. Her return manifestly checked hard words between Jett and his wife. Milly took up her tasks where they had been interrupted, but with this difference, that she had become alive to the situation among these hide thieves. Jett's status had been defined, and the woman was no doubt culpable with him. Catlee's blunt corroboration of Milly's fears had awakened her spirit; and the possibility of winning this hardened man to help her in her extremity had inspired courage and resolve. All in a flash, then, it seemed she was the girl who had written that brave letter to Tom Doan.

Supper was cooked and eaten. The men, except Catlee, were not hungry as usual, and appeared to be wearing off the effects of hard drinking. They spoke but seldom, and then only to ask for something out of reach on the spread canvas. Darkness settled down while Milly dried the pans and cups. Catlee came up with a huge armload of wood, which he dropped with a crash, a little too near Pruitt to suit his irascible mood.

"Say, you Missouri hay seed, can't you see my feet?" he demanded.

"I could if I'd looked. They're big enough," retorted Catlee. "I ain't wonderin' you have such a care of them."

"Ain't you? Shore I'd like to know why?" queried Pruitt.

"I reckon what little brains you've got are in them."

"You damn Yank!" ejaculated the little rebel, as amazed as enraged. "I've shot men for less'n thet."

"Reckon you have," rejoined Catlee with slow, cool sarcasm. "But in the back! . . . An' I'm lookin' at you."

There was not the slightest doubt of Catlee's emergence from the character of a solid dull teamster into something incalculably otherwise. Jett rolled out his loud, harsh laughter. It amused him, this revolt of the stupid farmer. Likewise it showed his subtle change. Was there reason for him to invite antagonism among his men? Assuredly there was strong antagonism toward him. Follonsbee gazed in genuine amaze at Catlee, and slowly nodded his lean buzzard-like head, as if he had before in his life seen queer things in men. As for the fiery little rebel, he was instantly transformed, in his attitude toward Catlee, from a man who had felt a raw irritation, to one who hated and who doubted. However, Follonsbee read the erstwhile Missouri farmer, Pruitt got only so far as a cold and waking doubt. Enmity was thus established and it seemed to be Pruitt's natural mental attitude, and to suit Catlee better than friendliness.

Milly heard and saw this byplay from the shadow beyond the camp-fire circle. If that were Catlee's answer to her appeal, it was a change, sudden and bewildering. The thrill she sustained was more like a shudder. In that moment she sensed a far-reaching influence, a something which had to do with future events. Catlee stalked off into the gloom of the cotton-wood, where he had made his bed.

"Rand, are you sure thet feller, is what you said he was—a Missouri farm hand, tired of workin' for nothin'?" demanded Follonsbee.

"Hank, I ain't sure of anythin' an' I don't give a whoop," replied the leader.

"Thet's natural, for you," said the other, with sarcasm. "You don't know the West as I know it. Catlee struck me queer. . . . When he called Pruitt, so cool-like, I had come to mind men of the Cole Younger stripe. If so——"

"Aw, it's nothin'," cut in Pruitt. "Jett spoke my sentiments aboot our Yankee pard. It r'ils me to think of him gettin' a share of our hide money."

Jett coughed, an unusual thing for him to do. "Who said Catlee got a share?" he queried, gruffly.

Follonsbee lifted his lean head to peer at the leader. Pruitt, who was sitting back to a stump, his distorted face gleaming red in the camp-fire light, moved slowly forward to gaze in turn. Both men were silent; both of them questioned with their whole bodies. But Jett had no answer. He calmly lit his pipe and flipped the match into the fire.

"Shore, now I tax myself, I cain't remember thet anybody said Catlee got a share," replied Pruitt, with deliberation. "But I thought he did. An' I know Hank thought so."

"I'd have gambled on it," said Follonsbee.

"Catlee gets wages, that's all," asserted the leader.

"Ahuh! . . . An' who gets *his* share of the hide money?" demanded Pruitt.

"I do," rejoined Jett, shortly.

"Jett, I'm tellin' you that's in line with your holdin' out money for supplies at Sprague," said Follonsbee, earnestly. "You was to furnish outfit, grub, everythin', an' share even with all of us, includin' your woman. You got your share, an' her share, an' now Catlee's share."

"I'm willin' to argue it with you, but not on an equal divvy basis."

There followed a long silence. The men smoked. The fire burned down, so that their faces were but pale gleams. Milly sought her bed, which she had made in the wagon. Jett had sacrificed tents to make room for equal weight of buffalo hides. He had unrolled his blankets under the wagon, where the sullen woman had repaired soon after dark. Milly took off her boy's shoes and folded the coat for a pillow, then slipping under the blankets she stretched out, glad for the relief.

How different, lying out under the open starry sky! She liked it. The immense blue dome was alight, mysterious, beautiful, comforting. Milly said her short prayer, childish and loyal, somehow more than ever helpful on this eventful night. Often, before she had met the Hudnalls and Tom Doan, she had omitted that little prayer, but never since she had learned from them the meaning of friendship and love.

The night was warm; the leaves of the cottonwoods near by rustled softly in the breeze; insects were chirping and a night bird was uttering plaintive notes.

Jett, Follonsbee, and Pruitt remained around the camp fire, quarreling in low voices; and that sound was the last Milly heard as slumber claimed her.

Milly's eyes opened to the bright light of day, and pale-blue sky seemed canopied over her. Not the canvas roof of her tent! Where was she? The smell of cottonwood smoke brought her with surging shock to realization. Then Jett's harsh voice, that had always made her shrink with fear, sent a creeping fire along her veins.

She lay a moment longer, calling to the spirit that had awakened last night; and it augmented while she seemed to grow strangely older. She would endure; she would fight; she would think. So that when she presented herself at the camp fire she was outwardly a quiet, obedient, impassive girl, inwardly a cunning, daring woman.

Not half a dozen words were spoken around the breakfast canvas. Jett rushed the tasks. Sunrise shone on the three wagons moving south at a brisk trot.

Milly had asked Catlee to fix her a comfortable place in the back of Jett's wagon. He had done so, adding of his own accord an improvised sun shade of canvas. She had watched him from the wagon seat, hoping he would speak to her or look at her in a way that would confirm her hopes. But the teamster was silent and kept his head lowered. Nevertheless, Milly did not regard his taciturnity as unfavorable to her. There had been about Catlee, last night when he had muttered: "So that's how a good girl feels," a something which spoke to Milly's intuition. She could not prove anything. But she felt. This man would befriend her. A subtle unconscious influence was working on his mind. It was her presence, her plight, her appeal.

Milly thought of a thousand plans to escape, to get word to Doan, to acquaint buffalo-hunters with the fact of her being practically a prisoner, to betray that Jett was a hide thief. Nothing definitely clear and satisfactory occurred to her. But the fact of her new knowledge of Jett stood out tremendously. It was an infallible weapon to employ, if the right opportunity presented. But a futile attempt at that would result fatally for her. Jett would most surely kill her.

It seemed to Milly as she revolved in mind plan after plan that the wisest thing to do would be to play submissive slave to Jett until he reached the end of the drive south; and there to persuade Catlee to take her at once to Hudnall's camp, where she would betray Jett. If Catlee would not help her, then she must go alone, or, failing that, wait for Tom Doan to find her.

Before the morning was far advanced Jett gave wide berth to an oncoming outfit. Milly was not aware of this until the unusual jolting caused her to rise to her knees and look out. Jett had driven off the main road, taking a low place, where other drivers had made short cuts. Four freight wagons, heavily laden with hides, were passing at some distance to the right. The foremost team of horses was white—Milly thought she recognized it as Hudnall's. Her heart rushed to her lips. But she had seen many white teams, and all of them had affected her that way. If she leaped out and ran to find she was mistaken, she would lose every chance she had. Besides, as she gazed, she imagined she was wrong. So with a deep sigh she dropped back to her seat.

The hours passed quickly. Milly pondered until she was weary, then fell asleep, and did not awaken until another camp was reached. And the first words she heard were Jett's speaking to Follonsbee as he drove up abreast the leader, "Wasn't that Hudnall's outfit we passed?"

"First two teams was," replied Follonsbee. "That young skinner of Hudnall's was leadin', an' that ugly-face cuss was drivin' the second team. I didn't know the other outfits."

Milly had to bite her lips to repress a scream. Jett was clamboring down from the seat above. The woman, grumbling under her breath, threw out the canvas bags of utensils, that clinked on the ground. Milly hid her face as Mrs. Jett descended from the seat. Then, for a moment, she shook like a leaf with the violence of her emotions. So near Tom! Not to see his face! It was heartrending. She lay prostrate, with her mind in a whirl. Of the many thoughts one returned—that Tom would reach Sprague's Post next

day and get her letter. That thought had strength to
impart. He would lose no time following, perhaps
would catch up with Jett before he got to the Pease
River, and if not then, soon afterward. This thought
sustained her in a trying moment.

The weakness passed, leaving her somewhat thick
witted, so that as she climbed out of the wagon she
nearly fell, and later her clumsiness at her assigned
camp tasks fetched a reprimand from Mrs. Jett. Soon
the men were back from attending to the horses, and
this evening they were hungry. Meeting outcoming
freighters with buffalo hides had for the moment
turned the minds of Jett and his two lieutenants from
their differences.

"How many hides in them outfits?" queried Jett.

"It weren't a big haul," replied Follonsbee.

"Shore was big enough to make us turn off the
road," said Pruitt, meaningly.

Jett glared at him. Then Catlee drawled: "Funny
they didn't see us. But we went down on our side
some. That first driver was Hudnall's man, Tom
Doan."

"Ahuh! Well, suppose it was?" returned Jett, non-
plussed at this remark from the habitually unobserving
Catlee.

"Nothin'. I just recognized him," replied Catlee,
casually, as he lowered his eyes.

When he raised them, a moment later, to look across
the canvas supper cloth at Milly, she saw them as
never before, sharp as a dagger, with a single bright
gleam. He wanted her to know that he had seen Tom
Doan. Milly dropped her own gaze and she spilled a
little of her coffee. She dared not trust her flashing
interpretation of this man's glance. It seemed like a
gleam of lightning from what had hitherto been dead
ashes. Thereafter he paid no attention to her, nor to
any of the others; and upon finishing the meal and
finishing his chore of cutting firewood, he vanished.

Jett and his two disgruntled men took up their quarrel and spent a long, noisy, angry hour round the camp fire.

The next day came and passed, with no difference for Milly except that Catlee now avoided her, never seemed to notice her; and that she hung out her red scarf, with a hopefull thrill in its significance. Then one by one the days rolled by, under the wheels of the wagons.

Seven days, and then the straggling lost bands of buffalo! The hot, drowsy summer air was tainted; the gently waving prairie bore heaps of bones; skulking coyotes sneaked back from the road. A thousand times Milly Fayre looked back down the endless road she had traveled. No wagon came in sight!

Noon of the ninth day brought Jett within sight of the prairie-wide herd of buffalo. He halted to point it out to his sullen, unseeing men; and later he reined in again, this time to turn his ear to the hot stinking wind.

"Aha! Listen," he called back to Follonsbee.

Milly heard the boom-boom-boom-boom of guns, near and far, incessant and potent. Strangely, for once she was glad to hear them!

All that hot midday she reclined on the improvised seat in her wagon, holding her scarf to her nostrils and looking out occasionally at the sordid ugliness of abandoned camp sites. The buffalo-hunters had moved on up the river, that now showed its wandering line of green timber.

Milly took a last backward gaze down the prairie road just as Jett turned off to go into the woods. Far away Milly saw a dot on the horizon—a white and black dot. Maybe it was Tom Doan's horses and wagons! He could not be far behind. It was as well now, perhaps, that he had not caught up with Jett. The buffalo range had been reached; and it could not be long before her situation was changed.

Jett drove off the prairie, into the timber, along a well-defined shady road where many camps had been pitched, and then down into the brakes. Brutal and fearless driver that he was, he urged his horses right through the tangled undergrowth, that bent with the onslaught of the wagon, to spring back erect after it had passed. Follonsbee came crashing next. Jett drove down into the bottom lands, thick and hot and aromatic with its jungle of foliage. He must have had either wonderful judgment as to where it was possible for horses to go, or an uncanny luck. For he penetrated the heavily wooded brakes clear to a deep shining river.

Milly would not allow herself to be unduly distressed because Jett meant to hide his camp, for she knew that any one hunting wagon tracks and camps would surely not miss his. In a way Milly was glad of the shade, the murmur of the river, the songs of birds, the absence of the stench. A camp on the edge of the prairie, with the rotten carcasses of buffalo close at hand, the dust and heat, the flies and bugs, would be well-nigh unendurable.

Jett halted his team in a shady glade of cottonwoods just back from the river and Milly then discovered that this was the scene of Jett's previous encampment. His tents and fireplace, boxes and bales, evidently had not been molested during his absence.

"Turn the horses loose an' unload the wagons," he ordered his men. "I'll take a look for my saddle horses."

"No fear of horses leavin' grass an' water," rejoined Follonsbee. "But there might be hoss thieves on the range."

"Haw! Haw!" laughed Pruitt, in his mean way. "Shore you know these heah buff-hunters are all honest men."

Jett strode off into the green brakes. The men unloaded the wagons and set the boxes and bags of supplies under a cottonwood. Mrs. Jett opened a tent near the fireplace.

"Miss," said Catlee, "the canvas wagon cover you had before got ripped to pieces. There ain't any tent for you till that one's mended."

"Can't I stay in the wagon?" she asked.

"Don't see why not. We'll hardly be movin' or haulin' very soon."

It was late in the afternoon when the rays of the sun began to lose heat. Milly was sorely in need of a little freedom of limbs. She had been cramped and inactive so long. So she walked to and fro under the trees. This camp was the most secluded Jett had ever chosen—far from the prairie, down in the brakes at the edge of the river, hidden by trees from the opposite densely foli-aged bank. If it had not hinted of a sinister meaning and was not indeed a prison for Milly she could have reveled in it. If she had to spend much time there she would be grateful for its quiet, cleanliness, and beauty. She strolled along the green bank until Mrs. Jett curtly called her to help get supper.

About the time it was ready Jett returned, with muddy boots and clothes covered with burrs and bits of brush.

"Found all the horses except the bay mare," he announced. "An' to-morrow we can go back to work. I'm aimin' at hard work, men."

"Huh! I'd like to know what you call all we've done," returned Follonsbee.

"Wal, Jett, there shore won't be *any* work aboot heah till you settle up," added Pruitt, crisply.

Jett's huge frame jerked with the shock of surprise and fury he must have felt.

"So that's it?" he queried, thickly. "Waited till you got way down here!"

"We shore did, boss," returned Pruitt.

In sullen silence then Jett began and finished his supper. Plain it was he had received a hard, unexpected blow, that he seemed scarcely prepared to cope with. He had no further words with his men, but he drew his wife aside; and they were in earnest conversation when Milly fell asleep.

Next day brought forward a situation Milly had not calculated upon. Jett had no intercourse whatever with his men, and saddling his horse rode off alone. The woman sulked. Follonsbee and Pruitt, manifestly satisfied with their stand, played cards interminably, now and then halting to talk in low tones over something vital to them. Catlec rigged himself a crude fishing tackle and repaired to the river bank, where he found a shady seat within sight of the camp.

Milly was left to herself. Her first act, after the tasks of the morning were ended, was to hang up her red scarf in a conspicuous place. Then she had nothing to do but kill time. With the men in camp, this was not easy. Apparently she had liberty. No orders had been given her, but perhaps this was owing to the timid meekness she had pretended. She might have wandered away into the brakes or have trailed the wagon tracks up to the prairie. But she could not decide that this was best. For the present she could only wait.

Already the boom of guns floated in on the summer air from all sides, increasing for a while, until along the upriver prairie there was almost continuous detonation. Every boom, perhaps, meant the heart or lungs of a noble animal torn to shreds for the sake of his hide. As Milly settled down again to the actual presence of this slaughter she accepted the fact with melancholy resignation.

In the course of her strolling round the camp Milly gravitated toward Catlee, where he sat contentedly smoking his pipe and fishing. She watched him, trying to make up her mind to approach him on the subject nearest her heart. But she knew the men and Mrs. Jett could see her and that any such action might arouse suspicion. Therefore she desisted. Once Catlee turned, apparently casually, and his gray gaze took her in and the camp. Then he winked at her.

That droll action established anew Milly's faith in an understanding between her and this man. She had no assurance that he would help her, but there was a secret between them. Milly felt more than she could prove. The incident made the long day supportable.

Chapter XIV

JETT's outfit fell into idleness for more days than Milly could remember. She waited for time to pass, and no one would have suspected her longing. When Jett returned to camp from one of his lonely rides Milly would hear his horse breaking the brush along the trail, and she could never repress a wild throb of hope. It might be Tom! But it was always Jett.

One day Jett returned in great perturbation, apparently exhausted. His horse was jaded. Follonsbee and Pruitt were curious, to no end, for Jett did not vouchsafe any explanation. Whatever had happened, however, brought about a change in him and his habits. He stayed in camp.

The business of hide-hunting had been abandoned; not improbably in Jett's mind for a temporary period, until his men weakened. But they did not weaken; they grew stronger. More days of this enforced idleness crystallized a growing influence—they would never again follow the extraordinary labors of hunting and skinning buffalo. Whatever had been Jett's unity of outfit was destroyed.

Milly heard the woman tell Jett this, and the ensuing scene had been violent. It marked, further, the revealment of Mrs. Jett's long-hidden hand in the game. She was the mainspring of Jett's calculated mechanism, and when the other men realized it, it precipitated something darkly somber into the situation. Follonsbee and Pruitt had manifestly been playing a hand they felt sure would win. Jett could no longer hunt hides, or steal them, either, without his men. All of these lonely rides of his had been taken to find other accomplices, whom Follonsbee and Pruitt knew could not be obtained there on the buffalo range.

Milly heard the bitter quarrel which ensued, between Jett and his wife and the two lieutenants. Catlee was always there, listening, watching, but took no part in any of their talks or quarrels. He was outside. They did not count him at all. Yet he should have been counted immeasurably, Milly concluded. Like herself, Catlee was an intense, though silent, participator in this drama.

The content of that quarrel was simple. Jett had weakened to the extent of wanting to settle in part with his men. Follonsbee and Pruitt were not willing to take what he offered, and the woman, most tenacious and calculating of all of them, refused to allow Jett to relinquish any share of their profits.

There was a deadlock, and the argument put aside for the present. Follonsbee and Pruitt walked away from camp; Jett and his wife repaired to their tent where they conversed heatedly; Catlee and Milly cooked the supper. Milly did not know when the absent men returned.

Next day the atmosphere of Jett's outfit had undergone further change. The leader was a worried and tormented man, beset by a woman with will of steel and heart of hate; and he saw opposed to him Westerners whose reaction now seemed formidable and deadly. That had roused an immovable stubbornness in him.

Milly saw the disintegration of this group, and what she could not divine herself she gathered from study of Catlee. Indeed, he was the most remarkable of the outfit—he whom the others never considered at all. Not that Milly could understand her impressions! If she tried to analyze Catlee's effect upon her it only led to doubt. As for Jett and his men, they were a divided outfit, wearing toward dissolution, answering to the wildness of the time and place. The evil that they had done hovered over them, about to enact retribution.

Milly began to dread the issue, though the breaking up of this outfit augured well for her. Then any day Tom Doan, with Hudnall and his men, might ride into Jett's camp. That meant deliverance for her, in one way or another. If Jett refused to let her go she had but to betray him. Milly held her courage all through this long ordeal, yet she felt more and more the looming of a shadow.

Toward the close of that afternoon the tension relaxed. Follonsbee and Pruitt sauntered off with their heads together; Jett fell asleep under a cottonwood and his sullen wife slouched into her tent; Catlee sat on a log by the river bank, not fishing or smoking, but deep in thought.

Milly, answering the long-resisted impulse, slipped to his side.

"Catlee, I must tell you," she whispered. "This—all this I've gone through has got on my nerves. I've waited and hoped and prayed for Tom Doan. . . . He doesn't come. He has missed this road. I might have stood it longer, but this fight between the Jetts and his men wears on me. I'm scared. Something awful will happen. I can't stand it. . . . I know you're my friend—oh, I know it! . . . But you must help me. Tell me what you think. Tell me what to do. It's all so wild—so strange. . . . That awful woman! She eyes me so—as if she guessed what the men are not thinking of *now*, but would be soon. . . . Catlee, you're no—no—you're not like these people. But whatever you were—

or are—remember your mother and save me before— before——"

Milly's voice failed her. Liberating her fears and hopes had spent her force in expression.

"Lass, have you said all you want to?" queried Catlee, in tense undertone.

"Yes—yes—I could only repeat," faltered Milly, but she held out trembling hands to him.

The man's face underwent a change not on the surface. It seemed light, agitation, transpiring beneath a mask.

"Don't go out of my sight!" he said, with ringing sharpness that made her gasp. Then he turned away, imperturbable as ever.

But Milly had seen or heard something terrible. She backed away from Catlee, sensing this was what he wanted her to do. Yet not out of his sight! What had he meant by that? It signified a crisis nearer than even her fears had presaged, and infinitely worse. All the time he had known what was to happen and all this time he had been her friend. This was what had been on his mind as he watched and listened.

Returning to the wagon that was her abode, she climbed to the seat and sank there, with wide eyes and beating heart. She could see Catlee sitting like a statue, staring into the river. Mrs. Jett came out of her tent, with slow, dragging step, and a face drawn, pale, malignant. Her eyes were beady, the corners of her hard mouth curved down. Heavy, slovenly, she moved to awaken Jett with a kick of foot no less gentle than her mien.

"Come out of it, you loafer," she said. "My mind's made up. We'll break camp at daylight to-morrow. . . . As you ain't got nerve to kill these men, you can have it out with them tonight. But I'm keepin' the money an' we're goin' to-morrow."

"Ahuh!" ejaculated Jett, with a husky finality.

The habit of camp tasks was strong in her, as in all of her companions. Methodically she bestirred herself round the boxes of supplies. Catlee fetched firewood as if he had been ordered to do so. Follonsbee and Pruitt returned to squat under a cottonwood, with faces like ghouls. Jett went into his tent, and when he came out he was wiping his yellow beard. He coughed huskily, as always when drinking.

For once Milly made no move to help. No one called her. It was as if she had not been there. Each member of that outfit was clamped by his or her own thoughts. Supper was prepared and eaten in a silence of unnatural calm. Lull before the storm!

Catlee brought Milly something to eat, which he tendered without speaking. Milly looked down into his eyes, and it seemed to her that she had been mistaken in the kindly nature of the man. As he turned away she noticed a gun in his belt. It was unusual for buffalo-hunters to go armed in such manner.

After supper Mrs. Jett left her husband to do her chores, and slouched toward her tent with a significant, "I'm packin' an' I want to get done before dark."

Milly saw Follonsbee motion for Pruitt and Catlee to draw aside. When they had gone, in separate directions, Follonsbee approached Jett.

"Rand, it's the last deal an' the cards are runnin' bad," he said.

"Ahuh!" ejaculated the giant, without looking up.

"Your woman has stacked the deck on us," went on Follonsbee, without rancor. "We ain't blamin' you altogether for this mess."

"Hank, I'm talked out," replied Jett, heavily.

"You've been drinkin' too much," went on the other, in conciliatory tones, "but you're sober now an' I'm goin' to try once more. Will you listen?"

"I ain't deaf."

"You'd be better off if you was. . . . Now, Rand, here's the straight of it, right off the shoulder. You've done us dirt. But square up an' all will be as before. We've got another chance here for a big haul—four thousand hides if there's one, an' easy. Use your sense. It's only this greedy woman who's changed you. Beat some sense into her or chuck her in the river. It's man to man now. An' I'm tellin' you, Pruitt is a dirty little rebel rattlesnake. He'll sting. I'm puttin' it to you honest an' level-headed. If this goes on another day it'll be too late. We're riskin' a lot here. The hunters will find out we're not killin' buffalo. We ought to load up an' *move*."

"We're goin' to-morrow," replied Jett, gloomily.

"Who?"

"It's my outfit an' I'm movin'. If you an' Pruitt want to stay here I'll divide supplies."

"You're most obligin'," returned Follonsbee, sarcastically. "But I reckon if you divide anythin' it'll be money, outfit, an' all."

"There's where the hitch comes in," snarled Jett.

"Are you plumb off your head, man?" queried the other, in weary amaze. "You just can't do anythin' else."

"Haw! Haw!" guffawed Jett.

Follonsbee dropped his lean vulture face and paced to and fro, his hands locked behind his back. Suddenly he shouted for Pruitt. The little rebel came on the run.

"Andy, I've talked fair to Jett, an' it ain't no use," said Follonsbee. "He an' the woman are breakin' camp to-morrow."

"Early mawnin', hey?" queried Pruitt.

"Yes, an' he's offered to let us stay here with half the supplies. I told him if he divided anythin' it'd be money, outfit, an' all."

"Wal, what'd he say then?"

"That here was just where the hitch come in. I told him he couldn't do anythin' else but divide, an' then he haw-hawed in my face."

"You don't say. Wal, he ain't very perlite, is he? . . . Hank, I'm through talkin' nice to Jett. If I talk any more I'll shore have somethin' hard to say. Give him till mawnin' to think it over."

Pruitt's sulky temper was not in evidence during this

short interview. Milly could not see his face, but his tone and the poise of his head were unlike him.

"Will you fellars have a drink with me?" asked Jett, in grim disdain.

They walked off without replying. Milly peered round. Catlee leaned against a tree close by, within earshot, and the look he cast at Jett was illuminating. Jett was new to the frontier, though he had answered quickly to its evil influence. But otherwise he had not developed. The man's quick decline from honest living had been the easiest way to satisfy a naturally greedy soul. Drink, the rough life of the open, had paved the way. His taking to this frontier woman was perhaps the worst step. And now the sordid nature of him lowered him beneath these thieves, who had probably put the evil chances in his way. But Jett did not understand Western men, much less desperadoes such as Follonsbee and Pruitt manifestly were.

Darkness settled down over the camp and the river. The crickets and frogs were less in evidence with their chirping and trilling. The camp fire had died out, and soon the dim light in Jett's tent was extinguished. The lonely night seemed to envelop Milly and strike terror to her soul. What was the portent of the wild mourn of the wolves? Yet there came a mounting intuitive, irresistible hope—to-morrow she might be free. Somewhere within a few miles Tom Doan lay asleep, perhaps dreaming of her, as she was thinking of him.

Milly heard Catlee's stealthy tread. He had moved his bed near her wagon, and his presence there was significant of his unobtrusive guardianship. It relieved her distraught nerves, and soon after that her eyelids wearily closed.

Milly awoke with a start. The stars above were wan in a paling sky; a camp fire crackled with newly burning sticks; the odor of wood smoke permeated the air. The wagon in which she lay was shaking. Then she heard the pound of hoofs, the clink and rattle of harness, a low husky voice she recognized. Jett was hitching up.

With a catch in her breath and a gush of blood along her veins Milly raised herself out of her bed and peered over the side of the wagon. The dark, heavy form of Mrs. Jett could be discerned in the flickering light of fire; contrary to her usual phlegmatic action, she was moving with a celerity that spoke eloquently of the nature of that departure. Apparently none of the others were stirring. Milly moved to the other side of the wagon and peered down, just making out Catlee's bed under the cottonwood. A dark form appeared against the dim background. Milly saw it move, and presently satisfied herself that Catlee was sitting on his bed, pulling on his boots.

Jett's huge figure loomed up, passing the wagon. Milly dropped down, so she would not be seen. He spoke in the low, husky voice to the woman. She did not reply. Presently Milly heard again the soft thud of hoofs, coming closer, to cease just back of her wagon. Next she heard the creak and flop of leather. Jett was saddling the fast horses he used in hunting. Again Milly cautiously raised her head. She saw Jett in quick, sharp, decisive, yet nervous action. He haltered both horses to the back of the wagon, and slipped nose bags over their heads. The horses began to munch the oats in the bags.

In a moment more Jett approached the wagon and lifted something over the footboard, just as Milly sank back into her bed. His quick heavy breathing denoted a laboring under excitement. She smelled rum on him. He disappeared, and soon returned to deposit another pack in the back of the wagon. This action he repeated several times. Next Milly heard him fumbling with the wire that held the water keg to the wagon. He tipped the keg, and the slap and gurgle of water told of the quantity.

"Half full," he muttered to himself. "That'll do for to-day."

His heavy footsteps moved away, and then came sound of his hoarse whisper to the woman. She replied:

"Reckon they'll show up. We'll not get away so easy, if I know men in this country. You'd better keep a rifle in your hand."

"Boh!" burst out Jett, in disgusted doubt of her, himself and the whole situation.

"Eat an' drink now, pronto," she said. "We won't stop to wash an' take these things. I packed some."

The boil of the coffee pot could be heard, and then a hot sizzle as the water boiled over into the fire. Some one removed it. Again Milly peeped out the wagon side. Dawn was at hand. All was gray, shadowy, obscure beyond the trees, but near at hand it was light enough to see. Jett and the woman were eating. His rifle leaned against the mess box. They ate hurriedly, in silence.

Just then a low rumble like thunder broke the stillness of the morning. Deep, distant, weird, it denoted a thunderstorm to Milly. Yet how long and strangely it held on!

Jett lifted his big head like a listening deer.

"Stampede, by gosh! First one this summer. Lucky it's across the river."

"Stampede!" echoed the woman, slowly. "Hum! . . . Are there lots of buffalo across here?"

"They'd make a tolerable herd if they got bunched. I ain't in love with the idee. They might start the big herd on this side. We're aimin' to cross the prairie to the Red River. An' even if we had two days' start, a runnin' herd would catch us."

"I don't agree with you, Jett," remarked the woman. "Anyway, we're goin', buffalo or no buffalo."

Milly listened to the low, distant rumble. What a strange sound! Did it not come from far away? Did she imagine it almost imperceptibly swelled in volume? She strained to hear. It lessened, died away, began again, and though ever so faint, it filled her ears.

Imperceptibly the gray dawn had yielded to daylight. The Jetts had about finished their meal. Whatever was going to happen must befall soon. Milly strove to control her fearful curiosity. Her heart beat high. This issue mattered mightily to her. Peeping over the far side of her wagon, she saw Catlee sitting on his bed, watching the Jetts from his angle. He saw Milly. Under the brim of his sombrero his eyes appeared to be black holes. He motioned Milly to keep down out of sight. Instinctively she obeyed, sinking back to her bed; and then, irresistibly impelled, she moved to the other side, farther up under the low wagon seat, and peeped out from under it.

At that juncture Pruitt and Follonsbee strode from somewhere to confront the Jetts. Milly would have shrunk back had she not been as if chained. The little rebel struck terror to her heart. Follonsbee resembled, as always, a bird of prey, but now about to strike.

"Jett, you ain't bravin' it out?" asked Pruitt, cool and laconic. "Shore you ain't aimin' to leave heah without a divvy?"

"I'm leavin' two wagons, six hosses, an' most of the outfit," replied Jett, gruffly. He stared at Pruitt. Something was seeking an entrance into his mind.

"You're lucky to get that," snapped the woman.

"Listen to her, Hank," said Pruitt, turning to Follonsbee.

"I'm listenin', an' I don't have to hear no more. She stacked this deal," replied Pruitt's comrade, stridently. Only the timbre of his voice showed his passion; he was as slow and easy as Pruitt.

"Talk to me," shouted Jett, beginning to give way to the stress of a situation beyond him. "Let my wife——"

"Wife? Aw, hell," interposed Pruitt, contemptuously. "This Hardin woman ain't your wife any more'n she's mine. . . . Jett, you're yellow, an' you're shore talkin' to men who ain't yellow, whatever else they are."

Jett cursed low and deep fumed in his effort to confront these men on an equality. But it was not in him. Fiercely he questioned the woman, "Did you tell them we wasn't married—yet?"

"Reckon I did. It was when you was silly over this black-eyed step-daughter of yours," she replied suddenly.

Assuredly Jett would have struck her down but for the unforgettable proximity of Pruitt and Follonsbee. The latter laughed coarsely. Pruitt took a stride forward. His manner was careless, casual, but the set of muscles, the action of him, indicated something different.

"Jett, did *you* tell your woman you wanted to get rid of her—so's you could have your black-eyed wench?" demanded the little rebel, with all his insolent meanness. "You shore told us—an' you wasn't so orful drunk."

The woman seemed to tower and her face grew black.

"I didn't," yelled Jett.

Wordlessly the woman turned to question these accusers.

"Jett's a lyin' yellow skunk," declared Pruitt. "He shore meant to give the girl your place. 'Cause he wouldn't give her to me or Hank heah!"

"It's true," corroborated Follonsbee. "It's Jett an' not us who's lyin'. Why, I wouldn't lie to save both your dirty lives."

That convinced the woman, and she turned on Jett with incoherent fury. He tried to yell a break into her tirade; and not till he had seized her in brutal hands, to shake her as if she had been a rat, did she stop. Then, after a pause, in which she glared at him with the hate of a jade, she panted: "I'll put—that little hussy's eyes out. . . . An' Rand Jett—*you'll* never—get a dollar of this hide money!"

"Shut up or I'll mash your jaw!" he shouted, hoarsely.

"Haw! Haw!" laughed Follonsbee, in glee that seemed only in his tones. He did not move hand or foot.

"Jett, I'm shore hopin' we can leave you to this sweet lady," cut in Pruitt, "for you deserve it. But I'm feared your bull-headedness will aboot force our deal. . . . Once more an' last time, damn you—will you divvy hide-money, outfit, an' supplies, as you agreed?"

"Naw, I won't," declared Jett, fiercely. He looked a driven man; and strangely his gaze of hate was for the woman and not the man who menaced him.

"Then we'll take it all!" flashed Pruitt, ringingly.

In violent shock Jett wheeled to face Pruitt, at last with comprehension. What he saw turned his skin white back of his yellow beard. His large, hard, bright blue eyes suddenly fixed in wild stare on Pruitt. And he began to shake. Suddenly he dove for his rifle.

Milly's gaze had been riveted on Jett. Dimly she had seen Pruitt, but not to note look or action. Her fascinated spell broke to a horror of what was coming. Swiftly she dropped down to cover and wrapped her head in the blankets of her bed. Tightly she pulled them over ears and eyes, and twisted and rolled. And deep concussions seemed to beat at her brain. The wagon lurched. The blackness that enveloped her was not all from the blankets. Her senses seemed whirling dizzily. Then heart, pulse, thought returned to degree of discrimination.

She listened. There was no sound she could discern while under the folds of blankets. She was suffocating. She threw them off. Then, fearfully she lay there. All was still. No sound! A low thunder of stampeding buffalo floated across the river. Milly listened for voices. The camp appeared deserted. Had these men run off into the brakes? Sullen, sousing splashes in the river under the bank transfixed her into blank, icy horror. Something was ended. She could only wait, lying there in a tremble.

Suddenly she heard a soft step close to the wagon. Then Catlee's hat and face appeared over the side. He looked down at her with eyes the like of which Milly had never seen in a human.

"Lass, it's half over, but the worst's to come," he whispered, and with dark, gray gleaming gaze on her, bright, almost smiling, he dropped down out of her sight. He had not seen her desperation. He had not appealed to her to bear up under this tragedy. His look, his whisper, had made of her a comrade, brave to stand the outcome. Likewise they were a warning for herself to interpret, a suggestion of his imminent part in this terrible affair. They strung Milly's nerves to high tension. What might her part be? Compared with this experience, the West had dealt to women fatality and catastrophe which dwarfed hers. Life was sweet, never more so than at that moment, when memory of Tom Doan flashed back to her. She felt the grim and somber presence of death; she felt the imminence of further developments, sinister, harrowing, revolving more around her. Must she surrender to her emotions? Milly bit and choked them back. She needed all the strength, will, nerve possible to a woman; and in her extremity, with a racked heart, and unseeing eyes on the cottonwoods above, she propelled her spirit with the thought of Tom Doan, to endure or achieve anything.

Low voices diverted the current of her mind. Some persons, at least two, were returning from the river bank. Milly sat up, to look over the wagon-side. Follonsbee and Pruitt were entering the camp clearing. Neither Jett nor the woman was to be seen. Milly suffered no shock, she had not expected to see them. Pruitt was wet and muddy to his hips.

". . . Shore may as well stay heah an' hunt hides, same as the other outfits," he was saying.

"I'm ag'in' stayin'," replied Follonsbee.

"Wal, we won't argue aboot it. Shore I ain't carin' much one way or other," responded Pruitt.

They reached the camp fire, the burned-out sticks of which Pruitt kicked with a wet boot. Follonsbee held his hands over the heat, though they could not have been chilled. The morning was warm. Milly saw his hands quivering very slightly.

"Shore we ought to have got that job off our hands long ago," said Pruitt. "Wal, Hank, heah's my idee. Let's pull out, ford the river below, an' strike for the Brazos. There's buffalo, an' this main herd won't be long comin'."

"Suits me good," responded the other, in relief. "Now let's have everythin' clear. We've shared the hide money Jett's woman had. How about the rest of the outfit?"

"Same way, share an' share alike."

"Ahuh. The deal's made. Shake on it," said Follonsbee, extending his hand.

Pruitt met it halfway with his own.

"Hank, we stuck together for aboot two years, an' I reckon we're a good team."

"How about the girl?" suddenly demanded Follonsbee.

Their backs were turned to Milly, who heard this query with the sharp ears of expectation. She was fortified by her own resolve and the still hidden presence of Catlee.

"Wal, if I didn't forgit aboot our black-eyed wench!" ejaculated Pruitt, slapping his leg.

"Toss you for her—or cut the cards?" asked Follonsbee, with his sleek, narrow, beak-like head lowered.

"No, you won't. Yo're shore too lucky. . . . We'll share the girl same as the rest of the outfit."

"All right. It'll be a two-man outfit, half of everythin' for each—even the girl. Then we can't squabble. . . . But say, we forgot Catlee. Where the hell's he been?"

"Reckon he was scared. Mebbe he's runnin' yet."

"Nope. I tell you, Andy, your hate of Yanks has got

you figgerin' this Catlee wrong," protested Follonsbee.

"That farm hand!" retorted Pruitt, with infinite disgust.

"Farm hand nothin'," replied the other bluntly. "I don't know *what* he is, but he's got me figgerin'. We'd better give him a hoss an' pack an' turn him loose."

Pruitt pondered this suggestion for a moment and then somberly shook his head. That idea did not appeal to him, while at the same time it manifestly introduced another and uncertain element into the situation.

Milly heard quick, rustling footsteps behind her. Catlee appeared round the wagon, with a gun leveled low in his right hand. Follonsbee saw him first and let out a startled exclamation. Pruitt jerked up. Then he froze.

"Howdy, men!" was Catlee's greeting, in a voice these companions evidently had never heard him use before.

Follonsbee uttered a gasp of amazed conviction.

"Andy! I *told* you!"

Pruitt scarcely moved a muscle, unless in the flicker of an eyelash. He did not change expression. He hissed out, "Who'n hell are you *now?*" That was his swift acceptance of Follonsbee's reiterated hints.

"Small matter," replied Catlee, as with weapon quiveringly extended he sheered round squarely in front of Pruitt, "but if it'd please you to be acquainted with me at this late day—you can bow to Sam Davis."

"Ahuh! Late pard of the Youngers," retorted Follonsbee, going white in the face.

"Reckon I'm used to hard company," whipped out Catlee, stingingly, "but never yet took to sharin' innocent little girls!"

Pruitt suffered no suggestion of Follonsbee's weakening to the power of a name, whatever it was. The leveled weapon, covering him and his comrade, was the great factor in his reaction. Not for the slightest fraction of a second did he take his dancing, furious gaze from Catlee. The uselessness of more words seemed marked in his almost imperceptible gathering of muscular force. All the power of sight and mind was transfixed on Catlee's eyes, to read there the intent that preceded action. He chose an instant, probably the one in which Catlee decided, and like a flash threw his gun.

As it left his hip and snapped, Catlee's gun crashed. The force of the bullet knocked Pruitt flat.

"Hur-ry Hank!" he yelled, in fierce, wild tone of terrible realization, and flinging the empty weapon he had forgotten to load he lurched like a crippled panther to get his hands on Jett's rifle.

Milly saw only the intrepid Pruitt, but she heard Catlee's second shot and the sodden thud of Follonsbee falling. He made no outcry. Pruitt's actions were almost too swift to follow—so swift that Catlee missed him, as with spasmodic dive he grasped and carried Jett's rifle over the mess box. Up he sprang, grotesque, misshapen, yet wonderfully agile, to discharge the heavy rifle even as he received Catlee's fire square in his chest. Staggering backward, he dropped the weapon, his arms spread, and he seemed falling step by step. An awful blankness blotted out the ferocity of his crooked face. Step by step, he fell backward over the bank into the river. A sounding splash followed his disappearance.

Milly's set gaze wavered. A silence intervened. Her lungs seemed to expand. The appalling fixidity of her attention broke with a shock and she looked for Catlee. He lay on the ground beside the camp fire. His hand twitched—released the smoking gun. Milly leaped out of the wagon and ran to him.

She knelt. His hat was off, his face vague, changing. The gray storm of his eyes seemed fading.

"Oh—oh—Catlee!" cried Milly, poignantly.

"Good luck," he whispered. His lips set, his eyelids

fluttered—all his body quivered to a relaxation. He had been shot through the breast.

"My God! how awful! . . . He's dead! They're all dead. I'm left—alone. It's over. . . . Brave Catlee! Oh, he saved me! . . . But what can I do? I——"

Milly's outburst was silenced by the shrill neigh of one of the horses hitched to the wagon. It was a neigh that heralded sight or scent of another horse. Wild and sharp then pealed out a whistling answer from across the river.

Milly bounded erect to peer out under the cotton-woods, thrilling with joy. But her joy sustained a bewildering check, and it died when steadier glance revealed mounted Indians riding down into the river. For one moment Milly stared, biting her fingers in her horror; then the spirit born of these trying hours ran through her like a white flame, and climbing to the seat of the wagon she whipped up the reins.

Her instinct was to escape. She had no time to think of a better way. And the horses, restive, not wholly recovered from fright, needed no urging. They broke into trot, dragging the saddled animals behind the wagon. Out of the clearing, into the brakes they crashed, and were hard to hold. Road there was none, but a wide lane of crushed weeds and brush marked where Jett had driven the wagon in, and later had ridden to and fro on horseback. The team followed it and they tore through the bending clumps of brush that hung over it and bumped over logs. Branches of trees struck Milly as she passed, blinding her for a moment. When he could see clearly again the horses were no longer in the lane through the brush. They had swerved to one side or the other, she did not know which. But she kept her sense of direction: to the right was down river, and to the left was the prairie, the main herd of buffalo, and the camps of the hunters.

She must get out into the open quickly. If the Indians had not heard her drive away there would be a little time before they would strike out on her trail through the brakes.

"Oh, I forgot," she cried. "They heard the horse neigh." And with a sinking of her daring spirit she let the horses have free rein. They quickened their gait, but showed no sign of bolting. They wanted to get out of that jungle, and they broke a path through thickets, over rotten logs, and under matted hanging vines. Milly had all she could do to keep from being torn from her seat.

They got by the worst of the brakes and Milly saw light ahead low down through the trees, but it seemed to be in the wrong direction. She should turn more to the left. Her efforts to head the iron-jawed team in that direction were unavailing. They kept to a straight course, out into the light. But this open had deceived Milly, and probably the horses also. It was a wide bare strip of sand where a tributary of the Pease flowed in wet season. Here the horses slowed to a dragging walk, yet soon crossed the sand to enter the brakes again.

Here in the shade and dust, and the *mêlée* of threshing branches round her face, Milly lost all sense of the right direction. She realized her peril, yet did not despair. Something had always happened; it would happen to save her again.

Suddenly a crashing of brush in front of her stopped her heart. She almost fell back into the wagon. A huge brown buffalo bull tore ahead of her, passing to the left. Milly recovered. Then again she heard crashing ahead of her, to one side, and more at a distance. There were buffalo in the brakes.

Above the swish of brush and rattle of wagon and pound of hoofs she began to hear a low, rumbling thunder, apparently to the fore and her right.

"They said stampede!" she cried fearfully.

Her horses heard it and were excited, or else the scent and proximity of stray buffalo had been the cause of their faster, less regular gait. Milly essayed again to swerve them to the left, but in vain. And indeed that left side grew more and more impractical, owing to obstructions which shunted the horses in an opposite direction. Quite unexpectedly then they burst out of the brakes into open prairie.

Milly was as amazed as frightened. The plain was so dusty she could not see a mile, and strings of buffalo were disappearing into a yellow broken pall. They appeared to be loping in their easy, lumbering way. The thunder was louder now, though still a strange low roar, and it came out of the dust curtain which obscured the prairie. The horses, snorting, not liking dust or buffalo, loped for a mile, then slowed to a walk and halted. Milly tried to get her bearings. The whole horizon to fore and right was streaky with dust and moving buffalo. From behind her the line of river timber extended on her right to fade in the obscurity of dust. This established her position. She had crossed the brakes of the tributary and was now headed east. The buffalo were then coming out of the south and they were crossing the Pease. Milly realized that she was far out of her proper course and must make a wide turn to the left, cross the dry stream-bed, and then go up the river to the camps of the hide-hunters.

Suddenly she missed something. The two saddle horses! They had broken off in the rough ride. Milly looked back at the dark, ragged line of the timber from where she had come. The air was clearer that way. Movement and flash attracted her gaze. She saw animals run out into the open. Wild, lean, colored ponies with riders! They stretched out in swift motion, graceful, wild, incomparably a contrast to the horses of white hunters.

Milly realized she was being pursued by Indians.

Chapter XV

MILLY screamed at the horses and swung the lash, beating them into a gallop. The lightly loaded wagon lurched and bounced over the hummocky prairie, throwing her off the seat and from side to side. A heavy strain on the reins threatened to tear her arms from their sockets.

It was this physical action that averted a panic-stricken flight. The horses broke from gallop into run, and they caught up with scattered groups and lines of buffalo. Milly was in the throes of the keenest terror that had yet beset her, but she did not quite lose her reason. There were a few moments fraught with heart-numbing, blood-curdling sensations; which on the other hand were counteracted by the violence of the race over the prairie, straight for the straggling strings of the buffalo herd. The horses plunged, hurtling the wagon along; the wind, now tainted with dust and scent of buffalo, rushed into Milly's face and waved her hair; the tremendous drag on the reins, at first scarcely perceptible, in her great excitement, began to hurt hands, wrists, arms, shoulders in a degree that compelled attention. But the race itself, the flight, the breakneck pace across the prairie, with stampeding buffalo before and Comanche Indians behind—it was too great, too magnificent, too terrible to prostrate this girl. Opposed to all the fears possible to a girl was the thing roused in her by love, by example of a thief who had died to save her, by the marvel of the moment.

Milly gazed back over her shoulder. The Comanches had gained. They were not half a mile away, riding now in wide formation, naked, gaudy, lean, feathered, swift and wild as a gale of wind in the tall prairie grass.

"Better death among the buffalo!" cried Milly, and she turned to wrap both reins around her left wrist, to lash out with the whip, and to scream: *Run! Run! Run!*

Buffalo loped ahead of her, to each side and behind, in straggling groups and lines, all headed in the same direction as the vague denser bunches to the right. Here the dust pall moved like broken clouds, showing light and dark.

She became aware of increasing fullness in her ears. The low rumble had changed to a clattering trample, yet there seemed more. The sound grew; it came closer; it swelled to a roar; and presently she located it in the rear.

She turned. With startled gaze she saw a long, bobbing, black, ragged mass pouring like a woolly flood out over the prairie. A sea of buffalo! They were moving at a lope, ponderously, regularly, and the scalloped head of that immense herd crossed the line between Milly and the Comanches. It swept on. It dammed and blocked the way. Milly saw the vermillion paint on the naked bodies and faces of these savages as they wheeled their lean horses to race along with the buffalo.

Then thin whorls of rising dust obscured them from Milly's sight. A half mile of black bobbing humps moved between her and the Comanches. She uttered a wild cry that was joy, wonder, reverence, and acceptance of the thing she had trusted. Thicker grew the dust mantle; wider the herd; greater the volume of sound! The Comanches might now have been a thousand miles away, for all the harm they could do her. As they vanished in the obscurity of dust so also did they fade from Milly's mind!

Milly drove a plunging maddened team of horses in the midst of buffalo as far as the eye could see. Her intelligence told her that she was now in greater peril of death than at any time heretofore, yet, though her hair rose stiff and her tongue clove to the roof of her mouth, she could not feel the same as when Pruitt had parceled her, share and share with Follonsbee, or when those lean wild-riding Comanches had been swooping down on her. Strangely, though there was natural terror in the moment, she did not seem afraid of the buffalo.

The thick massed herd was on her left, and appeared to have but few open patches; to the fore and all on the other side there were as many gray spaces of prairie showing as black loping blotches of buffalo. Her horses were running while the buffalo were loping, thus she kept gaining on groups near her and passing them. Always they sheered away, some of the bulls kicking out with wonderful quickness. But in the main they gave space to the swifter horses and the lumbering wagon.

The dust rose in sheets now thin, now thick, and obscured everything beyond a quarter of a mile distant. Milly was surrounded, hemmed in, carried onward by a pondering moving medium. The trampling roar of hoofs was deafening, but it was not now like thunder. It was too close. It did not swell or rumble or roll. It roared.

A thousand tufted tails switched out of that mass, and ten times that many shaggy humps bobbed in sight. What queer sensation this action gave Milly—

queer above all the other sensations! It struck her as ludicrous.

The larger, denser mass on the left had loped up at somewhat faster gait than those groups Milly had first encountered. It forged ahead for a time, then gradually absorbed all the buffalo, until they were moving in unison. Slowly they appeared to pack together, to obliterate the open spaces, and to close in on the horses. This was what Milly feared most.

The horses took their bits between their teeth and ran headlong. Milly had to slack the reins or be pulled out of the seat. They plunged into the rear of the moving buffalo, to make no impression otherwise than to split the phalanx for a few rods and be kicked from all sides. Here the horses reared, plunged, and set out above the steady roar a piercing scream of terror. Milly had never before heard the scream of a horse. She could do nothing but cling to the loose reins and the wagon seat, and gaze with distended eyes. One of the white horses, Jett's favorite, plunged to his knees. The instant was one when Milly seemed to be clamped by paralysis. The other white horse plunged on, dragging his mate to his feet and into the race again.

Then the space around horses and wagons closed in, narrowed to an oval with only a few yards clear to the fore and on each side. Behind, the huge, lowered, shaggy heads almost bobbed against the wagon.

The time of supreme suspense had come to Milly. She had heard buffalo would run over and crush any obstruction in their path. She seemed about to become the victim of such a blind juggernaut. Her horses had been compelled to slacken their gait to accommodate that of the buffalo. They could neither forge ahead, nor swerve to one side or other, nor stop. They were blocked, hemmed in, and pushed. And their terror was extreme. They plunged in unison and singly; they screamed and bit at the kicking buffalo. It was a miracle that leg or harness or wheel was not broken.

A violent jolt nearly unseated Milly. The wagon had

been struck from behind. Fearfully she looked back. A stupid-faced old bull, with shaggy head as large as a barrel, was wagging along almost under the end of the wagon-bed. He had bumped into it. Then the space on the left closed in until buffalo were right alongside the wheels. Milly wrung her hands. It would happen now. A wheel would be broken, the wagon overturned, and she . . . A big black bull rubbed his rump against the hind wheel. The iron tire revolving fast scraped hard on his hide. Quick as a flash the bull lowered head and elevated rear, kicking out viciously. One of his legs went between the spokes. A crack rang out above the trample of hoofs. The bull went down, and the wagon lifted and all but upset. Milly could not cry out. She clung to the seat with all her strength. Then began a terrific commotion. The horses plunged as the drag on the wagon held them back. Buffalo began to pile high over the one that had fallen, and a wave of action seemed to permeate all of them.

Those rushing forward pounded against the hind wheels, and split round them until the pressure became so great that they seemed to lift the wagon and carry it along, forcing the horses ahead.

Milly could not shut her eyes. They were fascinated by this heaving mass. The continuous roar, the endless motion toward certain catastrophe, were driving her mad. Then this bump and scrape and lurch, this frightful proximity of the encroaching buffalo, this pell-mell pandemonium behind, was too much for her. The strength of hands and will left her. The wagon tilted, turned sidewise, and stopped with a shock. An appalling sound seemed to take the place of motion. The buffalo behind began to lift their great heads, to pile high over those in front, to crowd in terrific straining wave of black, hideous and irresistible, like an oncoming tide. Heads and horns and hair, tufted tails, a dense, rounded, moving, tussling sea of buffalo bore down on the wagon. The sound was now a thundering roar. Dust hung low. The air was suffocating. Milly's nose and lungs seemed to close. She fell backward over the seat and fainted.

When she opened her eyes it was as if she had come out of a nightmare. She lay on her back. She gazed upward to sky thinly filmed over by dust clouds. Had she slept?

Suddenly she understood the meaning of motion and the sensation of filled ears. The wagon was moving steadily, she could not tell how fast, and from all sides rose a low, clattering roar of hoofs.

"Oh, it must be—something happened—the horses went on—the wagon did not upset!" she cried, and her voice was indistinct.

But she feared to rise and look out. She listened and felt. There was a vast difference. The wagon moved on steadily, smoothly, without lurch or bump; the sound of hoofs filled the air, yet not loudly or with such a cutting trample. She reasoned out that the pace had slowed much. Where was she? How long had she lain unconscious? What would be the end of this awful race?

Nothing happened. She found her breathing easier and her nostrils less stopped by dust and odor of buffalo. Her mouth was parched with thirst. There was a slow, torrid beat of her pulse. Her skin appeared moist and hot. Then she saw the sun, quite high, a strange magenta hue, seen through the thin dust clouds. It had been just after daylight when she escaped from Jett's camp. Ah! she remembered Catlee!—Sam Davis, one of Younger's clan! . . . Hours had passed and she was still surrounded by buffalo. The end had not come then; it had been averted, but it was inevitable. What she had passed through! Life was cruel. Hers had been an unhappy fate. Suddenly she thought of Tom Doan, and life, courage, hope surged with the magic of love. Something had happened to save her.

Milly sat up. She saw gray prairie—and then, some

fifty yards distant, the brown shaggy bodies of buffalo, in lazy lope. The wagon was keeping the same slow speed. Milly staggered up to lean against the seat and peer ahead. Wonderful to see—Jett's white team was contentedly trotting along, some rods in the rear of straggling buffalo. She could scarcely believe what she saw. The horses were no longer frightened.

On the other side wider space intervened before buffalo covered the gray prairie. She could see a long way—miles, it seemed—and there were as many black streaks of buffalo as gray strips of grass. To the fore Milly beheld the same scene, only greater in extent. Buffalo showed as far as sight could penetrate, but they were no longer massed or moving fast.

"It's not a stampede," Milly told herself in sudden realization. "It never was. . . . They're just traveling. They don't mind the wagon—the horses—not any more. . . . Oh, I shall get out!"

The knotted reins hung over the brake, where she had left them. Milly climbed to the driver's seat and took them up.

The horses responded to her control, not in accelerated trot, but by a lifting of ears and throwing of heads. They were glad to be under guidance again. They trotted on as if no buffalo were near. It amazed Milly, this change. But she could tell by the sweat and froth and cakes of dust on them that they had traveled far and long before coming to this indifference.

Milly did not drive the horses, though she held the reins taut enough for them to feel she was there; she sat stiff in the seat, calling to them, watching and thrilling, nervously and fearfully suspicious of the moving enclosure which carried her onward a prisoner. Time passed swiftly. The sun burned down on her. And the hour came when the buffalo lumbered to a walk.

They were no different from cattle now, Milly thought. Then the dust clouds floated away and she could see over the backs of buffalo on all sides, out to the boundless prairie. The blue sky overhead seemed to have a welcome for her. The horses slowed down. Gradually the form of the open space surrounding the wagon widened, changed its shape as buffalo in groups wandered out from the herd. Little light tawny calves appeared to run playfully into the open. They did not play as if they were tired.

Milly watched them with a birth of love in her heart for them, and a gratitude to the whole herd for its service to her. No doubt now that she was saved! Nearly a whole day had passed since the Indians had seen her disappear, and leagues of prairie had been covered. The direction she was being taken was north, and that she knew to be favorable to her. Sooner or later these buffalo would split or pass by her; then she would have another problem to consider.

But how interminably they traveled on! No doubt the annual instinct to migrate northward had been the cause of this movement. If they had stampeded across the Pease, which had not seemed to her the case, they had at once calmed to a gait the hunters called their regular ranging mode of travel. Her peril at one time had been great, but if this herd had caught her in a stampede she would have been lost.

The stragglers that from time to time came near her paid no attention to the horses or wagon. They were as tame as cows. They puffed along, wagging their big heads, apparently asleep as they traveled. The open lanes and aisles and patches changed shape, closed to reopen, yet on the whole there was a gradual widening. The herd was spreading. Milly could see the ragged rear a couple of miles back, where it marked its dark line against the gray prairie. Westward the mass was thick and wide; it was thin and straggly on the east. Northward the black creeping tide of backs extended to the horizon.

Milly rode on, escorted by a million beasts of the plain, and they came to mean more to her than she could understand. They were alive, vigorous, self-sufficient; and they were doomed by the hide-hunters. She could not think of anything save the great, shaggy, stolid old bulls, and the sleeker smaller cows, and the tawny romping calves. So wonderful an adventure, so vast a number of hoofed creatures, so strangely trooping up out of the dusty river brakes to envelop her, so different when she and they and the horses had become accustomed to one another—these ideas were the gist of her thoughts. It was a strange, unreal concentration on buffalo.

The afternoon waned. The sun sank low in the west and turned gold. A time came when Milly saw with amaze that the front leagues of buffalo had disappeared over the horizon, now close at hand. They had come to the edge of the slope on river brake. What would this mean to her?

When the wagon reached the line where the woolly backs had gone down out of sight Milly saw a slope, covered with spreading buffalo, that ended in a winding green belt of trees. In places shone the glancing brightness of water. Beyond, on a level immense plain, miles and miles of buffalo were moving like myriads of ants. They were spreading on all sides, and those in the lead had stopped to graze. The immensity of the scene, its beauty and life and tragedy, would remain in Milly's memory all her days. She saw the whole herd, and it was a spectacle to uplift her heart. While the horses walked on with the buffalo streaming down that slope Milly gazed in rapt attention. How endless the gray level prairie below! She understood why the buffalo loved it, how it had nourished them, what a wild lonely home it was. Faint threads of other rivers crossed the gray; and the green hue was welcome contrast to the monotony. Duskily red the sun was setting, and it cast its glow over the plain and buffalo, stronger every moment. In the distance purple mantled the horizon. Far to the northwest a faint dark ruggedness of land or cloud seemed limned against the sunset-flushed sky. Was that land? If so it was the Llano Estacado.

Milly's horses reached the belt of trees, and entered a grove through and round which the buffalo were traveling. She felt the breaking of the enclosure of beasts that had so long encompassed her. It brought a change of thoughts. She was free to let the remainder of the herd pass. Driving down, behind a thick clump of cottonwoods she turned into a green pocket, and halted. Wearily the horses stood, heaving, untempted by the grass. On each side of Milly streams and strings and groups of buffalo passed to go down into the river, from which a loud continuous splashing rose. She waited, watching on one side, then the other. The solid masses had gone by; the ranks behind thinned as they came on; and at last straggling groups with many calves brought up the rear. These hurried on, rustling the bush, on to splash into the shallow ford. Then the violence of agitated water ceased; the low trample of hoofs ceased.

Silence! It was not real. For a whole day Milly's ears had been filled and harassed by a continuous trample, at first a roar, then a clatter, then a slow beat, beat, beat of hoofs, but always a trample. She could not get used to silence. She felt lost. A rush of sensations seemed impending. But only a dreamy stillness pervaded the river bottom, a hot, drowsy, thick air, empty of life. The unnaturally silent moment flung at her the loneliness and wildness of the place. Alone! She was lost on the prairie.

"Oh, what shall I do now?" she cried.

There was everything to do—to care for the horses, and for herself, so to preserve strength; to choose a direction, and to travel on and on, until she found a road that would lead her to some camp or post. Suddenly she sank down in a heap. The thought of the enormous problem crushed her for a moment. She was in the throes of a reaction.

"But I mustn't *think*," she whispered, fiercely. "I must *do*!"

And she clambered out of the wagon. The grove sloped down to the green bench where she had waited for the buffalo to pass. Grass was abundant. The horses would not stray. She moved to unhitch them, and had begun when it occurred to her that she would have to hitch them up again. To this end she studied every buckle and strap. Many a time she had helped round horses on the farm. The intricacies of harness were not an entire mystery to her. Then she had watched Jett and Catlee hitch up this team. Still, she studied everything carefully. Then she unbuttoned the traces and removed the harness. The horses rolled in a dusty place which the buffalo had trampled barren, and they rose dirty and yellow to shake a cloud from their backs. Then with snorts they trotted down to the water.

Milly was reminded of her own burning thirst, and she ran down to the water's edge, where, unmindful of its muddy color, she threw herself flat and drank until she could hold no more. "Never knew—water—could taste so good," she panted. Returning to the wagon, she climbed up in it to examine its contents. She found a bag of oats for the horses, a box containing utensils for cooking, another full of food supplies, a bale of blankets, and lastly an ax and shovel.

"Robinson Crusoe had no more," said Milly to herself, and then stood aghast at her levity. Was she not lost on the prairie? Might not Indians ride down upon her? Milly considered the probabilities. "God has answered my prayer," she concluded, gravely, and dismissed fears for the time being.

In the box of utensils she found matches, which were next to food in importance, and thus encouraged she lifted out what she needed. Among the articles of food were a loaf of bread and a bag of biscuits. Suddenly her mouth became flooded with saliva and she had to bite into a biscuit. There were also cooked meat and both jerked venison and buffalo. Salt and pepper, sugar, coffee, dried apples she found, and then did not explore the box to the uttermost.

"I'll not starve, anyway," murmured Milly.

Next she gathered dry bits of bark and wood, of which there was abundance, and essayed to start a fire. Success crowned her efforts, though she burned her fingers. Then, taking up the pail, she descended the bank to the river and filled it with water, which was not clarifying in the slow current. Returning, she poured some into the coffee pot and put that in the edge of the fire. Next, while waiting for the water to boil she cut strips of the cooked buffalo meat and heated them in a pan. She had misgivings about what her cooking might be. Nevertheless, she sat down presently and ate as heartily as ever before in her life.

Twilight had fallen when she looked up from the last task. The west was rose with an afterglow of sunset. All at once, now that action had to be suspended, she was confronted with reality. The emotion of reality!

"Oh, I'm lost—alone—helpless!" she exclaimed. "It's growing dark. I was always afraid of the dark."

And she shivered there through a long moment of feeling. She would be compelled to think now. She could not force sleep. How impossible to fall asleep! Panthers, bears, wildcats, wolves lived in these river brakes. She felt in her coat for the little derringer. It was gone. She had no weapons save the ax, and she could not wield that effectively.

Yet she did not at once seek the apparent security of her bed in the wagon. She walked about, though close by. She peered into the gathering shadows. She listened. The silence had been relieved by crickets and frogs. Slowly the black night mantled the river bottom and the trains of stars twinkled in the blue dome.

The presence of the horses, as they grazed near, brought something of comfort, if not relief. She remembered a dog she had loved. Rover—if she only had him now! Then she climbed into the wagon, and without removing even her boots she crawled into the blankets. They had been disarranged in the rough ride. She needed them more to hide under than for warmth. The soft night seemed drowsily lulling.

Her body cried out with its aches and pains and weariness, with the deep internal riot round her heart, with throb of brain. Not all at once could she lie still. But gradually began a slow sinking, as if she were settling down, down, and all at once she lay like a log. It was too warm under the blanket, yet when she threw it back and saw the white stars, so strange, watchful, she grew more aware of her plight and covered her face again. At length her body relaxed to the point where it was no longer dominating with its muscular sensations. Then her mind grew active— reverted to the terrible tragedy of Jett's outfit. Catlee! . . . All the time he had watched over her. He had killed for her—and died for her. A man who confessed he had never been anything else than bad! Something great loomed in Milly's simple mind. Could Jett have had any good in him? . . . She prayed for their souls.

They had left her alone, and she must find her way— whither? And into that dark gulf of mind flashed the thought and the vision of Tom Doan. Milly began to weep. It was too terrible, the remembrance of him, and his love and kisses, of his offer of marriage and his plan for their home. Terrible to dwell upon when she was lost in the prairie. She might never see him again! But she must try with all her power to find her way out.

"I—will try—for him!" she sobbed, and remembered her prayers. Then grief and worry succumbed to exhaustion; she drifted into slumber.

The singing of birds awakened Milly. The sun had risen; the green leaves were fluttering with a silken rustle. It took a moment for realization of her situation to rush into thought. Yet the darkness of mind, the old reluctance to return to consciousness, was absent this morning.

When she got to her knees, and knelt there, stretching her bruised and cramped muscles, she looked over the wagon to see the white horses grazing near under the cottonwoods. Sleek gray deer were grazing with them, as tame as cattle. A rabbit crossed the aisle of green. The morning held a strange bright beauty and peace.

Milly brushed out her tangled short curls. Her face was burned from the wind and sun of yesterday's ride. Then she climbed out of the wagon, ready for the day. She did not have to dress, and she thought bathing her face might make the sunburn worse.

First she put a quart of oats in each nose bag, and carried them out to the horses. She did not need to go far. Both horses saw her and came to meet her; and slipping the nosebags in place, she led them to the wagon and haltered them. Breakfast did not take long to prepare and eat. Then she cleaned the utensils, packed them away in the box, shook out her blankets, and rolled them. This left the task which worried her—that of hitching up.

But when she came to undertake it she found that she remembered where every part of the harness belonged. To lift the heavy wagon tongue and hold it while she snapped the hooks into rings required all her strength.

"There!" she muttered, with something of pride and wonder. "Now what?"

Was the wagon all right? She walked around it, as she had seen Jett do. One spoke had been broken out of the left hind wheel; other than that she could not see any damage. Jett had greased the wagon wheels the day before his intended departure. Nothing more to do but start! Milly was almost overcome at the thought. It seemed incredible that she would dare to drive across the prairie.

"I can't stay here. I'd be as badly off as on the

move," she burst out, desperately. "Oh, I must go! But where—how?"

She wrung her hands and fought her fears. A terrible problem confronted her. Yet was it as perilous as when she was practically a prisoner in Jett's outfit. Again she remembered that her prayers had been answered. Suppose she was only a timid weak girl? Could she not make herself do what any boy might do? Once and for all she drove herself passionately into a spirit of daring and faith. She resolved to feel these, even though she had to endure agonies of dread.

Then she plumped to her knees before a little bare spot of sand, and gazing down at it she thought with all her might. Not for nothing had she been keen to observe men in camp, when they talked about roads, trails, places. Jett had been poor at direction and location, but Follonsbee had the whole buffalo country in his mind. Milly had seen him draw maps in the dirt. To this end she took up a stick.

"The west is there," she said thoughtfully. "I saw the sun set. Then the north is there. Northwest is my direction. It was ten days' travel from Pease River to Sprague's Post. . . . Here's the Pease."

And she drew a line in the sand.

"Yesterday I came thirty miles—maybe forty, almost due north, to this stream. Then I'm here." She made a dot in the sand, and another line representing the stream. "I don't dare try to find my way back to the buffalo camps. I might meet the Indians. I must not follow this stream west. I must cross it and head northwest. I must cross every stream I meet. When I reach one too deep to ford I must follow along it till I find a place."

Milly's reasoning was the result of her experience with the Jett outfit. It took no particular degree of intelligence to calculate about where she was on the prairie and what to do to get out. The great task was to accomplish what her judgment dictated. She had traveled enough over the untrodden prairie to have some faint conception of the enormity of what faced her. Thought of meeting with buffalo-hunters persistently flaunted hopes. They encouraged her, but she could not trust to them. This Texas prairie covered a vast space, and in it she was lost.

"That's all!" she said, blankly.

The moment of decision had come. Milly drew a deep breath and flung wide her arms, with hands clenching. How she hated to leave the apparent protection of these friendly cottonwoods! Then, with a great throb in her breast, she turned to mount the wagon.

Not reluctant indeed were the horses. They had grazed and drunk their fill and they knew their noses were pointed homeward, away from the buffalo fields. Milly had all she could do to hold them. She drove out of the grove, to the right where the buffalo had worn a wide trodden belt down to the stream. The last fifty yards were quite downhill. Milly reined in to scrutinize her first obstacle of the day.

Thousands of buffalo had forded the stream here. Far as she could see, the banks on both sides were trodden fresh and dark with tracks. At this point the stream was perhaps three feet deep and forty wide; nothing for strong and nimble buffalo to ford. But these buffalo had not been hampered with a wagon. Still, the crossing was not especially bad. Jett would not have given it a second glance. He would have plunged across. The sandy bottom would assuredly be hard packed. Milly had only to start right, not too carefully, and to keep the horses going.

She threw on the brake and called to the horses. "Get up! Whity! Specks! . . . Easy now!"

They trotted down the slope—faster—faster. Milly leaned back on the reins. Her face blanched. Her teeth clenched. It was fearful, yet it roused defiance. She could drive them. They were eager, unafraid. The wagon propelled them. Plunge! the water crashed and splashed high. And the wagon bounced after them, to souse into the stream, over the front wheels. Milly was deluged. For an instant she could not see for water in her eyes, for the flying spray. But she called to the horses. They took the stream at a trot. It was no deeper than their knees, and they sent sheets of muddy water ahead of them. The opposite bank was low, easy for them; and Milly, before she realized it, pulled up on the level open prairie.

"Easy, and I got a bath!" she cried, exultantly. "Oh, Whity and Specks, I love you!"

She searched for her scarf to wipe her wet face and hair. But it, too, like her little gun, was gone. She had lost it. No! She recalled that she had left it tied on the hoop of the wagon cover in Jett's camp. The memory startled her. Suppose Tom Doan should at last find Jett's camp and see her red scarf. But that misery for him could never be. The Indians would have made blackened embers of that camp.

Milly took her direction from the sun and drove out upon the prairie. It was a gray, beautiful plain, luxuriant with ripened grass, sloping very gently to the north. Far to the eastward she espied the black horizon—wide line of buffalo. They had grazed down the stream. In the bright sunlight the whole panorama was splendid and stirring to Milly.

The horses started at a trot, and in the thick grass slowed to a steady brisk walk. The wagon was light, the ground level; and this powerful team had no serious task ahead of them, if they were only guided aright. Milly was excited, thrilled, and yet troubled. The adventure was tremendous, but the responsibility too great except for moments of defiance or exaltation. She could not all the time remain keyed up with a spirit that was unquenchable.

Several miles of travel brought her to the summit of the gradual slope of valley, and here, as on the side from which she had come, she obtained a commanding view of the surrounding country. It was grand, but she had eyes only for the northwest. Across the leagues of billowy prairie, so gray and monotonous and lonely, there stood a purple escarpment, remote and calling. It was the Llano Estacado. Milly recognized it, and seemed for an instant to forget the sense of being lost. But it was far away, and the northern end disappeared in purple haze. On the other hand it was a landmark ever present from high points, and somewhere between it and her present position ran the road of the buffalo-hunters.

To her left meandered the green line of trees, like a fringed ribbon on the soft gray of prairie, and it headed toward the Staked Plain, where she knew all these Texas streams had their source.

"I could reach the road to-day or to-morrow, if I drove straight west," soliloquized Milly.

It was a sore temptation, but her good sense forbade her take such added risk. The Comanches were between her and the buffalo camps. She must aim diagonally across the prairie, toward the extreme northwest corner of the escarpment, and perhaps four or five days she would strike the road. Then she would know the camping grounds, and would surely fall in with oncoming hunters or outgoing freighters. To find water at night, and to cross such streams as she met—these were her present problems.

Meanwhile, as she drove on, thinking only of this incredible journey, she could not help seeing and being momentarily thrilled by the wild creatures of the prairie.

Sleek gray, white-rumped antelope scarcely bothered to trot out of her path, and with long ears erect they watched her pass. Wild? These beautiful prairie deer were not wild. Milly believed she could in time have had them eating out of her hand, like she had the squirrels and birds at the Pease River camp. It was men who made animals wild.

She ranged the wide gray expanse for sight of buffalo. There were none. She saw a band of coyotes sneaking round the antelope. Farther on she espied a gaunt wolf, almost white, watching her from a ridge-top. Rabbits were always scurrying from before the horses, and prairie birds flitted out of the grass. Once Milly saw a red hawk poised in midair, fluttering its wings with marvelous rapidity, and then it shot down like a streak, to strike the grass and rise with a tiny animal in its talons. Always beauty and life present, and with them, cruelty—death!

Milly drove from early morning until an hour before sunset, when she reached the only water of the day. It was a pond in a shady stream-bed. There were fringes of hackaberry brush along the banks, but no sheltering trees. Farther west some six or eight miles she thought she espied the green of timber, but that was far away and off her line of direction. She must take what afforded; and to this end she unhitched, turned the horses loose, and made the simple preparations for her own wants.

Whity and Specks, as she had christened the horses, after drinking at the pond returned to linger near the wagon. They manifested extraordinary interest in Milly and even got in her way.

"What's the matter with you white-faced beggars?" she asked. "It's oats you want, yes? Well, I'm not going to let you eat all the oats right away."

Yet she was not proof against their nosing round her. Long had she been gentle and kind to these horses— the more so because of Jett's brutality. They knew her well, and now that she was master they began to prove the devotion of dumb brutes. Milly gave them sparingly of the oats, and petted them, and talked the more because solitude had begun to impinge upon her mind.

This sunset hour found her tired after the long day's drive. With change of action, followed by food and drink she needed, there came a rally of spirits. Darkness soon hid the lonely, limitless expanse from Milly's gaze, and then it seemed the night was lonelier. Only a faint murmur of insects! She would have welcomed a mourn of wolf, or even a cry of panther. A slight breeze fanned the red embers of the meager fire. She went to bed afraid of the silence, the night, afraid of sleep, yet she could not keep her eyes open or stay the drowsy fading away of senses.

Next morning Milly was up early, and on the way before sunrise. She started well. But at the end of the first hour she ran into rough prairie, hindering travel. The luxuriant prairie grass failed and the gray earth carried only a scanty covering. The horses plowed up dust that rose and blew back upon her; the sun grew hot and glaring; and there was a wide area of shallow washes, ditches, gullies, like the depressions of a washboard. Having plodded miles into this zone, she could not turn back, unless absolutely balked, so she applied herself to careful driving, and kept on, true as possible to the distant purple landmark.

The strong horses, used to a heavy hand, could not altogether be controlled by Milly, and they plunged into many places without her sanction. What with holding the reins as best she could, and constant heed to brake and distance, and worry lest she would damage a wheel, she was in grievous straits most of that day. It passed swiftly, swallowed up in miles of hard going, and left no time for scanning the prairie or fearful imaginings. It was work.

Toward evening she drew out of this zone and came presently to good grass once more, and just at dusk hauled up to a timber belt that bordered water. The thirsty horses stamped to get down to it. Milly labored to unhitch them, and when the task was done she sank to the ground to rest. But she was driven to secure firewood while there was light enough. She felt too tired to eat, yet she knew she must eat, or else fail altogether of strength. The long hanging to the reins was what had exhausted Milly. Her hands hurt, her arms ached, her shoulders sagged. Driving that iron-mouthed team was a man's job. Milly was no weakling, but her weight and muscular force were inadequate to the demand of such driving.

Supper, bed, night, sleep—they all passed swiftly, and again the sun rose. Milly could not find a place to ford the stream. It was not a depth of water that prevented, but high banks unsafe to attempt. For miles she drove along it, glad of the green foliage and singing birds and wild creatures, and especially glad that its course for most of the morning ran a little west of north. When, however, it made an abrupt turn to the west, she knew she must cross. She essayed the best ford she could find, made it safely, wet, shaken, frightened, and nearly pulled apart. On that far side she rested in the shade, and wept while she ate.

When about to start again she remembered that the men had never passed a stream or pond without watering the horses. Whereupon she took the bucket and went down to fill it. Four trips were necessary to satisfy the thirst of Whity and Specks. She had done well.

"We had two dry camps between Sprague's and the Pease," she said, and thought she must not forget that.

The afternoon drive began favorably. The sun was somewhat hazed over, reducing the heat; a level prairie afforded smooth travel; the horses had settled down into steady stolid work. The miles came slowly, but surely.

Milly's courage had not failed, but she was beset by physical ills, and the attendant moods, fancies, thoughts that could not everlastingly be overcome. She grew to hate the boundless prairieland, so barren of life, of any color but gray, of things that might mitigate the deceit of distance. Nothing save gray level and purple haze! It wore on her, ever flinging at her the attributes of the prairie openness, a windy vastness, empty of sound, movement, the abode of solitude, the abode of loneliness. Lonely, lonely land! She was as much lost as ever. There was no road, no river, no camp, no mountain, only the dim upflung false Llano Estacado, unattainable as ever.

But while Milly succumbed to her ills and her woes the horses plodded on. They knew what they had to accomplish, and were equal to it. They crowded the hours and miles behind them, and bore Milly to another watercourse, a wide glade-bordered enlargement of a stream, where ducks and cranes and kingfishers gave life to the melancholy scene.

While she performed her tasks the lake changed from blue to gold, and at last mirrored the rose of sunset sky. Then dusk fell sadly, and night came, dark, lonely, pierced by the penetrating trill of frogs and the dismal cry of a water fowl. They kept Milly awake and she could not shake the encroachment of morbid thoughts. Where was she? What would become of her? The vast gloomy prairie encompassed her, held her a prisoner, threatened her with madness. She had feared Indians, rivers, accidents, but now only the insupportable loneliness. Would she not die of it and be eaten by buzzards? The stars that had been so beautiful, watching, helpful, now seemed pitiless, remote, aloof, with their pale eyes on her, a girl lost on the endless prairie. What was beyond those stars? Not a soul, no kindly great spirit to guide her out of this wilderness? Milly prayed once more.

She dragged herself from bed next day, long after sunrise, and had spirit to begin the ordeal, if her flesh was weak.

Whity and Specks waited in camp for their oats. Milly scorned herself for dreading they would run away, leaving her utterly alone. She fed them and caressed them, and talked as if they were human. "You belong to me," she said. "I was Jett's stepdaughter. He's gone. And you're mine. . . . If you ever get me out of this——"

But she did not think she would ever get out now, unless Providence remembered her again. She had no hunger. A fever consumed her and she drank copiously of water. Hitching up was a dragging job. The heavy wagon tongue nearly broke her back. At last she was in the driver's seat. Whity and Specks started of their own accord, splashed across the shallow lake, and pulled up on the gray flat expanse.

Milly was either ill or almost spent, she did not know which. She had power to sit up, hold the reins, guide the horses toward that futile illusive landmark days away on the horizon, but she could not control her mind.

The wandering roll of prairie-land mocked her with its shining gray distances, its illusive endlessness, its veils of heat. The hot sun rose, glared down, slanted to the west, and waned. She found no water that sunset. The horses had no drink. Milly mixed their oats with water from the keg. Hunger exceeded all her sensations, even the pains; and tenaciously she clung to her one idea of effort, to keep trying, to follow judgment she had made at the outset. She ate, and crawled into her wagon-bed, no longer afraid of night and loneliness. So tired—so tired she wanted to die!

But the sun awakened her and the will to go on survived. The faithful horses waited, whinnying at her approach. Mechanically she worked, yet was aware of clumsiness and pain; that she must water them that day. The prairie smoked with heat. It beckoned, flaunted, slanted to the hot steely sky. She closed her eyes and slept with the reins in her hands; she awakened to jolt of wagon and crunching of stone. Thunder rumbled out of the sky and clouds obscured the sun. She drove into a storm, black, windy, with driving sheets of cool rain and white zigzag ropes of lightning, crashing thunder, long roll across the heavens. She was drenched to the skin and strangely refreshed. That fiery band round her head had snapped and gone. The horses splashed into a buffalo-wallow and drank of the fresh rain water.

Away the storm rolled, purple clouds and pall of

drifting gray and sheets of flame. The north showed blue again, and presently the sun shone. The horses steamed, the prairie smoked. Milly's clothes dried as the gray miles passed behind the tireless team.

The day's journey ended at a river, and as if her troubles need be multiplied, it was unfordable at that point. Milly camped. And the morning found her slower, stiffer, yet stern to go on. This river, too—could it have been the Louisiana Red?—had a northwest trend. All day she followed it, often in the shade of trees. No tracks, no trails, no old camps—the region was like a luxuriant barren land.

Next morning she found a disused buffalo ford. The tracks were old. They stirred her sluggish blood, her submerged hopes. She gained a little therefrom. If only she could drop the reins and rest her hands, her arms! But the faithful horses had to be guided. Would she ever come to a road? Was this whole world devoid of the manifestations of travel? Miles and miles, as gray, as monotonous as a dead sea!

Then she drove into a zone of buffalo carcasses, and was startled into wonder, hope, wild thought. Where was she? Fifty—maybe a hundred miles east of the Staked Plain, and still lost! These carcasses were black and dried; they had no odor; they were ghastly heaps of bones and hides. She drove ten miles across this belt of death and decay; and no sign of horse or wagon cheered her aching sight.

Milly lost track of hours, days, time. Sunset, a camp by water, black night with hateful stars, the false dawn, day with its gray leagues and blistering sun, the white horses forever moving on and on and on, night, blackness, light once more, and horrible weary pangs.

"What's this?" cried Milly, and wide flew her eyes. She was lying back in the wagon, where she had fallen from faintness. She remembered. It had been early morning. But now the sun was high. The wagon creaked, swayed, moved on to strange accompaniment—*clip-clop, clip-clop, clip-clop*. The horses were

trotting on hard road. Was she dreaming? She closed her eyes the better to listen. Clip-clop, clip-clop, clip-clop! This was no lying trick of her jaded ears, worn out from silence.

"Oh—thank Heaven!" panted Milly. "It's a road—a road!" And she struggled to rise. Gray endless prairie, as always, but split to the horizon by a white hard road! She staggered to the seat. But driving was not necessary. The reins were looped round the brake. Whity and Specks needed no guidance now, no urging, no help. They were on the homeward stretch. With steady clip-clop they trotted, clicking off the miles. Whity was lame and Specks had a clanging shoe, but these were small matters.

Milly sank down overwhelmed with joy. On the Fort Elliott road! The Llano Estacado showed no longer the deceiving purple of distance. It showed gray and drab, shadowy clefts, rock wall and canyons. She forced herself to eat and drink, though the dried meat and bread were hard to swallow. She must brace up. Many were the buffalo-hunters who traveled this road. Surely before the hour was gone she would see a white wagon on the horizon. Milly lifted her head to gaze backward, toward the south, and then forward toward the north. The prairie was still a lonely land. Yet how different!

She rested, she thought, she gazed the hours away; and something came back to her.

Afternoon waned and sunset came; and with the fading of rosy and golden light the horses snorted their scent of water. Milly was stronger. Hope had wonderfully revived her. And she called to the horses.

Another horizon line reached! It was the crest of one of the prairie slopes. Long had it been unattainable, hiding while it beckoned onward. A green-mantled stream crossed just below. Milly's aching and exhausted heart throbbed to sudden recognition. She had camped here. She knew those cottonwoods. And strong sweet wine of renewed life fired her veins.

Whity and Specks remembered. This was the cold sweet water from the uplands, well loved by the buffalo. They snorted and lifted dusty, shaggy hoofs, to plod on and stop. Milly looked down on the green bank where Catlee had voiced his sympathy.

Another sunset, one of gold and red out of purple clouds, burned over the prairie-land. The sloping shadows crept along the distant valleys; the grassy undulating expanse shone with dusky fire. And a winding river, like a bright thread, lost itself in the far dim reaches.

Milly Fayre drove Whity and Specks across the cattle-dotted pasture which flanked the river banks outside of Sprague's Post.

Horses mingled with the cattle. Between the road and the cottonwoods camps sent up their curling columns of blue smoke. Tents gleamed rosily in the sunset glow. Dogs ran out to herald the coming of another team. Curious buffalo-hunters, on the way south, dropped out to halt Milly. Natives of the Post strolled across from the store to question the traveler from the buffalo fields.

"Howdy, sonny!" greeted a white-haired old Westerner, with keen blue eyes flashing over weary horses, and wagon with its single occupant. "All by yourself?"

"Yes," replied Milly, amazed to hear her husky voice.

Men crowded closer, kindly, interested, beginning to wonder.

"Whar you from?" queried the old man.

"Pease River," replied Milly.

"Aw, say now, sonny, you're——" Then he checked his query and came closer, to lay a hand on the smoking horse nearest to him. The rugged faces, some bronzed, some with the paleness that was not long of the prairie, were lifted to Milly. They seemed beautiful, so full of life, kindness, interrogation. They dimmed in Milly's sight, through her tears.

"Yes, Pease River," she replied, hurriedly and low. "My outfit fought—killed one another. . . . Comanches swam the river. . . . I drove Whity and Specks through the brakes. . . . The Indians chased us. . . . We ran into stampeded buffalo. . . . Driven all day— surrounded—dust and roar. . . . Oh, it was terrible! . . . But they slowed up—they carried us all day— forty miles. . . . Since then I've camped and driven— camped and driven, days, days, days, I don't— know—how—many!"

A silence ensued after Milly's long poignant speech. Then the old Westerner scratched his beard in perplexity.

"Sonny, air you jest foolin' us or jest out of your haid? You shore look fagged out."

"It's—gospel—truth," panted Milly.

"My boy," began the kindly interrogator, with graver voice, and again his keen gaze swept over grimy horses and travel-worn wagon.

"Boy!" exclaimed Milly, as spiritedly as her huskiness would permit. "I'm no boy! . . . I'm a girl—Milly Fayre."

Chapter XVI

Tom raised himself as high as he dared and studied what he could see of the field in the direction of the bluff. A man might trust himself boldly to that jumble of rocks. Accordingly he crawled on hands and knees to the end of this stone-like corral, and there, stretching on his left side, with left hand extended and right dragging his rifle, he crawled as swiftly and noiselessly as possible. He peered only ahead of him. There was no use to look at the aisles between the rocks at the right and left, because he had to pass these openings, and looking was not going to help him. Trusting to luck and daring he went on, somehow conscious of a grim exultance in the moment. Fear had left him. At the outset he had a few thoughts of himself—that he could only die once, and if he had to do so now it would be for his comrades. Milly Fayre's dark haunting eyes crossed his memory, a stabbing, regretful pain; and for her he would have embraced any peril. Some way these Comanches had been the cause of Milly's flight, if they had not caught her. To them he owed loss of her. And he wanted to kill some of them. But all he asked was luck and strength enough to get back with the water.

After those few flashing thoughts all his senses were fixed on the physical task ahead of him. He had to go swiftly and noiselessly, without rest. His efforts were supreme, sustained. Coming back he would adhere to Pilchuck's advice, but on the way out he could not take it, except in the matter of laying a line of small stones as he progressed.

After the first ten or a dozen rods were behind him there came an easing of a terrible strain. His comrades behind him were shooting now something like a volley, which action he knew was Pilchuck's way of diverting possible discovery from him. The Indians were shooting more, too; and he began to draw considerably away from the cross-fire. He heard no more bullets whiz over his head. As it was impossible to crawl in a straight line, owing to rocks impeding his progress, he deviated from the course set by Pilchuck. This entailed a necessity of lifting himself every few moments so that he could peep over the rocks to keep the direction of the bluff. These wary brief actions were fraught with suspense. They exposed him perilously, but were absolutely imperative.

Bolder he grew. He was going to succeed in this venture. The sustained exertion threatened collapse, yet he still had strength to go on. A few more rods might safely earn rest! The burning sun beat down pitilessly. Tom's tongue hung out, dripping a white froth. His heart expanded as if trying to burst bands of steel. Despite the sternest passion of will he could not help the low gasping intake of air or the panting expulsion. A listening Indian within fifty yards could have heard him. But he kept on. His wet hand and wrist gathered a grimy covering of dust. His rifle grew slippery from sweat from his other hand. Rocks obstructing his advance, the narrow defiles he had to squeeze through, the hard sharp edges tearing his shirt, the smell of the hot earth, the glaring sun—all seemed obstacles that put the fact of Indians in the background.

Again Tom lost his direction. He was coming to a zone more open, and surely not far from the bluff that was his objective point. Usually he had chosen a high and large stone from which to peep. At this juncture not one of such size was available. Low down along the side of a flat stone he peered out. All he could see was a rather wide space, not thickly studded with rocks. But from that angle the bluff was not in sight.

Almost spent from his long crawl, with both muscle and will about played out, he raised himself to locate the bluff. Not on the right side! Dropping down, he crawled the few feet to the left end of this rock, and kneeling sidewise he raised himself again to look over.

Something like a sharp puff of wind whipped by. He heard a hiss. Then he felt a shock, solid, terrific, followed by a tearing burning pain across his back. Almost the same instant came the bursting crack of a rifle. Swift as light Tom's sight took in the open ahead. A half-naked Indian, red skinned, snake-like, stood with smoking rifle, a wild and savage expectation on his dark face.

Tom fell flat behind the rock, all the power of his mind in supreme and flashing conflict against the stunning surprise. It galvanized him. One second he gripped his rifle hard, cocked it, while his muscles gathered and strung for a mighty effort.

Tom leaped up and shot in the same action. It seemed he did not see the Indian clearly until after the discharge of the rifle. The Indian's gun was leveled. But it flew aside, strangely, as if propelled. And on the same instant there was a metallic crack. Tom's bullet had struck the breach of the Indian's gun and had glanced.

The Indian gasped and staggered. He seemed to push his gun away from him. It fell to the ground. Blood gushed from his mouth. He had been mortally wounded. His dark face was terrible to look upon. He was swaying, yet he snatched out a knife and made at Tom. A black flame of hate burned from his eyes.

For a second Tom stood transfixed. The Indian came lurching with the knife. Then Tom jumped just in time to avoid its sweep. Horror gave place to fury. He had no time to reload, so he whirled his rifle, making a club of it. But he missed the Indian, and such was the force of the blow he had aimed that he nearly lost his balance. As it was he righted himself to find the Indian lunging down with the knife.

Like a flash Tom's left hand caught the descending wrist and gripped it. Then he tried to swing the rifle with his right. But the Indian intercepted the blow and held the rifle.

Thus on the moment both were rendered helpless to force the issue. They held each other grimly.

"No—weyno!" gasped the Indian, thickly.

"Comanche! You're—no good—yourself!" panted Tom.

It was a deadlock. Tom exerted himself to the utmost to hold that quivering blade back from his body. He saw the advantage was on his side. Blood poured from a wound in the Indian's throat. The nearness of it, the terrible nature of the moment, the unabatable ferocity and courage of his red adversary were almost too much for Tom. He all but sank under the strain.

Then came a sudden shuddering convulsion on the part of the Indian, a last supreme effort. It was so great that it broke Tom's hold. But even as the Indian wrenched free his strength failed. The corded strung muscles suddenly relaxed. His working, fiercely malignant visage as suddenly set somberly. He dropped the knife. He swayed and fell.

Tom bent over him. The Indian gazed upward, conscious. Then the hate in his dark eyes gave way to a blankness. He was dead. Tom stared, slowly realizing.

In a moment more he was alive to the situation. He had conquered here. But he was not yet out of danger.

Still, if any Indians had seen this encounter they would have shot him before this.

Crouching down, Tom peered round until he had again located his objective point. Then he ran as fast as his spent strength permitted and soon reached the red bluff. But he did not locate the hiding place of the horses until Jake Devine saw him and called. Tom staggered round the bluff and into the pocket where the horses were concealed.

Devine came rattling down from a ledge where evidently he had been watching. Then Al Thorndyke, the other guard, appeared from the opposite quarter. They ran to Tom.

"Say, you're all bloody!" declared Jake, aghast.

"Tom, I seen thet fight," added Thorndyke, sharply. "But I couldn't shoot fer fear of hittin' you."

"I'm hit—I don't know—how bad," panted Tom. "But it can't—be very bad. . . . Hurry, boys. I came after water. Tie me up. I've got to rustle back."

"We'll shore go with you," said Devine.

They tore Tom's shirt off. It was wringing wet and as red as a flag.

"Reckon you sweat a heap," put in Thorndyke, encouragingly.

Tom winced as one of them ran a finger in the wound on his back.

"Nothin' bad. Long deep cut," said Devine. "Fetch water, Al."

The two men washed Tom's wound and bandaged it tightly with a scarf.

"I've got to take some canteens back," declared Tom.

"I'll go. You stay with Al," replied Devine.

"Wal, I ain't a-goin' to stay. I've got to git in thet fight," asserted Thorndyke.

"Listen to the shootin'," exclaimed Devine.

Tom heard a rattling volley of Creedmoors, punctuated by the sharper, lighter cracking of Winchesters. It was certainly an exciting sound.

"But I wasn't told to fetch you," protested Tom.

"Thet don't make no difference. What's the use of us hidin' here? If the Comanches found us we couldn't hold the horses. We'd just be goners. Out there we can git in the fight."

Devine's logic was unanswerable. So Tom made no further objection. The three men took two canteens each, and their rifles, and hurried forth.

Tom led the way. It was easy walking, but when he reached the point where he thought it needful to stoop, the hard work commenced. The heavy canteens swung round and hung from his neck.

He reached the spot where he had fought the Comanche, and here he crouched down. Devine and Thorndyke came up with him. The Indian lay stark—his eyes wide open—his hands spread.

"Fellars, I'll fetch thet Indian's gun an' belt," said Devine, practically.

Tom wondered how Devine could pack these in addition to the load he already carried. But the stocky little man appeared equal to the occasion. Soon Tom lay flat to crawl like a snake. It was well that he had laid a trail. Tom kept the lead, ten feet in front of Thorndyke, who was a like distance ahead of Devine. Tom had to stop every little while to rest. His lungs appeared to stand the test, but his muscles were weak. Still he knew he could make the distance. The long drink of water he had taken had revived him.

Whenever Tom halted to rest he would listen to the shooting. His followers would creep up to him and make some comment. They were eager to join the fray.

"Tom, I reckon you're tuckered out," whispered Thorndyke, on the last of these occasions. "But do your damndest. For we're shore needed."

Thus admonished, Tom did not rest again, though he crawled less violently, trying to husband what strength he had left. The return had not been so exciting, and for that reason was harder work. It was different. Nothing but bullets could have stopped him.

They had crawled close to where Pilchuck and his men were shooting, and therefore within the zone of the Indians' fire, when a bullet kicked up the dust in front of Tom. He hesitated. Then a bullet clipped the crown of his hat. This spurred him to a spasmodic scrambling forward to cover behind a boulder. From there Tom squirmed round to look back. Jake Devine was kneeling with leveled rifle, which on the instant belched fire and smoke. Jake dropped down and crawled forward. His face was black and his eyes blazed.

"Thet redskin is feed fer lizards," he said, grimly. "Go on, Tom."

Tom recalled the fact that Devine was a frontiersman, used to fighting Indians. So he crawled on, inspired by a sense of such companionship. Bullets now began to sing and hum overhead, and to spang from the rocks. Jake prodded Tom's feet.

"Tom, you're slower'n molasses," said Jake. "Reckon you don't mind this sort of thing. But, by golly! I'm scared. An' Al is hangin' on to my boots."

Sometimes Jake would give Tom a shove, rooting his face in the dust. "Crawl, you belly-whopper!" he whispered, gayly. And then he would call back to Thorndyke. "Come on, Al. Dy'e you want to git plugged all to yourself?"

At last Tom and his comrades reached the smoky place that marked Pilchuck's position.

"I ain't hankerin' fer this part of the job," said Devine. "Suppose they take us fer redskins."

But Pilchuck was too wise a leader to allow blunders of that nature. He was on the lookout, and his grimy, sweaty, stern face relaxed at sight of Tom.

"Shore was good work, Tom," he said. "It's next door to hell here. Hurry to Ory an' Roberts."

Tom hurried to where the young man lay, under a

sunshade Roberts had rigged up with his shirt and a stick. Roberts gave Tom a husky greeting. Manifestly his voice was almost gone. Ory's face was pale and clammy. When Tom lifted his head he opened his eyes and tried to speak. But he could not.

"Ory, here's water," said Tom, and held a canteen to the boy's pale lips.

Never until that moment had Tom appreciated the preciousness of water. He watched Ory drink, and had his reward in the wan smile of gratitude. "Much obliged, Tom," whispered Ory, and lay back with a strange look. Then he shut his eyes and appeared to relax. Tom did not like the uneasy impression he received on the moment, but in the excitement he did not think any more about it.

Roberts handed the canteen to the other wounded fellow and watched him drink. Then he slaked his own thirst.

"Say!" he ejaculated, with a deep breath. "Thet shore was all I needed."

The white-headed old plainsman crawled over for his share.

"Son, them canteens will lick Nigger Horse," he said.

"What! Are we fighting that chief?" queried Tom, in amaze.

"Accordin' to Pilchuck we're doin' jest that," responded the plainsman, cheerfully. "Old Nigger an' a thousand of his redskins, more or less."

Then Tom crawled to the vantage point behind the rock he had used before, and gave himself up to this phase of the fight. It did not take longer than a moment to realize what Pilchuck had meant. There was scarcely a second without its boom of Creedmoor or crack of Winchester. A little cloud of white smoke hung above every boulder. Tom exercised the utmost vigilance in the matter of exposing himself to the Indians' fire. He was almost spent, and suffering ex-

cruciating pain from his wound. How infernally hot
the sun burned down! His rifle and the stones were as
fire to his hands. But as he began to peer out for an
Indian to shoot at, and worked back into the fight, he
forgot his pangs, and then what had seemed the into-
lerable conditions.

Tom grew intensely absorbed in his own little part in
this battle. With the smell of gunpowder and smoke
clogging his nostrils, with the thunder of the Creedmoors behind him, with the circling rattle of the Winchesters out there in the hot haze of the sun, he gave
them but vague attention. He applied himself to an
intent watchfulness, and a swift aim and shot at every
moving thing in the direction he covered. It grew to be
a grim duel between him and Indians he knew saw
him. Like him they had to expose themselves somewhat to get in a shot. But as it was imperative to be
swift their aim was necessarily erring. Nevertheless,
bullets spat the dust from Tom's rock, sometimes
within a few inches of his head. What a tingling sense
of justice and deadly wrath these roused in Tom! It
made the fight even. He welcomed these bullets, because they justified his own. He caught glimpses of
shiny rifle barrels, of black sleek heads, of flashes of
brown; and toward these, whenever possible, he directed his aim. Whether or not he ever hit his mark he
could not tell. But he believed his bullets were making
it hot for several Comanches.

Slowly the pitch of the fight augmented, until it was
raging with a reckless fury on part of the Comanches,
and a desperate resistance on that of the besieged.
Sooner or later Tom was forced to realize in his own
reactions the fact that the fighting and the peril had
increased to an alarming extent. A stinging bullet
crease in his shoulder was the first awakening shock he
sustained. He had answered to the Indians' growing
recklessness. He had been exposing himself more and
redoubling his fire. He had missed Indians slipping

stealthily from boulder to boulder—opportunities that only intense excitement and haste had made him fail to grasp. Then, when he crouched back, forced to cover, aghast at this second wound, he became fully aware of the attack.

The Comanches had pressed closer and closer, now better concealed by the pall of smoke that overhung the scene.

"Hold your fire! Look out for a charge!" yelled Pilchuck in stentorian voice.

The booming of Creedmoors ceased, and that permitted a clearer distinguishing of the Indians' fire. Their Winchesters were rattling in a continuous volley, and a hail of lead whistled over and into the boulder corral. Manifestly the Indians had massed on the west side, between Starwell's position and Pilchuck's. This occasioned the leader to draw up his men in line with Tom's fortification. Closer and hotter grew the Indians' fire. Through the blue haze of smoke and heat Tom saw dim swiftly moving shapes, like phantoms. They were Comanches, gliding from covert to covert, and leaping from boulder to boulder. Tom's heart seemed to choke him. If the Indians were in strong enough force they would effect a massacre of Pilchuck's men. Suddenly, as Tom dwelt fearfully on such contingency, the firing abruptly ceased. A silence fraught with suspense ensued, strange after the heavy shooting.

"It's a trick. Look sharp!" Pilchuck warned his men.

"Wal, seein' this fight's ag'in' the exterminatin' of the buffalo, I reckon old Nigger Horse will do or die," said Jake Devine.

"If you'd ask me I'd say these hoss-ridin' redskins was up to their last dodge on foot," averred the old white-headed plainsman.

"Look out it's not *our* last dodge," replied Pilchuck.

Scarcely had he spoken when the Indians opened up with a heavy volley at alarmingly close range. Pilchuck shouted an order that was not intelligible in the cracking of firearms. But only its content was needed. The big buffalo guns answered with a roar. In another moment the firing became so fast and furious that it blended as a continuous thundering in Tom's ears. He saw the rush of the Indians, incredibly swift and vague through the smoke, and he worked his rifle so hard that it grew hot. Above the roar of guns he heard the strange ear-splitting yell of the Comanches. Almost at the same instant smoke veiled the scene, more to the advantage of the white men than the red. The Creedmoors thundered as continuously as before, and the volume of sound must have been damning to the desperate courage of the Comanches. Perhaps they had not counted on so strong a force and resistance. Their war-cry pealed to a shrill pitch and ceased; and following that the rattling volleys fell off. Then Pilchuck ordered his men to stop shooting.

Tom saw the old white-haired plainsman stand up and survey the smoke-hazed slope. Then he dropped down.

"Fellars, they're draggin' off their dead an' crippled," he said. "They're licked, an' we ought to chase them clear to their hosses."

"Right," replied Pilchuck, grimly. "But wait till we're sure."

Tom could not see anything of the retreat, if such it was. The smoke mantle was lifting above the boulders. With the sudden release of strain the men reacted according to their individual natures. Those new to such fighting were silent, as was Tom, and lay flat. Jake Devine was loquacious in his complaints that he had not downed any Comanches. The old plainsman urged Pilchuck to chase the Indians. Then when the receding fire of the enemy ceased altogether Tom heard yells close at hand.

"That's Harkaway," said the scout eagerly, and he called out a reply.

Soon Harkaway and his men came stooping and

crawling to join Pilchuck. They were panting from exertion.

"Boss—they're—workin' down," he said, breathlessly.

"Mebbe it's a trick," replied the wary scout. "I'll sneak out an' take a look."

Tom drew back from his position and eased his cramped limbs. His shirt was wet with blood. Examination showed his second bullet wound to be a slight one, but exceedingly annoying. He got Devine to tie it up, running a scarf under his arm and over his shoulder.

"Wal, a couple more scratches will make an old residenter out of you, Tom," he said, dryly.

Tom was about to make some fitting reply when Pilchuck returned in haste.

"Men, it's goin' to be our day," he said, his gray eyes alight with piercing intensity. "If we rout old Nigger Horse it'll be the first victory for the whites in this buffalo war. Us hunters will have done what the soldiers couldn't do. . . . Harkaway, you stay here with two of your men to guard these cripples. All the rest of you grab extra cartridges an' follow me."

Tom was not the last to get his hands into that cartridge bag, nor to fall in line after the scout. Once out of the zone of smoke, he was thrilled to see Indians disappearing over the edge of the slope. There was a good deal of shooting below, and the unmistakable booming reports told of Creedmoors in action. From the sound Tom judged Starwell had changed his position. But this could not be ascertained for sure until the brow of the slope was reached. Pilchuck advanced cautiously, gradually growing bolder as ambush appeared less probable, and the time came when he broke into a run.

"String out, an' come fast," he called back.

Tom fell in behind Jake Devine, and keeping some paces back he attended to the difficulty of running over the rough ground. Thus it was he did not look up until he reached the edge of the slope. Here he found Pilchuck and some of the men in a group, gazing, talking, and gesticulating all at once. Tom's breast was heaving from the hard run. He was hot and wet. But it was certain that a reviving thrill ran over him. The Comanches were in retreat. There was no doubt of that. It was still an orderly retreat, with a line of warriors guarding the rear. Tom saw Indians dragging and carrying their wounded and dead; others were gathering in the horses; and the mass was centered in the middle of the encampment, where there were signs of great haste.

One by one Pilchuck's arriving men added to the group on the slope.

"Starwell has the idea," declared Pilchuck. "See. He's moved this way an' down. He can still cover that gate an' also reach the camp."

"Jude, we shore hev our chance now," spoke up the old white-haired plainsman.

"I reckon," replied the scout. "Now listen, men. When I give the word we'll charge down this hill. Each an' every one of you yell like the devil, run a dozen jumps, drop down on your knee an' shoot. Then load, get up, an' do the same over again. Head for that pile of rocks this side of Starwell's position."

Silence followed the scout's trenchant speech. Then ensued a tightening of belts, a clinking of cartridges, a rasping of the mechanism of the Creedmoors. Tom was all ready, quivering for the word, yet glad of a few moments' rest. Pilchuck and the old plainsman stood close together, keen eyes on the Indian encampment. The sun was low over the escarpment to the west and it was losing its heat. The canyon seemed full of golden lights and blue haze, through which flashed and gleamed moving objects, horses, Indians, collapsing tepees, a colorful and exciting scene. The rear guard of Indians backed slowly to the center of the encampment. Their horses were being brought in readiness. Tom could not help but see the execution of a shrewd

Indian brain. Still, there were signs of a possible panic.
Already the Comanches had suffered in this fight, as
was manifested by the number of those incapacitated,
and which had to be packed off. Already the far slope
of the canyon was covered by ponies dragging travois.

The sudden breaking up of the rear guard, as these
Indians leaped for their horses, was a signal for Pilchuck.

"Charge, men!" he yelled, harshly, and plunged
down the slope.

"Hi, fellars," shouted Jake Devine, "old Nigger
Horse is my meat!"

In a moment Pilchuck's men were spread out on the
jump, yelling like fiends and brandishing their weapons. Tom was well to the fore, close behind Devine
and Pilchuck. Their heavy boots sent the loose stones
flying and rattling down the hill. White puffs of smoke
showed suddenly down in the encampment and were
followed by the rattle of Winchesters. Presently Pilchuck plunged to a halt and, kneeling, leveled his
Creedmoor. His action was swiftly followed by his
men. His Creedmoor boomed; that of Devine and the
plainsman next, and then the others thundered in
unison. It was a long-range shot and Tom aimed generally at the commotion in the encampment. Pandemonium broke loose down there. All order seemed to
vanish in a rushing *mêlée*. Pilchuck leaped up with a
hoarse command, which his men answered in wild
exulting whoops. And they plunged again down the
slope, faster, rendered reckless by the success of their
boldness.

Tom felt himself a part of that charging line of
furious buffalo-hunters, and had imbibed the courage
of the mass. Like the others, he had calculated on the
Indians charging back to meet them, thus precipitating
a pitched battle. But this was not the case. The Indians
began returning the fire from all parts of the canyon. It
was a hasty action, however, and did not appear

formidable. They were now bent on escape. That gave irresistible momentum to the charge of Pilchuck's force. Starwell and his men, seeing the Indians routed, left their covert and likewise plunged down, firing and yelling as never before.

Tom, following the example of the men before him, ran and knelt and fired four times in rapid succession on the way down to the level floor of the canyon. By this time all the Indians were mounted and the mass of them abandoned the idea of a slow climb up the opposite slope. They broke for the canyon gate. This meant they had to lessen the long range between them and Pilchuck's force, a fact that did not daunt them. Their lean, racy mustangs were quickly in a running stride, and each rider was presenting a rifle toward the enermy.

"HOLD HERE, MEN!" bawled Pilchuck, stridently. "If they charge us take to the rocks!"

Tom no longer heard the bang of any individual gun, not even his own. And he was loading and firing as fast as possible. A roar filled his ears, and the ground seemed to shake with the furious trample of the mustangs racing by. How long and low they stretched out—how lean and wild their riders! What matchless horsemen these Comanches! Even in the hot grip of that fighting moment Tom thrilled at the magnificent defiance of these Indians, courting death by that ride, to save their burdened comrades climbing the slope. Some of them met that death. Tom saw riders throw up their arms and pitch headlong to the ground. Mustangs leaped high, in convulsive action, and plunged down to roll over and over.

Tom seemed aware of the thinning of Pilchuck's ranks. And when the order came to run down the canyon to prevent a possible massacre of Starwell and men, who had impetuously advanced too far, some were left behind. From that moment Tom lost clear perception of the progress of the fight. The blood rage that obsessed the frontiersmen was communicated to him. He plunged with the others; he felt their nearness; he heard their hoarse yells and the boom of their guns; but he seemed to be fighting alone for the sake of the fight itself. The last of that mounted band of Comanches swooped across toward Starwell's men, driving them to the rocks. Pilchuck's force, charging down the level, came abreast of them, and there in the open a terrible, brief, and decisive battle ensued.

If the Comanches had not halted in the face of the booming Creedmoors there would have been an end to Pilchuck's buffalo-hunters. They would have been run down. But the Indians were not equal to victory at such cost. They shot as they had ridden, furiously, without direct attention. As for the white men, fury made them only the more efficient. They advanced, yelling, cursing, shooting and loading as men possessed of devils. The smoke and din seemed to envelop Tom. His gun scorched his hands and powder burned his face. When he reloaded he seemed to reel and fumble over his breech-lock. The compact mass of Indians disintegrated to strings and streams, vague, not so close, lean wild savage figures hard to aim at. Then something struck Tom and the vagueness became obscurity.

When Tom returned to consciousness he felt a dull pain, and a thickness of mind that did not permit him to establish a clear conception of his whereabouts or what had happened. He was being carried; voices of men fell upon his ears; daylight seemed fading into a red duskiness. A blankness intervened, then again he dizzily awoke. He was lying on his back and a dark bluff rose above him. Then he became aware of cold water being dashed in his face, and a familiar voice.

"Tom's not bad hurt," said Jake Devine. "Thet last bullet bounded off'n his skull. He shore is a hard-headed fellar."

"Aw! I reckon I'm glad," replied Pilchuck. "Looked to me like he'd gone."

"Nope. He'll come round tip-top. . . . I'm a son-of-a-gun if he ain't come to right now! Hey, Tom!"

"I'm all right, thanks," said Tom, weakly. "How'd we make out?"

Whereupon Devine began an eloquent account of how they had stood off Nigger Horse and two hundred braves, had whipped them, and finally routed them completely with a considerable loss. But Devine omitted to mention what Pilchuck's force had suffered.

Though feeling considerable pain and much weakness through loss of blood, Tom was able to eat a little, after which effort he fell asleep.

Daylight brought clear consciousness to him, and one glance round at his lame and bandaged comrades gave an inkling of what the victory over Nigger Horse had cost. Not a man had escaped at least one wound! Burn Hudnall had escaped serious injury. Tom missed familiar faces. But he did not make inquiries then. He submitted to a painful treatment of his wounds. Then he was glad enough to lie quietly with closed eyes.

Later that morning he had strength enough to mount his horse and ride with the slow procession back to the permanent camp. He made it, but prayed he would have no more such ordeals. The shady, cool camp with its running water was a most soothing relief. One by one the injured were made comfortable. It was then Tom learned that seven of Pilchuck's force had been killed in the fight. Ory Tacks had been the first to succumb. Thus Tom had verification of his fears. Poor, brave, cheerful Ory! These heroic men would find graves on the spot where they had helped to break forever the backbone of the Comanches' hostility.

Pilchuck visited with the injured men that day. His sternness had vanished.

"Boys," he said, "I never expected any of us to get out of that fight alive. When those yellin' devils charged us I thought the game was up. We did well, but we were mighty lucky. It's sad about our comrades. But some of us had to go an' we were all ready.

Now the great good truth is that this victory will rouse the buffalo-hunters. I'll go after more men. We'll shore chase the Comanches an' Kiowas off the Staked Plain, an' that will leave us free to hunt buffalo. What's more important, it will make Texas safe for settlers. So you can all feel proud, as I do. The buffalo-hunters will go down in history as havin' made Texas habitable."

Chapter XVII

In 1876 more than two hundred thousand buffalo hides were shipped east over the Santa Fe Railroad, and hundreds of thousands in addition went north from Fort Worth, Texas.

For this great number of hides that reached eastern and foreign markets there were at least twice the number of hides sacrificed on the range. Old buffalo-hunters generally agreed on the causes for this lamentable fact. Inexperienced hunters did not learn to poison the hides, which were soon destroyed by hide bugs. Then as many buffalo were crippled as killed outright and skinned, and these wounded ones stole away to die in coulees or the brakes of the rivers. Lastly, a large percentage of buffalo were chased by hunters into the quagmires and quicksands along the numerous streams, there to perish.

1877 saw the last of the raids by Comanches and Kiowas, a condition brought round solely by the long campaign of united bands of buffalo-hunters, who chased and fought these Indians all over the Staked

Plain. But this campaign was really a part of the destruction of the buffalo, and that destruction broke forever the strength of these hard-riding Indians.

In the winter and spring of that year the number of hide-hunting outfits doubled and trebled and quadrupled; and from the Red River to the Brazos, over that immense tract of Texas prairie, every river, stream, pond, water-hole and spring, everywhere buffalo could drink, was ambushed by hunters with heavy guns. The poor animals that were not shot down had to keep on traveling until the time came when a terrible parching thirst made them mad. Then, when in their wanderings to find some place to drink, they scented water, they would stampede, and in their madness to assuage an insupportable thirst, would plunge over one another in great waves, crushing to death those underneath.

Tom Doan, during the year and a half of the Indian raids, fought through three campaigns against Comanches, Kiowas, and Llano Estacado Apaches.

Pilchuck's first organizing of buffalo-hunters into a unit to fight Comanches drove the wedge that split the Indians; and likewise it inspired and roused the hide-hunters from the Territory line to the Rio Grande. Thus there was a war on the several tribes, as well as continued slaughter of the buffalo.

In the spring of 1877, when, according to the scouts, the backbone of the Southwest raiding tribes had been broken, Tom Doan bade good-by to Burn Hudnall, his friend and comrade for so long. Dave Stronghurl had months before gone back to Sprague's Post to join his wife, and Burn, now that the campaign had ended, wanted to see his wife and people.

"I reckon I'm even with the Comanches," he said, grimly. That was his only reference to his father's murder.

"Well, Burn, we've seen wild life," mused Tom, sadly. "I'm glad I helped rout the Comanches.

They've been robbed, I suppose, and I can't blame them. But they sure made a man's blood boil for a fight."

"What'll you do, Tom?" queried Burn.

Doan dropped his head. "It'd hurt too much to go back to Sprague's Post—just yet. You see, Burn, I can't forget Milly. Of course she's dead long ago. But then, sometimes I see her in dreams, and she seems alive. I'd like to learn the truth of her fate. Some day I might. Pilchuck and I are going south to the Brazos. The last great hunt is on there."

"I'm goin' to settle on a ranch at Sprague's," said Burn. "Father always said that would be the center of a fine cattle an' farmin' district some day."

"Yes, I remember. It used to be my dream, too. But I'm changed. This roving life, I guess. The open range for me yet awhile! Some day I'll come back."

"Tom, you've money saved," returned Burn, thoughtfully. "You could buy an' stock a ranch. Isn't it risky carryin' round all your money? There's worse than bad Comanches now in the huntin' field."

"I've thought of that," said Tom. "It does seem risky. So I'll ask you to take most of my money and bank it for me."

"It's a good idea. But see here, old man, suppose you don't come back? You know, we've seen things happen to strong an' capable men down here. Think how lucky we've been!"

"I've thought of that, too," said Tom, with gravity. "If I don't show up inside of five years invest the money for your children. Money's not much to me any more. . . . But I'm likely to come back."

This conversation took place at Wheaton's camp, on the headwaters of the Red River, in April. A great exodus of freighters was taking place that day. It was interesting for Tom to note the development of the hide hauling. The wagons were large and had racks and booms, so that when loaded they resembled hay wagons, except in color. Two hundred buffalo hides to a wagon, and six yokes of oxen to a team and twenty-five teams to a train! Swiftly indeed were the buffalo disappearing from the plains. Burn Hudnall rode north with one of these immense freighting outfits.

Tom and Pilchuck made preparations for an extended hunt in the Brazos River country, whence emanated rumors somewhat similar to the gold rumors of '49.

While choosing and arranging an outfit they were visited by a brawny little man with a most remarkable visage. It was scarred with records of both the sublime and the ridiculous.

"I'm after wantin' to throw in with you," he announced to Pilchuck.

The scout, used to judging men in a glance, evidently saw service and character in this fellow.

"Wal, we need a man, that's shore. But he must be experienced," returned the scout.

"Nary tenderfoot, scout, not no more," he grinned. "I've killed an' skinned over four thousands buffs. An' I'm a blacksmith an' a cook."

"Wal, I reckon you're a whole outfit in yourself," rejoined Pilchuck, with his rare broad smile. "How do you want to throw in?"

"Share expense of outfit, work, an' profit."

"Nothin' could be no more fair. I reckon we'll be right glad to have you. What's your handle?"

"Wrong-Wheel Jones," replied the applicant, as if he expected that cognomen to be recognized.

"What the hell! I've met Buffalo Jones, an' Dirty-Face Jones an' Spike Jones, but I never heard of you. . . . Wrong-Wheel Jones! Where'd you ever get that?"

"It was stuck on me my first hunt when I was sorta tenderfooty."

"Wal, tell me an' my pard here, Tom Doan," continued the scout, good-humoredly. "Tom, shake with Wrong-Wheel Jones."

After quaintly acknowledging the introduction Jones said: "Fust trip I busted a right hind wheel of my wagon. Along comes half a dozen outfits, but none had an extra wheel. Blake, the leader, told me he'd passed a wagon like mine, broke down on the Cimarron. 'Peared it had some good wheels. So I harnessed my hosses, rode one an' led t'other. I found the wagon, but the *left hind wheel* was the only one not busted. So I rode back to camp. Blake asked me why I didn't fetch a wheel back, an' I says: 'What'd I want with *two* left hind wheels? I got one. It's the right one thet's busted. Thet left hind wheel back thar on thet wagon would do fust rate, but it's on the wrong side.' An' Blake an' his outfit roared till they near died. When he could talk ag'in he says: 'You darned fool. Thet left hind wheel turned round would make your right hind wheel.' An' after a while I seen he was right. They called me Wrong-Wheel Jones an' the name's stuck."

"By gosh! it ought to!" laughed Pilchuck.

In company with another outfit belonging to a new-comer named Hazelton, with a son of fifteen and two other boys not much older, Pilchuck headed for the Brazos River.

After an uneventful journey, somewhat off the beaten track, they reached one of the many tributaries of the Brazos, where they ran into some straggling small herds.

"We'll make two-day stops till we reach the main herd," said Pilchuck. "I've a hankerin' for my huntin' alone. Reckon hide-hunters are thick as bees down on the Brazos. Let's keep out of the stink an' musketeers as long as we can."

They went into camp, the two outfits not far apart, within hailing distance.

It was perhaps the most beautiful location for a camp Tom had seen in all his traveling over western Texas. Pilchuck said the main herd, with its horde of hide-hunters, had passed miles east of this point. As a consequence the air was sweet, the water unpolluted, and grass and wood abundant.

Brakes of the tributary consisted of groves of pecan trees and cottonwoods, where cold springs abounded, and the deep pools contained fish. As spring had just come in that latitude, there were color of flowers, and fragrance in the air, and a myriad of birds lingering on their way north. Like the wooded sections of the Red River and the Pease River Divide had been, so was this Brazos district. Deer, antelope, turkey, with their carnivorous attendants, panthers, wildcats, and wolves, had not yet been molested by white hunters.

Perhaps the Indian campaigns had hardened Tom Doan, for he returned to the slaughter of buffalo. He had been so long out of the hunting game that he had forgotten many of the details, and especially the sentiment that had once moved him. Then this wild life in the open had become a habit; it clung to a man. Moreover, Tom had an aching and ever-present discontent which only action could subdue.

He took a liking to Cherry Hazleton. The boy was a strapping youngster, freckle faced and red headed, and like all healthy youths of the Middle West during the 'seventies he was a worshiper of the frontiersman and Indian fighter. He and his young comrades, brothers named Dan and Joe Newman, spent what little leisure time they had hanging round Pilchuck and Tom, hungry for stories as dogs for bones.

Two days at this camp did not suffice Pilchuck. Buffalo were not excessively numerous, but they were scattered into small bands under leadership of old bulls; and for these reasons offered the conditions best suited to experienced hunters.

The third day Tom took Cherry Hazleton hunting with him, allowing him to carry canteen and extra cartridges while getting valuable experience.

Buffalo in small numbers were in sight everywhere, but as this country was rolling and cut up, unlike the Pease prairie, it was not possible to locate all the herds that might be within reaching distance.

In several hours of riding and stalking Tom had not

found a position favorable to any extended success, though he had downed some buffalo,. and young Hazleton, after missing a number, had finally killed his first, a fine bull. The boy was wild with excitement, and this brought back to Tom his early experience, now seemingly so long in the past.

They were now on a creek that ran through a wide stretch of plain, down to the tributary, and no more than two miles from camp. A large herd of buffalo trooped out of the west, coming fast under a cloud of dust. They poured down into the creek and literally blocked it, crazy to drink. Tom had here a marked instance of the thirst-driven madness now common to the buffalo. This herd, numbering many hundreds, slaked their thirst, and then trooped into a wide flat in the creek bottom, where trees stood here and there. Manifestly they had drunk too deeply, if they had not foundered, for most of them lay down.

"We'll cross the creek and sneak close on them," said Tom. "Bring all the cartridges. We might get a stand."

"What's that?" whispered Cherry, excitedly.

"It's what a buffalo-hunter calls a place and time where a big number bunches and can be kept from running off. I never had a stand myself. But I've an idea what one's like."

They crept on behind trees and brush, down into the wide shallow flat, until they were no farther than a hundred yards from the resting herd. From the way Cherry panted Tom knew he was frightened.

"It is sort of skittish," whispered Tom, "but if they run our way we can climb a tree."

"I'm not—scared. It's—just—great," rejoined the lad, in a tone that hardly verified his words.

"Crawl slow now, and easy," said Tom. "A little farther—then we'll bombard them."

At last Tom led the youngster yards closer, to a wonderful position behind an uprooted cottonwood, from which they could not be seen. Thrilling indeed was it even for Tom, who had stalked Comanches in this way. Most of the buffalo were down, and those standing were stupid with drowsiness. The heat, and a long parching thirst, then an overcharged stomach, had rendered them loggy.

Tom turned his head to whisper instruction to the lad. Cherry's face was pale and the freckles stood out prominently. He was trembling with wild eagerness, fear and delight combined. Tom thought it no wonder. Again he smelled the raw scent of buffalo. They made a magnificent sight, an assorted herd of all kinds and ages, from the clean, glossy, newly shedded old bulls down to the red calves.

"Take the bull on your right—farthest out," whispered Tom. "And I'll tend to this old stager on my left."

The big guns boomed. Tom's bull went to his knees and, grunting loud, fell over; Cherry's bull wagged his head as if a bee had stung him. Part of the buffalo lying down got up. The old bull, evidently a leader, started off.

"Knock him," whispered Tom, quickly. "They'll follow him." Tom fired almost simultaneously with Cherry, and one or both of them scored a dead shot. The buffalo that had started to follow the bull turned back into the herd, and this seemed to dominate all of them. Most of those standing pressed closer in. Others began to walk stolidly off.

"Shoot the outsiders," said Tom, quickly. And in three seconds he had stopped as many buffalo. Cherry's gun boomed, but apparently without execution.

At this juncture Pilchuck rushed up behind them.

"By golly! you've got a stand!" he ejaculated, in excited tones for him. "Never seen a better in my life. Now, here, you boys let me do the shootin'. It's tough on you, but if this stand is handled right we'll make a killin'."

Pilchuck stuck his forked rest-stick in the ground, and knelt behind it, just to the right of Tom and

Cherry. This elevated him somewhat above the log, and certainly not hidden from the buffalo.

"Case like this a fellow wants to shoot straight," said the scout. "A crippled buff means a bolt."

Choosing the bull the farthest outside of the herd, Pilchuck aimed with deliberation, and fired. The animal fell. Then he treated the next in the same manner. He was far from hurried, and that explained his deadly precision.

"You mustn't let your gun get too hot," he said. "Over-expansion from heat makes a bullet go crooked."

Pilchuck picked out buffalo slowly walking away and downed them. The herd kept massed, uneasy in some quarters, but for the most part not disturbed by the shooting. Few of those lying down rose to their feet. When the scout had accounted for at least two dozen buffalo he handed his gun to Tom.

"Cool it off an' wipe it out," he directed, and taking Tom's gun returned to his deliberate work.

Tom threw down the breech-block and poured water through the barrel, once, and then presently again. Taking up Pilchuck's ramrod Tom ran a greasy patch of cloth through the barrel. It was cooling rapidly and would soon be safe to use.

Meanwhile the imperturbable scout was knocking buffalo down as if they had been tenpins. On the side toward him there was soon a corral of dead buffalo. He never missed; only seldom was it necessary to take two shots to an animal. After shooting ten or twelve he returned Tom's gun and took up his own.

"Best stand I ever saw," he said. "Queer how buffalo act sometimes. They're not stupid. They know somethin' is wrong. But you see I keep knockin' down the one that leads off."

Buffalo walked over to dead ones, and sniffed at them, and hooked them with such violence that the contact could be heard. An old bull put something apparently like anger into his actions. Why did not his comrade, or perhaps his mate, get up and come? Some of them looked anxiously round, waiting. Now and then another would walk out of the crowd, and that was fatal for him. Boom! And the heavy bullet would thud solidly; the buffalo would sag or jerk, and then sink down, shot through the heart. Pilchuck was a machine for the collecting of buffalo hides. There were hundreds of hunters like him on the range. Boom! Boom! Boom! boomed out the big fifty.

At last, after more than an hour of this incredible stolidity to the boom of gun and the fall of their numbers, the resting buffalo got up, and they all moved round uneasily, uncertainly. Then Pilchuck missed dead center of a quartering shot at a bull that led out. The bullet made the beast frantic, and with a kind of low bellow it bounded away. The mass broke, and a stream of shaggy brown poured off the flat and up the gentle slope. In a moment all the herd was in motion. The industrious Pilchuck dropped four more while they were crowding behind, following off the flat. A heavy trampling roar filled the air; dust, switching tufted tails, woolly bobbing backs, covered the slope. And in a few moments they were gone. Silence settled down. The blue smoke drifted away. A gasp of dying buffalo could be heard.

"Reckon I never beat this stand," said the scout, wiping his wet, black hands. "If I only hadn't crippled that bull."

"Gosh! It was murder—wusser'n butcherin' cows!" ejaculated the boy Cherry. Drops of sweat stood out on his pale face, as marked as the freckles. He looked sick. Long before that hour had ended his boyish sense of exciting adventure had been outraged.

"Lad, it ain't always that easy," remarked Pilchuck. "An' don't let this make you think huntin' buffalo isn't dangerous. Now we'll make a count."

One hundred and twenty-six buffalo lay dead in space less than three acres; and most of them were bulls.

"Yep, it's my record," declared the scout, with satisfaction. "But I come back fresh to it, an' shore that was a grand stand. Boys, we've got skinnin' for the rest of to-day an' all of tomorrow."

The two outfits gradually hunted down the tributary towards its confluence with the Brazos. As the number of buffalo increased they encountered other hunters; and when May arrived they were on the outskirts of the great herd and a swarm of camps.

Hide thieves were numbered among these outfits, and this necessitated the consolidation of camps and the need for one or more men to be left on guard. Thus Tom and Cherry often had a day in camp, most welcome change, though tasks were endless. Their place was at a point where the old Spanish Trail from the Staked Plain crossed the Brazos; and therefore was in line of constant travel. Hunters and freighters, tenderfeet and old timers, soldiers and Indians, passed that camp, and seldom came a day when no traveler stopped for an hour.

Cherry liked these days more than those out on the range. He was being broken in to Pilchuck's strenuous method and the process was no longer enticing.

Once it happened that Cherry and Dan Newman were left together. Tom had ridden off to take up his skinning, in which he had soon regained all his old-time skill, but he did not forget to admonish the boys to keep out of mischief. Wrong-Wheel Jones, who had been recovering from one of his infrequent intemperate spells, had also been left behind. When Tom returned he found Jones in a state of high dudgeon, raving what he would do to those infernal boys. It was plain that Wrong-Wheel had very recently come out of the river, which at this point ran under a bank close to camp. Tom decided the old fellow had fallen in, but as the boys were not to be found, a later conclusion heaped upon their heads something of suspicion. At last Tom persuaded him to talk.

"Wal, it was this way," began Wrong-Wheel, with the air of a much-injured man. "Since I lost them two hundred hides—an' I know darn well some thief got them—I been drinkin' considerable. Jest got to taperin' off lately, an' wasn't seein' so many queer things. . . . Wal, to-day I went to sleep thar in the shade on the bank. Suthin' woke me, an' when I opened my eyes I seed an orful sight. I was scared turrible, an' I jest backed off the bank an' fell in the river. Damn near drowned! Reckon when I got out I was good an' sober. . . . An', say, what d'ye spose them boys done?"

Wrong-Wheel squinted at Tom and squirted a brown stream of tobacco into the camp fire.

"I haven't any idea," replied Tom, with difficulty preserving a straight face.

"Wal," went on Jones, "you know thet big panther Pilchuck shot yestiddy. Them boys hed skinned it, shot-pouched it, as we say, an' they hed stuffed it with grass, an' put sticks in fer legs, an' marbles fer eyes. An' I'm a son-of-a-gun if they didn't stand the dummy right in front of me, so when I woke I seed it fust, an' I jest nat'rally went off my head."

Another day an old acquaintance of Tom's rode in and halted on his way to Fort Worth.

"Roberts!" exclaimed Tom, in glad surprise.

"Just come from Fort Sill," said Roberts, evincing equal pleasure. "An' I have shore some news for you. Do you remember old Nigger Horse, the thief of that band of Comanches we fought—when I had this heah arm broke?"

"I'm not likely to forget," replied Tom.

"Wal, the Comanches that are left are slowly comin' in to Fort Sill an' goin' on the reservation. An' from some of them we got facts aboot things we never was shore on. The soldiers lately had a long runnin' fight with old Nigger Horse. Some sergeant killed the old chief an' his squaw, an' that shore was a good job."

"Nigger was a bad Comanche," agreed Tom. "Did you ever hear any more about Hudnall's gun?"

"Shore. We heerd all aboot it, an' from several bucks who were in our fight where I had my arm broke, an' other fights afterwards. . . . I reckon you remember Hudnall had a fine gun, one shore calculated to make redskins want it. An' possession of that rifle was bad medicine to every consarned Indian who got it. Nigger Horse's son had it first. He was the brave who led that ride down the canyon to draw our fire. He shore had spunk. Wal, I reckon he was full of lead. Then an Injun named Five Plumes got it. 'Pears we killed him. After that every redskin who took Hudnall's rifle an' cartridges got his everlastin'. Finally they quit usin' it, thinkin' it was bad medicine. Now the fact is, those Comanches who used Hudnall's gun got reckless because they had it, an' laid themselves open to our fire. But they thought it had a spell of the devil."

Chapter XVIII

The middle of July found Tom Doan and Pilchuck far down on the Brazos, in the thick of the slaughter. Thirty miles of buffalo-hunters drove the last great herd day by day toward extermination.

If the weather had been uncomfortable in midsummer on the Pease River Divide, here it was worse than hot. Moreover, up there in earlier days the hunting had been comparatively easy. Here it was incessant toil. The buffalo had to be chased.

The prairie was open, hot, dusty, an vast. Always the buffalo headed to the wind; they would drink and graze, and go on, noses to the breeze. If the wind changed overnight, in the morning they would be found turned round, traveling toward it. All day they grazed against it. They relied on their scent more than on sight or hearing; and in that open country the wind brought them warning of their foes. But for the great number of hide-hunters these buffalo might have escaped any extended slaughter.

The outfits were strung along the Brazos for many miles; and as the buffalo had to drink they were never

far from water. Thus a number of hunters would get to
them every day, kill many on the chase, and drive
them on to the next aggregation of slayers.

Tom Doan had been in hard action for over two
months; and he and Pilchuck and Jones had killed
thirty-nine hundred and twenty buffalo, losing only a
small percentage of skins. Their aim was to last out the
summer and fall if endurance could be great enough.
They had no freighting to do now; they sold their hides
in bales on the range.

The days grew to be nightmares. As the buffalo were
driven up the river, then back down, and up again, the
killing was accomplished for weeks in a comparatively
small area. It got to be so that Tom could not ride many
rods without encountering either a pile of bones, or
rotten carcass, or one just beginning to decompose, or
a freshly skinned one torn over the night before by the
packs of thousand of coyotes that followed the herd.
Some days hundreds of newly skinned buffalo shone
red along with the blackened carcasses over a stretch
of miles. Buzzards were as thick as bees. And the
stench was unbearable. The prairie became a
gruesome, ghastly shambles; and the camps were almost untenable because of flies and bugs, ticks and
mosquitoes. These hunters stuck to a job that in a
worthy cause would have been heroic. As it was they
descended to butchers, and each and all of them sank
inevitably. Boom! Boom! Boom! All day long the
detonation filled the hot air. No camp was out of
hearing of the guns. Wagons lumbered along the dusty
roads. All the outfits labored day and night to increase
their store of hides, riding, chasing, shooting, skinning, hauling, and pegging, as if their very lives de-
pended upon incessant labor. It was a time of carnage.

Long had Tom Doan felt the encroachment of a
mood he had at one time striven against—a morbid
estimate of self, a consciousness that this carnage
would debase him utterly if he did not soon abandon it.

Once there had been a wonderful reason for him to give up the hunting. Milly Fayre! Sometimes still her dark eyes haunted him. If she had not been lost he would long ago have quit this bloody game. The wound in his heart did not heal. Love of Milly abided, and that alone saved him from the utter debasement of hard life at a hard time.

One morning when he drove out on the dust-hazed, stinking prairie he found a little red buffalo calf standing beside its mother, that Tom had shot and skinned the day before. This was no new sight to Tom. Nevertheless, in the present case there seemed a difference. These calves left motherless by the slaughter had always wandered over the prairie, lost, bewildered; this one, however, had recognized its mother and would not leave her.

"Go along! Get back to the herd!" yelled Tom, shocked despite his callousness.

The calf scarcely noticed him. It smelled of its hide-stripped mother, and manifestly was hungry. Presently it left off trying to awaken this strange horribly red and inert body, and stood with hanging head, dejected, resigned, a poor miserable little beast. Tom could not drive it away; and after loading the hide on the wagon he returned twice to try to make it run off. Finally he was compelled to kill it.

This incident boded ill for Tom. It fixed his mind on this thing he was doing and left him no peace. Thousands and thousands of beautiful little buffalo calves were rendered motherless by the hide-hunters. That was to Tom the unforgivable brutality. Calves just born, just able to suck, and from that to yearlings, were left to starve, to die of thirst, to wander until they dropped or were torn to shreds by wolves. No wonder this little calf showed in its sad resignation the doom of the species!

August came. The great herd massed. The mating season had come, and both bulls and cows, slaves to the marvelous instinct that had evolved them, grew slower, less wary, heedless now to the scent of man on the wind.

At the beginning of this mating time it was necessary to be within a mile or less to hear the strange *roo roo roo—ooo*. This sound was the bellow of a bull. Gradually day by day the sound increased in volume and range. It could be heard several miles, and gradually farther as more and more bulls bellowed in unison. Roo roo roo—ooo!—It began to be incessant, heard above the boom! boom! boom! of guns.

The time came when it increased tremendously and lasted day and night. Tom Doan's camp was then ten miles from the herd. At that distance the bellow was as loud as distant thunder. ROO ROO ROO—OOO! It kept Tom awake. It filled his ears. If he did fall asleep it gave him a nightmare. When he awoke he heard again the long mournful roar. At length it wore upon him so deeply that in the darkness and solitude of night he conceived the idea he was listening to the voice of a great species, bellowing out for life—life—life.

This wild deep *Roo—ooo* was the knell of the buffalo. What a strange sound, vastly different from anything human, yet somehow poignant, tragic, terrible! Nature had called to the great herd; and that last million of buffalo bellowed out their acceptance of the decree. But in Tom's morbid mind he attributed vastly more to this strange thunder, which was not the trampling thunder of their hoofs. In the dead of night when the guns were silent he could not shake the spell. It came to him then how terribly wrong, obsessed, evil were these hide-hunters. God and nature had placed the wonderful beasts on earth for a purpose, the least of which might have been to furnish meat and robe for men in a measure of reason. But here all the meat was left to rot, and half the hides; and the remaining half went to satisfy a false demand, and to make rich a number of hunters, vastly degraded by the process.

Roo—ooo—ooo! Tom heard in that the meaning of a
futile demand of nature.

Tom Doan and Pilchuck reined their horses on the
crest of a league-sloping ridge and surveyed the buffalo range.

To their surprise the endless black line of buffalo
was not in sight. They had moved north in the night.
At this early morning hour the hunters were just riding
out to begin their day's work. No guns were booming,
and it appeared that Tom and the scout had that part of
the range to themselves.

"Wal, we spent yesterday peggin' hides in camp, an'
didn't think to ask Jones if the buffalo had moved,"
remarked Pilchuck, reflectively.

"The wind has changed. It's now from the north,"
said Tom.

"Shore is. An' the buffs will be grazin' back pronto.
That is, if they *are* grazin'!"

"Any reason to doubt it?" asked Tom.

"Wal, the breedin' season's just about ended. An'
that with this muggy, stormy, electric-charged mornin'
might cause a move. Never in my huntin' days have I
seen such a restless queer herd of buffalo as this one."

"No wonder!" exclaimed Tom.

"Wal, it ain't, an' that's a fact. . . . Do I see hosses
yonder?"

Tom swept the prairie with his glass.

"Yes. Hunters riding out. I see more beyond.
They're all going downriver."

"Come to think of it, I didn't hear much shootin'
yesterday. Did you?"

"Not a great deal. And that was early morning and
far away," replied Tom.

"Buffs an' hunters have worked north. Let's see.
The river makes a bend about ten miles from here, an'
runs east. I'd be willin' to bet the herd hasn't turned
that bend."

"Why?"

"Because they'll *never* go north again. For two months the trend has been south, day by day. Some days a wind like yesterday would switch them, but on the whole they're workin' south. This ain't natural for midsummer. They ought to be headed north. 'Course the mob of hunters are drivin' them south."

"But how about to-day?" inquired Tom.

"Wal, I'm shore figgerin'. Reckon I can't explain, but I feel all them outfits ridin' north will have their work for nothin'."

"What will we do?"

"I'm not carin' a lot. Reckon I've sickened on this job, an' I shore know that, when I stay a day in camp."

Tom had before noted this tendency in the scout. It was common to all those hunters who had been long in the field. He did not voice his own sentiment.

"I've been wantin' to ride west an' see what that next ford is goin' to be like," said the scout, presently. "We'll be breakin' camp an' movin' south soon. An' the other side of the river is where we want to be."

For the first time Tom experienced a reluctance to a continuation of the old mode of traveling south. Why not turn north once more? The thought was a surprise. There was no reason to start north, unless in answer to the revulsion of hide-hunting. This surely would be his last buffalo hunt. But he did not think it just to his partners to quit while they wanted to keep on. His reflection then was that Pilchuck was wearing out, both in strength and in greed.

They rode west, aiming to reach the river some four or five miles farther on.

It was a cloudy, sultry summer morning, with storm in the air. The prairie was not here a beautiful prospect. Tom seemed to gaze over it rather than at it. Westward the undulating gray rise of ground stretched interminably to a horizon bare of landmarks. Far in the east rays of sunlight streamed down between sullen, angry, copper and purple-hued clouds. The north threatened. It was black all along the horizon. Still, oppressive, sultry, the air seemed charged.

From time to time Pilchuck turned in his saddle to gaze backward along the empty range, and then up at the cloudbank. It appeared to Tom as if the scout were looking and listening for something.

"What're you expecting?" queried Tom, yielding to curiosity. "A thunderstorm?"

"Wal, I'll be darned if I know," ejaculated Pilchuck. "Shore I wasn't thinkin' about a storm. Wasn't thinkin' at all! Must be just habit with me. . . . But now you tax me, I reckon I'm oneasy about that herd."

Pilchuck led west farther than he had calculated, and struck the river at a wonderful place where the prairie took a sudden dip for miles, sheering steeply to the shallow water. Here was the buffalo ford, used by the herds in their annual migrations. Trees were absent, and brush and grass had not the luxuriance common to most stretches of river bank. From prairie rim to margin of river sloped a long steep bank, even and smooth; and at one point the wide approach to the ford was split and dominated by a rocky eminence, the only high point in sight along the river.

The place seemed dismal and lonely to Tom, as he sat on his horse while Pilchuck forded the river. Contrary to most river scenes, this one was lifeless. Not a bird or animal or a fish or turtle in sight! Loneliness and solitude had their abode in this trodden road of the buffalo.

At length the scout returned and rode up to Tom.

"Wal, I wouldn't care to get a team stuck in that sand," he remarked. "It shore ain't packed none. . . . Lend me your glass."

The scout swept a half circle of the horizon, and finally came to a halt westward, at a point on the prairie some distance from the river.

"See some small bunches of buffalo," he said. "Let's ride up on them, make our kill, skin what we get, an' pick them up with the wagon on our way south to-morrow."

"You're the boss," replied Tom.

"Wal, I wish some one was bossin' me," returned Pilchuck, enigmatically.

They trotted off over the gray prairie, and after traveling a couple of miles, could see the buffalo plainly. Meanwhile a slight breeze began to blow from the north.

"I'll be darned!" ejaculated Pilchuck, with annoyance. "Wind's turned again. If it blows stronger we'll not slip up on this bunch."

Another mile brought increase of wind, and the wary buffalo, catching the scent of the killers, loped away over the prairie. Pilchuck watched them in disgust. "Run, you old dunder-heads! Run clear across the Rio Grande! . . . Tom, I reckon we're all spoiled by the past easy huntin'. It'll never be easy again. An' somehow I'm glad. Let's work back."

They turned about to face the breeze, now quite strong, cooler, with a heavy scent of rotting buffalo carcasses.

"Faugh!" exclaimed the scout. "I'd rather have nose an' eyes full of cottonwood smoke."

Tom's quick ear caught a very low rumble of thunder. He turned his head. The sound had ceased. It had come on a stronger puff of wind.

"What'd you hear?" inquired the scout, whose eye never missed anything.

"Thunder."

"Wal, it does look stormy. But I never trust thunder in this country," replied the scout, significantly.

He halted his horse; and Tom did likewise. They gazed at the north. Dull, leaden mushrooming clouds were moving toward them, not rapidly, but steadily, in heavy changing forms. They merged into a purple-black mass down which streaked thin zigzag ropes of lightning.

"Storm all right," observed Pilchuck. "Listen."

After a moment in which nothing was heard save the heaving of horses, the rattle of bridle, and creak of leather, the scout dismounted.

"Get off, Tom, an' walk away from the horses. . . . Listen now."

Presently Tom again heard the low dull rumble.

"There," he said.

"Shore. That's genuine thunder, an' it means rain for this stinkin' dusty hot range. . . . Listen some more, Tom."

The two men stood apart, Pilchuck favoring his right ear, Tom his left; and they remained motionless. Several times the mutter of thunder, distinct now to Tom, caused the scout to nod his head.

"Reckon that's not what I'm expectin'," he said, gloomily. "An' we've no time to stand here all day. . . . Listen hard, Tom. You're younger than me."

Tom's sluggish blood quickened a little. He had been two years with this old plainsman, during which there had been numberless instances of his sagacity and vision, and remarkable evidences of experience. Pilchuck was worrying about that herd of buffalo. Thereupon Tom bent lower, held his breath, and strained his ear with all intensity possible. Again he heard the muttering long rumble—then the beat of his heart, the stir of his hair over his temple—the sweep of wind. Thunder again! That was all; and he abandoned the strain.

"Nothing but storm," he told Pilchuck.

"I reckon my ears are old, an' my imagination makes me think I hear things," returned the scout. "But a moment ago . . . Try again. I want to be *shore*."

Thus incited, Tom lent himself to as sensitive and profound listening as was possible for him. This time he seemed to hear the thunder as before, somewhat louder; and under it another, fainter sound, an infinitely low roar that did not die out, that went on and on, deadened by another mutter of thunder, and then, when this was gone, beginning again, low, strange, unceasing.

Then he straightened up and told Pilchuck what he had heard. How sharply and intelligently the scout's gray eyes flashed! He made no reply, except to raise one of his brawny hands. Leaving it extended, he froze in the attitude of an Indian listening. Tom again lent his ear to the strengthening breeze. Thunder—then long low menacing roar—thunder again—and roar! He made his own deductions and, lifting his head, waited for the scout to speak. Long did Pilchuck maintain that tense posture. He was a slow, deliberate man on occasions. Sometimes he would act with the most incredible speed. Here he must have been studying the volume, direction, distance of this thrilling sound, and not its cause. Suddenly his big brown hand clenched and shot down to crack into the palm of the other. He wheeled to Tom, with gray lightning in his eyes.

"Stampede! . . . The whole herd!" he ejaculated. "I've been expectin' it for days."

Then he gazed across the northern horizon of the prairie round to a point due east.

"You notice we can see only four or five miles," he said. "The prairie rises slow for about that distance, then dips. That'd deaden sound as well as hide any movin' thing. We can't be shore that herd is far away. . . . Funny how we run into things. Reckon we'd better ride!"

They mounted, and were off at a gallop that gave place to a run. Tom had lost his fleet, faithful Dusty, and was now riding a horse strong and sound and fairly fast, but no match for Pilchuck's hunter. So Tom fell behind gradually. He did not goad the horse, though he appreciated Pilchuck's brief hint of danger.

The scout rode east, quartering toward the river, and passed a couple of miles out from where he and Tom had stopped at the ford. Tom gradually fell behind until he was fully a quarter of a mile in the rear. As long as he could keep Pilchuck in sight he did not have any anxiety about the separation. The horse could run, and he was sure-footed. Tom believed he would acquit himself well even in a grueling race with the buffalo. It seemed strange to be running away from an unseen danger. While riding he could not hear anything save the rhythmic beat of hoofs and rush of wind. He observed that the direction Pilchuck had chosen was just a point east of the center of the black storm cloud. Far to its right showed the dim fringe of river timber. There was a wide distance between the end of that cloud and the river, most of which was gently sloping prairie. He had a keen eagerness to know what could be seen beyond the long ridge-top.

Next time he gazed at Pilchuck he was amazed to see him pulling his horse to a halt. Tom rode on with eyes now intent. The scout reined in and leaped out of the saddle. He ran a few paces from the horse, and stopped to lie flat on the ground. Tom realized that Pilchuck was listening with ear close to the earth. The action startled Tom. Not improbably this situation was growing serious. Pilchuck lay a moment, then got up and stood like a statue. Then he abruptly broke his rigid posture and leaped astride. But instead of riding off he waited there, face to the north. Tom rapidly overhauled him and pulled his mount to a stand.

"Jude, what's wrong?" he called, sharply.

"I ain't shore, but I'm damned scared," replied the scout.

"Why? I can't see or hear anything."

"See that yellow dust way to the right of the black sky. Look! It's movin'!—I'm afraid if we go farther this way we'll get headed off an' run into the river. We could cross, but it'd take time, an' when we got over we might have to run south. That'd never do. We've got to go east or west."

"Jude, I hear a roar," said Tom.

"Shore. So do I. But it was the movin' dust that stopped me. . . . Keep still now an' let me figger. If I've any prairie cunnin' left we're in a hell of a fix. We've got to do what's right—an' quick."

Therefore Tom attended to sight of the low, rounded, yellow cloud of dust. It did move, apparently slowly, and spread to the right. Against the background of purple sky it held something ominous. Tom watched it rise gradually to the left, though in this direction it did not spread along the prairie so rapidly. The ground sloped that way, and the ridge-top stretched higher than the level to the east, where the dust now rolled plainly. The roar was a dull distant rumble, steady and ear-filling though not at all loud. It was a deceiving sound, and might be closer than it seemed or farther away.

Suddenly it became loud. It startled Tom. He turned to see what Pilchuck made of that. The scout sat his fidgety horse, with his head extended, his long neck craned forward: Suddenly he jerked back as if struck.

"Doan, look!" he shouted, in a tone Tom had never heard. His voice seemed to merge into a rolling rumble.

Tom wheeled. Along the whole of the prairie horizon had appeared a black bobbing line of buffalo. Above them rose the yellow dust, and beyond that spread the storm-cloud of purple. The ragged front of the herd appeared to creep over the ridge-top, like a horizon-wide tide, low, flat, black. Toward the west the level gray horizon was being blotted out with exceeding swiftness, as the herd came in sight. It spread like a black smoke, flying low. To the east the whole space before noted by Tom had been clouded with black and yellow. The front line of the herd, then, did not appear to be straight across: it was curving from the right.

One moment Tom gazed, rapt, thrilling, then his blood gushed hot. The great herd was at last on the stampede. Not five miles distant, running downhill!

"By God! we're in a trap!" yelled Pilchuck, hoarsely. "We've only one chance. Follow me an' ride!"

He spurred and wheeled his horse and, goading him into a run, headed for the river ford. Tom spurred after him, finding now that his horse, frightened by the roar, could keep up with Pilchuck's. They ran straight away from the eastern front of the herd, that was curving in and quartering away from the western front. Tom had ridden fast before, but Pilchuck's start bade fair to lead him into the swiftest race of his experience on the range. He was aware of drawing away somewhat from the roar in the rear; on his right, however, the sound augmented. Tom gazed around. His eyes, blurred from the rush of wind, showed a league-wide band of black, sliding down the prairie slope, widening, spreading. He did not look behind.

Pilchuck's fleet horse began to draw ahead. The old scout was riding as he had never ridden away from Comanches. Tom remembered what fear these old plainsmen had of the buffalo stampede. It was the terror of the plains, more appalling than the prairie fire. Comanches could be fought; fires could be outridden or back-fired, but the stampede of buffalo was a rolling sea of swift insane beasts. With spur and fist and voice Tom urged his horse to its utmost, and kept the distance between him and Pilchuck from widening farther.

Both horses now were on a headlong run strained to the breaking point. The wind hissed by Tom's ears, swayed him back in his saddle. On both sides the gray prairie slid by, indistinct, a blurred expanse, over which he seemed to sail. He could not see the river depression, but before long he made out the rocky eminence that marked the site of the ford. Pilchuck's intention now was plain. At first Tom had imagined the scout meant to try to cross the river ahead of the herd; now, however, he was making for the high point of rock. This realization unclamped Tom's cold doubt. If the horses did not fall they could make that place of safety. Pilchuck was fifty feet ahead, and not only was he driving the horse at breakneck speed, but he was guiding him over what appeared to be the smoother ground. Tom caught the slight variations in the course and the swervings aside; and he had only to follow.

So they flew. The gray mound of rock seemed close, the prairie flashing by, yet how slowly the distance lessened. Tom saw Pilchuck turn. His brown face gleamed. He waved his hand. A beckoning and an encouragement! Peril was not over, but safety was in sight. Then the scout leaned back, pulling the horse to his haunches, on which he slid to a stop. Over Pilchuck's head Tom saw the pale brightness of water. The river! Behind Tom rolled a rumbling thunder, strange to hear with his ears full of rushing wind. He dared not look back.

The straining horse broke his stride, caught it again, stretched on, and plunged to the bare rise of rocky ground. Tom hauled with all his strength on the bridle. He checked the maddened animal, but could not stop him. Pilchuck stood ten feet above the bank. He had dismounted. Both hands were uplifted in a gesture of awe. Tom leaped off just as his horse slowed before the first rocky bench. Dragging him up, Tom climbed to Pilchuck, who seemed to yell at him. But Tom heard no voice. The rocky eminence was about half an acre in extent, and high enough above the bank to split the herd. Tom dropped the bridle and whirled in fear and wonder.

His first thought when he saw the ragged, sweeping tide of beasts, still a third of a mile distant, was that he would have had time to spare. The herd had not been so close as his imagination had pictured.

Pilchuck dragged at Tom, pulling him higher on the rock. The scout put his mouth close to Tom's ear and manifestly yelled. But Tom heard no voice; felt only a soundless, hot breath. His ears were distending with a terrific thunder. His eyes were protruding at an awful spectacle.

Yet he saw that sweep of buffalo with a marvelous distinctness, with the swift leap of emotion which magnified all his senses. Across the level front of his vision spread a ragged, shaggy black wall of heads, humps, hoofs, coming at the speed of buffalo on the stampede! On a hard run! The sea of bobbing backs beyond disappeared in a yellow pall of dust curled aloft and hung low, and kept almost the speed of the front rank. Above the moving mantle of dust, farther back, showed the gray pall of storm. Lightning flashed in vivid white streaks. But there was no thunder from above. The thunder rolled low, along the ground.

Spellbound Tom gazed. He was riveted to the rock. If he had not been he would have fled, up, back, away from that oncoming mass. But he could only gaze, in a profound consciousness of something great and terrifying. These buffalo might not split round the higher ground; those in line might run over the rock. What an end for hide-hunters! Killed, crushed, trampled to jelly, trampled to dust under the hoofs of the great herd! It would be just retribution. Tom felt the awful truth of that in his lifting heart. It was mete! The murderous hide-hunters, money-grubbers, deserved no pity. He could not feel any for himself. How furiously angry that curling surf of woolly heads and shiny horns and gleaming hoofs! On! On! On! The thundering herd! How magnificent and appalling!

Suddenly his ears ceased to function. He could no longer hear. The sense had been outdone. There was no sound. But he saw the mighty onsweep, majestic, irresistible, an army of maddened beasts on the stampede, shaking the earth. The rock under his feet began to tremble. It was no longer stable. He felt the queer vibrations, and the sensation added to his terror.

Transfixed, Tom awaited the insupportable moment for the rolling front ranks to reach the rock, either to roll over it like a tidal wave, or split round it. The moment was an age. Pilchuck was holding to him. Tom was holding to Pilchuck. The solid earth seemed about to cave in under them. Shaggy black heads bobbing swiftly, gleam of horns, and flash of wild eyes, hoofs, hoofs, hoofs sweeping out, out, out—and the awful moment was at hand.

The shaggy flood split round the rock and two streams of rounded woolly backs, close-pressed as water, swift as a mill-race, poured over the bank toward the river.

Pilchuck dragged Tom away from the back position to the front of the rock. As if by supernatural magic the scene was changed. Below, far on each side, the mass of buffalo spilled over the embankment to plunge into the river. Up and down the water line spread white splashes; and over and into them leaped the second ranks of buffalo, too close to miss the first. Then what had momentarily been ranks on the slope closed up into solid mass of black. Bulge and heave— great sheets of muddy water—a terrible writhing massing forward along that irregular front! Then the tide of buffalo swept on, over, once more a flat, level multitude of heads and humps, irrepressible as an avalanche. They crossed the river on the run; the stampede had been only momentarily retarded. Downriver, below the ford, far as eye could see, stretched lines of buffalo swimming, swiftly, like an endless flock of enormous geese. Upriver stretched the same, as far as eye could see. The slope of the prairie to the water was one solid mass of buffalo, moving as one beast, impelled by motive as wild as the action. Above swept the dust, blowing as a storm wind from the prairie, and, curling like a yellow curtain of smoke, it followed the buffalo across the river up the long slope, and out upon the prairie.

Tom and Pilchuck were on that level between the moving dust above and the moving buffalo below. All view back toward the prairie whence the herd rolled was soon obliterated. Likewise the front ranks of the great mass disappeared on the opposite side, under this accompanying mantle. But the river, for a while, lay clear to their gaze, miles up and miles down, and all visible space of water and ground was covered with buffalo. Buffalo more numerous than a band of ants on the march!

Tom sank down, overcome by the spectacle, by the continuous trembling of the earth under him, by the strangulation which threatened, by the terrible pressure on his ear-drums.

Suddenly night seemed to intervene. A gale swooped the dust away across the river; and in place of a yellow curling curtain of dust there came a slanting gray pall of rain. It blackened as the light grew less. Blazing streaks of lightning played through the gray gloom. But if there was thunder above, it could not be heard in the thunder below.

Pilchuck drew Tom under a narrow shelf of rock, where, half protected from the deluge, they crouched in the semi-darkness. What seemed hours passed. Yet there was no end to the passing of the great herd. The rain ceased, the sky lightened and cleared, and clearer grew the black mantling of prairie and river. All was buffalo, except the sky. Then the sun broke out of the clouds.

Tom's stunned senses rallied enough for him to appreciate the grandeur and beauty suddenly given the scene by a glorious sheen of gold and purple, streaming down from the rifts between the clouds. The dust was gone. The thousands of shining black backs moved on and on, rapidly, ponderously, swallowed up by the haze of the disappearing storm. And still the buffalo came over the prairie, obscuring the ground.

But at last the time came when the mass showed breaks in the ranks, and then, in the rear line, more ragged than had been the fore. Tom's hearing seemed gradually to be restored. That, he realized, was only the diminishing of the vast volume of sound to the point where it was no longer deafening. It was a blood-deadening thunder that gradually lessened as the end of the herd rolled on from the prairie, down over the bank, and across the river.

The thundering herd swept on out of sight. And the thunder became a roar, the roar a rumble, and the rumble died away.

Pilchuck rose to his lofty height and peered across the river, into the gray haze and purple distance that had swallowed up the buffalo. He seemed to be a man who had lived through something terrible.

"The last herd!" he said, with pathos. "They've crossed the Brazos an' they'll never come back. . . . The storm of rain was like the storm of lead that'll follow them."

Tom also got dizzily to his feet and faced the south. What he felt about the last herd could not be spoken. He had been spared a death he felt he deserved; and he had seen a mighty spectacle, incalculable in its spiritual effect. All in vain was the grand stampede of that thundering herd. It must drink, it must graze—and behind would troop the ruthless hunters of hides. But Tom had seen and felt its overpowering vitality, its tremendous life, its spirit. Never would he kill another buffalo! And a great sadness pervaded his mind. As he stood there, trying to form in words something to say to Pilchuck, a huge old buffalo bull, one of the many that had been mired in the sand, floundered and wallowed free, and waddled to the opposite shore. Stupidly he gazed about him, forlorn, alone, lost, a symbol of the herd that had gone on without him. Then he headed south out into the melancholy gray of the prairie.

"Jude, I'm—going—north!" exclaimed Tom, haltingly, full of words that would not come.

"Shake!" replied the old scout, quick as a flash, as he extended his brawny hand.

Chapter XIX

FROM the crest of the long prairie slope, beginning to color brown and gold in the September sun, Tom Doan gazed down at the place that had been Sprague's Post. It had grown so as to be almost unrecognizable. Ranches dotted the beautiful sweep of fertile land. Near at hand, the river wound away, hidden in green foliage, and far out on the plain it glistened in the sunlight.

Despite the keen pang in Tom's heart, and the morbid reluctance to return that had abided with him, strangely he found he was glad. The wildness of the buffalo range, loneliness and silence and solitude, and the loss that he felt was irreparable—these had dwarfed his former kindliness and hopefulness, and his old ambition to know the joy of his own home and ranch. But might there not be some compensation?

The long wagon train of hides and camp outfits lumbered across the prairie to enter the outskirts of the Post and haul up on the green square between the town and the river. Huts and cabins had taken the place of tents. Still there were new wagons and outfits belonging to hunters bound for the buffalo range. Tom wanted to cry out about the pains and blunders they were so cheerfully and ignorantly traveling to meet.

Big wagon trains such as this one were always encountered at the Post. News traveled ahead of such large caravans; and there was a crowd on the green. There were half a dozen wagons ahead of the one Tom drove, and the last of these was Pilchuck's. The lean old scout was at once surrounded by hunters eager to learn news of the buffalo range.

Tom saw Burn Hudnall and Dave Stronghurl before they saw him. How well they looked—fuller of face and not so bronzed as when they had ridden the open range! Eager and excited also they appeared to Tom. They would be glad to see him. If only he could avoid meeting their women folk! Then Burn espied him and made at him. Tom dropped the knotted reins over the brake with a movement of finality, and stepped down out of the wagon.

"Howdy, boys! It's sure good to see you," he said, heartily.

They grasped him with hands almost rough, so forceful were they; and both greeted him at once in a kind of suppressed joy, incoherent and noisy, all the more welcoming for that. Then they hung on to him, one at each side.

"Say, have you boys taken to drink?" retorted Tom, to conceal how their warmth affected him. "I haven't just come back to life."

"Tom, I—we—all of us was afraid you'd never come," burst out Burn. "You look fine. Thin, mebbe, an' hard. . . . My Gawd! I'm glad!"

"Tom—I've got a baby—a boy!" beamed Dave, his strong smug face alight.

"You don't say! Dave, shake on that. . . . I'm sure glad. How time flies! It doesn't seem so long——"

"We've got other news, but the best of it'll keep till we get to the ranch," interrupted Burn. "Tom, I've got that five hundred acres father liked so well. Remember? You can buy next to me, along the river. Dave has thrown in with Sprague. The town's boomin'! We've a bank, a church, and a school. An' wait till you see the teacher! She's——"

He rambled on, like a boy, to be silenced by Dave's look. Then Dave began, and being more practical he soon got out Tom's bag and gun and roll of blankets.

"You're comin' with us this hyar very minnit," he concluded, as Tom tried to make excuses. "Burn, grab some of his outfit. Reckon this team an' wagon belongs to Pilchuck?"

"Yes, it does," replied Tom.

"Come along, then, you buffalo-chasin', Comanche-ridin' Llaner Estacador," went on Dave. "We've orders to fetch you home before these hyar town girls set eyes on you."

They dragged Tom and his belongings out of the crowd, pushed him up into a spring-wagon, and while Burn piled his baggage in the back, Dave climbed up beside him and started a team of spirited horses out along the river road.

If the welcome accorded Tom by Burn and Dave had touched him, that given by their women folk reached deeply to his heart. They were all at the front of Burn's fine ranch house. Burn's wife was weeping, it seemed for joy; and Sally Hudnall gave Tom a resounding kiss, to his consternation. Mrs. Hudnall, whose motherly face showed the ravages of grief, greeted him in a way that made Tom ashamed of how he had forgotten these good people. She took possession of him and led him indoors, ahead of the others. They had all seemed strange, hurried, suppressing something. They were not as Tom remembered. Alas! had he grown away from wholesome simplicity? They wanted to welcome him to their home.

Mrs. Hudnall shut the door. Tom had a sense that the room was large, lighted by windows at each end. Clearing his throat, he turned to speak. But Mrs.

Hudnall's working face, her tear-wet eyes, made him dumb. There was something wrong here.

"Tom, you're changed," she began, hurriedly. "No boy any more! I can see how it hurts you to come back to us."

"Yes, because of—of Milly," he replied, simply. "But you mustn't think I'm not glad to see you all. I am. You're my good friends. I'm ashamed I never appreciated you as I should have. But that hard life out there——"

"Don't," she interrupted, huskily. "You know how it hurt me. . . . But, Tom, never mind the past. Think of the present."

"My heart's buried in that past. It seems so long ago. So short a time to remember! I——"

"Didn't you ever think Milly might not have been lost?" she asked.

"Yes, I thought that—till hope died," replied Tom, slowly.

"My boy—we heard she wasn't killed—or captured—or anything," said Mrs. Hudnall, softly.

"Heard she wasn't? My God! That would only torture me," replied Tom, poignantly. He felt himself shaking. What did these people mean? His mind seemed to encounter that query as a wall.

"Tom, we *know* she wasn't," flashed the woman, with all the ecstasy in face and voice.

He staggered back suddenly, released from bewilderment. He realized now. That had been the secret of their excitement, their strangeness. His consciousness grasped the truth. Milly Fayre was not dead. For an instant his eyes closed and his physical and spiritual being seemed to unite in a tremendous resistance against the shock of rapture. He must not lose his senses. He must not miss one word or look of this good woman who had given him back love and life. But he was mute. A strong quiver ran over him from head to foot. Then heat and pulse leaped in exquisite pain and maddening thrill.

"Milly is here," said Mrs. Hudnall. "We tried again and again to send you word, but always missed you. Milly has lived here—ever since she escaped from Jett—and the Indians. She has grown. She's taught the school. She is well—happy. She has waited for you—she loves you dearly."

Voice was wrenched from Tom. "I see truth in your face," he whispered, huskily. "But I can't believe. . . . Let me *see* her!"

Mrs. Hudnall pushed back the door and went out. Some one slipped in. A girl—a woman, white of face, with parted lips and great, radiant black eyes! Could this be Milly Fayre?"

"Oh—Tom!" she burst out, in broken voice, deep and low. She took a forward step, with hands extended, then swayed back against the door. "Don't you—know me?"

"I'd lost all hope," whispered Tom, as if to himself. "It's too sudden. I can't believe . . . You ghost! You white thing with eyes I loved!"

"It's your Milly, alive—alive!" she cried, and ran to envelop him.

Later they stood by the open window watching the sun set gold over the dim dark line of the Llana Estacado. She had told her story. Tom could only marvel at it, as at her, so changed, so wonderful, yet sweet and simple as of old.

"You shall never go back to the buffalo range," she said, in what seemed both command and appeal.

"No, Milly," he replied, and told her the story of the stampede of the thundering herd.

"Oh, how wonderful and terrible!" she replied. "I loved the buffalo."

Mrs. Hudnall called gayly to them from the door. "Tom—Milly, you can't live on love. Supper is ready."

"We're not hungry," replied Milly, dreamily.

d when we met in secret under the cotton-
? Those moonlight nights!"

o, I never forgot anything," she whispered, her
going down on his shoulder.

ell—since to-morrow is your nineteenth birth-
and I've lost you for an endless hateful year—
ry me tomorrow. Will you?"

Yes!"

"Yes, we are," added Tom, for⟨
. . . Milly, I'm starved. You know
A year and a half on hump steak!"

"Wait. I was only teasing," she w⟨
downcast eyes, like midnight under t
leaned a little closer to him. "Do you r⟨
my birthday?"

"I never knew it," he replied, smiling.

"It's to-morrow."

"You don't say. Well, I did get back a
time. Let's see, you're eighteen years old."

"Ah, you forget! I am nineteen. You lost me
a year."

"But, Milly, I *never* forgot what was to hav⟨
your eighteenth birthday, though I never kne⟨
date."

"What was to have been?" she asked, shyly, wi⟨
slow blush mantling her cheek.

"You were to marry me."

"Oh, did I promise that?" she questioned, in pr⟨
tended wonder.

"Yes."

"Well, *that* was for my eighteenth birthday. You
never hunted me—you hunted only buffalo. You might
have had me. . . . But now you shall wait till—till I'm
twenty."

"Milly, I hunted for you all through summer, fall,
winter. And my heart broke."

"But—but I can only marry you on a birthday," she
replied, shaken by his words, and looked up at him
with dusky, eloquent eyes.

"Dear, I'm so happy to find you alive—to see you
grown into a beautiful woman—to know you love
me—that I could wait for ten birthdays," he said,
earnestly. "But why make me wait? I've had a lonely
hard life out there in the buffalo fields. It has taken
something from me that only you can make up for. I
must go back to my dream of a ranch—a home, cattle,
horses, tilling the soil. Have you forgotten how we